PRAISE FOR S
– THE ROWLAND SI

'Well-researched and atmospheric, with a brisk pace, colourful characters and charming period dialogue' – *Age*

'Glossy, original and appealingly Australian'
– *Australian Women's Weekly*

'There are a lot good crime writers in Australia and Gentill is up with the pack, providing interesting characters, punchy plots, a lively and witty style, and some sobering reflection on dangerous times in our history'
– *Sydney Morning Herald*

'It takes a talented writer to imbue history with colour and vivacity. It is all the more impressive when the author creates a compelling narrative'
– *Australian Book Review*

'I must confess I've become rather fond of artist Roland Sinclair and his bohemian friends who divide their time globetrotting, solving murder mysteries' – *Herald Sun*

'Containing an intriguing mystery, a unique sense of humour and a range of historical characters, this is a highly recommended read for lovers of Australian fiction' – *Canberra Times*

'Again, Gentill has turned her deft touch to weave little-known details of Australian political intrigue into an engrossing, easy-read mystery novel'
– *Daily Telegraph*

'Gentill has written an absorbing story about a crucial but underwritten slice of Australian history' – *The Courier Mail*

'Gentill immerses us in an unfamiliar world that quickly becomes one we willingly reside in' – *Herald Sun*

'This is the ninth book in Sulari Gentill's outstanding Rowland Sinclair series, which once again provides the reader with a slick and entertaining story that expertly combines exciting history detail with a scintillating mystery. An enjoyable example of good Australian fiction'
– *Canberra Weekly*

'Gentill is already hitting her straps and readers have noticed'
– *Sydney Morning Herald*

The Rowland Sinclair Mysteries

A MURDER UNMENTIONED

SULARI GENTILL

A ROWLAND SINCLAIR MYSTERY

The Crime & Mystery Club
Harpenden
crimeandmysteryclub.co.uk

First Published by Pantera Press

ISBN
978-0-85730-367-7 (print)
978-0-85730-368-4 (ebook)

2 4 6 8 10 9 7 5 3 1

Typeset in 12pt Adobe Jenson
by Avocet Typeset, Bideford, Devon, EX39 2BP
Printed and bound by CPI Group (UK) Ltd, Croydon CR0 4YY

For more information about Crime Fiction go to @crimetimeuk

For Leith,
for so many good reasons
and because this book made her cry.

Prologue

If Henry Sinclair had been a different man, he might have taken a step back. He might have quailed a little as the gun was cocked, or at least proceeded with some small deference to the weapon. But he was the man he was. And instead Henry laughed—a mirthless blast of scorn, his eyes narrowing with a cold cruel fury.

"By God, I'll make you regret—"

The shot was unexpected. Death took him by surprise... and so quickly, that he had no time to wonder at a murderer's defiance.

1

SYDNEY GIRLS

❖

TO FLY FOR THEIR BREAD AND BUTTER

Two Sydney girls, Miss Nancy de Low Bird, aged 18, Manly, and Miss May Bradford, are working hard to win their 'B' (commercial) aviation licences. When they win them they plan to take up flying as a profession. Both are pupils of the Kingsford Smith flying school.

Nancy Bird, who won her 'A' licence in September, now has it endorsed (50 hours flying solo) so that she can take up passengers, but she cannot obtain her 'B' licence until she is 19 next October. Her age is a handicap to her ambition, which is to secure all engineers' licences, but she must be 21.

Morning Bulletin, 1933

Edna Higgins clasped the hat to her head as she watched the racing-green Gipsy Moth glide gradually back to the Mascot Aerodrome. She waved more out of exhilaration than any expectation that her salute would be seen. Beside her, Milton Isaacs attempted to push a particularly ugly greyhound back into the yellow Mercedes. The misshapen dog resisted, straining against the lead in its desperation to chase the biplane. The poet dragged the greyhound back, cursing as his immaculate cravat was pushed awry in the battle.

The *Rule Britannia* touched gently down onto the tarmac and taxied to a stop. Charles Kingsford Smith climbed out of the passenger seat, pausing to speak at length, and by his posture, quite stridently, to the pilot before he jumped down from the fuselage.

A girl in overalls emerged from the hangar. "He banked too hard on the turn," she said, grimacing. "Smithy's letting him have it!"

"Really?" Clyde Watson Jones folded his brawny arms. His weathered face creased into sceptical lines. "You could tell that from here?" he asked.

"Of course," she replied.

Loyal Clyde rolled his eyes. Some pilot's daughter no doubt, convinced she knew everything about flying. As far as he could tell, the flight had been perfect; the Gipsy Moth soaring into the sky, executing several acrobatic manoeuvres and then returning to the ground in a series of precisely angled glides and turns. Clyde had been impressed though not surprised.

Rowland Sinclair pulled himself out of the cockpit, patting the *Rule Britannia*'s fuselage affectionately before he strode over to greet his friends.

The ecstatic greyhound broke away from Milton, hurling itself at its master, who reeled backwards under the impact. "Lenin, settle down mate," Rowland said uselessly as the dog writhed with the momentum created by the movement of its overlong tail and tried to pull the leather gloves from his hands. He laughed, giving in and allowing himself to be mauled with the robust affection. Eventually Lenin calmed and having claimed a glove, retreated to the car to chew it in peace.

Rowland removed his aviator cap and goggles. He was boyishly elated. Milton clapped him enthusiastically on the back.

"Well that was a fine thing to see, Rowly!"

Edna embraced him. "I was completely terrified you were going to fall out when the plane turned upside down," she said.

"I banked a little hard on the turn," Rowland admitted. "I wouldn't have tried the acrobatics if Smithy hadn't been on hand to tell me what to do."

The girl smiled smugly.

Rowland noticed, wincing as he realised his mistake had not escaped Nancy Bird's sharp skyward eye. He introduced his fellow student of Kingsford Smith's flying school. "Miss Bird is a flying prodigy," he said. "She wouldn't have so royally cocked up the turn."

"I've had an extra month's lessons," Nancy Bird conceded graciously.

"You're a pilot?" Clyde looked the diminutive young woman up and down. She was barely five foot tall and wore her hair in braids. "How old are you?"

"Clyde! You can't ask a lady that!" Edna was indignant.

"I'm eighteen," Nancy replied, raising her chin defiantly.

Rowland sighed. "It's embarrassing... shown up by a child."

"I am not a child!" she returned. He laughed and then, so did she.

Rowland had taken an immediate liking to Nancy Bird. The girl was aptly named, giddy for the clouds with what seemed a natural affinity for flying machines. She'd made clear from the start that she intended to obtain her commercial flying licence, to seek a career in aviation, to set records and win races, while the likes of him were content to simply fly well enough for their own amusement.

If Rowland had not been a Sinclair perhaps he might have sought his fortune in aviation, but as it was, his fortune had been amply made by his grazier forebears. And as much as flight stirred his blood, it did not run in his veins and define his view in the way that paint and canvas did. Even fifteen hundred feet in the air he'd found himself composing a portrait of Kingsford Smith against an inverted horizon. He'd landed exhilarated but already he longed to take out the sketchbook he carried in his breast pocket and somehow capture the love of speed and freedom in the lines of the airman's craggy face.

Milton handed him a glass of champagne whilst Edna found a bottle of ginger beer for Nancy in the abundant hamper packed by Rowland's housekeeper.

The poet put one arm about Rowland's shoulders and raised his glass with the other. "Thou wast not born for death, immortal Bird!"

"Keats," Rowland murmured. His friend had been reading Keats of late. Milton's reputation as a poet was earned primarily through a propensity to borrow shamelessly from the English bards with neither public nor private acknowledgement that the words were not his. "Are you referring to me or Nancy?"

"I'd be delighted to propose an appropriate salutation to the exceptional young lady," Milton said, winking at Nancy Bird. "But I thought that first we should toast the fact that you didn't die."

"Hardly reason enough!" Kingsford Smith declared as he joined them. "But you may want to celebrate that Mr. Sinclair's licence is now endorsed so he may take his biplane and a passenger up whenever he pleases." The aviator accepted a glass of champagne and raised it towards Rowland. "Just watch your turns, Sinclair... the Moth's instruments are very sensitive." He rapped his knuckles against the long bonnet of the yellow Mercedes. "It's not the same as steering one of these hefty contraptions."

Rowland's brow rose.

"You want to get yourself a vehicle with good British engineering," Kingsford Smith continued, warming to his subject. "Still I suppose all these automobiles will be obsolete in time."

Rowland muttered something unintelligible.

Edna smiled. Rowland did not receive any criticism of his beloved motor kindly. "You could fly back to *Oaklea* this year, Rowly," she said, deciding to direct the conversation away from the slandered automobile.

With the Yuletide approaching, Rowland Sinclair and his houseguests would soon part for the holidays. Clyde would return to

Batlow in the high country to visit his parents. As Edna's father was away, she and Milton planned to spend Christmas at a succession of decadent Sydney soirees. Rowland, however, was expected at the family property in Yass, from which his brother Wilfred reigned over the Sinclair empire.

"I suppose there are plenty of places to land at *Oaklea*." Rowland considered the proposition seriously.

"You could take Ernie for a ride," Clyde suggested. "The little bloke would be thrilled."

"Yes, but I'm not entirely sure Wil would be," Rowland replied. Ernest was the elder of his two nephews but still only six years old. Although Rowland's place in the oversubscribed Kingsford Smith Flying School had been arranged through Wilfred Sinclair's considerable connections, he doubted his brother would be willing to entrust Ernest to him and the *Rule Britannia* just yet.

They remained at the Mascot hangar for some time, celebrating Rowland's licence and then watching as Nancy Bird took the Gipsy Moth up. Kingsford Smith provided a commentary as Bird plunged the biplane into more acrobatic manoeuvres, pointing out how the young woman was manipulating the joystick and foot controls to achieve the loops and rolls.

There were moments when Edna just could not look, sure that the biplane would meet tragedy, and others when she gazed as mesmerised as the men.

As the afternoon began to slip reluctantly into evening, the Gipsy Moth was returned to her hangar. Rowland took the wheel of the Mercedes while Edna and Milton fought over the front passenger seat. On this occasion Edna prevailed. They drove Nancy Bird home, before returning to the Woollahra mansion which had been the principal residence of Rowland Sinclair and a succession of artists, writers and poets over the past three years. His current houseguests had more or less become permanent instalments at *Woodlands House* though others came and went from time to time.

It had been the cause of significant friction between the Sinclair brothers that Rowland had converted the grand Sydney estate into some kind of artistic commune, which seemed to exist in a constant state of scandal. In recent years, many heated words had been exchanged over occasional salacious snippets in *Smith's Weekly* or the *Truth*; rumours of naked women, wild parties and decadent immorality that mortified Wilfred but to which Rowland seemed indifferent if not amused.

The newly licensed pilot and his friends were greeted at the entrance vestibule by the upright character and stern visage of Rowland's housekeeper. Mary Brown had served at *Woodlands House* since well before the war, maintaining what decorum she could with a vexed silence and pointed exhalations of despair.

"Thank goodness you're here, Master Rowly," she said, addressing him in the manner she had since he was a child. "Colonel Bennett has come to call upon you. He insisted on waiting."

"Bennett..." Clyde's brow furrowed. "He's not...?"

"Lucy's father?" Rowland finished the question for him. "Yes, I'm afraid he is."

Lucy Bennett was his sister-in-law's chum, a young woman of excellent breeding whom well-meaning Kate Sinclair seemed determined Rowland should marry. Somehow Kate's hope had become an expectation, one which Lucy herself now seemed to share. For the life of him, Rowland could not think of one thing he might have said or done that may have led either lady to believe he had any interest in marrying Lucy Bennett.

"What do you suppose he wants?" Edna asked quietly.

Rowland groaned. Clyde grasped his friend's shoulder sympathetically and Milton grinned. They all had a fairly good idea.

"I'd best go talk to him," Rowland muttered, removing his leather aviator jacket and exchanging it for the grey tweed he'd left on the coat stand. "Is he in the drawing room, Mary?"

"No, sir. I did not think the drawing room fit for company. Colonel Bennett is waiting in the library."

Rowland smiled slightly at his housekeeper's less than subtle rebuke. The drawing room enjoyed excellent light and so he used it as a studio. The fine furniture shared space with his easels and paint boxes, while canvases in progress leant against the expensively papered walls. To Rowland's mind it was still perfectly comfortable and now remarkably functional.

The library was another matter altogether. The room had been his father's and though Henry Sinclair had been dead since 1920, it remained unchanged. Before Henry's death, Rowland had only ever been summoned to the library when his father was displeased. All things considered, it was possibly a more fitting venue for the delicate conversation he was about to have.

Edna grabbed his arm as he turned to go. "You will be kind, won't you, Rowly?"

Milton laughed. "Kind? For God's sake, Ed, that's the least of our worries. Rowly will probably agree to wed the girl so she doesn't think him impolite!"

Edna smiled. "Oh dear, you're probably right." Rowland's excessive courtesy had got him into trouble before.

Even Clyde agreed. "Every girl you meet seems to become convinced you want to marry her, mate... It probably wouldn't hurt to be marginally rude."

"Yes, you're all very amusing," Rowland returned, mildly offended. None of the misunderstandings to which they were alluding was his fault. "I'd better disillusion Colonel Bennett before this gets out of hand." He wasn't sure how he could possibly do it kindly.

2

CENTRE PARTY

---◆---

ERIC CAMPBELL'S
NEW PROPOSAL

SYDNEY, Monday

The formation of what will be termed the Centre Party, with its ultimate objective the abolition of machine politics by the institution of vocational representation was outlined by Mr. Eric Campbell at a large and representative meeting of the New Guard tonight. The hall was packed with men wearing arm bands of numerous colours, while all entrances were strongly guarded by bands of coatless men dressed in white shirts.

Addressing the gathering, Mr. Campbell referred to the "great god of the U.A.P. with feet of clay and a head of concrete" and the "high priests Stevens and Lyons, who are nothing more than a pair of mummers." ...

Amongst the objects of the proposed Centre Party as outlined by Mr. Campbell, were the unity of political, industrial, cultural and moral functions of the State, repeal of all Socialist legislation, indissoluble co-operation of capital and Labour in all industries, non-payment of members of Parliament, elimination of unemployment by efficient and economic government and development of the country's resources and the freeing of industry from unjust and inequitable taxation.

The Canberra Times, 5 December 1933

Morris Bennett had taken the chair behind the desk and was ensconced with his pipe and a cup of tea. He stood as Rowland entered, the smart abrupt movement of a military man.

"Colonel Bennett," Rowland extended his hand.

"Rowland my boy, there you are!" Bennett grasped Rowland's hand in both of his and shook it warmly.

"Can I offer you a drink, sir?"

"Why, yes, dear boy!" Bennett replied enthusiastically. "I expect that we will have something to toast quite soon." He exhaled contentedly. "I've always thought a man should have a son... of course the good Lord deigned to give me daughters!" Bennett sat back and cleared his throat. "I must say I am very happy we're having this conversation, Rowland, very happy indeed."

For a brief moment Rowland seriously considered making his excuses and leaving. But what reason could he possibly concoct to suddenly rush from his own house? So he poured a glass of Scotch for Bennett and fortified himself with gin.

"To what exactly do I owe the pleasure, Colonel Bennett?" he asked deciding to get straight to the point.

Bennett frowned then. "I had hoped that you might have presented yourself as soon as you returned from abroad, Sinclair."

"I see." Rowland took a deep breath. "I'm sorry, sir, but—"

"Apology accepted, Sinclair. After all a man must attend to business first, no matter what the ladies want, eh?" He sighed. "Did I tell you that I have four daughters, Sinclair? Four!" Bennett shook his head as if the gravity of his misfortune yet astounded him. "Still, they're not bad gels if you can bear all the silly nonsense that they go on with."

Rowland tried again. "Colonel Bennett, I have the greatest respect for your daughter—"

"Of course these things must be done properly, but Lucy would never forgive me if I stood in your way, which I can tell you, Rowland,

I'm not inclined to do. I knew your father you know… fine man. I expect you're cut from the same cloth."

Rowland tensed slightly. "I don't think I am, sir."

Bennett laughed. "I recall dining at *Oaklea* in Henry's time." He closed his eyes to savour the memory with his Scotch. "Extraordinary property. Splendid grounds, magnificent mechanised woolshed— twenty stands—simply superb… and the house itself…" His eyes shone, moist with emotion. "A stately oasis of British elegance and gentility in the Australian wilderness. Your father was an exemplary host, my boy… the finest of everything in abundance… and your dear mother, as gracious as she was beautiful. What wonderful, wonderful times they were."

Rowland drained his glass of gin silently.

Bennett leant forward and lowered his voice. "I understand that you have been meeting with members of the government since you got back."

"How did—" Rowland began uneasily.

The colonel grinned and tapped his nose. "I'm not without connections, you know. I presume you are contemplating a career in politics. A fine ambition, my boy. I expect I could be of some assistance to you on that account."

Rowland almost laughed. He had, since returning to Sydney, approached every sitting member of the parliament to whom he could gain access to press his concerns about the excesses of the German government. The process had not left him with a particularly warm opinion of the esteemed members of the United Australia Party. Entering parliament himself was the furthest thing from his mind. "I'm afraid—"

"You'll find Lucy an invaluable asset in that regard." Bennett advised. "A wife can be very near as useful to a politician as his lodge."

"Sir, I don't think you understand…"

"But I do… it seems not so long ago that I spoke to my Marjorie's father. And now—"

Bennett stopped as the door burst open. Milton and Clyde stumbled in, each carrying several canvases.

"Where do you want these, Rowly?" Milton asked, holding up a painting of Edna.

Bennett's moustache bristled, as he studied the vibrant nude rendered in oil. She stood emblazoned on the canvas with her arms outstretched, beguiling, unashamed and utterly naked. The retired colonel moved his gaze systematically over the other paintings, flinching as he beheld each new nude.

Rowland stared at his friends bewildered.

"We've simply run out of space in the drawing room… we'll have to hang these here," Clyde said, holding a pastel piece up against the wall.

Bennett's face began to flush.

"Oh hello. What are you all doing in here?" Edna walked in. She bestowed Bennett with an enchanting smile.

Still confused, Rowland introduced his friends.

Bennett looked from Edna's face to the paintings.

She laughed. "You've recognised me, Colonel Bennett. They're excellent likenesses are they not? No one paints me with quite the intimacy that Rowly does. Why there's no part of me that he does not know."

Bennett blustered incomprehensibly.

Milton, Clyde and Edna then fell into a rather animated conversation about the works, recounting the arduous hours Edna was called on to spend naked as she modelled for Rowland. They reminisced about the other models that Rowland used from time to time.

Bennett's face was entirely red but for his lips, which were pressed into a hard white line.

"Oh, is that the time?" Milton said suddenly, with a deliberate scrutiny of his watch. "We'd best be on our way." He nodded at Bennett and apologised. "You'll have to excuse Clyde and me, Colonel. Party meeting, you know."

It was probably then that Bennett noticed the red Communist badge pinned to Milton's lapel. He gasped audibly.

Milton smiled, breathed onto the badge and polished it with the velvet sleeve of his jacket. He addressed Rowland. "We'll get this lot up when we get back, if that's all right with you, comrade."

"Why this is outrageous!" Bennett exploded. "How dare you come here! Sinclair, I trust you are about to call someone to throw these... these trespassers out."

Rowland replied quite calmly. "They're not trespassers, Colonel Bennett. They live here."

For a moment, Bennett seemed to lose his breath. "Here... under your father's roof? Have you taken leave of your senses, boy?"

"*Woodlands* is no longer my father's house, Colonel Bennett. The gentlemen and Miss Higgins reside here on my invitation."

"And you will not withdraw it?" Bennett demanded.

"Not under any circumstances."

"Well then, Sinclair, I regret to say that I cannot allow a man of such poor judgement, such undesirable associations, to... to marry *my* daughter. I will thank you to withdraw your attentions forthwith."

"As you wish, Colonel Bennett," Rowland said slowly.

Bennett seized his bowler from the desk, and slammed it onto his head. "I have no doubt that Lucy will be distressed, but surely not as appalled as your dear father would have been, Rowland. Henry was an upstanding man, a figure of decorum and respectability... as is your brother. But you, my boy, are a great disappointment!"

The colonel pushed angrily past Clyde and stalked out of the library.

Nobody said anything, waiting in silence as they listened to Mary Brown ushering the implacable Bennett out.

"Well, we arrived in the nick of time," Milton observed finally, shaking his head at Rowland. "A few more minutes and you would have been engaged!"

"Don't be ridiculous." Rowland's response was somewhat ungrateful. "I was fine."

"Fine? You didn't want to marry her, did you, Rowly?" Clyde asked, dubiously.

"Of course not! I was just trying to find a courteous way to—"

"You can't do these things politely, mate. Trust me, I know." Milton sighed deeply.

Clyde snorted.

"It's much better for Lucy this way, Rowly," Edna assured him.

"I beg your pardon?"

"Well having one's father forbid an association is tragic and romantic, but it's not humiliating."

Rowland considered her words. There was sense in them. The intervention of his friends had relieved him from having to tell Colonel Bennett, his sister-in-law and Lucy herself that he had never intended to propose marriage.

"Yes, I expect you're right." He leant back against the desk, smiling as he recalled the look on Bennett's face when he realised Edna was the woman in the paintings. He glanced at Milton and Clyde. "And do you actually have a party meeting?"

"Not till tomorrow... that was just in case he was willing to forgive your scandalous paintings," Milton replied grinning.

"We were ready to tell him I'd converted you, if it became necessary," Clyde added gravely.

"Good Lord! I'm lucky he didn't shoot me as it was." Rowland had never before thought of using Clyde's Catholicism as a defence against would-be fathers-in-law. The idea had its merits. He shook his head. "I still don't believe I needed rescuing, but thank you for your efforts, regardless."

"Rowly darling, whatever's the matter?" Edna asked peering down at him from over the top of his newspaper.

"Ed... I didn't see you," Rowland said, shamefaced, as he lowered the broadsheet which had caused him to curse out loud. He stood hastily. "I'm sorry. I..."

Edna folded her arms and waited impatiently for him to finish apologising. She couldn't have cared less about the profanity. He had, after all, believed he was alone. She simply wished to know what had inspired him to use it.

"That mad—" Rowland caught himself and started again. "Eric Campbell intends to field a party in the next election," he said, handing her the paper so she could read the article for herself. "It seems that he was so impressed by what the Nazis have done in Germany that he's decided to try it here."

Edna glanced through the news story. They had made an enemy of Colonel Eric Campbell, founder and leader of the New Guard, at a time when he was at his most powerful, and New South Wales had appeared on the brink of civil war. The association had ended particularly badly for Rowland, and though Wilfred Sinclair had intervened to broker an agreement which would keep his brother out of gaol, they all knew it was a fragile and bitter peace. Although the membership of Campbell's movement had declined since the dismissal of Jack Lang, whose controversial premiership of New South Wales had united the establishment against him, there were still New Guardsmen keen to settle the score against Rowland Sinclair.

Neither had Rowland let the matter rest. Indeed they'd all embarked to Germany just months before because he was determined to foil Campbell's plans to forge alliances with the Germans and prevent him bringing Nazism to Australia. They had thought they'd succeeded.

"I suppose standing for election is better than organising a coup d'état."

Rowland frowned. "We can't be sure he's not."

Edna put down the paper and fell into the wing-backed armchair in which she often posed for Rowland. The leather was softened with age and marked in places where even Mary Brown had been unable to remove a careless splash of paint.

A life-sized portrait of the late Henry Sinclair, sitting in that same chair, glared down at the sculptress from the wall opposite. Edna tilted her head to study Rowland against that imposing, disapproving image of his father. Aside from the distinctive blue, which characterised the eyes of all the Sinclair men, Rowland and his father seemed to have had little physically in common.

"Who painted that portrait, Rowly?" she asked as he sat down again.

Rowland glanced back at the painting. "That's a William McInnes." He smiled. "Father didn't have much time for him... thought him too young to paint well."

Edna laughed. McInnes had won the Archibald Prize six times already and was one of the country's most acclaimed portrait artists. Still, he would have been in his early twenties when he'd painted Henry Sinclair. "It's such a fierce painting. Is it a good likeness?"

"Yes."

"Did he like it... your father?"

"It used to hang in his study at *Oaklea*, so I presume he did."

"At *Oaklea*? Then what's it doing here?" Edna asked, surprised. She'd assumed that Rowland kept the portrait in his studio amongst all his own work because it had always hung there. It intrigued her that he would install it himself.

Rowland's smile was brief. "My father always liked to keep an eye on me."

Edna wondered if she had misjudged Henry Sinclair. Rowland rarely spoke of his father but that need not, of itself, mean their relationship had been strained. Perhaps it was a silence born of loss. Perhaps, beneath the outward severity, Henry Sinclair's was an artistic soul. Rowland's talent, Edna reasoned, must have come from somewhere. "It's a shame he didn't live to see your work, Rowly," she said quietly.

Rowland frowned, his jaw tightened. "It's not a shame at all, Ed." He retrieved the jacket he had thrown over the back of his chair.

"Where are you going?" Edna asked uneasily.

"I have an appointment in the city."

"Rowly, I'm sorry if I—"

Rowland stopped, realising that she believed she'd offended him somehow, that he'd been unintentionally abrupt. He moved to sit directly opposite Edna and answered the question she'd not yet asked. "My father would not have approved of my work, Ed. He would not have tolerated it."

"But you didn't paint when he was alive."

"No, I was only fifteen when Father died. Still, I did plenty of other things he disapproved of."

Edna glanced up at the portrait. "You don't take after him at all?"

"No. I don't think so."

"I'm glad."

"To be honest, I am too." He checked his watch. "Now, I really am late."

"Who are you going to see?"

"Eric Campbell."

"Campbell? Rowly, I don't think that's such a—"

"It's not a private audience, Ed. He's delivering another one of his stirring speeches," Rowland replied dryly.

"Even so," Edna persisted, convinced that Rowland's determination to personally foil Campbell at every turn was ill advised. "He's a dangerous man, Rowly."

Rowland nodded. "Yes, I believe he is. And I don't think he's finished. I just want to know what he's thinking."

"They won't let you—"

"I'll be a face in the crowd, Ed. It's been nearly two years since I crossed the New Guard… de Groot and half the executive have resigned or been expelled—no one will notice me."

Edna studied him for a moment, and then she stood. "Well, we'd better get going then."

"I didn't mean…"

Edna retrieved her gloves from the sideboard. "I can't think of anything I'd rather be doing than listening to Mr. Campbell give a speech," she said grimacing. A thought occurred to her and she glanced down at her simple cotton dress. It was a little faded and a couple of seasons out of style. "Where is Mr. Campbell giving this speech, Rowly… should I change?"

Rowland contemplated the sculptress. He had seen her nearly every day for almost three years. She lived in his house, was his model and his muse. Yet even now, just looking at her took his breath. "No, don't change."

3

SUED LEADER OF NEW GUARD

£401 5/8 FOR ALLEGED LEGAL EXPENSES

SYDNEY, Sept 21

The case in which John Francis Dynon had sued Eric Campbell, leader of the New Guard, for £401 5/8, alleged to have been expenses incurred in the defence of the plaintiff and other members of the New Guard who were convicted at the Central Court of having assaulted Alderman J. Garden in May of last year, was brought to an end by the announcement of Mr. Justice Halse Rogers in the Supreme Court today that the matter had been settled out of court. The terms of the settlement were not disclosed.

Kalgoorlie Miner, 1933

The barrel-chested men who guarded the entrance to the hall were noticeably uniformed by their lack of jackets and the coloured armbands which stood out against the crisp white of exposed shirtsleeves. They stopped Rowland and Edna, silently cutting them out of the crowd of New Guardsmen and curious citizens streaming into the hall.

Rowland cursed under his breath, grabbing Edna's hand and turning to leave.

"Sinclair!" One of the jacketless guardsmen smiled broadly as he barred Rowland's way.

"Hodges," Rowland replied pulling Edna behind him. The guardsman was one of many Rowland had met when he'd infiltrated the New Guard. His cover was, of course, no longer intact and the New Guard knew well that Rowland Sinclair had been a spy in their midst. Many believed he had tried to assassinate their leader.

Hodges conferred quietly with a couple of his colleagues.

"You'd better come with me," he said curtly.

"I don't think so," Rowland replied. "We might just be on our way."

Hodges' eyes narrowed. "There are three thousand right thinking men here... what do you suppose would happen if they knew who you were, that you were the Red mongrel who tried to kill the commander?"

Rowland said nothing, furious with himself for so carelessly bringing Edna into danger. Campbell's men were not averse to violence.

"Very well," he said slowly. "But allow Miss Higgins to leave first."

"No, I think I'll stay," Edna was defiant.

"Ed—"

"We're not going to let your young lady go just yet," Hodges interrupted. "If you make us drag you, she could get hurt."

Rowland flared. "Touch her and I'll—"

"Ten seconds and I'll announce who you are and leave you to it," Hodges threatened.

"Rowly..." Edna glanced back into the hall at the packed assembly of guardsmen all chanting for Campbell.

Rowland squeezed her hand. The sculptress was right. They would have to take their chances with Hodges.

A dozen guardsmen escorted them to an anteroom adjoining the hall. Hodges entered first, and after a brief interval Rowland and Edna were ushered in. Eric Campbell stood before a full-length mirror, grooming his moustache.

"Sinclair," he said coldly, regarding them first in the mirror. He turned. "And your charming fiancée… or has Miss Higgins become Mrs. Rowland Sinclair since we last had the pleasure?"

"No," Rowland said curtly. He was fairly sure Campbell knew that Edna had never been his fiancée. "What do you want, Campbell?"

"I could ask the same thing of you," Campbell said turning back to the mirror to adjust his tie. He didn't wait for Rowland to respond. "This is a day of significance Sinclair, an historic day. Today we will take the first step towards smashing the corrupt machine of party politics from within. Democracy has had its chance. Australians deserve a better system."

"This won't work," Rowland said. "Not here."

"I met some gentlemen in Germany who might disagree," Campbell replied. "Mr. Hitler's government worked within the system to deliver the change the German people wanted… I see no reason why the Centre Party supported by the New Guard can't do the same here."

"You can't seriously be looking to emulate the Nazis!" Rowland said angrily. "For God's sake, man, Hitler is—"

Hodges pushed him back. "Shut your Red trap, Sinclair."

Rowland might have thrown a punch then and there if Edna was not still holding onto his hand.

"You'll find, Sinclair," Campbell said, with a restraining grip on Hodges' shoulder, "that there'll be no receptive ear for your Bolshevik slander here."

Edna tried. "Mr. Campbell, you don't understand. We were in Germany…"

"So was I, Miss Higgins. And let me tell you I was impressed. In orderliness and cleanliness, the Germans have no equal! They are happy and content and prosperous."

"And what about the German Jews, Mr. Campbell—are they happy and content?" Edna asked.

Campbell's reply was smooth, practised. "The only Jews I saw were eating in restaurants... fat, well-dressed people who scoffed at notions that they were persecuted in any way!"

Rowland shook his head. "Don't bother, Ed. The man is an idiot, too vain to recognise what's in front of his nose."

Campbell's face hardened. "What's in front of my nose, Sinclair, is a spoiled Red sympathiser, a traitor!" He took a step towards Rowland. "You are not welcome here amongst the noble and decent men of the New Guard, *comrade*. Go back to your shirking Commie mates and wait for the judgement day that's coming to you!"

"I won't be waiting quietly, Campbell," Rowland's voice was thick with contempt. "You go ahead and follow Mr. Hitler's plan, copy his every move, but you'll find it won't work in Australia!"

Campbell smiled. "You might care to watch yourself. Some of the lads quite earnestly believe you got off too lightly last time we crossed paths. They may decide to deal the justice that most loyal, right thinking men believe you deserve."

"Rowly, let's just go," Edna said before he could respond. She grabbed his arm. "Rowly!"

Rowland nodded slowly. They'd already pushed their luck.

Four guardsmen, including Hodges, escorted them out of the anteroom, accompanying them down the street, well away from the crowds gathered around the hall in which Eric Campbell's parliamentary ambitions would be launched.

"Right, Sinclair," Hodges snarled. "Get lost!" He half turned away and then changed his mind.

"Rowly!" Edna screamed as the guardsman swivelled and swung.

Rowland ducked, pushing Edna back with his left arm whilst he led with his right. Of course, there were four New Guardsmen, and they closed in.

"Oi!" A shout from behind them.

"Harry!" Edna responded as she recognised the first of the two burly men now charging the affray. Harcourt Garden would help them.

With the odds now almost equal, the guardsmen pulled back and the confrontation turned into a heated skirmish of words, and even that was curbed in profanity by the presence of Edna.

After a sufficiency of threats had been duly exchanged, the guardsmen departed, telling themselves and each other that they had put the fear of God into Rowland Sinclair.

Harcourt Garden slapped Rowland on the back and introduced him to his companion, Paul Bremner, a solid swarthy Union man with a Communist badge pinned to his flat cap. "This is the bloke who tried to shoot that Fascist bastard Eric Campbell a couple of years ago... before old Jock got worked over by the bloody Boo Guard!" he told Bremner proudly. Harcourt's father, Jock Garden, was a founder of the Communist Party of Australia and a vocal proponent of the Left. He'd been brutally ambushed outside his own home by a group of hooded vigilantes whose connection to Campbell and the New Guard was widely known, if never proved.

"I didn't shoot anyone," Rowland corrected the record as he shook hands with Harcourt Garden's mate.

"We've given you points for trying," Garden said, slinging his arm around Rowland's shoulders.

"What happened? Did ya miss?" Bremner asked, grinning.

"No. I got shot," Rowland said wearily.

Edna looked at him in horror. "I can't believe you're bringing that up again!"

Rowland smiled. Edna hated being reminded that she'd shot him. "I should buy you gentlemen a drink, I suspect," he said, judiciously changing the subject.

The task of so thanking their saviours was, however, complicated by Edna whose presence, and refusal to sit by herself in the ladies' bar, precluded a simple stop at the nearest pub. It was Bremner who suggested the wine bar not far from Trades Hall. The décor was on the sparse side of rudimentary, but the venue was full. Men and women gathered about the small round tables in conspiratorial groups. Whether or not they were actually conspiring was hard to tell—they could well have been discussing the cricket—but in the smoke filled haze of the Communist haunt it was not hard to imagine that the odd plot was being hatched. Rowland Sinclair's party shared a bottle of McWilliams red while they talked of Campbell's political aspirations. Garden and Bremner were inclined to dismiss them as a joke. Rowland, less so. He told Garden of the persecution of trade unionists and dissidents they had seen in Germany, of Dachau and the men forced into hiding. Garden ranted his outrage, Bremner smouldered quietly. And so the morning was passed.

It was nearly noon before Rowland and Edna stood to depart under a chorus of protests and entreaties that they stay for one more drink.

Rowland purchased another bottle for Garden and Bremner to enjoy in their absence.

Bremner raised his glass in thanks. "You watch yourself, Sinclair. The Boo Guard is looking for an enemy. With Premier Lang gone they may just decide that you'll do in a pinch."

The black police vehicle was parked conspicuously in the driveway.

Edna sighed. "What do you suppose Milt's done now?"

"It's probably Delaney," Rowland replied hopefully. He and the detective had helped each other in the past and Delaney occasionally dropped by for a drink.

But it was not Delaney. Detectives Gilbey and Angel had just arrived and were on hand to meet Rowland at his door.

Mary Brown's lips were pursed tightly as Rowland greeted the policemen and introduced Edna. "I'm so glad you're back, Master Rowly—Mr. Sinclair has telephoned thrice this morning!" the housekeeper exclaimed, determinedly dealing first with what she believed the more important matter.

"Wil…?" Rowland stood aside for the detectives to enter. Mary Brown had allowed Wilfred the title of Mr. Sinclair when their father had passed—to her mind there could only ever be one. "If you'd step this way, gentlemen. Thank you, Mary. I'll telephone Wil shortly."

Gilbey and Angel declined refreshments, scrutinising the drawing room as they took the seats Rowland offered. Tubes of pigment, brushes, palettes and various items of artistic paraphernalia sat atop French polished sideboards. The light, coming through the large bay windows by which Rowland's easels were positioned, was softened by the generous canopies of the jacaranda trees outside. Even so, the view of *Woodlands'* manicured lawns was not obscured. Rowland's latest work sat on the largest easel… a dark, moody piece of a naked nymph asleep on a forest floor—a strangely elevated perspective like that of a voyeuristic god. Rowland had begun the painting leaning precariously over the balustrade of the staircase with Edna posed below, on the floor of the hall.

"And how may I be of assistance, gentlemen?" Rowland asked, sitting beside Edna on the settee.

"We'd like you to assist with some enquiries, Mr. Sinclair." Detective Angel cleared his throat and glanced at Edna.

Gilbey studied the sculptress. "The matter is somewhat sensitive, Mr. Sinclair. Perhaps Miss Higgins should—"

"Please go ahead, detectives," Rowland said, mildly curious now.

Angel nodded curtly and proceeded. "What can you tell us about the evening your father, the late Henry Sinclair, was murdered, Mr. Sinclair?"

Edna stiffened. She looked to Rowland for some sign that there was a mistake. Henry Sinclair had died of a heart attack, or old age or something equally unremarkable.

For a moment, Rowland didn't say anything. Then, "That was thirteen years ago, detectives."

"Are you saying you don't remember the night your father was killed?" Gilbey asked.

"I'm wondering why, after all this time, you are questioning me about that night?"

"There's been a development."

"What development?"

"Your father's gun has been found. We believe it was the weapon that killed him."

"I see."

"Aren't you going to ask where it was found, Mr. Sinclair?" Angel studied him too sharply.

Rowland answered calmly, coldly. "I assume you're going to tell me."

Gilbey and Angel exchanged a glance. "At the bottom of the dam closest to the main house at *Oaklea*."

Rowland sat back slowly. "When? When was it found?"

"Early yesterday. They're draining the dam for some landscaping works apparently."

Rowland paused and then he nodded at each of the policemen. "Thank you for letting me know, gentlemen."

"Regrettably, Mr. Sinclair, we did not come to inform you, but to ask you about what you remember from that night. A question you've not answered as yet."

"I was fifteen at the time, detective. I believe I was in bed when Father died. I'm not sure I remember anything at all."

"That seems unlikely if you don't mind my saying, sir."

"It may indeed seem unlikely to you, sir, but it is so."

"Why were you in Yass, Mr. Sinclair?" Gilbey took out a notebook. "Your father was killed during the school term. You were at Kings were you not?"

Rowland's face hardened perceptibly. "I'd been sent down."

"You were expelled?"

"Yes."

"Why?"

Rowland rolled his eyes. "I'd started a poker club among the boarders—I was fifteen."

"Are you saying you've reformed, Mr. Sinclair?"

"Not at all, detective, but I am more discreet."

Gilbey looked archly at Edna. He stood and, stepping over to the easel, inspected the painting. "Is this your work, Mr. Sinclair?" he asked scrutinising the naked nymph so closely that his nose collected some still wet oil paint on its tip.

"Yes."

"Interesting subject. Do you often paint dead bodies?"

Rowland's brow rose.

Edna left the settee to join the detective. "That's Shakespeare's Titania, Detective Gilbey," she whispered. "From *A Midsummer Night's Dream*—she's asleep. Rowly's been painting a series inspired by literary heroines… only Ophelia is dead."

"Of course," Gilbey said brusquely. "I am myself very familiar with the works of William Shakespeare. This is quite an interesting, may

I say, lustful depiction, both poignant and shocking in its dedication to the intimacies of the female form."

Rowland blinked. Apparently the detective was also an art critic.

Angel stared at his colleague, clearly appalled.

Gilbey stood back from the painting and moved his attention instead to the portrait of Henry Sinclair. "Is this—"

"Yes," Rowland replied.

Gilbey nodded slowly, though he did not seem inclined to examine that painting in the same depth.

"If you don't mind my saying, Mr. Sinclair, you don't seem particularly excited by the discovery of your father's gun," Angel quite decidedly directed the conversation away from the artwork.

"Excited?" Rowland made no attempt to hide his scorn. "The burglar who killed my father has had thirteen years to make his escape!"

"Why do you believe a burglar killed your father, Mr. Sinclair?" Gilbey asked sharply.

"There were some valuables taken from the house... I can't remember what exactly they were."

Gilbey wrote in his notebook.

"Is there something more, detective?" Rowland asked suspiciously.

"Several items of silverware and an antique carriage clock were found with the gun."

"Well, there you go."

Gilbey raised his hand. "It's understandable that a killer would seek to rid himself of the murder weapon, but why would he discard the fruits of his burglary?"

"Perhaps he panicked."

"Perhaps he never had any interest in the silver."

"What are you saying, detective?"

"Do you have any idea, Mr. Sinclair, who might have wanted your father dead?"

The pause was so slight that only Edna noticed it.

"I really wasn't privy to my father's affairs." He shrugged. "But I have it on good authority that he was a paragon of virtue and respectability."

Gilbey studied Rowland, his eyes piercing beneath a furrowed brow.

Rowland exhaled impatiently. "If there's nothing further, detectives..."

"Not for now, Mr. Sinclair," Angel said, closing his notebook as he stood. Gilbey followed suit.

Rowland waited as Mary Brown showed the policemen to the door, stepping into the hallway as soon as he heard the door close. Wordlessly he picked up the telephone receiver to book a call through to *Oaklea*.

4

TREE PLANTING

At a lecture on trees given before the Trained Gardeners Association (Old Burnley Students), Miss Edna Walling, the well-known garden designer, said:

"It may seem rather obvious to say that tree-planting in the suburbs is usually a very different matter to tree-planting in the country, but it is not until you are faced with a few acres instead of the accustomed suburban block that the important part trees play in developing large acreages of the country is recognised.

"Even when the supply of labour for the maintenance of an extensive garden scheme is available, nothing will produce a richer or more dignified effect than wood land or a little forest."

The Australasian, 1933

Edna sat curled in the winged-back armchair pondering the police visit. Rowland's telephone conversation with Wilfred had been brief, and then he'd disappeared. It was all somewhat unusual.

Clyde and Milton returned first, a little merry after a party meeting which had apparently been conducted in a public bar. Edna duly informed them of the police visit to *Woodlands*. Like her, neither man had been aware that Rowland's father had died in circumstances that were anything other than ordinary.

"So he was shot?" Milton asked. "In his own home?"

"Apparently." Edna looked out of the window hoping to see Rowland. "Rowly was fifteen."

"And now the police have surmised that he was shot with his own gun?"

"That's what I gathered."

"What did Rowly say?"

"Not a great deal."

Clyde looked up, surprised. "If it were my old dad, I wouldn't rest till…" He scratched his head. "Perhaps it's just the shock."

Milton pondered the portrait of Henry Sinclair. "Where is Rowly, Ed?"

"I don't know, he just vanished," she replied, unable to keep the worry out of her voice. It was not like Rowland.

"He can't have gone far," Clyde observed. "His car's still in the drive."

Edna nodded. The engine of Rowland's flamboyant yellow Mercedes was in any case so loud she would have heard it.

"Rowly's a grown man," Milton said, pouring himself a drink from one of the well-stocked decanters which graced the sideboard. "And we, dear friends, are not his keepers."

It was nearly dark by the time Rowland finally returned. Lenin was with him. The greyhound padded wearily into the drawing room and collapsed onto the rug, glaring resentfully at his master before closing his eyes.

Rowland's houseguests descended from different parts of the mansion where they had been carrying on in an attempt to appear unconcerned about his absence.

"Where have you been?" Edna blurted. "We were beginning to worry… oh my Lord, what have you done to Lenin?"

Rowland glanced at his dog, splayed gracelessly on the Axminster, his tongue lolling out of his head in a manner that looked more like death than slumber. He smiled. "I took Len for a walk," he said, removing his jacket and hanging it on the edge of an easel. "We might have gone a bit further than he's used to."

"Forget about the flaming dog," Clyde muttered. "You all right, Rowly?"

"Ed's told you then?" Rowland loosened his tie. "Yes, I'm well. I just needed to clear my head. I haven't really thought about all that in a while."

"Did Wilfred—" Edna began as Milton poured Rowland a drink.

"Find the gun?" Rowland finished. "No, apparently it was some gardener that Arthur retained."

Arthur Sinclair was Rowland's cousin, a solicitor who had stepped in to keep an eye on the property and old Mrs. Sinclair when both Wilfred and Rowland had been abroad. Apparently he had not yet left.

Edna took Rowland's hand. "I'm so sorry, Rowly... this must be horrible for you."

Rowland squeezed her hand warmly, before releasing it to take the drink that Milton held out to him. "It's fine, Ed. I'm just annoyed that all this is being dredged up for nothing."

"For nothing?" Edna said alarmed he could be so indifferent to such a staggering tragedy.

Rowland sighed. "It was thirteen years ago, Ed. There were no witnesses. Whoever shot Father is long gone, regardless of what gun he used." He sat down, swirling his glass distractedly. "Wil wants me to return home to Yass straight away."

"Because of this investigation?"

"Possibly... either that or my sister-in-law has unearthed another old school chum she feels I should marry."

Edna's brow furrowed slightly. "Oh dear, you don't suppose Kate will be cross about Lucy, do you?"

"How could she possibly be cross?" Rowland said innocently. "It's Colonel Bennett who put an end to it all."

"So are you going?" Clyde asked.

Rowland grimaced. There were a few parties he'd planned to attend before retreating to the more sober celebrations at the family estate. Still… "Yes," he said.

His friends did not try to persuade him otherwise. As much as Rowland appeared to dismiss it, the reinvestigation of Henry Sinclair's murder had clearly shaken him.

"Did the police find out anything at all when your father was first killed, Rowly?" Edna asked.

"Ed!" Clyde scowled at the sculptress. "For pity's sake…"

"It's all right, Clyde. It's a fair question." Rowland put down his glass. "But to be honest, I don't know. I boarded a boat to England the day after my father's funeral."

"The day after? Where the hell were you going in such a hurry?" Milton blurted.

Clyde swatted Milton. "You're as bad as Ed," he muttered, appalled by the poet's lack of sensitivity.

"I suppose it would seem rather odd," Rowland conceded. He tried to explain. "Wil sent me to school in London. I expect he was trying to protect me from all the fuss."

Edna stood with her hands on her hips, her eyes fierce and disapproving. Rowland continued, aware that the sculptress had always thought Wilfred's actions, in this respect, cruel. "Wil had a lot to contend with… the investigation, the property, Father's affairs, not to mention my mother—he wasn't trying to be unkind."

"You were a boy who'd just lost his father," Edna replied, unmoved by his defence. "He sent you away to grieve with strangers."

"It wasn't that simple, Ed."

Edna paused and then let well enough alone. She had no wish to make the situation more difficult with her outrage on his behalf. "When are you going to Yass, Rowly?" she asked.

"I can fly to *Oaklea* tomorrow."

"That soon?"

Rowland smiled. "Did you have plans for me?"

"Of course!" she said perching on the upholstered arm of his chair. She sighed. "I'll have to make do with Milt, I suppose."

"You should be so lucky," Milton muttered indignantly. "You will find that I am very much in demand these days. I may well be busy."

Rowland glanced at Edna regretfully. He had promised to escort the sculptress to the Christmas Ball to be held at the Domain. Not that she would have any trouble replacing him, whether or not Milton was busy—which he somehow doubted.

"I am sorry, Ed," he said.

Edna's face softened. "Oh darling, you have no reason to be. You will be all right, won't you, Rowly?"

"Yes, I will… I am." He slung back the remnants of his drink and smiled at the sculptress. "This is just one of those things, Ed. Wil will probably have cleared it up before I've landed at *Oaklea*."

Rowland banked left and assessed the landscape below the *Rule Britannia*. Someone had let a mob of merinos into the paddock in which he'd been told to land.

"For pity's sake!" There were too many to risk hoping the creatures had sense enough to get out of his path. The only remaining option was the cleared ground near the billabong, but that would mean a five-mile walk to the house.

Cursing, he cut back the engine and began his descent into the wind.

The fence-line was new. Not that Rowland would have, in any case, been familiar with the fence-lines of *Oaklea* but perhaps if the barbed wire had had time to rust he may have seen it before it was too late.

He pulled hard on the joystick, in a desperate attempt to raise the plane's nose. *Rule Britannia* pitched upwards but not enough to clear the fence. The wheels clipped the top wire and the fuselage shook as the undercarriage dragged along the barbs.

The impact slowed the Gipsy Moth and forced her nose even higher. Rowland gunned the engine hoping a burst of speed would soften the landing. It may have done so, but the landing was hard regardless. The Moth bounced and careered precariously until Rowland managed to regain control and bring her to a stop just short of the water.

Rowland heaved himself out of the fuselage, wincing as he moved the knee which had slammed against the underside of the dashboard when the plane had touched down. He ignored the damage to himself and inspected that sustained by his plane. One tyre had blown and the fabric of the fuselage near the tail was torn where it had been ripped on the barbs.

Rowland limped over to check the fence. Incredibly it seemed perfectly intact despite its brief tussle with the *Rule Britannia*. He removed his cap and goggles, relieved. This was embarrassing enough without having to tell Wilfred that he'd destroyed the fence as well.

Returning to the Gipsy Moth, Rowland retrieved the Gladstone bag he'd stowed in the passenger compartment. Clyde would drop off his trunk and the Mercedes in a couple of days, before catching the train on to Kunama, near Batlow.

"I'll be back for you, sweetheart," he said tossing the aviator cap and goggles into the cockpit and extracting his hat from the bag.

Removing his leather flying jacket, he slung it over his shoulder and set out in the direction of the main house.

The day was warm and the countryside had already taken on a mantle of summer gold. The new green growth coming up amongst the longer yellowed stalks spoke of recent rain despite the ripening of the landscape. Some of the paddocks Rowland cut through were stocked. The lambs, no longer tiny, were still with their mothers and the mobs were sleek on the rich pastures of *Oaklea*.

He'd been walking for nearly an hour when the workman hailed him. "Hey! What are you doing here?"

Rowland stopped and waited for the man to approach. He wasn't about to announce his arrival by shouting across the paddocks.

He realised it was a woman only when she stood before him. Rowland supposed she was about forty, though he couldn't be sure. Tall and broad shouldered, wearing jodhpurs into which was tucked a man's shirt, rolled up at the sleeves. A large sketchbook was clamped under her arm and a small paintbox and brushes protruded from various pockets. She peered curiously at him from beneath a thick, blunt fringe of dark hair.

"I say, are you lost?" she asked. "You're on private property, you know."

Rowland removed his hat. "I'm not lost, Miss..."

"Walling," she said, offering him her hand. "Edna Walling. And who are you?"

"Rowland Sinclair, Miss Walling. How do you do?"

"Well, well... another blue-eyed Sinclair!" Edna Walling looked him up and down. "Good Lord, you've hurt yourself!" she said, noticing his trousers were ripped and bloody at one knee.

"It's just a graze," Rowland replied. "I belted it against the dashboard when I clipped the fence."

"You've had a motor accident..."

"A plane actually," Rowland said, sheepishly. "I was forced to improvise. For some reason Wil's had stock placed in the paddock I planned to use for landing."

"Oh, that would be my fault, I'm afraid." Walling uncapped the canteen she'd had slung across her body and offered him a drink. "We moved them there when we began draining the dam so we weren't having to rescue the silly creatures from the mud constantly."

Rowland realised then with whom he was speaking. "You must be the *gardener chap* that Arthur retained," he said smiling.

She laughed. "In a manner of speaking."

"Are you painting?" Rowland asked, glancing at the sketchbook.

"Just some plans for the grounds." She opened the sketchbook so he could see.

Rowland dropped his coat and took the book to examine the watercolour more carefully. It was an aerial plan of the grounds at *Oaklea*… though he recognised only Wilfred's rose gardens and the grand oaks which lined the drive to the house. Edna Walling had taken those bones and added sweeping stone walls and extensive new plantings. The plans she had created in detailed watercolour were of themselves beautiful—fluid, and balanced with an innate sense of space and light. They conjured the garden she'd designed. Rowland was spellbound.

At Walling's invitation, he turned the page to view the plans for the dam paddock. The small dam was gone in this second watercolour, replaced by a cobble-edged pond, surrounded by terraced gardens.

"Why, these are magnificent," Rowland said. "Has Wil seen them?"

"If you mean Mr. Wilfred Sinclair, yes, of course. We've already started work draining the old dam."

Rowland remembered the gun. "You found the revolver."

"Yes. It was quite the surprise. I took it to Mr. Sinclair and he called the police."

"Wil?" Rowland's eyes narrowed.

"No, the other Mr. Sinclair."

"I see."

"I should let you get on," Walling said, taking back her sketchbook. "I expect they're wondering why you haven't turned up at the house."

5

A LITTLE NONSENSE

HONEST LABOURER

"These barbed-wire fences bean't no good," said the farm labourer. "I wouldn't have one of 'em on my place if I had my way."

"Why not?" inquired the stranger. "They are cheap and strong and keep cattle in better than anything else."

"That may be, sir," replied the rustic, "but a man can't sit down to rest on 'em."

Molong Express, 1938

The old housekeeper threw open the door. Every part of her plump person seemed to beam. Rowland forgot he was on the threshold of his brother's house, where propriety was paramount and a certain reserve preferred, and he embraced her warmly, wholeheartedly. She clasped his face delighted. "Mr. Rowland! Now don't you look a sight! My goodness what have you done to yourself?"

"It's just a scrape, Mrs. Kendall."

"You boys—tearing headlong about the place as if the world was on fire. It's a wonder you don't do yourself serious harm!"

Rowland allowed her to fuss over him as she always had. Though she at least allowed him the title of "Mr.", Alice Kendall had somehow missed that he was no longer twelve years old, smoothing and chiding him as if he were a child, promising to bake him a special batch of shortbread that very same afternoon. Still, her unrestrained motherly welcome reminded him that *Oaklea* had once been his home.

"Uncle Rowly!" Ernest Sinclair came hurtling down the grand staircase. He stopped abruptly and raised his small fists. "Put up your dukes."

"Ernest Aubrey Sinclair!" Kate descended the stairs more slowly behind him. "Is that any way to speak to, let alone to greet your uncle?"

Rowland laughed, dropping gingerly onto his uninjured knee to move Ernest's fists a touch higher and adjust his stance. He'd been teaching his nephew the basics of boxing. Ernest, in his way, applied himself to the sport with solemn diligence.

"That's better," Rowland said when he was satisfied with Ernest's fighting posture. "You don't want to overbalance when you swing."

Ernest thus sorted, Rowland stood to greet his sister-in-law. "Hello Kate. You look well." The swell, which had first become noticeable on Kate Sinclair's slim frame as they were all sailing home from Britain, had become much more pronounced in the two months since they'd returned.

"Did you have a good flight? We were expecting you earlier, Rowly," she said as he kissed her cheek. "Wil thought you might have lost your way."

"Not quite," Rowland replied.

Kate turned to her son. "Ernie darling, if you've quite finished challenging your uncle to fisticuffs, perhaps you might accompany him into the library to see Daddy, while Mrs. Kendall and I see about luncheon. Is that your bag, Rowly? Just leave it here... I'll have one of the maids attend to it."

Ernest took Rowland's hand, pulling him gently but insistently into the hallway.

"Rowly!" Wil was seated on the studded chesterfield. He ground his cigarette into the ashtray of the chrome stand beside him and stood. "We were wondering what had become of you."

Rowland shook his brother's hand explaining quickly why he'd been delayed.

Wilfred frowned. "Sheep? Lord knows what that Walling woman is up to now. We'll be lucky if we have any paddocks left for the bloody stock!"

"Actually I ran into Miss Walling on the walk up to the house," Rowland said. "I must confess I thought her plans rather splendid."

Wilfred sighed. "Yes, yes, she does seem to know what she's doing," he said vaguely. "Kate's idea, you know. Apparently this Miss Walling has a popular column in some publication called *Home Beautiful*. McNair is beside himself. I've had to intervene to prevent him digging trenches to defend the flaming vegetable garden!"

Rowland smiled as his brother mentioned the intemperate one-armed gardener. Having seen service on the Western Front with Wilfred Sinclair, McNair had returned more than just physically damaged. He'd worked at *Oaklea* for the past decade, obsessively planting potatoes and pumpkins on every unattended square of ground.

Wilfred paused to send Ernest off to play. "It was Miss Walling who found Father's gun," he said when they were alone.

Rowland nodded. "She did mention that. And then Arthur called in the police."

"Naturally."

Rowland rubbed the back of his neck. "God, I thought this was finished thirteen years ago, Wil."

Wilfred gripped his brother's shoulder. "You mustn't worry, Rowly. I'll handle it."

"I say, Wilfred—oh, hello." A gentleman of about Wilfred's vintage strode into the library before Rowland could reply. He was, in fact, quite like Wilfred physically. His fair hair was slicked sharply back and his tie sat perfectly against a starched white shirt and, behind wire-rimmed spectacles, his eyes were the same dark, distinct blue that seemed to mark all Sinclair males. He had a similar upright neatness about his person to Wilfred Sinclair, but his smile was more boyish, broad and uncontained.

"Well, well, Cousin Rowland," he said, extending his hand. "I haven't seen you since you were in knee pants! Good Lord, look at you!" He glanced up pointedly at Rowland's height. "They obviously had you on better pasture than Wilfred and me. And the spitting image of poor Aubrey... it's uncanny!"

"They were always quite alike," Wilfred agreed.

"Hello, Arthur." Rowland regarded curiously the cousin whose story had become a precautionary tale in Sinclair family folklore.

Arthur Sinclair had only recently come back into the Sinclair fold after being disinherited before the war for what Wilfred called an "inappropriate association". It may have been that Edward Sinclair, Arthur's father, had not intended to permanently cut off his only child—previous generations of Sinclairs had often used disinheritance to control their sons. Unfortunately, Edward's unexpected death had intervened before the falling out could be resolved or forgiven, and his considerable personal fortune had reverted to his elder brother, Henry Sinclair, becoming part of the great estate that Wilfred now controlled.

Rowland expected that Arthur's current residency at *Oaklea* was Wilfred's way of compensating their cousin for the harshness of their fathers and the anomalies of the succession.

"Young Ernest said he saw your biplane over an hour ago," Arthur continued. "But when you didn't turn up we thought it must have been the boy's imagination. He's been frightfully excited about your visit, hasn't he, Wilfred?"

"Indeed."

"I had to bring her down near the billabong," Rowland said. "Actually I had rather a rough landing. I'm afraid the plane will need a bit of attention."

"You crashed?" Wilfred said, alarmed. He stepped back to look at his brother, noticing the blood on the knee of Rowland's trouser for the first time. "Good Lord, why didn't you say? I thought Kingsford Smith taught you to fly that contraption! I'll send for a doctor."

"I don't need a doctor, Wil," Rowland protested. "It's a graze, that's all. I just haven't had a chance to clean up. But if you could send a lorry to pick up *Doris*, I'd be grateful."

"*Doris*?"

"The plane—she thinks *Rule Britannia* is a daft name. Asked me to call her *Doris* now that we're on more intimate terms."

Wilfred stared at him. Arthur laughed.

"Yes, of course," Wilfred said eventually. "I'll send some men to bring her in. You'd best get cleaned up. Kate will expect us all at luncheon soon."

Rowland knotted his tie hastily, aware that Kate was waiting luncheon on him. Still, it would not have done to sit at his brother's table in a state of dishevelment. He had been given his old bedroom which, aside from new wallpaper and the addition of a shaving mirror to the marble-topped washstand, remained essentially unchanged. The brass bed under which he'd occasionally hidden as a child, still creaked, the oak wardrobe and tallboy still smelled of lavender oil; the heavy Persian rug still caught on the door if you weren't careful. Perhaps it was this business about his father's gun, but the familiarity of it was a little unnerving.

He grabbed the cufflinks he'd left on his last visit from the drawer of the dumb valet, and was still adjusting them when he walked into the drawing room for a customary drink before being seated.

"Aubrey! When did you arrive?" Elisabeth Sinclair clapped her hands joyfully as he entered.

Rowland barely blinked. "Just a short while ago, Mother," he said as he bent down to kiss her cheek. It had been many years since his mother had recognised him for himself, insisting instead that he was the son she'd lost to the Great War. What Elisabeth Sinclair thought had happened to her youngest son was unclear. It appeared she'd forgotten that Rowland ever existed.

The confusion may initially have been born of the marked resemblance between Rowland and the late Aubrey Sinclair, but the delusion had become fixed in Elisabeth's mind and she would not now countenance that he was anyone else. Rowland had long given up trying to remind his mother who he was.

He talked with her for a while, not really impersonating Aubrey but without challenging her mistake. And so the conversation was easy—until she asked him to play for her. Aubrey had been quite the musician, an excellent pianist, and Elisabeth Sinclair was adamant.

"I don't play, Mother."

"Don't be absurd, Aubrey! You play beautifully."

Rowland looked to Wilfred for help.

"Kate will want us to sit down soon I expect," Wilfred intercepted.

Elisabeth Sinclair's green eyes flashed. She straightened. "Yes, well I don't want to be a bother. We don't want to upset Kate, do we?"

"Now I didn't mean—" Wilfred began.

"I'm afraid I'm feeling rather tired." Elisabeth stood. The gentlemen followed suit. "I might take luncheon in my room. I'm sure Kate won't be too upset by my absence."

"Come now, Mother." Wilfred tried in vain to persuade her to change her mind.

Elisabeth refused to hear him. "Arthur, darling, would you be a dear and have Mrs. Kendall send something up on a tray?"

"Er… yes… of course, Aunt Libby," Arthur agreed awkwardly, as she left the room.

Rowland glanced at his brother.

Wilfred sighed. "Mother is becoming more difficult," he said quietly. "It's hardest—she's hardest—on Kate. I suspect she doesn't remember how much she liked her."

"What else has she forgotten?" Rowland asked. His mother had been fragile for some time, but they had hoped it would not get worse.

"She has good days and bad days, Rowly. Both seem to be worse than they once were."

"Can I pour you a whisky, Rowland?" Arthur asked in an apparent effort to soothe the situation with alcohol.

"Whisky… no," Rowland replied, flinching instinctively at the thought.

"I think you'll find Rowly would prefer a sherry or whatever it is the ladies are drinking these days," Wilfred said tersely.

Rowland ignored his brother and helped himself from a bottle of gin. For some reason Wilfred seemed to believe that a dislike of whisky was some unforgivable failure of character.

Arthur laughed. "Give him time, Wil. Young Rowland's only twenty-eight. I couldn't bear whisky until I was thirty." He raised his charged glass. "Then I realised what I'd been missing."

"One can only hope," Wilfred muttered.

Arthur nodded towards the portrait of Kate and Ernest Sinclair hanging above the mantelpiece. The composition was tender—Ernest asleep in his mother's arms. The brushwork was soft, loose. It captured Kate as a young woman becoming aware of her own power and place, gentle, timid but protective and imbued with a kind of gracious strength. "I believe that particular piece is your work, Rowland."

"Yes, it is."

"Why it's simply superb. Quite extraordinary."

Wilfred cleared his throat.

"It must be said, Wil." Arthur continued, regardless. "Business and whatnot is perfectly all right for the likes of us, but your brother is a real talent. God knows where it came from… I've never heard of another Sinclair who could draw anything more than a cheque."

"Possibly because they were more usefully occupied?" Wilfred said testily.

"Usefully occupied… Good Lord, Wil, look at that painting and tell me he should have been doing something else! I look at it and think, by Jove, Wilfred Sinclair is the luckiest man in the empire."

Wilfred glanced at the portrait and despite himself, his eyes softened. "Yes, well I suppose it did come out rather well."

Rowland watched the exchange silently, bemused by Arthur's lavish praise and Wilfred's barely discernible, and hardly unequivocal, approval. The sentiment of the first and the expression of the second were somewhat unexpected.

Kate joined them, having settled the children to eat in the scullery, and they proceeded into the dining room where Alice Kendall had laid out what was more a banquet than luncheon, even at opulent *Oaklea*.

"It appears Mrs. Kendall is pleased to have you home," Wilfred said, regarding the feast comprised of all Rowland's favourite dishes.

Over the meal, which, on account of its abundance, was necessarily a long one, Rowland became reacquainted with Arthur Sinclair who had been excluded from the Sinclair family over twenty years before. It appeared that his cousin had sought his fortune abroad with just enough connections remaining to secure a position articled to a solicitor. The war had intervened and Arthur Sinclair had joined the British army and distinguished himself in France. He had returned to complete his clerkship and had in time established a successful practice of his own in London, returning to Australia just the year before and settling in Melbourne.

"It was rather fortunate that Arthur was able to keep an eye on the place while we were both abroad," Wilfred said, frowning.

Rowland glanced guiltily at Kate, guessing that Wilfred was referring more to their mother than *Oaklea*. Wilfred, and therefore his wife, had always taken responsibility for Elisabeth Sinclair, managing her frailty in a manner that kept her condition from public knowledge and maintained her dignity.

Despite this, Kate still seemed manifestly frightened of her mother-in-law, and, on occasion, Elisabeth Sinclair forgot that she was no longer mistress of *Oaklea*. In the past, any potential conflict had been tempered, if not completely avoided, by Elisabeth's genuine fondness for Kate. Now Rowland wondered if that had changed.

He was aware that by refusing to live on the property, he had effectively abdicated shouldering much of the strain involved with his mother's condition. Perhaps he should take her back to *Woodlands* with him, for a while at least.

Tentatively he suggested it.

Wilfred rolled his eyes. "For pity's sake, Rowly! Do you propose to have our mother live with you and your idle Communist friends? I suspect, seeing for herself what you've done to her house would be one tragedy too far!"

Kate was quiet.

"I'm sure I could—" Rowland began.

"Don't be ridiculous! Mother doesn't even remember who you are, not to mention the fact that you run *Woodlands* in a manner that is hardly appropriate for the residence of a lady!"

"Wil…" Kate touched her husband's arm, startled by the harsh frankness of his words.

Rowland said nothing, seething.

"You know," Arthur Sinclair interrupted the tension. "I would be very pleased to have Aunt Libby stay with me whenever… whenever she needs a change of scenery." He waited while one of the maids took his plate. "We do rub along rather well, and it won't be far away."

Rowland's face was unreadable. It was true that while his mother had forgotten him, she remembered fondly her nephew by marriage who had been cut out of their lives two decades ago—a stinging irony he was trying valiantly not to hold against Arthur.

"If you'll excuse me, gentlemen, I might go and check on the children," Kate said.

"Yes, of course." Wilfred stood to pull out her chair.

"Kate seems a trifle quiet," Arthur whispered as they watched her go.

Wilfred nodded. "I suspect she finds Yass a little dull and lonely after the excitement of our time abroad." He lit a cigarette. "I've organised a small surprise which should cheer her up."

"You cousin, are a prince among men!" Arthur rose from the table. "I have some business in Yass, so I might leave you chaps to it. Wil, do you mind if I—"

"Not at all. Take the Continental," Wilfred replied. There were several Rolls Royce limousines garaged in the *Oaklea* stables. The Phantom II Continental was Wilfred's particular favourite.

When Arthur too had departed, Wilfred took Rowland into his study. Clearly there was much on his mind.

Rowland assumed the seat his brother offered him and watched as Wilfred paced. He was feeling restless himself but they couldn't both pace without risk of collision.

"Look, Rowly, I expect that by now the police will have realised this new investigation into Father's death is futile but, if they haven't, I think we should be crystal clear about what happened."

"I see," Rowland said. He clenched a fist in his hair, his face unguarded for the first time. He was worried. "Just tell me what you want me to say, Wil."

Wilfred sat. He fixed his eyes on Rowland's. "You were in bed when you heard the gunshot. You did not leave your room until I came to tell you there had been a break-in and that Father had been shot and killed."

"Is that all?"

"Yes. I'll deal with the rest of it."

Rowland nodded. "Very well."

"I don't want you to worry, Rowland. I'll take care of this. Just keep your head."

6

GOLF HINTS

———◆———

Art of Putting
USEFUL PRACTICE
(By S.R. HOWARD.)

There is no part of the game which is so vital to a player's
success as putting. When played badly it causes more
aggravation than the misplaying of longer shots. When
a player gets out of the double-figure handicap class an
analysis of his score will show that half of his strokes will
be putts.

Dungog Chronicle, 19 May 1931

The yellow Mercedes slowed to halt outside the chapel on
Oaklea. The small sandstone church sat alone amongst sheep
paddocks and occasional stands of gum trees from which cicadas
raised the background scream of an Australian summer. The
building was encircled by the private cemetery in which Sinclairs had
been interred for generations.

The driver's-side door was swung open, and Clyde Watson Jones
stepped out. A greyhound followed him, its excessive tail already
wagging furiously. Clyde smoothed back his hair before replacing his
hat and adjusting his tie.

He'd called at the homestead, knocking bashfully at the tradesman's entrance where he'd been greeted by Alice Kendall. She'd plied him with tea and cake and informed him that Mr. Rowland was visiting his father's grave. Not wanting to announce his arrival in the absence of the friend who'd invited him, Clyde had followed the housekeeper's directions to the chapel.

He'd been both surprised and relieved to learn Rowland was here. His friend's apparent lack of interest in Henry Sinclair's murder had unsettled Clyde. It was not the way one expected a son to behave. But visiting graves was. Perhaps it was the shock of learning the gun had been found, or simply that insane upper class stoicism that had initially made Rowland seem so indifferent.

Clyde held tightly to Lenin's collar as they walked around behind the chapel to the main part of the picket-fenced cemetery. The dog struggled against the restraint as they sighted his master—by a grave and on his knees. Clyde held the dog back, respectfully allowing Rowland a private moment of prayer.

Less considerately, Lenin barked.

Rowland looked up. "Clyde!" he said pulling his arm out of the dirt and walking over the grave at which he'd been kneeling to greet his friend. He slipped the golf ball into his pocket before he offered Clyde his hand. "How are you? Hello Len."

The hound responded with a demented excitement, leaping and writhing with such pure joy that he seemed unable to proceed with any composure at all. It took a time to calm him. It was while Rowland was thus occupied that Clyde noticed the golf clubs. They were propped against a marble headstone at the apex of which was mounted a gilded angel who appeared to be wearing Rowland's jacket.

"Rowly, what the dickens were you doing?"

Rowland looked up from his dog. He pulled the golf ball from his pocket. "I was retrieving my ball... that hole's a few inches deeper than I remember. I hope it hasn't attracted a resident."

"What?"

"A snake."

"No, I mean... what are you doing here?"

"Playing golf with Aubrey," Rowland said, pointing out a bronze and sandstone memorial a few yards away. The inlaid portrait of a young soldier might have been Rowland Sinclair, so striking was the resemblance.

"And exactly how often do you golf with your late brother?"

"We try to play a round whenever I'm back in Yass."

"Rowly, mate, this is a cemetery."

Rowland smiled. "Yes... it's more putting and chipping practice than an actual game of golf." He retrieved his jacket from the headstone, revealing the inscription: "Henry John Sinclair, 6th July 1851 – 13th March 1920". There was something more below that began with the word "Beloved", but which had otherwise been so badly chipped as to render the original lettering illegible.

Rowland fetched a putting iron, dropped the golf ball on to the grass before him and, lining up his shot, swung. The ball hit the headstone like a bullet. "Beloved" became "Belove".

"You've lost your mind!" Clyde accused.

Rowland laughed but he offered no explanation. "Did you have a good run?"

"Yes, not bad. I'm early in fact."

"Good! Can you stay a while? I might need your help with something."

"I'm not playing golf in a cemetery. I'll have enough explaining to do when I face the Almighty as it is!"

"No, not golf. Something else."

"Then, sure. I could catch a train tomorrow or the next day if your brother doesn't mind my sleeping in one of his sheds."

"He mightn't, but I would," Rowland replied. "I'm sure we can find you an actual bed."

"In that case, what do you need?"

"I'll show you." Rowland gathered his golf clubs and stowed them in a rough shed behind the chapel. He patted his brother's memorial affectionately, before heading back to the Mercedes. Slipping behind the wheel, he drove them to what was technically a separate holding. *Emoh Ruo* had been purchased by Wilfred a couple of years previously and, with it, the *Rule Britannia*. Past the now uninhabited homestead was a cluster of sizeable sheds.

Rowland keyed the padlock that secured the largest shed, and opened the doors wide to allow light into what was a makeshift hangar.

Clyde whistled. "What the hell happened to her?"

"I landed a bit hard and clipped a fence on the way down," Rowland confessed. "I've managed to procure a replacement tyre through the local flying club—it'll be here tomorrow morning."

"Any other damage?"

"I'll need to patch the fuselage…"

Clyde nodded, running his hand over the rips in the body's fabric. "You'll need some linen canvas and a couple of coats of dope. You're damn lucky the wire didn't go over the wheel—you'd have flipped old *Doris* completely."

Rowland nodded. "It was a new fence," he said in his own defence. "I didn't see it until it was too late."

Clyde squatted before the damaged wheel. "We might as well get started then." He removed his jacket and rolled up his shirtsleeves. Rowland followed suit.

Having worked for a time in a motor mechanic's workshop,

Clyde had acquired an understanding of machines, and the virtue of improvisation.

And so they remained in the shed, jacking up the *Rule Britannia* and determining how to remove the shredded wheel. As they worked, Clyde brought Rowland up to date with goings on in Sydney: Edna had won a part in another film.

"I think she must die in this one," he said, grimacing. "She's been rehearsing her final moments in the drawing room… sounds like it may be a painful demise. Your housekeeper is not happy. That's why I had to bring the dog with me. Miss Brown is quite clearly fed up with the strays you bring home."

Rowland laughed. Over the years Edna had procured the odd acting role in local amateur productions and been an extra on one or two films. Perhaps it was because she approached the roles like an excited child at play that none of them took it seriously.

They'd only just managed to remove the wheel when Wilfred's Continental approached. The racing green duco was coated with a thick layer of red-brown dust. The chauffeur opened the door, and Wilfred and Arthur Sinclair stepped out.

"Good Lord, she's a beauty!" Arthur said admiringly. "What a jolly ship!"

"She will be once Clyde and I fix my little mishap," Rowland said smiling. Wilfred had never appreciated the biplane sufficiently. It pleased Rowland that Arthur, at least, could give the aircraft her due. "And what are you gentlemen doing out here?"

"We've stopped in to see what you were up to, on our way to the house," Wilfred said. "I thought Arthur might like to take over the *Emoh Ruo* homestead since he plans to stay on in Yass."

"As long as you don't have any objections, Rowland," Arthur added hastily. "Wilfred assures me that you have no intention of taking over the place yourself… but if you've changed your mind—"

"God, no!" Rowland glanced at Wilfred, more disconcerted by the fact that his brother had not mentioned that he planned to offer Arthur a house on what was now the greater Sinclair property, than by the offer itself. "I'm happy where I am."

While Clyde showed Arthur what they were doing to repair the biplane, Wilfred took the opportunity to pull Rowland aside. "I am informed that Campbell, Campbell and Campbell is preparing to take action against you for slander and libel."

Rowland frowned. Campbell, Campbell and Campbell, as the name suggested, was Eric Campbell's law firm.

"Let him sue."

"For God's sake, Rowly, can't you just leave this alone? Campbell's Centre Party will amount to nothing. You are making yourself a target for no reason at all!"

"But what if it doesn't amount to nothing, Wil?" Rowland asked, shaking his head.

Wilfred looked at him thoughtfully. "I know you're still smarting after what happened in Germany but there are better ways of taking a stand against him, Rowly. All you're doing at the moment is inviting the New Guard to silence you one way or another."

"I am not afraid of those—"

"This is not the time to call out all your enemies!" Wilfred stopped as Clyde and Arthur emerged from the shed. "We'll talk about this later. At least you can't get into any more trouble while you're here!"

Rowland could hear the bubbling chatter of his nephews as he came down the stairs. They were in the conservatory with Clyde who was telling them some kind of country yarn, spinning it out with amusing voices and imitations. His tale was consequently interrupted by Ernest's giggles and questions and exclamations of thrilled horror. Ewan, who was only eighteen months old, babbled and clapped with equivalent enthusiasm.

Rowland smiled. Clyde had a way with children. He expected that his fellow artist would be the first of them to settle down and do that for which his long-suffering Catholic mother prayed. He knew that Clyde's sweetheart, a young woman by the name of Rosalina Martinelli, was of the same mind, though Clyde himself was in less of a hurry. Indeed, Clyde had been playing a game of matrimonial duck and weave since they'd returned from abroad.

They'd come in only a short while earlier to clean up and dress for dinner. Rowland's trunk had, by then, been collected from the Mercedes, taken up to his room and unpacked. Kate had welcomed Clyde to *Oaklea* and ensured he was comfortably accommodated in one of its many guest rooms.

They were dining formally that evening. Rowland's dinner suit had, of course, been in the trunk Clyde had delivered with the Mercedes. Clyde's not untirely unfounded conviction that any interaction with the upper classes, however brief, would require formal attire, meant he had also brought his own.

It was when Rowland was about to join Clyde and the boys in the conservatory that he heard the commotion at the front door and Kate, breathless with excitement. "Oh Wil, how could you not tell me? What a truly wonderful surprise!"

"I thought you might like the company, Katie," Wilfred replied. Rowland could hear the warmth in his brother's voice. It was always the way when Wilfred Sinclair spoke of, or to, his wife and sons.

Rowland hung back, allowing them that moment alone. He may have continued in to join Clyde if he hadn't heard a vaguely familiar voice shriek, "Kate, darling!"

And then, Kate's response. "Lucy, how simply wonderful to see you!"

Rowland closed his eyes and cursed under his breath. With everything that had happened he had completely forgotten to mention his awkward conversation with Colonel Bennett to his brother and sister-in-law.

"Rowly!" Wilfred caught sight of him as they walked through into the drawing room. "You remember Miss Lucy Bennett…"

Lucy gasped. She had arrived dressed for dinner, in voluminous, emerald-green taffeta and jewels. Perhaps it was the influence of the season, but she reminded Rowland of a blonde Christmas tree.

"A pleasure to see you again, Miss Bennett," he said uncomfortably.

Lucy stared at him. Some moments later, it seemed she might speak, but instead her eyes brimmed with tears and she pushed past Rowland to run up the stairs in quite obvious distress.

Dumbfounded, Wilfred and Kate watched her go.

"Oh… oh dear," Kate said eventually. "I'd best go after her." She set off up the stairs in concerned pursuit.

Wilfred grabbed Rowland's arm, furious. "What the hell did you do to that girl?"

"Nothing," Rowland replied, shaking off Wilfred's grip. "Her father asked me never to see her again."

"What! Why? If you've—"

"For God's sake, Wil!" Rowland said, affronted. "Colonel Bennett came to see me. Somehow he'd got the impression that I wanted to marry his daughter, which I can assure you, I do not!"

Wilfred cursed. "Why didn't you tell me you'd jilted the poor girl?"

"I didn't jilt her… I've never had any—"

"She's Kate's dearest friend, Rowly. Why would you—no wonder she—" He stopped as a thought occurred to him. "If you refused her, why did Bennett feel the need to forbid you seeing her again?"

"I hadn't had the chance to tell him when he met my friends and decided I was not a fit and proper suitor for his daughter."

"Well, that part is perfectly understandable," Wilfred growled. He sighed. "The poor wretch probably believes I've orchestrated this encounter in defiance of her father's wishes."

"I'll leave," Rowland offered.

"Bloody hell, Rowly, why can't you do anything without a public scandal? Colonel Bennett will unleash the dogs of war when he hears you're here."

"I can be gone before she comes down for dinner," Rowland said again, but Wilfred was not listening to him. Kate and Lucy were descending the stairs arm in arm.

"Gentlemen, you must forgive me," Lucy said, when they'd come down. "It's been a frightful trip. I'm afraid I was tired and overwrought. You must think me terribly silly, Mr. Sinclair."

"It's wonderful to have Rowly and Lucy visiting at the same time, don't you think, Wil?" Kate's enthusiasm was distinctly forced. "The four of us will make such a jolly party."

Wilfred cleared his throat, glaring at Rowland. "Don't forget Arthur, my dear."

"Or Clyde," Rowland added. "Indeed, I might just go and tell him that we'll be going in for dinner," he said, taking the opportunity to retreat, for a while at least. "What would you like done with the boys, Kate?"

"Oh, I'd better have them taken up to the nursery," Kate replied. "Nanny de Waring will have their supper waiting."

"Clyde and I will do that," Rowland volunteered, already on his way to the conservatory. "It'll give you and Miss Bennett a chance to get reacquainted."

7

THE HOME CIRCLE

A SIGN OF TRUE LOVE

Rarely, indeed almost never, is it of any use for a man to ask advice as to how he shall manage a proposal of marriage to the woman of his choice. Books of etiquette, with formulas for every occasion, counsel from obliging and deeply interested friends, however experienced, alike are of little or no avail to "him who lacks a tongue."

Shyness is, above all, a distinguishing characteristic of true love, and the man who has most cause highly to esteem himself is often the one who is most diffident, who will stammer and blush like a bashful schoolboy in the presence of the woman whom he believes to be the paragon of her sex and who all the while, if the truth were known, may be longing to help him out with his faltering speech.

Camperdown Chronicle, 1934

Ewan Sinclair shrieked in delight as he was hoisted onto Clyde's broad shoulders. He grabbed a chubby fistful of the artist's sandy hair and bounced. Ernest punched into Rowland's open palms, his face fierce and clenched in concentration.

"Good show, Ernie!" Rowland said as his nephew managed a jab without closing his eyes. "What did I tell you? Your aim's rather better when you can see."

Ernest nodded thoughtfully.

"Come on then, Sonny Jim." Rowland got up off his knees. "Your supper's waiting and Clyde and I have to go in to dinner."

"Are you going to marry Aunt Lucy?" Ernest blurted.

Rowland was startled enough to answer bluntly, "No."

"Oh. Are you sure, Uncle Rowly?" Ernest's small brow furrowed with concern. "Aunt Lucy is very suitable."

Clyde smothered a snigger. Rowland stared at his nephew, wondering what adult conversations the boy might have overheard.

"I'm sure she is, Ernie, but I'm afraid that I'm not."

Ernest nodded solemnly. "Oh, I see." He took Rowland's hand. "Will you tell Nanny de Waring that you kept us playing so she won't be cross?"

"That I can do."

"And that we needn't go to bed straight after supper?"

"That might be trickier." Rowland grabbed Ernest and slung the boy over his shoulder. "When did you become such a scamp?" he asked as Ernest writhed and squealed.

And so the younger Sinclairs were delivered somewhat raucously to the sanctuary of the nursery so that the adults could go about the business of dinner.

Kate's other dinner guests had arrived by the time Rowland and Clyde made their way down. Kate had, like any good hostess, attempted to alleviate the gender imbalance by inviting Miss Edna Walling to join them. Lucy's surprise arrival had happily evened the numbers exactly, so now each lady had a gentleman to escort her into the dining room.

The seating arrangements placed Rowland between Lucy Bennett and Edna Walling. Resigned now to an awkward evening, he just hoped for the best.

Clyde took his place on the other side of the garden designer. The two seemed to find each other good company from the outset.

Unlike Rowland, Clyde painted landscapes and so perhaps it was this appreciation of nature that each recognised in the other. It may also have been a certain discomfiture in the rarefied atmosphere of an *Oaklea* dinner party. Sun-bronzed and straight-backed, Edna Walling looked as out of place in the constriction of her fussy lace-trimmed gown as Clyde had always seemed in a dinner suit, however well-tailored.

In the absence of any protocol on how to proceed, Rowland decided to carry on as if he had never spoken with Colonel Bennett. Perhaps Lucy, too, wished to relegate the whole embarrassing incident to the past. After all, it was quite possible that her overzealous father had acted of his own accord.

Lucy's behaviour did, in fact, reassure him on this account. She was as cheerfully vacuous as ever. She asked about his time abroad, enquiring after fashions and acquaintances she'd made during her own season in London, and extolling over Kate Sinclair's presentation at court. Of course, nobody mentioned the murders. They were, after all, at dinner.

Elisabeth Sinclair was also her best self this night, the charming hostess who had once claimed a place at the pinnacle of gracious society. Rowland had vague memories of his mother thus when he'd been very young—long before the war, when his brother and father had been alive. Wilfred expertly managed the conversation so that her inescapable frailty, her inability to acknowledge Rowland with anything but Aubrey's name, and Aubrey's life, was barely noticed.

As the main course was being cleared, Elisabeth Sinclair bid them all good night. "Late nights and Mrs. Kendall's desserts are best enjoyed by the young," she said, smiling warmly. All the gentlemen stood, volunteering to see her to her rooms, but it was Arthur's arm she chose.

"Your mama seems well tonight, Mr. Sinclair," Lucy said once Elisabeth had left the room.

Rowland nodded. "She does." He presumed that, despite

Wilfred's efforts, the malady of his mother's memory was something of which Lucy was aware.

"She has been rather unwell, I believe."

"For quite a while," Rowland murmured more to himself than anyone else.

"Kate believes that it would be easier if your mama had another daughter-in-law."

"She said that?"

"Not exactly, but I know Kate would love nothing more than to have another woman in the family."

"I expect she would."

Lucy giggled.

Rowland looked desperately for some way to steer the subject to one less personally threatening. As luck would have it, he overheard a snippet of Clyde's conversation which served the purpose admirably.

"A project of this size must be daunting, Miss Walling. When we were abroad we visited whole countries smaller than *Oaklea*!"

"Fortunately, Mr. Watson Jones, we are not converting the entire property into garden, just the immediate grounds, which already have excellent bones. I'm just adding a few highlights."

"You must have Miss Walling show you her plans, Clyde," Rowland interjected. "They're quite splendid."

Kate nodded. "I'm very much looking forward to seeing it all in place."

The garden designer sighed. "We would be progressing a great deal more quickly if the jolly police would stop bothering me about that old gun!"

Wilfred cleared his throat.

"That Gilbey chap," she continued, "is insisting the area be sieved before he'll let me get on with building the ponds. You'd think I'd dug up Tutankhamun's tomb!"

The table fell silent as the Sinclairs struggled for an appropriate response.

In the end, Rowland leaned over and said quietly, "I'm afraid, Miss Walling, that the police believe our late father was killed with that gun."

Edna Walling turned quite crimson. "Oh, my Lord, how clumsy of me. I had no idea... I hope you can forgive my lack of tact."

"Not at all, Miss Walling. You weren't to know," Wilfred said. "Indeed it was remiss of us not to have told you sooner since you did us the service of finding the weapon."

Dessert was served: an extraordinary construction of meringue, brandied pears and caramel sauce.

Edna Walling was noticeably quiet.

"Please don't feel badly," Rowland whispered to the embarrassed garden designer. "My father died a long time ago. It's not a fresh wound by any means."

"You can always trust me to drop a clanger!" Edna lamented.

Rowland laughed, taking up his dessert fork. "Tell me, Miss Walling, what exactly did the police want?"

"All sorts of daft information, Mr. Sinclair. What vegetation has been removed, whether the dam was visible from the house, how long it would take to get from the house to the dam, whether the dam was visible from the workmen's cottages... I'm afraid they must have mistaken me for a surveyor!"

"I imagine it must be testing your patience, Miss Walling, but I'm sure the matter will be put to rest soon."

"Do you expect they'll find your father's murderer quickly, Mr. Sinclair?"

Rowland shook his head. "No. I don't expect they'll find him at all."

"You're being rather pessimistic, don't you think, old chap?" Arthur said, having returned to the table. He smiled broadly.

"Wouldn't it be something if, after all these years, justice could finally be done?"

"It's quite frightening to think that a man was murdered in this very house." Lucy shuddered. "I'm quite sure I won't sleep at all tonight."

"Well, perhaps we should talk of a more pleasant subject." Wilfred's tone was not that of mere suggestion.

"Oh yes, let's," Kate said. "Miss Walling you must tell us more about your work. How exactly does one construct a dry rock wall?"

Rowland stepped out onto the verandah. The night air was perfumed with the heady scent of his brother's prized roses. Closest to the house the blooms were red. Wilfred had planted them for Kate.

Rowland smiled as he pondered the remontant tribute. It was hard to believe stern, pragmatic Wilfred Sinclair was capable of so romantic a gesture.

After dinner the ladies had retired to the drawing room leaving the men at the dining table with their brandy and cigarettes. Rowland alone did not smoke. Perhaps it was the cigarette fumes, but he'd felt a sudden need for fresh air. And so he'd excused himself.

"Rowland." Lucy Bennett stepped out after him.

He was as startled by her use of his Christian name as by her emergence. "Miss Bennett."

"We're alone, my darling. Finally." Lucy closed her eyes and inhaled deeply. "I'm not going to cry, I promise." She moved towards him. "Oh, Rowland, what are we going to do?"

"Do?"

"About Pater... his opposition to us." She ran her hand over the silk of his lapel.

For some moments, Rowland could think of nothing which would help him. And then he pulled himself together. "He's your father, Miss Bennett. We have to respect his wishes."

She smiled, fluttering her eyelids in a manner Rowland had once assumed an involuntary twitch, but had since discovered was intended to be flirtatious. "You wouldn't have organised this tryst if you intended to respect his wishes, my darling."

"I can assure you I didn't—"

"You don't need to deny it, Rowland. Knowing you'd defy Pater for us only makes me love you more."

A voice from the darkness, a timely intrusion. "Rowly, is that you?"

"Clyde!" Rowland responded with an unmistakeable note of "thank God" in his voice. "Miss Bennett and I were just taking some air. I say, why don't you join us?"

It was not so dark that Rowland couldn't see Clyde's grin.

"I'd best get back to the ladies before they wonder what has become of me," Lucy said casting a resentful glance Clyde's way. "Good evening, gentlemen."

"Well?" Clyde asked when she was gone.

"Miss Bennett seems to believe that it's only her father keeping us apart."

"Oh... sorry."

Rowland leaned back against a verandah post. "She has consequently concluded that the two of us happening to be here at the same time is some sort of illicit tryst!"

Clyde rubbed his brow , his lips pursed as he tried not to laugh. "So what are you going to do?"

"I'm hoping Wil will feel honour-bound to inform Colonel Bennett that I'm here."

"And if he doesn't?"

Rowland shrugged. "I'll tell Miss Bennett that I'm Catholic."

Rowland and Clyde were just setting out to complete the repairs to the *Rule Britannia* when the telephone call came through. Wilfred signalled them to wait.

"What's wrong?" Rowland asked as Wilfred slammed down the receiver.

"Detectives Gilbey and Angel are on their way."

"Here?"

"Yes. They've been despatched from Sydney to deal with Father's murder."

"What do they want? I've already—"

"Someone has apparently come forward."

"Who? And what the hell have they come forward with?"

"I presume we'll know soon enough," Wilfred replied calmly.

Rowland cursed.

Wilfred ignored him. "I think it may be prudent to have Arthur sit in."

"Arthur?"

"He's a solicitor, Rowly."

Gilbey and Angel were not alone. Clyde had been about to join the ladies when all the policemen were shown into the library—the detectives, two uniformed constables and one other, a large, barrel-chested man who had gone to seed. He was perhaps sixty, his suit as worn as his countenance. His hands trembled slightly and the veins at his temples seemed to visibly pulse. Clyde saw Rowland tense, he noticed his friend's face. And so he stayed.

Detective Angel introduced the fifth man. "I believe you may know Mr. Charles Hayden."

"Whoa, Rowly!" Clyde grabbed Rowland as he launched himself at Hayden. The constables moved quickly to protect their informant and restrain his attacker.

"What the hell is this man doing on my property?" Wilfred turned on Gilbey.

"Perhaps we should have conducted these enquiries at the station," Gilbey said, standing his ground. "Mr. Hayden has made a statement. We hoped we might gauge your reactions to his story." Gilbey looked at Rowland. "I suppose we have already, but I had thought you'd like to hear what he had to say first."

Wilfred's face was stony. "You had no business bringing this man into my house. Be assured that I will be speaking to the commissioner, if not the premier, about this outrage."

"Wilfred." Arthur Sinclair intervened to soothe his cousin. He spoke quietly. "If this chap's made a statement, it may be in our interests to hear him out. If he's lying or just making mischief we can establish that before matters get out of hand."

"I can warrant that he will be making mischief!" Wilfred replied.

"Even so, Wil, you'll not be giving him a hearing that he hasn't already had. Let's deal with the scoundrel now and then this investigation, such as it is, can resume without distraction." Arthur plied his persuasion firmly.

Eventually Wilfred conceded. "Very well—"

"Wil—no!" There was a palpable dismay in Rowland's voice, a wounded rage in his eyes.

"Arthur may be right, Rowly," Wilfred said. "The sooner we deal with this mongrel, the sooner we can despatch him." He addressed the policemen coldly. "You can unhand my brother now."

The constables who held Rowland looked to Gilbey for his approval. He nodded cautiously. "You should understand, however, Mr. Sinclair, that this man is under the protection of the New South Wales Police Department." He turned to Wilfred. "Perhaps we should sit down."

Wilfred directed them to the long polished meeting table which ran parallel to the south wall of the library, and around which, at one time or another, had sat the most powerful men in the country.

The Sinclairs sat on one side, the two detectives and Hayden on the other.

Unsure of his place in this, but unwilling to leave Rowland to it, Clyde remained, standing unobtrusively with the constables. He'd never before seen Rowland look quite like this—it wasn't so much anger as unbridled loathing.

"Perhaps if Mr. Hayden was to begin by reiterating the statement he gave to Detective Angel last evening."

Wilfred snorted, but otherwise did not object.

Hayden fidgeted with the brim of the hat he clutched in his lap. He did not look at Rowland.

"Could you tell us how you knew the deceased, the late Mr. Henry Sinclair, who died on or about the thirteenth of March 1920, Mr. Hayden?" Angel prompted.

Hayden straightened. He focussed on the detective. "I was in the employ of the late Mr. Henry Sinclair for sixteen years, as the manager here at *Oaklea*. Mr. Sinclair engaged my services in 1904, before Rowland Sinclair was born."

"Are we in agreement thus far?" Gilbey asked Wilfred.

"Yes."

"And what were your duties, Mr. Hayden?" Angel prompted again.

Hayden recited a long list of managerial responsibilities, including crop and breeding programmes, at pains to point out his contribution, Henry Sinclair's reliance on him and his loyalty to the family.

"And did you have any duties of a more personal nature, Mr. Hayden?"

Hayden nodded. "You've gotta understand Henry Sinclair was not a young man. He'd always been strict with his boys but Master Rowland was a lot younger than his brothers… and the boy was a handful."

The constables took a precautionary step closer to Rowland at this point.

"What was it Henry Sinclair required of you in relation to his son?"

"This wasn't until after the Great War had started, mind," Hayden said licking his lips. "Mr. Sinclair would call me in to discipline the boy."

"Discipline how?"

"With a belt."

"Would you be more specific, Mr. Hayden?"

Hayden tilted his head to one side. "About two, maybe three inches wide… long enough to go around a girth of a stock horse…"

Gilbey cleared his throat. "Could you be more specific about how exactly this arrangement worked," he corrected.

"Oh. Mr. Sinclair would send word that I was needed at the house. I knew what he meant. I'd go to the tack shed and pull a surcingle from one of the stock saddles and then report to Mr. Sinclair's study. The boy would take his shirt off, brace himself against the armchair, and I would give him a thrashing." He looked at Rowland. "I was just doing my job. Mr. Sinclair would've sacked me if I refused."

"Was it always in the study?"

"Mostly. Once in the shearing shed."

"Why the shearing shed?"

"One of the shearers, bloke called Barrett—gun shearer—had been teaching the boy to shear, for a lark. Mr. Sinclair didn't like it. He sacked the man and had me thrash the boy right there in front of the gang." He shuddered. "If it hadn't been such a big shed, those blokes might have strung me up for what Mr. Sinclair had me do. As it was, what happened to the boy reminded them of their place."

Clyde was unsure if it was the past injury or the humiliation of having this all aired now that made Rowland look so murderously at Hayden. Wilfred's hand moved to his brother's shoulder, a gesture of solidarity, perhaps restraint.

"And what would Henry Sinclair do while you disciplined his son?"

"He'd read from the bible, until he'd decided it was enough."

"Did you never have pity on the boy, Mr. Hayden?"

Hayden looked around at the library and snorted. His lip curled. "Hard to pity a boy who'd eventually come into all this. Besides it weren't my place to feel sorry for Rowland. I was only doing what Mr. Sinclair wanted."

"I don't see what any of this has to do with—" Wilfred began.

"If you'll bear with us, Mr. Sinclair, you'll soon see," Gilbey said.

"Did Henry Sinclair call you to his study the evening he died?"

"Yes, sir. I'm not sure what the boy had done, but Mr. Sinclair was livid." Hayden twisted the brim of his hat and licked his lips. "He didn't want me to stop. I told him twice that I thought the boy had had enough but he ordered me to keep going, to keep laying on cut after cut." He rubbed his face. "I was just doing my job."

"Can you tell us what happened next, Mr. Hayden?"

"I was about to stop no matter what he said, I was, when Mr. Sinclair—Wilfred Sinclair—came in."

"And what did he do?"

"He walked in and belted me fair in the face. Nearly broke my nose. I was just doing my job."

"And then?"

"He picked up his brother."

"Picked up?"

"The boy had collapsed. Mr. Sinclair had to help him stand. He was in a pretty bad way… shaking, crying like a baby."

Rowland stood. "That's enough."

"Please sit down, Mr. Sinclair," Angel said. "You'll want to hear the rest of this."

Rowland stepped away from the table, seething. Clyde moved to go with him.

It was Arthur who reasoned with his cousin. "Let's hear him out, Rowland," he said quietly. "We'll deal with him later, once we know what exactly it is we're contending with."

Rowland glanced at Wilfred, who himself seemed in two minds as to whether to stay or walk out. Slowly, Rowland resumed his seat. He glared at Hayden until the man met his eye. "You'd do well to remember, Hayden, that I'm not fifteen anymore."

The informant cringed.

"I must caution you, Mr. Sinclair, that it is a crime to threaten or intimidate a witness," Gilbey warned.

Rowland did not respond, but there was nothing in his face to give Hayden any form of comfort.

"Go on, Mr. Hayden," Angel prompted as Hayden quailed.

"There was a row… one helluva row. Mr. Wilfred wanted me sacked. Threatened to rip off my arm if I ever raised it against his brother again. I won't repeat what he said to his father but he was bloody disrespectful. Mr. Sinclair said he would cut Mr. Wilfred off. Mr. Wilfred said he didn't care, then Mr. Sinclair said disciplining the boy was his right and duty. He told Mr. Wilfred to get out. Mr. Wilfred said he was not going to leave his brother to the mercy of a tyrannical bastard again. I left then… went home. I always tried not to get involved in the family's falling outs. You know, I was just doing my job."

"And then." There was a vaguely triumphant note to Angel's voice which heralded the point of Hayden's testimonial.

"I report for work the next morning and find that Mr. Sinclair was shot during the night. Mr. Wilfred tells me he's in charge five seconds before he sacks me... hands me my wages and another month's in an envelope and tells me to take my family and get off the property that day. I thought Henry Sinclair was hard but Mr. Wilfred put him in the shade. After he was done, I couldn't get a job anywhere. My wife took the children to live with her people—she never came back. I was just doing my flaming job!"

For a time there was silence, and then Angel said, "You can see gentlemen, that this puts a slightly different complexion on the assumption that your father was the victim of some random burglary."

8

"SPARE THE ROD?"

… "spare the rod and spoil the child," sometimes to his complete undoing. In the "absence of the birch behind the door," say some students of criminology, lies the explanation of why so many "young hopefuls" go wrong and end their days in prison… a writer in *The New York Herald* quotes Judge Alfred J. Talley, of the Court of General Sessions, New York, as saying that "there is just one kind of discipline that does work and that is corporal punishment. Lax parents make boy criminals…" Physical punishment has gone out of fashion; "moral suasion has taken the place of a whipping." But "what does one of the little fellows care about moral suasion? He would care a good deal about a sound thrashing… old-fashioned ideas of parental authority should be insisted on, and where it is resisted I see no better or surer way to enforce it than by judicious corporal punishment."

The Register, 1922

"So, gentlemen." Gilbey pressed his fingertips together. "Perhaps you would care to tell us about your movements that night."

Wilfred replied with a kind of ominous calm. "Delighted to answer your questions, detective, but Mr. Hayden can leave. His business is concluded and I see no reason to suffer his presence any longer."

"For God's sake, man!" Hayden exploded. "It's been nearly fourteen years. You've already destroyed me… replaced me with that bloody blue-eyed Jackie… and don't think I don't know why he was elevated above his station! That'd be a fine bloody scandal, wouldn't it?"

"That'll do, Mr. Hayden!" Gilbey said as both Rowland and Wilfred rose from their seats.

"I was just doing my job," Hayden whined, cowering as the Sinclair brothers loomed over him.

"Get off my property!" Wilfred spat.

Gilbey signalled to one of the constables. "Perhaps you could take Mr. Hayden to the car."

"That's right, get rid of Charlie Hayden. That'd be bloody right!"

Wilfred turned his back, refusing to acknowledge him any further. Rowland's wrath was barely contained. The constable grabbed Hayden by the arm and took him out.

"Do you deny any part of Mr. Hayden's account, gentlemen?" Angel asked when the door was closed.

Wilfred retook his seat. "No."

Angel waited for Rowland.

"No."

"Let's begin with you, Mr. Sinclair." Gilbey looked directly at Wilfred. "What did you do immediately after Mr. Hayden left that evening?"

"I took Rowly up to his room and sent for Dr. Oliver."

"How badly injured was your brother?" Angel asked.

"Badly enough. He was bleeding and confused."

"Did you stay with him?"

"Yes."

"Why?"

"For pity's sake… to make sure he was all right," Wilfred said irritably.

"Did you believe he was in any further danger?"

"I was determined that he would not be."

"When did you leave?"

"After Rowly fell asleep. Dr. Oliver had given him something, I expect."

"And what did you do then, Mr. Sinclair?"

"I telephoned our Uncle Rowland… my father's brother—he was Rowly's namesake. I was hoping he might speak to our father."

"To dissuade Henry Sinclair from cutting you off?"

Wilfred bristled. "If you knew my father, Detective Gilbey, you would know that threats of disinheritance were not unusual. No. I was trying to sort something out for Rowly. He and Uncle Rowland were close. I thought… to be honest, I can't recall what exactly I thought. It was over thirteen years ago."

"And what about you, Mr. Sinclair?" Gilbey said, turning to Rowland. "Perhaps Mr. Hayden has managed to jog your memory. When last we spoke you seemed to have forgotten rather a lot."

Rowland's voice was flat. "I was in my room, asleep, until Wil came in to tell me about the burglary."

"You didn't hear the gunshot?"

"Not that I can recall. It had been a long day, detective. I was exhausted."

"Did you know where your father kept his gun?"

"It was not a secret. Father stowed the guns in the utility room of the pantry."

"Did you know how to use a gun?"

"I was a cadet during the war."

"How did you feel about your father, Mr. Sinclair?"

A pause—silence strained by expectation. Rowland sat back in his chair. A single bead of sweat glistened on his brow.

"I'm not sure what you mean."

"It sounds like your father was very hard on you, Mr. Sinclair. Did you resent him for that?"

"I was fifteen, detective. I hated him."

It was nearly midday by the time they all emerged from the library. Wilfred had brought the interview to an abrupt close after Rowland's rather too honest declaration.

"For the love of God, Rowly," he whispered as they watched the police vehicle pull away. "What possessed you to say that? Can't you see how it looks?"

Rowland met his brother's eye. "After what that bastard Hayden told them, if I'd said anything else, Wil, they would have known I was lying."

"Yes. I expect you're right." Wilfred shook his head. "I should make some calls."

"To whom?"

"It's been far too long since I had a conversation with the Commissioner of Police. And I think it's time I spoke to our lawyers."

"In case this gets ugly."

"To make sure it doesn't."

"Wil." Kate Sinclair came out of the breakfast room into the hallway. She had Ewan in her arms. "Arthur said you'd finished. Have you eaten? I can have Mrs. Kendall prepare something."

Wilfred took Ewan from her. "You shouldn't still be carrying Ewan about, Katie," he said.

"You worry too much," she said, dusting some speck off his immaculate lapel. "I'm quite capable of hauling your giant son around."

Wilfred tapped Ewan on the nose. "Did you hear that, McDuff? Your mother has the strength of a horse."

Kate laughed. "Oh you think you're funny now, but you wait till he starts telling people his name is McDuff Sinclair! You'll only have yourself to blame!"

Rowland smiled.

"Lucy thought that she and Rowly might take the boys on a picnic today," Kate said. "They're Ewan's godparents after all."

"I'm afraid I've a damaged plane to work on," Rowland said quickly.

"But couldn't you attend to that tomorrow, Rowly?"

"Clyde needs to get on, and I'm not sure I could repair *Doris* without his help," Rowland lied. He was perfectly capable of changing the tyre and patching the canvas body on his own.

"Well, perhaps early this evening?"

"Rowly's had a rough morning, Katie," Wilfred intervened, hoisting Ewan onto his shoulders. "He might not be in the best mood to deal with this scamp and his brother. Let him go tinker with that aeroplane of his for a while."

"Oh dear, Rowly, I am sorry." Kate was too discreet to enquire what exactly had occurred that morning. She knew the police had called and assumed that Rowland had found himself in some scrape which required Wilfred's intervention. Her brother-in-law was, in some respects, wild, but Kate was convinced that with the right woman he would settle down.

Rowland glanced gratefully at Wilfred. "I'd better grab Clyde and get moving before the day is completely wasted," he said, checking his watch.

Wilfred nodded. "Go."

The day was hot and dry, unremarkable for Yass in December. Sheltered from the warm movement of air which passed locally for a breeze, the heat in the makeshift hangar was stifling. Rowland's greyhound lay under the plane looking balefully at the master who'd taken him from *Oaklea*'s cool verandahs to this place. Clyde had stripped down to his cotton singlet, Rowland to shirtsleeves, which he'd rolled to the elbow. Both men were damp with perspiration. Rowland had also managed to acquire quite a large amount of axle grease on his person.

Smiling, Clyde tossed him a rag. "You work like you paint, Rowly. I've never seen anyone make such a mess."

"You left all the filthy jobs to me," Rowland protested, wiping the oily graphite off his hands and neck. He wasn't entirely sure how he'd managed to get grease on his neck.

They had worked in almost total silence till now. For some reason, Clyde had decided to give the biplane a complete service, checking bungee straps and fuel lines in addition to replacing the tyre and repairing the fuselage. Rowland had been glad of the distraction, and Clyde's quiet, practical company.

"We're nearly done," Clyde said, ladling a drink out of the bucket they'd collected earlier from the rainwater tank attached to the shed. "Bloody hell, it's hot."

Rowland nodded. He took the ladle from Clyde, splashing the now tepid water on his neck and face.

"Rowly, can I ask you something?"

"Yes, of course."

"That bloke, Hayden, and your father… how long did that go on?"

Rowland stopped. He leaned against *Rule Britannia*'s lower wing. "My father was always strict. Wil and Aubrey protected me before the war, kept me out of his way… But then they all enlisted."

"And that's when he…?"

Rowland swallowed. His words were bitterly frank. "Father was always liberal with his walking cane, though he started really laying into me only when Aubrey died. But he had some kind of turn." Rowland frowned and rubbed the back of his neck. "That was when he decided his own hand was no longer firm enough, I suppose. He began using Hayden then."

"And no one knew?"

"Oh, plenty of people knew, just no one who could do anything about it. He was my father, Clyde, and he was Henry Sinclair."

"Did Wilfred know?"

"No. He was serving. It seemed to get better for a while when Wil returned, at least when he was at *Oaklea*. But then I was expelled and... well you heard Hayden."

"And it was Wilfred who told you about your father?"

"Yes."

"What exactly did he say?"

Rowland's brow rose, but he answered the question.

"He said that Father was dead, and I was not to worry. He wouldn't let me go downstairs."

"Why did you want to?"

"To make sure he was really dead, I think." Rowland's jaw hardened. "I know people say they hate this and that all the time, Clyde, but I meant it. I truly hated him."

Clyde winced. "You know what the police are thinking, don't you, Rowly?"

"That I killed him? Don't worry, old boy. Wil's handling it."

"It wasn't you I was—" Clyde stopped as one of the Sinclair cars sailed down the road on what appeared to be a tide of red dust. "Who is that?"

Rowland squinted. He could make out a flash of colour in the back seat. "Kate, I think... better get dressed."

Clyde cursed and pulled on his shirt while Rowland tried to find his tie.

The Rolls Royce eased to a stop and Samuels, Wilfred's elderly chauffeur, stepped out and opened the rear door. Lucy Bennett handed out a large basket before emerging from the leather interior, being careful not to catch her broad-brimmed hat. "Kate thought you gentlemen might enjoy some refreshment." She considered the state of them. "My goodness you have been working hard!"

"Miss Bennett," Rowland tried to keep the exasperation out of his voice. "What in heaven's name are you doing out here?"

"I brought the picnic, silly," Lucy chirped. "Surely there's some shade about somewhere to lay out a blanket."

"Not unless you want to picnic inside the shed," Rowland said. "It's very kind of you to go to such trouble, Miss Bennett, but Clyde and I are filthy. I don't think we're fit company, even for a picnic."

"Kate will never forgive me if I return without being able to report that you've eaten!" Lucy sashayed into the shed. "Why don't you gentlemen clean up, while I put out some sandwiches?"

Clearly she was not leaving.

Left with little choice, Clyde and Rowland walked around to the water tank to wash up. Clyde stuck his head under the tap, allowing the cool water to wash away the dirt and sweat of the afternoon's toil.

"You know, Rowly, we need more dope to finish repairing the fuselage. I might drive into Yass and fetch some."

"I'll come with you."

"One of us needs to stay here and attend a picnic."

Rowland groaned.

Clyde smiled. "I rather think you need to tell the poor girl the truth. Clearly, offending her father wasn't enough. You may just have to risk offending her."

"You're probably right." Rowland handed Clyde his pocketbook. "Try the stock and station agent—he flies a Tiger Moth himself." He glanced at the sky. "It'll be dark before you get back, so I suppose I'll see you at the house."

Clyde slapped him on the back. "Chin up, mate… and good luck."

So Rowland walked back into the shed alone. Lucy Bennett had laid out a blanket on the dirt floor and on it, placed plates of sandwiches, shortbread and bottles of lemonade. The chauffeur had taken the car a discreet distance from the shed.

"You've sent Mr. Watson Jones away," she gushed.

"I didn't send him anywhere, Miss Bennett, he had an errand to run."

"I must remember to ask him if he's of the Novocastrian Watson Joneses. Irma Watson Jones was at school with Kate and me. Lovely girl. Married a Macarthur, I believe. Do you suppose Mr. Watson Jones is related?"

"I don't believe so."

"Well, I think he's a wonderful friend to have given *us* this time alone." She held out her hand. "Come and sit with me, Rowland."

Rowland decided he'd best get straight to the point. He sat because it did not seem a conversation one should have while standing over a lady. "Miss Bennett, I'm afraid there's been a terrible misunderstanding."

"I'll say there has! Pater is convinced you're some kind of Communist pornographer."

"Pornographer?" Rowland was startled. "He called me a pornographer?"

"A Communist one!" she said, indignantly. "Your paintings, darling. Pater can be very old-fashioned. Perhaps if you were to paint landscapes or still life…"

"I'm afraid I don't paint trees… or fruit."

Lucy pouted. Her voice became childishly coy. "But couldn't you try for me, for us. Just for a teensy widdle while. Pweeese, Wowly."

Rowland blinked. Why the hell was she speaking like that? He shook his head in horror at both the request and the manner in which it was made. "No."

She sighed. "Oh darling, I'm so mad for you that I don't care that you're so dreadfully stubborn." She inched closer; her breath came quickly as she gazed up into his face. "You know, I believe I shall have my bridesmaids wear the same blue as your eyes."

Rowland looked away. Of course. Lucy's apparent obsession with him was about creating a matched set—to coordinate with Kate, the bridal party and quite possibly the curtains… she was probably planning blue curtains. "Miss Bennett, I'm afraid your father may be operating under a misimpression."

"I know, darling, I've tried to talk to him, told him we absolutely love each other to bits. I've cried, sworn I won't eat till I starve to death, but he's adamant you're a scoundrel."

"Miss Bennett, when your father called I had no intention of asking for your hand."

"Oh my darling, I've always known you were impulsive," she said, turning suddenly to clasp her hands behind his neck. "Wonderfully, romantically impulsive."

Rowland cracked. "For pity's sake, Miss Bennett, I am trying to say I am not, and never have been, in love with you!"

Lucy Bennett reacted as if he'd struck her. She recoiled wide-eyed and shaking. "But that's not true!" she whispered, pleaded.

"I assure you it is," he replied, but gently.

Lucy became strangely rigid as her hopes finally gave way. Silent tears cut a channel through the carefully applied layer of face-powder on her cheeks. Rowland offered her his handkerchief. Lucy clutched it to her breast, gasping and gagging as if his rejection was too bitter a fruit to be swallowed, crumpling finally into anguished wails.

Rowland couldn't help but feel a cad. He had not thought her feelings genuine. "Miss Bennett, please, your father is right. I'm not at all suitable for you."

He tried to help her up.

"Don't touch me!" she shrieked. "You toyed with my feelings... led me to believe..." Enraged, Lucy threw a bottle of lemonade at him and ran out of the shed.

Rowland, ducked, cursed, and followed her.

Sobbing inconsolably, Lucy ran directly to the waiting Rolls Royce. Samuels climbed out. Clearly disconcerted, the chauffeur looked from Rowland to the weeping woman who was waiting for him to open her door. Samuels had driven for many wealthy men. His face remained unreadable, his decorum unflustered. He opened the door for Lucy without a word and, turning his back on Rowland Sinclair, took his seat behind the wheel.

Rowland watched helplessly as the car pulled away, swearing as he realised he was now stranded a good five miles from the homestead.

Clyde pulled in outside the post office. He booked a call through to *Woodlands House* and waited until the operator put Milton on the line.

"What's wrong?" the poet asked immediately. The very fact that Clyde was telephoning from Yass did not bode well.

Clyde recounted what had occurred over the past days.

Milton was quiet. "How's Rowly?" he asked after a few moments.

"This is the problem, Milt. I know his old man was a mongrel, but Rowly doesn't seem the least bit interested in who killed him."

"God, Clyde, who could blame him? It sounds like the murderer did him a favour."

"Except, I think the police suspect Rowly. And he's quite happy to let Wilfred deal with it."

"That doesn't sound like a bad plan. Wilfred may be a capitalist bastard, but he's a powerful capitalist bastard."

"No, it isn't a bad plan. Unless, of course, it was Wilfred who murdered Henry Sinclair."

"Wilfred? Have you lost your mind?"

"Hear me out, Milt. Wilfred was about to be disinherited. If he had been, he would have lost everything and wouldn't have been able to help Rowly at all. Anyone can see he had more to gain from the old man's death than Rowly. Rowly was a battered kid, Wilfred a man just returned from the war. He packed Rowly off to England the day after the funeral; he sacked that bastard manager and ran him and his family out of Yass. It seems to me he got rid of anyone who might have heard Henry threaten to disinherit him."

"Or he was just protecting his brother."

"There's more to it," Clyde persisted.

"And Rowly doesn't see this?"

"He's not an idiot, Milt. Of course he does. But it's Wilfred."

"What about the lawyers? Surely—"

"I'm sure Wilfred will retain the best legal minds in Australia, but they'll be Wilfred's lawyers. Look, Milt, what worries me is that there's no one, including Rowly himself, who's going to put Rowly's interests first. He could go down for this. Fifteen is old enough to be convicted of murder and Rowly may just be willing to go to gaol to make sure that Wilfred doesn't hang."

Milton swore. "Ed and I will head out to you at Yass tomorrow. We'll think of some excuse to tell Rowly on the way. I'll call Delaney tonight—see if I can't find out why the police are suddenly so interested in a thirteen-year-old murder."

9

KENNEL *CHRONICLE*

DOINGS IN DOGGIE LANE
CANINE PSYCHOLOGY
Some Interesting Sidelights

Dogs have a colour complex. This is the view of a prominent member of the staff of the Royal Veterinary College, London.

The greyhound, for instance, cannot resist the impulse to chase small dogs and cats. They have been known to worry goats, especially white goats.

Sunday Times, 1937

Rowland felt a little guilty eating Lucy's picnic, but he was famished. Between them, he and Lenin polished off most of the basket's contents. It had cooled off marginally and, after the difficulty of the last couple of days, the shed was a peaceful refuge. He brooded for a time, furious that Hayden had emerged to resurrect the ghosts of a past he had tried hard to exorcise. The scars left by the vicious beatings of his youth were on his back where he couldn't see them. Until now, Rowland had put the memories where he couldn't see them, too.

"I doubt Lucy's coming back for us, old boy," he said, scratching the dog's one ear. "We'd best start back—it'll be dark soon."

Rowland decided to take the road rather than cut through the paddocks. It would make the walk longer but at least they wouldn't miss any car despatched to collect them.

He found a rope, a makeshift lead to prevent Lenin tearing after every rabbit they came across, and man and dog set off. Once the sun set, the evening became quite pleasant. There was no moon but the stars were many and spectacular, one of those vistas that Rowland had always thought unpaintable.

Lenin padded along quite happily for about a mile, straining against the rope at every movement in the grass. But then it seemed the past day's heat and the unexpected exercise took its toll. The dog's head began to droop pathetically and he whined from time to time.

"For pity's sake, Len, you're a greyhound. Well something like a greyhound," Rowland muttered as he realised the drag on the rope was now more to do with the dog wanting to stop, than rabbits. The hound's eyes glistened reproachfully up at him. "I know, it's my fault we have to walk, but I'm not carrying you."

They were nearly halfway back to *Oaklea* when Rowland caught sight of headlamps in the distance. "There you go, Len, you can quit your complaining. It looks like the cavalry's arrived."

He blanched as the vehicle approached. He knew it wasn't the Mercedes by the sound of its motor, but the glare made it impossible to see who was behind the wheel. Rowland waved. The car slowed to an idle.

"Come on, Len," he urged, tugging on the rope. Lenin whined and resisted in reply. Rowland was still arguing with the dog when the first shot cracked the night air. Instinctively, Rowland dropped down. He felt the whistle as the second shot passed his shoulder. Cursing, he tried to pull Lenin off the road but the dog would not stir. "Len!" he shouted. "Move!"

Lenin whimpered. The car's engine roared. A third shot, and a screech as the car swung around and sped back in the direction from which it had come.

But Rowland wasn't looking at the car. In the swing of the headlamps as the car turned, he'd seen the blood.

"Len, hang on mate," he said pulling out his lighter to inspect his dog in the feeble glow of its flame. Blood oozed from Lenin's bony hind. Swearing, Rowland pulled off his jacket and then his shirt. He pressed the shirt against the wound, and then wrapped the stricken hound in his jacket. Knowing the dog would respond to his voice, Rowland spoke calmly. "Helluva way to get me to carry you, mate." He heaved Lenin into his arms. "You're going to be all right... we've just got to get back."

Rowland continued on the dirt road as quickly as he could manage under the greyhound's weight. The road was rough here and he was forced to slow down and step carefully lest he stumble. Lenin became limp and somehow heavier.

"Come on, Len, talk to me," Rowland demanded as even the whimpering stopped.

Then he saw headlights again. For a moment, he panicked, looking frantically for some place to hide, some sort of cover. And then, he recognised the familiar attention-seeking scream of a supercharged motor. His car. He ran towards it.

The Mercedes stopped as it caught him in its headlamps. Clyde stepped out first and then a giant of a man, so dark that had he not been standing against the yellow paintwork he might have been invisible in the night.

"Harry!" Rowland exclaimed, recognising the shape of the shadow.

"Rowly, what the hell!" Harry Simpson said by way of greeting.

"Lenin's been shot," Rowland gasped.

"That was years ago, Rowly. Are you all right?"

"He means the dog," Clyde said. "Who would—"

"He's not moving," Rowland said as Harry took the dog from him.

Harry Simpson put his ear to the greyhound's muzzle. He listened, his face grim. "We'd better get your dog seen to quickly, Rowly."

Rowland sat by his dog's head, comforting and restraining the hound as Harry Simpson stitched the wound. The bullet had grazed but not lodged. Lenin had lost a good deal of blood, but thanks to Harry's needlework the wound would not be fatal.

"You gave me one helluva scare, you daft bloody dog," Rowland said gruffly as he stroked the animal's long muzzle.

They were in the manager's cottage reserved for Harry Simpson.

"I didn't expect to see you here, Harry," Rowland said.

The Aboriginal stockman washed his hands in an enamel basin. "Wil needed an extra man to oversee the stock while Bob Bowman deals with the harvest. Jim's got the stock in the high country well in hand—good man, that Jim—so I came down."

Clyde smiled. His brother, Jim, worked under Simpson on the Sinclair holdings in the high country. "It's a lucky thing you did, Harry. Old Len wasn't looking too chipper."

Harry Simpson frowned. "What happened, Rowly? Who shot your ugly dog?"

Rowland left his hand on Lenin. "I don't know." He told them about the car.

"So they were shooting at you?"

"Seems that way."

"Why?" Simpson asked.

"That rather depends on who it was, I suppose. There might be a few reasons."

Harry Simpson chuckled, his face creasing around blue eyes that were all the brighter for the darkness of the brow under which they were set. He reached over and ruffled Rowland's hair. "I've missed you, Gagamin."

Rowland smiled. "Thank you for fixing my dog, Harry."

"Looks like it's not the first time you broke him, Rowly," Simpson regarded the battle-scarred Lenin dubiously. "I had a dog with only one ear once. Lost the other in a fight with a cat." The stockman's shoulders slumped and he exhaled loudly. "He died eventually... I think it was the embarrassment." Simpson's eyes moved to the swastika-shaped scar of cigarette burns on Rowland's chest. "That's new, Gagamin. You had an interesting time in Germany then?"

"You could say that. I may have to borrow a shirt before we return to the house."

Rowland told him of the trouble they'd found in Munich, of what had happened to him. Simpson let him talk, cursing occasionally.

"And these fellas who did you over," he asked eventually, "what happened to them?"

"Well, one of them is Mr. Hitler's deputy." Rowland shrugged. "I don't know Harry. I'm hoping our escape was at least awkward for them, but who knows?"

Simpson studied him, assessing more than the physical scars. "Are you painting?" he asked.

Rowland nodded.

"Good," Simpson replied as if nothing more needed to be said.

Clyde watched the exchange, intrigued. Despite the fact that he'd been by Rowland's side in Germany and England, that he'd seen Rowland struggle with nightmares and sleeplessness, it had taken him weeks to realise that Rowland needed to paint to deal with the violence and fear of his encounter with Nazis. And yet Harry Simpson knew this instinctively.

"Does Wil know you're here, Harry?" Rowland stroked Lenin's muzzle, smiling as the dog's eyes rolled back with pleasure.

"Yes. I called the house when I got in," Simpson said. The manager's offices and cottages on *Oaklea* were equipped with telephones. He frowned. "Wil said that mongrel Hayden's turned up."

"They found Father's gun."

"How?" Simpson asked, clearly surprised.

"It was in the dam. And now they…"

"Well, don't you worry about it, Rowly," Simpson said after a moment. "Wil will deal with it." The stockman rubbed his jowl. "Who knew you were out there tonight, that you'd be walking back?"

"Clyde and I went out to work on the plane this afternoon. I expect Miss Bennett mentioned that she'd left me out there… among other things."

"Good Lord, I'd forgotten about Miss Bennett," Clyde said. "What happened? How did it go?"

Rowland told them.

Clyde grimaced. "Well at least it's done, Rowly. You can concentrate on finding someone far less suitable now."

Rowland sighed. "I'm sure Wil will have plenty to say on the matter."

"He told me to go get you when I pulled in," Clyde replied, smiling. "If he'd been too upset he'd have let you walk, I imagine. I'd just dropped in here to say hello to Harry when we heard the shots."

"And I take it you didn't see a motorcar coming the other way?"

"No, but we cut across past the shearing shed from here," Simpson said. "If they took the other lane…" He frowned. "We'd better let Wil know what's happened, and inform the police I suppose."

The gentle but persistent tapping woke him eventually. Reluctantly Rowland opened his eyes. It was barely light. It had been a late night, explaining the events to Wilfred and then the police, who seemed amused that he was reporting an assault upon his dog.

"Did the dog bark often at night? We find that disgruntled neighbours can often take matters into their own hands."

Too tired to argue with what he concluded was the force's most dimwitted constable, Rowland had let it go.

"Uncle Rowly, it's me, Uncle Rowly."

"Come in, Ernie."

Wilfred's elder son was still in his pyjamas.

"I came to check on… Lenin," he said, whispering the dog's name as if it were a profanity. Ernest tiptoed over to the chaise longue on which the injured hound had been settled.

"What are you doing out of bed, Ernie?" Rowland asked, as the boy scrutinised the dog anxiously.

"Is he alive, Uncle Rowly?"

"Of course—he's just asleep."

"I was worried," Ernest said, climbing onto Rowland's bed. "I heard Aunt Lucy crying and then Mummy started crying too."

Rowland groaned. "That probably wasn't about Lenin, Ernie."

"Was it about you, Uncle Rowly?"

"Possibly."

"Did you get shot too?"

"No, not this time."

"Have you fallen out with Aunt Lucy?"

"In a manner of speaking."

Realising that going back to sleep was probably not an option, Rowland sat up. "Would you keep an eye on Lenin while I get dressed?" he asked his nephew.

Ernest nodded, slipping off the bed to take up a vigil beside the slumbering hound. By the time Rowland had showered and dressed, the Sinclairs' nanny was searching for her missing charge. Charlotte de Waring had joined the *Oaklea* household only recently, after the family returned from abroad. Knowing his brother's preference for a certain moral severity in his staff, Rowland assumed that Kate must have selected the pleasant, loquacious young woman.

He watched, amused, as the nanny tried valiantly to invoke some sense of authority and control. "Ernest!" she exclaimed when the boy emerged from his uncle's room. "Whatever are you thinking going visiting in your pyjamas?"

"Uncle Rowly was in his pyjamas, too!" Ernest replied.

"It was five in the morning!" Rowland protested. "I was asleep."

"Why, you cheeky devil!" The nanny folded her arms in a manner designed to appear stern, and scolded Ernest in a tone too kind to have any disciplinary effect at all. "You can't be calling on a gentleman at that time!"

Rowland laughed. "Ernie was just keeping an eye on Len while I dressed," he said. "It was very thoughtful of him."

Ernest nodded solemnly.

Nanny de Waring's round, wholesome face softened. "Oh, yes… how is the poor creature, Mr. Sinclair? Mrs. Kendall has cooked up some bacon for its breakfast, I believe."

"I'm sure Len will make a complete recovery, Miss de Waring, particularly if there's bacon involved." Rowland moved back so she could see the hound. The nanny stepped past him to the chaise and knelt to fuss over the patient.

Lenin played his part, lifting his muzzle weakly to offer her a feeble lick.

"Poor, sweet puppy," she said stroking his head softly. "Who would do such a terrible thing?"

"I'm afraid I have no idea, Miss de Waring."

"Well, I must say that I can't think of anything more wicked than trying to murder an innocent animal!" The nanny placed her hands on her hips. "I hope they catch the scoundrel, Mr. Sinclair. Lord knows what he'll shoot next."

"Indeed."

She left her hands on her hips. "Now Master Ernest, do you propose to spend the day in your pyjamas?"

Rowland laughed. "Hurry up and get dressed, Ernie. We'd best go down to breakfast before all the bacon is requisitioned for Lenin."

"Miss Bennett hasn't left, has she?" Rowland caught his brother in the library.

"For God's sake, Rowly, don't tell me you've changed your mind?"

"About Miss Bennett? No."

"Then why—?"

"I know Kate was rather looking forward to her visit. Ernie mentioned they were both upset."

Wilfred sighed. "Lucy was under the impression that you admired her. I'm afraid Kate may have encouraged her in her devotion to you, expecting that you would eventually see sense." Wilfred scanned the shelves in search of a title. "I did warn Kate that seeing sense was not your strong suit, but she is optimistic by nature. As you can understand, Miss Bennett feels both disappointed and humiliated. Kate is also quite disappointed."

Rowland cursed. "That wasn't my intention, Wil. I wouldn't upset Kate for the world. I had hoped Colonel Bennett's disapproval would end the matter."

Wilfred's mouth twitched. "Unfortunately Lucy's romanticised her father's opposition. She's fond of novels, I believe." He found what he was looking for and pulled *An Account of the State of Agriculture and Grazing in New South Wales* by James Atkinson from the shelf. Rowland had seen the book in his brother's hand many times before. Wilfred put a great deal of stock in the wisdom of Atkinson and was known to quote the one-hundred-year-old text at length.

"You could give her that," Rowland suggested. "I'm sure Mr. Atkinson would cure her of sentimentality. Probably cure her of consciousness too."

"James Atkinson brought the Merino sheep to this country Rowly." Wilfred pointed out, unamused.

"The Merino? I thought that was Macarthur?" Rowland said, recalling absurdly that one of Lucy Bennett's ridiculous friends had married a Macarthur.

"Macarthur bought a lame ewe from James Atkinson's Saxon merino flock and—" Wilfred stopped, and regarded Rowland suspiciously over the top of his spectacles. "As much as I applaud your sudden interest in agriculture, I believe we were discussing this appalling situation between you and Miss Bennett!"

"Yes, of course. I should apologise," Rowland said, though he was not sure what for. He certainly did not want to retract his refusal. "I haven't seen Miss Bennett this morning, has she left?"

"Arthur invited Lucy to the pictures in town. He thought it might cheer her up. He's been very kind to her since yesterday's drama."

"Oh."

Wilfred regarded him sharply. "I think it was jolly nice of him."

"Yes, of course. He's a decent chap."

"We should talk about the shooting," Wilfred said, moving on brusquely.

Rowland agreed. "Sadly, I didn't see anything of use. I was dazzled by the headlamps and then…"

Wilfred nodded. "You know, Rowly, I expect it was some half-drunk hothead shooting at rabbits. I suppose he panicked when he heard you shout and fled. I've been planning to withdraw the permissions for shooting on *Emoh Ruo* in any case."

Rowland paused, more than a little surprised that Wilfred was taking the incident quite so casually. "I suppose you're right."

"Good. That's settled then. Now, there are some gentlemen whom I expect to call on you shortly. They telephoned last night to make an appointment."

"Who?" Rowland asked, guardedly.

"I'll let them explain when they get here," Wilfred replied. "I believe they could be very good for you. Give you some purpose."

Rowland groaned. "I'm not joining the Country Party."

Wilfred returned to the writings of James Atkinson. "It's not the Country Party. I doubt the U.C.P. would have you anyway. Just don't wander off."

10

TRESPASS NOTICE

ANY PERSON found fishing, shooting, or otherwise trespassing at EMOH RUO will be prosecuted. All previous permissions cancelled.

W.H. SINCLAIR

Riverina Advertiser, 1933

Rowland helped himself from the platters of cakes and pastries set out in preparation for Wilfred's mysterious guests. He broke a shortbread biscuit in half and gave the larger segment to the convalescing greyhound now settled beneath the table. The edges of a white damask tablecloth fluttered in the light breeze that cooled the broad verandah.

Clyde sat in a wicker armchair with a cup of tea and his legs stretched out like a man who had no intention of moving for quite some time. The verandah was certainly a great deal more pleasant than the iron shed in which he and Rowland had originally planned to spend the morning finishing work on the *Rule Britannia*.

"So who are these people Wilfred wants you to meet, Rowly?"

"No idea. He wouldn't say."

Clyde's brow rose. "He hasn't called in the church, has he?"

Rowland laughed. "I don't think so."

Clyde drained his tea and sighed in satisfaction. "Wilfred really believes that some local poacher shot at you by accident?"

"Not a poacher. A lot of people have permission to shoot on *Emoh Ruo.*"

"I don't know, Rowly… you don't look much like a rabbit to me."

"Rowly!" Kate Sinclair stepped out onto the verandah.

Clyde and Rowland stood hastily.

"Oh, there you are," she said.

"Good morning, Kate."

"Are you all right, Rowly? You're not hurt at all are you? How is Lenin?" Kate's concern bubbled out as she studied Rowland.

"I'm perfectly well, Kate. And Len is getting fat with all the bacon-flavoured sympathy he's been receiving."

Kate took a breath, relieved. "I'm so glad."

Rowland looked at his sister-in-law. She was, as always, dressed elegantly, in a simple cream sheath and embroidered shawl. Her make-up was flawless but there was just the slightest taint of red in the whites of her eyes. Ernest had said she'd been crying.

"Kate," Rowland said quietly. "I am dreadfully sorry about this business with Lucy Bennett. I didn't mean to make such a mess of it all."

Kate blinked. "Oh Rowly, are you absolutely sure you—"

"Yes, I am."

For a moment she looked away. The silence stretched awkwardly. "But why?" Kate blurted suddenly. "Lucy is so well suited to you… to us! I don't understand why you can't see that! What could you possibly want that you couldn't find in Lucy?"

Rowland's smile was fleeting and almost imperceptible. He'd never before heard Kate raise her voice. He found himself unexpectedly touched by her loyalty to her friend. "I want to be as in love with my wife as Wilfred is with his," he said.

Kate faltered.

"But, I should have been clear with Colonel Bennett," Rowland admitted. "I cannot tell you how sorry I am to have upset you and Miss Bennett."

Kate Sinclair's eyes filled and she pressed her lips together in an attempt to stop them trembling. Rowland gave her his handkerchief.

"Oh dear, I am sorry, Rowly. I just feel badly for poor Lucy—she is so very fond of you." She dabbed at her eyes. "It would have been perfect. I'm so glad you weren't hurt last evening. If you'll excuse me… I must be… excuse me…" Kate turned and hurried back inside the house.

Rowland groaned.

Clyde, who had tactfully decided to inspect the Staghorn fern which hung on the verandah post a few paces away, was philosophical. "There wasn't a lot else you could do, Rowly."

"I suppose not."

Clyde pointed to the car turning into *Oaklea*'s long drive. "Better look sharp, old mate. I believe the people Wilfred wants you to meet have arrived."

The black Chrysler pulled up in front of the house. Two men and a smartly turned out woman alighted. The elder of the gentlemen was burdened with two heavy leather briefcases.

"Good Lord, what's this?" Rowland murmured.

"They're not your lawyers are they, Rowly?" Clyde asked, squinting at the arrivals.

"I don't think so," Rowland replied. It had been a couple of years since he'd had dealings with the Sinclair solicitors, but he doubted very much that Kent, Beswick and Associates had taken on a female partner. And it was only ever the partners that called at *Oaklea*.

"Oh Rowly… you're here, very good," Wilfred came out onto the verandah. "I expect you'll find this extremely interesting."

He began the introductions with the gentlemen: Messrs Olaf Oberg and Charles Ludowici. Oberg cut a tall athletic figure and seemed about Wilfred's age. Ludowici was possibly ten years his companion's senior, though clearly, he deferred to Oberg. Both men sported moustaches and an air of robust goodwill.

"Allow me to present Mrs. Diana Drosher," Oberg said, taking over the introductions.

Diana Drosher smiled and nodded. "A pleasure to make your acquaintance, gentlemen."

Mrs. Drosher was neither old nor young, her manner was pleasant and everything about her well-groomed person was extremely neat, from the precise ordered crimp of her hair to the military shine of her patent leather shoes. She rather reminded Rowland of a Sunday School teacher. He began to wonder if he should have been so hasty to dismiss Clyde's concern that Wilfred had summoned the church.

"I'm afraid we're having a spot of bother with one of the harvesters, so I won't be able to stay." Wilfred turned to Clyde. "Indeed, Mr. Watson Jones, I was hoping I could prevail on you to accompany me—Rowly tells me you have a talent for mechanics."

"Yes... yes, of course, Mr. Sinclair," Clyde said, startled. He glanced at Rowland uncertainly.

"I'm sure Rowly can manage to entertain the gentlemen and Mrs. Drosher," Wilfred said, patting Rowland's back. "Kate will be down shortly. You can manage to pour tea till then, can't you, old chap?"

"I expect I can," Rowland said tightly.

"Good show. Well, we best be off. Come along, Mr. Watson Jones."

Oberg broke the awkward, tense silence left in Wilfred's wake. "Shall we sit down, Mr. Sinclair?"

"Yes, of course."

"Shall I pour?" Diana Drosher asked.

Rowland nodded, realising that he was the only one who did not know what this meeting was about. Clearly these people had conspired with Wilfred to get him alone. He slipped a finger sandwich to Lenin, taking perverse pleasure in the knowledge that he had an ally hidden beneath the table.

"Allow me to introduce myself and my colleagues more fully, Mr. Sinclair," Oberg said. "I have the very great honour of being president of an organisation known as the Sane Democracy League. Mr. Ludowici here is my vice-president and Mrs. Drosher is one of our most dedicated members. I wonder if you are aware of our activities?"

"I have seen your advertisements," Rowland said cautiously. The Sane Democracy League was, as far as he could tell, some form of conservative lobby group. They had peppered the print media during the reign of the last Labor government with various inflammatory depictions of the then premier, Jack Lang, and dire warnings of the destruction his government would bring. To be honest, Rowland had always considered the "Sane" part of their title highly suspect.

"Our mission, Mr. Sinclair," Oberg said solemnly, "is public education."

"You see, Mr. Sinclair," Ludowici took up the baton, "Communism plays on the naivety of the working man, it takes advantage of his trust to manipulate him into believing the employer is his enemy rather than the means by which he earns a living." He opened one of the briefcases and took from it several pamphlets and a book entitled *Sane democracy: some radio lectures conducted by the Sane Democracy League from the Trades Hall, Sydney*. "The S.D.L. believes in a dialogue between employer and worker. It is the intermediaries who foster misunderstanding and antagonism between the industry and its workforce."

Rowland accepted the cup of tea that Diana Drosher offered him. It was excessively sugared.

"Sadly, Mr. Sinclair," she said, "subversive elements have already gone a long way to creating an impenetrable barrier of mistrust."

"Subversive elements?" Rowland asked.

"The Communists, the trade unions and the Socialists, Mr. Sinclair. If they actually cared anything for the worker they would support trade and industrial growth, for how is the worker to prosper without a demand for his labour?"

"I'm not sure what this has to do with me, Mrs. Drosher."

"If you don't mind my saying Mr. Sinclair," Oberg said, smiling, "you have a certain reputation for maintaining unconventional friendships."

"I beg your pardon!"

"What Mr. Oberg means to say is that as an artist you are well-acquainted with and trusted by people who are susceptible to the divisive propaganda and rhetoric of the Left." Ludowici proceeded with more caution. "Of course with your background, your breeding and your education—I understand you are a man of letters—you, sir, are able to see through the manipulation of the Communists and recognise Bolshevik propaganda for the vile lie that it is."

Rowland concentrated on eating cake.

"Our aim, Mr. Sinclair, is to bring about a better understanding between employer and employee for the common good," Mrs. Drosher said earnestly. "Communism feeds on antagonism between the classes fuelled by militant unionism. The working class is being used by the Communists to further their ambitions of revolution. The S.D.L. seeks to redress that with education, empowering the working man and furthering the interests of every stratum of society."

Mrs. Drosher paused. It was a moment before Rowland realised that the silence was in expectation of some response from him. He feared arguing with the delegation would only prolong their visit and yet he could not bring himself to even feign agreement. So he attempted to return the S.D.L. to Wilfred.

"Perhaps you should be talking to my brother?"

"On the contrary, Mr. Sinclair," Oberg said. "It's you, with your contacts amongst the working classes, whom we believe would be ideal for our programme."

"We wouldn't be here, Mr. Sinclair," Ludowici assured him, "if we didn't believe you were the kind of patriotic citizen who could make a difference. This would be an opportunity to demonstrate to your countrymen that you are not a Communist."

Rowland's brow rose. "And why would I wish to do that, Mr. Ludowici?"

"Because the rumours surrounding your loyalties are dangerous to your interests, and those of your fine family. And because you could set an example to those in the arts community, persuade them of the errors of a Socialist life."

"I see."

Oberg leaned towards Rowland. "Mr. Sinclair, we understand from your brother that you have never been a member of the Communist Party, that you are not a Communist."

"That's true."

"Why?"

"I beg your pardon?"

"Why are you not a Communist? I imagine that you have very good reasons why you have chosen not to join your friends."

"It depends what you call a good reason, Mr. Oberg."

"I think it's because you value the British system of government, because you value democracy. Our league considers that a very good reason."

"Indeed. I don't mean to be rude, gentlemen, Mrs. Drosher, but what exactly do you want from me?" Rowland said, irritated to have a stranger tell him about his reasons. Oberg was not entirely wrong, but the presumption vexed him nonetheless.

"We'd like to invite you to attend a function the league will be hosting at the Wesley Methodist Hall in Burwood in the new year."

"I'm flattered that you'd come here personally to issue an invitation, but it seems rather a lot of trouble to ask me to a dance."

For a moment they stared blankly at him, and then, glancing at each other for confirmation, they laughed in unison.

"Very good, Mr. Sinclair, most amusing," Ludowici said, slapping his knee. He winked conspiratorially. "Of course it's not a dance but an educational debate, though might I say that our events do serve an invaluable social function—introducing young men and women of like minds."

"Your friends would be welcome as well," Mrs. Drosher added. "Your brother mentioned that you don't like to go anywhere without them."

Rowland blinked. It did sound like something Wilfred would say but he wasn't sure quite how he should respond.

"What you must understand," Mrs. Drosher persisted, "is that with information and education, otherwise decent men and women may be saved from the dry rot of Socialism. It is our duty to guide their thinking."

Rowland took a steadying breath. "With respect, Mrs. Drosher, some of the most informed and decent people I know are Socialists for that very reason—I feel no compunction to save them." Diana Drosher's hands flew to her mouth in a futile attempt to smother a gasp.

"I was in Germany recently," Rowland continued, his eyes flashing. "Mr. Hitler's Minister for Propaganda and Enlightenment is also very committed to warning people against Socialism, to guiding their thinking. May I be so forward as to suggest your organisation may better serve democracy by warning otherwise decent men and women about the dangers of Fascism!"

"The National Socialists of Germany—" Oberg began.

"Whatever it chooses to call itself, the government of Germany is not Socialist! It has far more in common with the system Eric Campbell and his New Guardsmen are advocating."

Why Lenin decided to emerge at that moment from beneath the table was hard to tell. Perhaps it was the anger in Rowland's voice, perhaps he assumed that his master needed help. The greyhound's long angular nose came first through the folds of the tablecloth. Rowland was unsure whether Mrs. Drosher was afraid of dogs, or whether the good lady did not recognise Lenin's one-eared, sharply conical head as that of a dog, but she screamed and dropped the teapot she was holding. Oberg, who was closest to her, was duly splattered with hot tea, as were the pamphlets and publications of the Sane Democracy League which he'd previously set out before him. Lenin, startled by the commotion and possibly a touch jumpy after being shot, panicked and attempted to climb into Rowland's lap.

Rowland tried valiantly to calm both the dog and Mrs. Drosher. And Ludowici extracted his handkerchief to mop tea off the pamphlets and Oberg.

Fortunately the scream had also summoned both Kate Sinclair and Mrs. Kendall.

"Oh dear," Kate said, taking in the wreckage. "What happened?"

Somehow, Rowland managed to pry Lenin off his lap so he could stand, apologising for his dog and introducing his sister-in-law at the same time.

"Please, think nothing of it," Oberg said, still dabbing tea from his jacket. "We really should be going in any case. We'll leave this material with you, Mr. Sinclair, and look forward to seeing you at the

Burwood debate." He glanced at the greyhound who was devouring the various cakes he'd upset onto the verandah boards. "A dog called Lenin," he said, smiling. "I like your sense of humour, Mr. Sinclair. I must say I can't think of a better name for a mongrel cur."

Rowland's eyes darkened a shade, but he elected not to defend Lenin's pedigree, such as it was. It was not really a fight he could win.

And so the esteemed executive of the league departed, leaving Rowland Sinclair to wonder what on earth his brother was up to now.

11

"ENGINEERED BY COMMUNISTS"

———————◆———————

SYDNEY, Wednesday

Mr. O.D.A. Oberg, president of the Sane Democracy League, says the strike movement has been secretly engineered by the Communist Party, whose agents have been at work for months among the miners, the transport workers, and generally in what are known as the "key" unions. Of this he had positive evidence.

Barrier Miner, 1932

Rowland sat in *Oaklea*'s well-lit parlour sketching Edna Walling at work through the window. The garden designer was dressed in what he'd come to observe as her customary style: a man's shirt, riding breeches and boots. A broad-brimmed straw hat shielded her face from the December sun as she directed a team of young men working on the construction of an arbour.

The spring had been warm and dry but the immediate grounds of the homestead were irrigated. The lush green of its lawns and beds was almost startling against the yellowed hills in the distance. The contrast served as a reminder that *Oaklea* was removed from the world outside.

Ernest sat with his face cupped in his hands, watching the movement of Rowland's pencil intently.

Wilfred and Clyde had not yet returned, and Kate's manner towards her brother-in-law had become distinctly cool and distant.

Ernest's admiring company was consequently a particularly welcome distraction. The boy demonstrated no interest in drawing, himself, but remained fascinated with what his uncle was doing.

Rowland glanced up when he heard the motor. A powder-blue Riley Lynx stopped hard in the gravelled driveway.

"I wonder who that is?" Rowland mused aloud.

"Oh, that's Aunt Lucy's motorcar," Ernest informed his uncle. "Her daddy bought it for her last month. It has special leather seats and came with wing screen swipers."

"I think you mean windscreen wipers, Ernie," Rowland said as Lucy and Arthur emerged from the sleek four-seater sedan. They stood by the automobile for a while chatting. Arthur leaned in to whisper in Lucy's ear and she laughed, patting his lapel as she did so.

Rowland raised his brows. "Good old Arthur," he said quietly.

Ernest pushed his nose against the window to watch the couple. "Aunt Lucy's not sad anymore," he reported.

"I'm glad to hear it, Ernie," Rowland replied, hoping the development would mean Kate might speak to him again.

Arthur and Lucy did not come into the house immediately but strolled arm-in-arm through the garden, stopping to talk with Edna Walling and the workmen.

"Daddy and Mr. Jones are back too," Ernest said, his face still glued to the glass.

"Capital," Rowland replied, closing his notebook and slipping the pencil into its spine. "Would you like to come out and see my aeroplane, Ernie?"

"Yes, Uncle Rowly, I would." Ernest nodded most emphatically.

"Very well, you'd best go tell Nanny de Waring that you're coming out with me. I must have a word with your father."

Ernest zoomed off, his arms outstretched, shouting for his nanny as he went. Rowland stepped in to the hallway just as Wilfred and Clyde entered the vestibule.

"Oh Rowly, hello." Wilfred hung his hat on the rack. "How was your meeting with Oberg?"

"We should probably have words about that."

"Don't you mean a word, old boy?"

"No, I mean words. What the devil are you playing at, Wil?"

Wilfred restrained a smile. "Shall we step into the library?" he suggested. "I'm sure Mrs. Kendall will bring Mr. Watson Jones a well-deserved cup of tea while you and I speak."

Clyde accepted the gentle nudge and announced he was going to check on Lenin.

"Right," Rowland said as soon as Wilfred closed the library door behind them. "What would possess you to give those people the impression that I might join them?"

"I take it they did not convince you of the importance of their purpose."

"For God's sake, Wil, I am not going to join some band of right-wing missionaries intent on converting the savage masses to what they consider the moral path."

"They are somewhat zealous, true."

Rowland stopped, surprised by Wilfred's vague agreement.

"I didn't arrange the meeting, Rowly. That was poor Lucy. Before the two of you fell out."

"What?"

"I believe she hoped the S.D.L. could *educate* you, and that your involvement with them would demonstrate to Colonel Bennett, once and for all, that you were not beyond redemption." He sighed. "Kate was possibly involved."

"But why did you—?"

"Remove Mr. Watson Jones and leave you to it? It was too late to tell Ollie Oberg and his colleagues not to call—they had come all the way from Sydney after all. And there truly was another breakdown with that blasted harvester. Mr. Watson Jones is quite a handy chap with machines. I can't imagine how he manages to remain unemployed!"

***

"Mr. Sinclair!" Edna Walling waved as Rowland walked towards his car.

He diverted to speak with her, leaving the driveway and walking down to the lawn where her gang of workers were constructing a substantial stepped pergola cutting through the axis of the garden.

"Good afternoon, Miss Walling," he said, removing his hat as he admired the progress.

The garden designer had installed round concrete pillars at ten-foot intervals, softened by sapling crossbeams. The walkway beneath was paved with bricks that led to stepping stones which themselves led to a small circular bed defined by a hedge planting of lavender. There was a gentle sculptural quality to the design.

"I have a friend who would love to see your work," Rowland said, thinking wistfully of Edna Higgins whose own art was so often created for gardens.

Edna Walling smiled. "And how is your dog, Mr. Sinclair? We heard that he was shot."

"I'm trusting Len will be perfectly well in a short while, Miss Walling, aside from becoming outrageously indulged."

"Can I ask who shot the poor creature, Mr. Sinclair?"

"I wish I knew, Miss Walling. Wil is convinced it was some poacher who thought Len was a rabbit."

"Blimey—he must've been blind!" The labourer's whisper was loud enough to carry the few yards from where he worked on one of the pergola's pillars. A lean, wiry man with snow white hair and a short grizzled beard.

"Blind drunk, more likely," added the younger man assisting him.

Edna Walling cleared her throat fiercely.

The men looked up, realising they'd been overheard. "I beg your pardon," the elder of the two stammered, clearly abashed. His leathered face was too tanned to show the blush his voice betrayed. "We meant the poacher, not Mr. Sinclair. Why he's a proper gentleman. We didn't mean to—"

"Not at all," Rowland smiled.

"May I introduce Victor Bates and Jack Templeton," Edna Walling said glaring at the outspoken pair. "They've joined us temporarily while my usual contractor is unwell."

Rowland offered the men his hand. "How do you do, gentlemen? Rowland Sinclair."

For a breath, Templeton, the younger man, stared at Rowland's hand, then he wiped his own and shook it. "I know who you are, Mr. Sinclair. I'm sorry if Vic here spoke out of turn —he's from Adelaide, I'm afraid... no decorum at all."

"Watch yourself, boy!" Bates poked his workmate and shook Rowland's hand himself. "Jacko thinks he's funny, but we didn't mean no offence."

"None taken," Rowland replied, laughing. "I misspoke myself. Poacher is probably not quite right. A number of people enjoy shooting rights on *Emoh Ruo* apparently. Perhaps some of them have poor eyesight."

"We did run into a couple of rabbit shooters when we were surveying the dam paddock," Edna Walling said thoughtfully. "Of course they refrained from shooting at us!"

"I'm glad to hear it," Rowland replied. "It was dark when Len and I were out," he added, though he wasn't entirely convinced of the explanation himself. "Fortunately, Lenin will pull up quite well, and I believe Wil intends to revoke the permissions to all shooting parties."

"Uncle Rowly!" Ernest Sinclair stood up in the passenger seat of the Mercedes as a reminder that he was waiting.

Rowland waved at his nephew and took his leave of Edna Walling and her workmen.

As there wasn't a great deal left to be done to restore the *Rule Britannia*, Rowland planned to take the biplane up, ostensibly for a test flight. Ernest, armed with his father's binoculars, was understandably impatient to be on their way. Mrs. Kendall had packed them a basket of cakes and shortbread, and Clyde had secured a wooden crate, containing three bottles of lemonade and another of ginger beer, to the running board.

It took less than an hour to finish patching the fuselage. Rowland and Clyde pushed the wood and canvas aircraft out of the shed. Rowland walked the paddock checking for holes or obstructions in the low stubble, anything large enough to interfere with a successful take-off. That done, he climbed into the pilot's seat and switched on the engine. Clyde spun the propeller and removed the wheel chocks before running back to watch with Ernest. Rowland turned the *Rule Britannia* into the prevailing headwind and opened up the throttle. Clyde and Ernest cheered as she left the ground.

Rowland tested the elevators and ailerons, banking hard in a series of turns. He could see Ernest on Clyde's shoulders, waving madly. He turned into the headwind again to land, double-checking for any troublesome fence-lines before he cut back the engine and began to glide towards the ground.

He landed softly, faultlessly, taxiing the biplane to rest in almost the same position as he started. Rowland climbed out of the cockpit, looking around for Clyde. It was only then he noticed another man a short distance behind Clyde and Ernest.

Tearing off his aviator cap and goggles, Rowland jumped down from the wing.

"What the hell are you doing here, Hayden?" he demanded.

Clyde and Ernest turned. Focussed on the flight of the *Rule Britannia*, they'd failed to notice Charlie Hayden, whose history as the manager of *Oaklea* had so interested the police.

Rowland strode past them towards the intruder.

"Ernie, stay here, mate," Clyde instructed as he set the boy down and started after Rowland.

Charlie Hayden dropped his cigarette stub onto the ground and crushed it with the ball of his foot. "Look, Mr. Sinclair, Rowland... I thought maybe you'd hear me out... for old time's sake—"

"I don't know why you'd think that, Hayden. I don't know why you'd think that I wouldn't want to kill you!"

Hayden backed away a step. "Because you're not like your father or your brother. You're not a complete bastard. And because you know who killed your father as well as I do!"

Hayden recoiled, staggering as Rowland's fist made contact with his jaw.

Clyde leapt to grab his friend before he could swing again.

"Leave off, Clyde," Rowland growled, his eyes fixed on Hayden who was spitting blood.

"Rowly!" Clyde did not loosen his grip. "Ernie... the boy's here. Is this something you want him to see?"

Rowland glanced at his nephew, who watched from just a few yards away, his small fists up in the fighting stance his uncle had taught him as he blinked back tears of horror and confusion. Rowland stopped pushing against Clyde and turned back to Hayden. "Get off this property!"

"If you'd only listen, Rowland. I was doing my job. You can't hold that against me!"

"On the contrary, Mr. Hayden, I do." Rowland's fists remained clenched as he lowered his voice. "I don't want to listen to your cock and bull theories, I don't want to talk to you and if I see you here again, I may just kill you. Now go!"

Hayden did not move. "You'll regret this, boy!" he spat blood into the dirt at his feet.

It was all Clyde could do to hold Rowland back then. Suddenly Hayden seemed to reconsider the wisdom of what he was doing and put up his hands. "I'm going… I'm going."

He turned and walked towards the road. They watched till he was out of sight.

"What do you think he's after?" Clyde whispered.

Rowland suppressed a curse. "I don't know, but the bastard's bloody lucky that you and Ernie were here."

Clyde smiled. "Well, Ernie anyway. I would have helped you bury him, otherwise."

Rowland laughed bitterly. "You may yet have to." He stepped back to Ernest and knelt to look his nephew in the eye.

"I'm sorry about that, Ernie. Are you all right?"

"That's the man who came to see Mummy," Ernest said shakily.

"He came to see your mother? When?"

"Yesterday."

"What did he want?"

Ernest's lower lip began to tremble. "I don't know."

"That's all right, mate," Rowland said more gently. "I can ask your mother."

"Why did you punch that man, Uncle Rowly?"

"I was angry."

"Why?"

Rowland hesitated, unsure how to respond. "I shouldn't have hit him, Ernie," he said in the end. "I'm sorry if I frightened you."

Ernest threw his arms around Rowland's neck and hugged him. Rowland was surprised and then ashamed. Whether by nature or training, Ernest was not generally demonstrative. The child must have been truly frightened by the violence.

He stood up with Ernest still in his arms. "Come on, you can ride in the cockpit while Clyde and I push *Doris* back into the shed."

12

DOCTOR SAYS:

---◆---

Weather Decides A Baby's Sex
(From Brooke McClure, *The Sunday Times* Special
U.S.A. Representative.)

NEW YORK, Saturday

Dr. William F. Peterson, pathology expert of Illinois University,
is convinced that the fact of a baby being born a boy or girl is
largely due to temperature.

He believes that, broadly speaking, girl babies are the result of
warm weather conditions and males the result of cold weather.

More geniuses as well as sub-normal babies are born when
weather conditions are unsettled, and he believes that Europe is
filled with so many turbulent figures because its climate is more
unsettled than the climate of many other parts of the world.

The Sunday Times, 1939

The two-ton Federal lorry looked entirely out of place with the
imposing elegance of *Oaklea* as a backdrop. Battered and patched
with mismatching timbers and tin-plate, it was a stark contrast to the
pristine duco of Lucy Bennett's Riley Lynx, beside which it was parked.
Rowland did not pay a great deal of attention to the lorry, assuming it
belonged to Edna Walling or one of her contractors. It was the third
vehicle that caught his attention: a black police car.

"It looks like Gilbey and Angel are back." He brought the Mercedes to a stop.

Clyde nodded. "You might want to have a word to them about this bloke Hayden," he said, frowning. "The man's got some hide turning up here again."

"I will," Rowland promised as he climbed out of the car.

He glanced up at *Oaklea*. In their absence a grand wreath had been hung on the front door and swags of holly beneath the windows. With all the drama he had almost forgotten it was nearly Christmas.

"Your poor mother will be wondering where you've got to," Rowland said guiltily. "You should have reached Batlow days ago, Clyde."

"Don't worry about it, Rowly—with all the wives and husbands and children, there are an awful lot of us now. I expect Mum's glad to have the extra bed until the last possible moment. And my sisters' boys won't be half-impressed when I tell them about how we fixed *Doris*."

Rowland had an idea. "Why don't I fly you up there? There must be somewhere near Batlow we could land."

For a moment Clyde considered it and then, reluctantly, he declined. "Nah, Rowly, I'd never hear the end of it. My old mum doesn't really approve of flying. She thinks it's blasphemous."

"Blasphemous?"

"She has this notion that the heavens are the dominion of the good Lord and we should not venture up there unless we're invited, or dead."

"I see," Rowland smiled. He'd met Mrs. Watson Jones. Clyde was probably wise to be cautious. "Come on, we'd best see what the constabulary wants this time." He looked thoughtfully at his nephew. "Ernie, why don't you investigate what Miss Walling and her band of gardeners are up to?" Rowland handed Ernest Mrs. Kendall's picnic basket which had, it turned out, been packed with enough cakes and shortbread to feed a dozen men. "See if they're hungry."

Ernest took the basket eagerly. He liked talking to the workmen. Miss Walling had let him plant the violets. Templeton and Bates always made him laugh, calling him "Ernest, Lord of *Oaklea*" or "Prince Short Pants" and requesting that he shift great boulders out of the way.

And so he set off happily, leaving his uncle and Clyde to see about the police.

"Rowly! Clyde!" Edna Higgins flung open the homestead door and launched herself at them, somehow managing to embrace them both simultaneously.

Milton came up behind the sculptress and shook Rowland's hand. "Lenin told us he took a bullet for you. How are you, Rowly?"

"I'm well…" Rowland replied, bewildered. "What are you both doing here?"

"Aren't you pleased to see us?" Edna asked, feigning hurt.

"Of course I am. I'm simply surprised. How did you get here?"

Milton pointed to the shabby Federal. "My cousin lent me his lorry, though I did have to promise him your car for his wedding in return."

"What?"

"He could hardly expect his bride to arrive in the Federal."

"Aren't you both supposed to be spending Christmas in Sydney?"

"Ed received an invitation to spend Christmas in Canberra," Milton replied.

"Do you remember Bertie Middleton, Rowly?" Edna asked casually.

Rowland did. Bertram Middleton had been one of the sculptress's many suitors… a writer, if memory served. "Yes, Middleton— whatever happened to him?"

"He moved to Canberra… something about inspiration for his novel."

"Canberra?"

Edna shrugged. "Where else would you write the Great Australian Novel?"

"I can think of a few places… he won't be hindered by distractions, I suppose."

She laughed. "Poor Bertie has been wretchedly lonely—he literally begged us to visit."

"Actually, he begged Ed," Milton corrected. "I'm just the chaperone."

"I see," Rowland said. It was a little startling to find them both here but it was the kind of impulsive thing they would do. And he was strangely relieved to see them. Of course he was less than pleased that Middleton seemed to be once again pressing his case. "I thought you had a film role?" he said to Edna.

Milton grinned, delighted. "They sacked her."

"Whatever for?"

"A creative disagreement," Edna declared loftily.

"She told the director that he was ridiculous," Milton revealed.

"Kenny Hall? Good Lord! Why?" Edna had always got on famously with Ken Hall.

"It's K.G. now," Edna said rolling her eyes. "He won't let anyone call him Kenny anymore."

"And that's why you told him he was ridiculous?" Rowland ventured.

"No, of course not. Kenny wasn't directing this film. This was Harry Southwell who wanted me to die like a lady."

"How else could you die?"

"Like someone actually dying!" Edna said, demonstrating by clutching her hands to her chest, gasping and stumbling in a wild but surprisingly convincing depiction.

Rowland grabbed her in case she fell off the verandah in the pursuit of realism. "Yes, I see."

"He wanted me to sigh and slip ethereally to the floor without mussing my hair or showing too much leg. It was quite absurd! Not even nuns die like that!"

Rowland was contemplating how exactly one would expect a nun to die when Kate Sinclair came to the door. She smiled nervously. "Is there some reason you're all standing at the threshold rather than coming inside?"

"No, of course not... sorry, Kate. Clyde and I were just taken a bit by surprise," Rowland said, standing back for Edna.

"I think that was the point," Kate said. Clearly, she too was surprised.

"We're so sorry to impose," Edna apologised directly to Kate. "There's nothing worse than people who drop in out of the blue— we just wanted to let Rowly know we were here and where we'd be staying."

Kate blushed. "Oh no, I didn't mean—you must stay with us, of course."

Edna shook her head. "That's very kind, but we wouldn't dream of imposing any further. We've taken rooms at the Royal in town. The manager remembered us, in fact."

"Of course he remembered us," Milton said indignantly. "How many of his establishment's guests do the good people of Yass attempt to tar and feather!"

"Oh, they didn't actually tar and feather you," Edna chided. "Don't be such a baby."

Wilfred Sinclair cleared his throat as he stepped into the entrance hall. "I would consider it a personal favour if you and Miss Higgins would stay at *Oaklea* while you are in Yass," he said firmly.

Rowland was once again surprised and he wasn't alone. Though Wilfred's opinion of his brother's friends had softened somewhat over the years, his attitude to them was closer to sufferance than anything else. Kate's invitation was probably compelled by courtesy but very few things ever compelled Wilfred Sinclair.

"But we couldn't—" Edna began.

"Nonsense, it would be more convenient for all concerned if you were to lodge here. Katie, my dear, perhaps you might speak to Mrs. Kendall about preparing guest rooms when she's finished with the detectives."

"Detectives!" Rowland tensed. "What do they want with Mrs. Kendall? Where are they?" He moved towards the kitchen.

Wilfred pulled his brother back. "They're questioning all the staff who were here the night Father died. We've been instructed not to interfere in any way, Rowly."

"And you agreed to that?"

"If I hadn't, they would simply have carted everybody back to the station for interviews," Wilfred replied firmly. "Perhaps you should all visit with mother in the drawing room until they're finished. I have some telephone calls to make."

"Don't you think—?"

"I think we should at least *appear* to co-operate with this nonsense," Wilfred said, making no attempt to mask his irritation. "Go, Rowly. I told you I would handle this."

Frustrated, Rowland did as his brother asked, retiring to the drawing room and reintroducing his friends to his mother. Elisabeth was as always delighted to meet "Aubrey's" young friends, though she had met them before on occasions she'd forgotten soon after.

Milton and Clyde chatted patiently and kindly with Rowland's ailing mother, and the poet was soon persuaded to play the piano since Aubrey never played for her anymore. Lenin had been settled

SULARI GENTILL

in a large basket by the hearth with blankets and cushions and every conceivable comfort. Rowland knelt to talk to him, and Kate Sinclair lowered herself into an armchair, looking exhausted and uneasy.

Edna went to her, taking both her hands. "You look all in, Kate. I'm going to fetch you a cup of tea."

"But Mrs. Kendall is being interviewed. Oh dear, I can't even offer you tea."

"I can make the tea," Edna said, patting Kate's hand.

"They're conducting the interview in the kitchen."

"They won't bother about a girl making tea," Edna replied with confidence.

"I'll go with you." Rowland stood.

"Don't be silly, Rowly." Edna dismissed the offer with a wave of her hand. "You, they will notice, and you can't make a decent pot of tea anyway." She looked at Kate and winked. "All those fancy schools and they didn't teach him one sensible thing!"

Kate smiled, and her reserve thawed.

Edna was gone much longer than Rowland expected. He was just preparing to go searching for her when she arrived with a large, heavily laden tray of the promised tea. She looked pale and shaken.

"Ed? What's wrong?" he whispered as he took the tray from her and set it on the sideboard.

She stared at him for a moment, and then impulsively she embraced him. "My God, Rowly, your father was a fiend, a brute," she whispered. "How could he?"

"I'm not sure what—"

Edna pulled back and looked into his eyes. "I heard Mrs. Kendall talking to the detectives, telling them…" She swallowed.

"Mrs. Kendall was always very protective of me, Ed. You mustn't—"

128

"The police are suggesting you killed your father," she blurted. "They believe you shot him."

Rowland frowned, glancing over his shoulder at the drawing room. Milton was now singing to his own piano accompaniment, and the mildly alarmed amusement of all. "Let's not upset my mother with this right now," he said.

"Yes, of course, but Rowly you must—"

"I will. I'll speak to Wil as soon as the police leave. You mustn't worry."

Edna seemed about to say something more, but she thought better of it. The sculptress poured tea instead and gave Rowland a cup for his mother. She took a cup to Kate.

"Who is that very demonstrative young woman, Aubrey?" Elisabeth Sinclair demanded when Rowland brought her the tea.

"That is Miss Higgins, Mother, I just introduced you."

"Oh did you? I must have forgotten." She patted the settee beside her and he sat obediently. "Your father would have considered her most improper, Aubrey."

"No doubt."

"I thought you and that lovely girl, Lucy, were about to announce your engagement. I'm sure your father would have approved."

"I am afraid reports of our fondness for each have been grossly exaggerated."

"Oh dear, that is a shame. Henry would have liked her, I think."

Rowland rubbed her hand absently, watching as Edna spoke with Kate. His sister-in-law seemed more relaxed now. She laughed at something Edna said, and patted her swollen belly. It was only then he realised she'd not mentioned one word about the impending addition since he'd arrived. Perhaps that was not something you spoke of in the presence of men. No wonder she'd been so desperate to have him bring Lucy Bennett into the Sinclair fold.

Kate slipped off her wedding ring and handed it to Edna. The sculptress released the clasp of the locket she always wore and looped the silver chain through the ring. She suspended it then over Kate's belly, allowing it to swing gently.

Kate giggled and for the first time she seemed to Rowland as young as Edna.

Clyde, who had also been watching, laughed. "You're not going to pay any attention to that old carnival trick are you, Mrs. Sinclair?"

"Don't listen to Clyde, he's always been a spoilsport," Edna said. "It's another boy!"

"Oh dear… really!" Kate said, smiling.

"I had three boys," Elisabeth Sinclair interrupted. "Three blue-eyed boys. Henry was so proud."

The room stilled; for a moment it seemed that no one breathed. Rowland pressed his mother's hand and Elisabeth Sinclair looked at him, her eyes bright and clear. She handed him her empty cup and saucer. "I'd like another cup of tea, Aubrey darling."

Rowland paused before he replied. "Yes, of course." He glanced at his watch—surely the police had finished with Mrs. Kendall by now. "I might pop out to the kitchen and see if the detectives are done."

"Actually, Rowly," Milton said, leaving the piano. "Might I have a quiet word before you go?"

"Yes, if you like." Rowland opened the door and allowed Milton to step out before him into the hallway.

Milton moved directly to the point. "Look, Rowly, I spoke to Delaney about this business concerning your father. He says that he's being kept out of the investigation."

Rowland shrugged. "Colin Delaney's not my personal detective, Milt."

"He did find out that the police received information that your father's murder had nothing to do with a robbery." The poet seized his friend's shoulder. "They suspect it was you. That's what they're investigating to establish. Delaney says Gilbey's an ambitious sod, Angel's not much better. Apparently the publicity this case could generate…"

Rowland rubbed his face. "They can investigate till hell freezes over, they won't find anything."

"I don't know, Rowly," Milton said, his face grim. "From what I gather, Eric Campbell's been in to see the commissioner about what he says is a 'campaign of harassment'. Wilfred's friends in the department are coming up against his enemies. Delaney's worried."

13

THE MIRROR OF
SOCIETY

By ANNE SEYMOUR

THIS week sees Mrs. Ernest Merriman, of Yass, staying in
Sydney with her sister, Mrs. C.G. Berge, with a specially fat
cheque, a result of the high wool prices, clasped in her hand,
ready to be spent on decorations and such for the Picnic Race
Ball. Mr. Merriman is the president of the race committee.

Australian Women's Weekly, January 1934

Gilbey and Angel confronted the Sinclair brothers in Wilfred's
study. Gilbey began quite affably, examining the Glover which
hung behind Wilfred's desk, and commenting quite extensively on
the artist's technique, until Wilfred lost patience and asked him
what he wanted.

"We tracked down Dr. Oliver," Gilbey informed them. "He
remembers the night in question and categorically denies giving
Rowland Sinclair any form of sedative."

Wilfred didn't falter. "It was an assumption—I may have been
mistaken."

"At 11 p.m. a Miss Jane Pell, then in your employ as an upstairs maid,
took a cup of tea to Mr. Rowland Sinclair's room. According to Miss

Pell, he was not there. As you are no doubt aware, Mr. Henry Sinclair was shot at ten past or thereabouts. Given Miss Pell's revelations, would you care to tell us where exactly you were, Mr. Sinclair?"

Rowland frowned. "I can't remember. The bathroom, perhaps."

"Well that's the interesting point, Mr. Sinclair." Angel flicked through his notebook. "Miss Pell states that she waited so that she could report back to Mrs. Kendall that you had taken the tea. She was in your room when she heard the fatal gunshot."

"She alleges," Wilfred said pointedly.

Gilbey flipped on a couple of pages. "Mrs. Kendall has just confirmed that she sent Miss Pell up to Mr. Sinclair's room with a cup of tea and that she does not recall seeing her again until after the gunshot."

Rowland stood and wandered over to the window. He stared out at the garden. Ernest was watering the new plantings under the supervision of Edna Walling. "Am I under arrest, detectives?"

"No, sir. Not yet. Considering what we have come to know about Henry Sinclair's treatment of you, we hoped you might take this opportunity to make a statement."

"Do you mean a statement or a confession, Detective Gilbey?"

"That would be up to you, Mr. Sinclair."

Wilfred intervened. His face was rigidly controlled but there was no mistaking his displeasure. "I believe this meeting is at an end, gentlemen. I will thank you to direct any future enquiries through our solicitors."

"It might be in your best interests—"

Wilfred opened the door. "Thank you, detectives. Allow me to show you out." His manner did not invite argument or even suggested that it was an option.

Gilbey and Angel exchanged a glance, and slowly stood to go. Wilfred accompanied them to the front door himself.

When he returned to the study, Rowland was still gazing out of the window. Edna and Milton had, it seemed, ventured into the garden. The sculptress was admiring the new walkway, and Milton appeared to be making some sort of speech from atop a mound of rocks awaiting incorporation into the dry wall.

"If that blasted fool is inciting my gardeners into some kind of Communist rebellion just days before Christmas—" Wilfred muttered.

"I thought you had finally warmed to my friends," Rowland said, more amused than surprised.

"What?"

"You invited them to stay here, in fact, you jolly well insisted."

Wilfred snorted. "It's no secret that Miss Higgins and that long-haired buffoon are friends of yours. In Yass they would embarrass us publicly. At least here, I can contain the damage."

Rowland's laugh was wry. He should have known. "Fair enough. Thank you anyway."

Wilfred sat down at the desk and waved him away. "You'd best go and supervise them," he said. "I'll speak to the solicitors again."

───────────   ───────────

Arthur Sinclair was waiting for Rowland when he came out of Wilfred's study. He pulled him aside. "I say, old man, don't you think it's a bit much to bring that Miss Higgins here?"

"I beg your pardon?"

"It's bad enough you jilt poor Miss Bennett, but to bring your... her rival... to the house and barely a day later—it's too bad, if you'll forgive my saying. It's not the way a gentleman should behave."

Rowland stared at his cousin. No one but Wilfred had ever even tried to speak to him this way before.

"This really isn't any of your business, Arthur."

"I'm a Sinclair, Rowland. Your behaviour reflects on us all. And may I tell you that you are trading a diamond for a shard of common glass!"

Rowland's eyes hardened. "Arthur, you are more than welcome to admire Miss Bennett, but you would be well advised to never again insult Miss Higgins in my presence."

"You are in no position to advise anybody. Do you have any idea of the spot in which you're putting poor Kate and Wilfred?"

"Who the hell do you think you are?"

Arthur shook his head. "I can't believe you'd introduce a woman like that to your mother."

Rowland grabbed Arthur by the lapel and shoved him up against the wall. Someone screamed behind him. The door to the study flew open. "Rowly! What the devil are you doing?" Wilfred was incredulous.

Rowland glanced at Lucy, who now stood in the hallway, and released his cousin. "Arthur and I are having a minor disagreement."

Lucy Bennett's face crumpled into tears and she turned and ran towards the stairs.

"For pity's sake! Have you no sense of common decency?" Arthur said, shaking Rowland off and setting out after Lucy.

Wilfred glared at his brother. "Just what is going on?"

Rowland unclenched his fist. "I believe that idiot Arthur fancies he's defending Miss Bennett's honour or some such thing."

Wilfred took a deep slow breath. "I suspect that Arthur has become rather fond of Lucy. I'll speak to him." He removed his spectacles and squinted at Rowland. "In the meantime perhaps you should stay out of his way."

"It would be my pleasure," Rowland replied, fuming quietly. "I might take Ed and the chaps into Yass tonight. We'll need to cancel

Ed and Milt's reservation at the Royal and pick up their luggage anyway. We could have dinner at the hotel and leave you and Kate in peace for an evening."

Wilfred nodded. "That's probably a wise idea. And why don't you take them over to the race meet in Bungendore tomorrow, as well? Perhaps by then things will have simmered down."

Rowland nodded. "Look Wil, about Arthur…"

"Don't worry, he'll get used to you."

———————————————   ———————————————

Edna looked tentatively into the kitchen.

Rowland sat at the scrubbed oak table watching as Mrs. Kendall worked. The soft pale flesh of her ample arms jiggled as she rolled out the pastry. Though she smiled now, her eyes were red and swollen. It was clear she'd been crying. The monogrammed corner of Rowland's handkerchief protruded from the pocket of her apron.

"Those officers just kept asking and asking," the faithful servant said as she worked the rolling pin. "Oh my dear, dear boy, I'll never forgive myself if—"

Rowland stood and put his arm protectively about her shoulders. "You mustn't upset yourself, Mrs. Kendall. I'm terribly sorry they spoke to you like that. I won't let it happen again."

"Oh Mr. Rowland, it's not me you should be worried about!" She dabbed her eyes with Rowland's handkerchief.

Edna cleared her throat, to let them know she was there.

Rowland turned. "Oh hello, Ed." He smiled. "I've persuaded Mrs. Kendall to bake us her delicious treacle tart for tomorrow."

"Tomorrow?"

"We're going across to the picnic races at Bungendore. Unless of course Middleton requires you immediately?"

"No. Bertie can wait," Edna said absently.

"Well if you want that treacle tart, you best get out of my kitchen!" Mrs. Kendall said, wiping a few specks of pastry flour from Rowland's lapel.

Rowland smiled, embracing the housekeeper warmly. "Stop worrying about me," he said. "I'll be fine."

Mrs. Kendall sighed, as she dusted off the flour which had just been transferred to Rowland's attire from her apron. "Go on with you then." She shooed them out of her kitchen in a manner that left them feeling more welcomed than expelled.

━━━━━━━━━   ━━━━━━━━━

Rowland elected not to risk any further scenes with Arthur or Lucy. He let Kate know that he was taking his friends into Yass to retrieve their chattels from the Royal. "We might as well stop for dinner there, rather than making you all wait for our return."

Kate looked relieved.

Inwardly, Rowland flinched, wondering if his relationship with his sister-in-law would ever be restored. He had always thought of Kate as an undeclared ally, tempering Wilfred's more disapproving moments with her fondness for her husband's errant brother.

"I'd best head off," Rowland said into the awkward silence.

"Where are you going, Uncle Rowly?" Ernest Sinclair came into the drawing room and sat on the floor beside Lenin's basket.

"Into town, Ernie. We won't be long."

"Will that man be there? The one you hit?"

"Ernest, your uncle doesn't go about hitting people," Kate said sternly.

"Actually Kate…" Rowland began sheepishly. He told her of the incident with Charlie Hayden.

"And you got into a fight? With Ernie there?"

"It wasn't a fight... but yes, I lost my temper. The man was trespassing," he offered weakly.

"Oh, Rowly."

"I'm sorry. You know I wouldn't have let anything happen to Ernie."

Kate sighed, summoning Ernest and hugging him protectively to her breast. "I suppose it can't be helped."

"Ernest mentioned that Charlie Hayden had been round here, to see you," Rowland said cautiously.

"Oh, him." Kate made the connection. "I found him on the verandah a couple of days ago, waiting. I asked him what he was doing here and he said he'd come to see me. He was hoping I could influence Wil in some way."

Silence was the most civil thing Rowland could offer at that point.

"Arthur came out and ordered him to leave," Kate continued. "I felt rather sorry for him after I got over the initial shock. He seemed almost hurt that we would want him off the property."

Rowland's eyes flashed. "You don't need to feel sorry for him, Kate. Does Wil know he was here?"

"To be honest, with all the excitement... and Lucy... I believe I forgot to mention it to him."

The subtle reproach hit its mark. "I'd better go. The others will be waiting." Rowland bent to pat Lenin and talk to his nephew. "Would you keep an eye on Len for me, Ernie?"

Ernest nodded, placing his arm around Lenin as a symbol of his commitment to the task his uncle had assigned.

"Do me a favour, Kate," Rowland said. "Would you inform Wil that Hayden came here... that he tried to speak to you?"

"Of course," she replied coldly. "Are you going to tell him that you got into a fight with Mr. Hayden in the presence of our son?"

Rowland looked at her, noticeably startled. Immediately, Kate seemed to regret the sharpness of her words, looking away from him, her hand over her mouth.

Rowland presumed that sometime after her last conversation with Lucy Bennett, his sister-in-law had resolved to be angry with him, to punish him for hurting her friend. But hostility was hard for Kate. It was not in her nature. He smiled. "You can tell Wil if you like. Otherwise I'll speak to him when I get back."

"I shall," she said without looking at him. "It's something he should know!"

Deciding that the exchange was not going to improve, Rowland bade Kate good night and walked out to his car. Edna handed him his driving gloves as he slipped behind the wheel. "Are you all right, Rowly?" she asked.

"Yes… I'm just beginning to fear that Kate will never forgive me for this debacle with Lucy."

"Of course she will," the sculptress replied. "She's just disappointed, and feels a trifle guilty."

"Guilty? Why should Kate feel guilty?"

"I suspect she encouraged Lucy to fall in love with you at least as much as she encouraged you to fall in love with Lucy. Sadly, it worked only in the former case. Now Lucy's heartbroken, or thinks she is, and as a result Kate feels terrible." Edna rubbed his arm. "She'll come round, Rowly."

"I hope so." He pulled away from the main house and drove the short distance to the manager's residence where Clyde and Milton had already called in on Harry Simpson. The three men were standing together on the verandah when the yellow Mercedes pulled in.

Harry Simpson removed his hat and took Edna's hand in his. "Miss Higgins. What a pleasure to see you again."

"Likewise, Mr. Simpson," Edna said, smiling warmly at the stockman. "Won't you come to dinner with us?"

"Thank you, but no." He took out a battered gold pocket watch to check the time. "I'm expecting Wil as soon as he can get away."

"Fishing?" Rowland asked.

Simpson nodded. "Full moon tonight. You know I had a dog that loved full moons. Must've been part wolf—used to howl like a mad thing. Startled a mob of cattle one night." He grimaced. "They trampled the noisy blighter… had to shoot him in the end."

"How simply awful," Edna exclaimed, though she had become accustomed to Simpson's stories of unfortunate dogs. "Why on earth are you and Mr. Sinclair fishing at night?"

"It's impossible for Wilfred to get away during the day what with harvest and a house full of Communists." Simpson chuckled.

Edna's brow furrowed gently. "Be careful. Whoever shot Lenin—"

"Don't you worry, Miss Higgins," Simpson reassured her. "I'm pretty hard to spot in the dark. Of course, Wil's a goner!"

For a moment Edna stared at him, unsure. Rowland grinned and shoved the stockman. Then Simpson giggled, his great broad shoulders bouncing, and he winked at Edna. "We'll be all right," he said once the paroxysm had passed. "Wil's pretty sure we won't have any more trouble."

14

EDITORIAL

———◆———

Evidently hoping to put a "smoke screen" to divert attention from the "salary grab," the Federal members are making bitter attacks on the newspapers which condemned their action, and there was talk of bringing one editor before the bar of the House.

Parliament would be wise not to take this action—it would appear ridiculous in addition to the manner in which it is already regarded following the increase in salaries. The members' best plan would be to keep quiet in the hope that the "grab" may be forgotten by election time—an air of injured innocence will not be accepted by the people in their present frame of mind.

The Post pays a tribute to Senator Charles Hardy for his wholehearted opposition to the "grab," and frankly admits that this is the first time during his political history that he has won our admiration.

Western Champion, 3 November 1933

The publican's wife was less than pleased to have the two-room booking cancelled so late. Of course Rowland paid for that night's accommodation and moreover added a generous gratuity for the inconvenience, but the gesture served only to irritate her further. It seemed to Margaret Sedgwick that Rowland Sinclair was still mixing in a bad crowd.

She'd hoped that the youngest of the Sinclair boys might finally have settled down into some semblance of respectability. With the decadent morality of young people, the town needed its better families to set an example. Lord knows, her own Richard could have done with a little virtuous leadership. In Henry Sinclair's day no one ever had cause to raise an eyebrow, but Wilfred was indulgent of his feckless younger brother. It was a crying shame!

A little grudgingly, Mrs. Sedgwick pointed the party from Sydney towards a dining room already bustling with travellers. It was well past six in the evening and the locals had departed from the public bar.

As Rowland was finalising the account, a couple came out of the dining room and proceeded towards the staircase which led to the Royal's labyrinth of guest rooms.

"Well, what do you know," Milton observed.

The gentleman walked past them with the jaunty confidence of a man who was sure of his evening's pleasure. Milton nudged Rowland. "Isn't that Senator Hardy?"

Rowland followed the direction of Milton's gaze. The contented gentleman was indeed Senator Charles Hardy Jnr. with whom they'd had a long, and not always happy, association. In fact, it was Hardy's speech, at the Yass Memorial Hall nearly two years previously, which had incited the townspeople to kidnap Milton in their enthusiasm to tar and feather a Communist. The young woman on Hardy's arm was clearly enraptured with his every word and gesture.

"That's not his wife, is it?" Milton's grin was sly, his manner quite gleeful.

"No," Rowland replied. In fact they had all met Mrs. Hardy. "She is not."

"In that case, I think we'd better say hello," Milton said, already striding over with his hand outstretched.

Clyde cursed under his breath, and they all followed—more to keep an eye on the poet than the senator.

"Senator Hardy!" Milton said loudly. "How are you, sir?"

Hardy stopped, startled. "Mr. Isaacs, Mr. Sinclair, and Mr. Watson Jones isn't it?" He shook their hands. "And the unforgettable Miss Higgins. Good Lord! What brings you all to Yass?"

"We're visiting Rowly," Milton replied.

Hardy's companion started up the stairs without him. "Don't be long, Chas," she purred.

"Just passing through myself, en route from Wagga," Hardy said when she'd gone.

"Oh. You're not staying?" Milton cast his eyes up the stairs.

"Me? No. I'll have to head back to Canberra. But I might pop up and say goodnight to… my sister." He slapped his forehead. "I am sorry, I should have introduced you to my sister. I have six of them you know."

"My goodness, six!" Milton replied. "You're a lucky man—I'm an only child myself."

"Well, we must get on to the dining room," Clyde said, glaring pointedly at the poet.

"Yes, we must." Rowland took Clyde's lead. "Good night, Senator Hardy. Please do give our regards to your sister."

Hardy grinned. It was more mischievous than embarrassed. "I shall. Indeed, I shall."

They left Hardy to his family reunion and continued into the dining area, finding a table which afforded a level of seclusion by virtue of its position in the ladies' bar. Separated from the main dining hall by stained glass concertina doors, it served their needs well.

Rowland was perfectly aware that his friends had questions and so he was not surprised when Edna opened in her customarily direct manner.

"Rowly, why do the police believe you killed your father?"

"Obviously, they're idiots."

"You can't shrug this off, Rowly," Milton warned. "Why have they suddenly come to the conclusion that you shot your old man?"

Rowland frowned. "There appears to be a barrage of witnesses coming out of the woodwork, who until now have held their peace."

"You mean Hayden?" Milton prompted.

"Clyde told you?"

"I'm sorry, mate," Clyde said. "I was worried about you and—"

Rowland waved away his friend's apology. "It saves me having to go into the whole ugly business again." He loosened his tie just slightly. "It's not only him. There's now a maid who says she remembers I was not in my room when Father was shot, and Dr. Oliver who confirms I wasn't sedated in any way."

"Doesn't it strike you as odd that they're all emerging now, Rowly?"

Rowland thought for a moment and then shook his head. "I guess Hayden's appearance is what made the police look into my story and hunt down the others. I don't even remember them questioning me back then."

"And this Hayden... why does he suddenly turn up after thirteen years?"

"I don't know. Perhaps he heard about Father's pistol being found."

Milton got up and checked that there was no one listening outside the door to the anteroom before he spoke. "Rowly, you know that we're with you no matter what you did. You do know that?"

Clyde turned on the poet. "Bloody hell, Milt! What do you mean by that?"

"We need to know the truth if we're going to sort this out."

"Are you out of your tiny drunken mind?"

"If I'd been in Rowly's place," Milton said, without taking his eyes off Rowland, "I might have shot the bast… him."

"Well, Rowly's not you!"

Rowland watched them argue. His face was unreadable, almost distracted.

It was Edna who intervened. "Stop," she said. The word was softly uttered yet somehow it had the force of a slap. Both Clyde and Milton fell silent. "We're not here to make things more difficult." She took Rowland's hand in hers. "We're worried about you, Rowly."

Rowland squeezed her hand as he met the poet's eye. "I didn't shoot him, Milt. Lord knows I thought about it. During all those beatings, I killed him over and over again in my mind… but someone else actually did it first."

Milton slapped him warmly on the back. "Good, we don't have to smuggle you out of the country to avoid the gallows, then. We've only been back a few months."

Rowland laughed. If it came to that Milton probably knew someone who could oblige. "Wil's handling it. He's called in an army of lawyers. There's more silk on his payroll than there is in all of China. It'll blow over."

Milton glanced at Clyde. "There's really only one way to make sure you don't go down for your father's murder, mate, and that's to find out who really did shoot him."

"I didn't kill my father—Gilbey and Angel will work that out eventually. As for who really did it," Rowland's bearing hardened, "I'm inclined to wish him the best of British."

The drive back from Yass to *Oaklea* was quiet, though the silence was not strained. They had all said everything they could, or would. Rowland knew full well now that his friends had dropped everything—abandoned Christmas plans, disappointed family and risked Wilfred's ire—simply because they thought he needed help. They'd done so without any idea of how they could help him. He appreciated it but, as much as he trusted them, this was a family matter.

It was quite late when they reached *Oaklea*. The evening was bright under the full moon that Harry Simpson had mentioned earlier. The house was still. Rowland turned off the engine.

"If we use the back door we won't have to wake everybody up," Rowland suggested. "Mrs. Kendall leaves it unlocked."

It was as they were cutting across the lawn that Rowland noticed the light in the south wing.

"Someone's up," he murmured. The south wing was where the nursery and the children's rooms were located. Perhaps Nanny de Waring was engaged in some late-night duty.

He looked again. There was something odd about the light... it wasn't steady. It flickered. And then he realised what it was.

"Fire... my God, it's on fire!" He turned to Edna. "Quick, go to the front door, wake everybody, pull the servant's bells—get them out!" Rowland began to run towards the glowing room. Clyde and Milton went with him.

At the window they could see into the room. The drapes and furnishings were ablaze. The fire had spread to an adjoining room. Rowland could see Ernest's rocking horse in the flames.

"Milt—it's spreading. We'll need men!"

Milton nodded. "I'll alert the managers."

Clyde pulled a capstone free from one of the newly constructed dry rock walls. "Stand clear, Rowly!" he warned as he threw the stone through the glass. The flames, fed anew, surged greedily towards the opening. Rowland ripped off his jacket and used it to protect his arm as he broke away jagged shards of glass. With the window broken, they could make out screams from inside.

Rowland hoisted himself in. Clyde followed.

"Where are they, Rowly?" Clyde shouted, gasping and coughing as the dense black smoke pushed into his lungs.

Rowland paused to cough and orient himself, to pick up the source of the screams. The wallpaper peeled and crackled off the upper walls as the wainscoting below scorched and split. The heat was immense.

"This way," he said moving towards the rooms on the left. The fire had not yet engulfed the short hallway and the door at the end of it was still shut. Rowland tried the handle but the door was locked. He could hear a child screaming clearly now. Desperately, he and Clyde charged the door. It gave. The room within was filled with smoke and, when they shut the door against the fire, black.

Clyde pulled the light switch to no avail. Rowland followed the cries and discovered Ewan in his bed by the window.

"Rowly, I found the nanny," Clyde called from the other side of the room.

Rowland opened the shutters. The moonlight faded the black marginally. Clyde held the semi-conscious nanny in his arms. She was coming round. "Ernest," she mumbled as she revived. "Ernie?" Then she screamed. "Ernest!"

Rowland put Ewan back onto the bed and grabbed a stool, using it to break the windows. They could hear the commotion and panic outside.

"Get them out," he said to Clyde, pulling a blanket from the bed. "I'll find Ernie."

"Upstairs," the nanny said. "His room is upstairs."

Rowland grabbed Clyde's arm. "Can you—?"

Clyde nodded. "Go."

Rowland gulped what air he could and opened the door, plunging back into the corridor and the burning sunroom. The fire had all but engulfed the room. Throwing the blanket over his head he made a blind dash for the stairs. The runner secured to the centre of the stairs was alight but the structure had not yet caught.

"Ernie!" Rowland took the stairs two and three at a time. The landing adjoining the first floor corridor was choked as smoke funnelled up the stairwell.

Rowland blinked, his eyes stung and watered as he tried to remember which room was Ernest's. The first door led to a storage room.

"Ernie!"

And then he heard the sobbing, terrified cry. "I'm here. I'm here!"

Rowland pushed open the second door. The smoke was less dense here. Ernest ran into his arms and clung there. Rowland shoved the door shut behind him and tried to think. He went to the window and looked out. The lawns were now teeming with men with buckets and fire blankets. The irrigation system had been mercilessly torn up to turn against the fire.

He could see Harry and Arthur trying to prevent Wilfred from running towards the building, Kate on her knees, hysterical... and then Clyde and Ewan, thank God. With Ernest still clinging to him, Rowland fumbled with the brass window fastenings. "Chin up, Ernie, I'm here now."

The smoke was now beginning to seep under the door and he could hear crashing on the floor below. Finally the window lifted.

A large bay window protruded from the wall directly below them. As with all the bays on this wing, the small area of its flat roof had been surrounded with a decorative wrought iron rail to define a false balcony. Rowland considered the drop from that roof. They would still be about twenty feet above the ground but perhaps he could lower Ernest down somehow.

"Ernie," he said into the boy's ear, "just hang onto me, mate. Don't let go, until I tell you."

Ernest whimpered but he nodded into Rowland's neck.

"Good man."

Rowland called out to his brother then. Wilfred heard him on the third frantic shout. For a moment, he simply stared in horror and disbelief and then as Rowland climbed out, he sprinted towards the window.

Rowland lowered himself and Ernest gingerly onto the roof of the bay, only too aware that the structure had not been designed to bear the weight of a grown man. He could feel the heat rising from the burning room beneath.

"Rowly, hang on!" It was Milton's voice. "We'll find a ladder."

"A rope," Rowland gasped, coughing now. "Get me a rope."

"Rowly!"

Rowland glanced down at his brother's ashen face. "Ernie's all right, Wil."

Milton returned with a coil of rope. "Ready?"

"Yes. Toss it up."

Rowland held onto Ernest with one arm and caught the rope with his other. The roof underfoot creaked and groaned. It took him several moments to pry Ernest from him. "Ernie, I'm going to lower you down to your father. I have to tie the rope around you."

"No!" Ernest tried to cling to him again. "I'm scared," he sobbed.

"Look down there, mate. You can see your father waiting for you. Don't worry, I won't let you fall."

Ernest looked, but to a small boy it seemed a great height and his father appeared very far away.

"Come on, mate, put your dukes up!"

Still crying, Ernest raised his fists in front of his face. "That's right, Ernie, a good boxer protects his head." Rowland tied the rope securely under his nephew's raised arms. He twisted the rope around his hand and forearm and began to lower the boy to the ground. Terrified, Ernest struggled and kicked, forcing Rowland to step back to keep from over-balancing. He felt the bay roof give way a little.

"Ernie! Don't move! Do you hear me? Don't move!" Wilfred roared, seeing what was happening.

His father's voice seemed to shock Ernest into compliance. Rowland worked quickly, against the heat, against panic. Men positioned themselves below ready to catch Ernest should the rope or Rowland give way.

The coir skinned Rowland's hands as it slid through. Ernest's eyes were closed and he cried for his mother. For a time everybody seemed to hold their breath. And then cheering as Ernest reached his father's outstretched arms.

Rowland stumbled, relieved, exhausted. He had been so determined to get Ernest out that now, with the boy safe, his body just wanted to stop, to rest. His head was beginning to swim.

"Rowly!" Wilfred did not pause to celebrate, handing his son to Arthur, and bellowing at his brother to pull himself together. The rope was sent back up.

Rallying, Rowland forced his limbs to move, this time to secure the rope to the balcony rail.

Below him the windows of the bay shattered outwards with the heat. The surge of flame forced the men on the lawn back. There wasn't time to think. Rowland swung himself over with only his grip on the rope to support him. He was about halfway down when the bay structure finally collapsed.

15

FIRST AID AT HOME

Asphyxia

Continuous insensibility when breathing is absent is known as asphyxia…

The treatment applicable to all cases of insensibility should be given. Ensure that breathing is possible, by making sure that the air passages are not obstructed, that pressure does not prevent the necessary expansion of the chest, and that there is abundance of pure air… To ensure the possibility of breathing, direct action should be as follows: Strangulation: Cut and remove the band constricting the throat. Hanging: Do not wait for the arrival of a policeman. Grasp the lower limbs and raise the body to take the tension off the rope, cut the rope, and free the neck… Suffocation by smoke or gases: Remove the patient into fresh air. Before entering a building full of smoke, tie a handkerchief (wet if possible) over the nose and mouth. Keep low, or even crawl, while in a room full of smoke or gas that rises.

The West Australian, November 1930

The Lister pumps which had been installed to irrigate the new garden designed by Edna Walling deluged the bay window and its surrounds with water as the structure disintegrated. In the fire, and smoke and water, there was a while where no one was sure what had happened to Rowland Sinclair.

His friends, his brother and Harry Simpson plunged into the chaos to find him.

Rowland was aware he was on the ground, and that he was having difficulty breathing. Beyond that, he could not seem to focus.

"Rowly, thank God!" Wilfred's voice.

Two sets of shoulders under his arms... he wasn't sure whose. And then the world became hazy and incomprehensible.

When Rowland was next aware, he was lying on the lawn a distance away from the burning wing. Every breath was painful, but it was air at least.

"Rowly?" Edna loosened his tie and released the first button of his shirt. She rubbed his back as he coughed violently. "Wilfred's just gone to check on Kate. Rowly? Can you hear me?"

Rowland nodded, falling back exhausted. His ears were ringing but he could hear Edna. He began to take in what was happening around him: people running, shouting, carrying buckets and blankets. Bells, sirens, someone barking orders. The cars had been driven up so that their headlamps could illuminate what the full moon didn't. He tensed when he saw the clergyman. "What the hell's the Canon doing here?"

Edna calmed him, stroking the hair away from his forehead. "He came to help with the fire, Rowly. No one's died."

"Oh... good." Rowland closed his eyes still unable to think clearly, but glad. Wilfred returned with a blanket, spoke to him briefly and was called away again. Edna cradled his head in her lap, answering his questions, telling him repeatedly that his nephews were safe. Later he would remember that she kissed him—tenderly—a kiss that was so out of context that he became sure he'd imagined the softness of her lips on his.

By the time Wilfred returned once more, the fog in Rowland's mind had cleared to some extent and he'd recovered enough clarity to recognise the bearded gentleman standing by his brother's side.

"Maguire," he said weakly, wondering how and from where Wilfred had managed to produce the renowned Sydney surgeon.

Maguire nodded and with no further pleasantry proceeded to examine Rowland. He addressed his findings directly to Wilfred as if his patient were a child. "I'm optimistic that his lungs have not been damaged. His ribs seem to have been bruised by the fall." Rowland gasped as Maguire poked him to illustrate his point. "The pain when breathing is related to that. And there's quite a tremendous bump on his head which is why he's so disoriented. Rope burns on his hands, a few minor lacerations—from falling on the glass, I presume—but miraculously he seems to have avoided any burns." He stood up, using his hat to dust off his trousers. "However, as I was always taught to be cautious, I want you to keep him quiet, see that he rests, send for me immediately if he loses consciousness or begins to vomit."

The surgeon moved on to attend the next casualty in what was beginning to resemble a field hospital.

"Give me a hand, Wil."

"Are you sure you should—"

"Yes. I am."

Rowland grabbed the hand Wilfred offered him and, slowly, pulled himself to his feet.

"Are you all right?"

Rowland nodded, gazing at the ruined wing where the fire had started and was now successfully confined. The fire fighters were working to keep the flames away from the sandstone walls of the older part of the house. "How's Kate... and Mother?"

"Mother is coping surprisingly well—more worried about the fire spreading to the stables than anything else. Kate will be all right now that the boys are safe."

Rowland flinched as another beam crashed in the inferno. "Good."

"I'm sending Kate, Mother, Lucy and the children to lodgings in town," Wilfred said grimly. "I want you to go with them."

Rowland shook his head. "No, I'm all right. I'd rather stay."

"Rowly, I need to oversee the mop up. I can't—"

"I don't need a nursemaid," Rowland said irately.

"Very well, just stay out of the way." Wilfred replied with his customary gruffness. Even so, he braced his brother's shoulder before he returned to direct the men now consolidating control of the fire and attempting to finally extinguish its flames.

Edna, who had somehow avoided being sent away with the women and children, slipped her hand into Rowland's. She looked critically into his face, frowning as she studied the bloody bruise on his brow now visible even against the soot. "Are you sure you're all right, Rowly?" She reached up to test the temperature of his forehead. "How do you feel?"

"Like the house fell on me… but otherwise fine. Where's—"

"Milt and Clyde are still helping out with the fire. Harry too, and Lenin is safely asleep in the back seat of your car." Edna pre-empted a number of questions. She rubbed his arm. "I'm so sorry, Rowly. It must be heartbreaking to watch your family home—"

He placed his arm around her shoulders. For a moment he fancied he could smell her rose scent through the smoke and the smoulder. "The older part of the house is untouched, see," he said, pointing. "Fortunately, the blessed fire seems to have been confined to that one wing." He surveyed the destruction. For some reason, he thought of Ernest's rocking horse in the flames. "I'm just jolly glad we came back from town when we did."

Edna shuddered. She had been present when Kate had realised both her children were inside the burning building. She'd watched

Kate's joy and her terror when Clyde had delivered Ewan with the news that Rowland and Ernest were still inside. "You're right, it could have been a lot worse."

They watched McNair, the one-armed gardener, limp between the pump and the flames with a wet hessian bag, cursing and beating the fire as if it were a cognisant enemy that could be turned back by the ferocity of his threats.

"Rowly!" Milton spotted them from amongst the men on a bucket line. He handed the tin pail to the next man in the line and ran over to shake his friend's hand.

Clyde too appeared from somewhere to clap Rowland on the shoulder. "Bloody hell, Rowly. That was too close, mate."

It was a few hours before Wilfred was satisfied that the fire was completely out. In that time many men stopped to shake Rowland Sinclair's hand and to confirm for themselves that he had survived what seemed impossible.

The grounds of *Oaklea* were crowded: all the men who worked on the property, Edna Walling and her contractors, neighbours, volunteers, the Yass Fire Brigade and reporters from local papers. Mrs. Kendall returned to her kitchen and, as the sun rose, tray after tray of fresh scones, sandwiches, treacle tarts no longer needed for the picnic races, and pots of tea were sent out to feed the hungry. With the danger over, the mood became almost festive. *Oaklea*, and more importantly, the children, had been saved.

Eventually the Sinclair men and their Sydney guests retired to the intact part of the house, to wash and change. Maguire returned to reassess Rowland's condition in the light of day. In between prodding and poking, the physician spoke cryptically to Wilfred of meetings and telephone calls. Rowland assumed that the influence of the estimable men of the Old Guard was being called to Wilfred's aid.

"If Gilbey and Angel don't pull their heads in, we'll have to have them shot!" Maguire muttered darkly.

"What?" Rowland demanded.

Wilfred smiled. "You'll find that Freddie is speaking in jest, Rowly."

"Of course," Rowland muttered. As a doctor, Maguire had the bedside manner of a melancholic executioner. Rowland had never even seen the man smile. That he was capable of jest was debatable.

"Yes, yes," Maguire said, accepting a cigarette and a light from Wilfred. He inhaled deeply and sighed. "We don't shoot people anymore."

Wilfred nodded and for a moment both men smoked and contemplated that regrettable fact.

Then the surgeon turned sternly to Rowland. "All frivolity aside, my boy, I'm prescribing bed rest for at least the next twenty-four hours. I do now suspect you may have cracked a rib in that fall, and whilst your lungs do not appear to be damaged, you did inhale a great deal of smoke." He drew again on his cigarette.

Rowland protested but, in honesty, he felt like he could easily sleep for a day. Any careless breath was still painful and he had a thumping headache. He didn't bother to put his shirt back on, falling onto the bed the moment Wilfred accompanied Maguire out. He might have slept then if Wilfred had not returned.

"Rowly, may I have a word?" he said taking the armchair beside the bed.

Rowland did not lift his face from the pillow. "What? Now?"

Wilfred cleared his throat. He stared at the livid rope burns on Rowland's forearms and hands, sustained in lowering Ernest to safety. "I am aware that I have not yet had the opportunity to thank you."

"For what?" Rowland murmured.

"For pity's sake, Rowly, you saved my children!"

"Clyde—"

"I've already spoken with Mr. Watson Jones."

"Really? What did he say?"

"Not a great deal. He seemed embarrassed."

Rowland closed his eyes. "Sounds like Clyde."

Wilfred struggled for words. "What you did, Rowly…"

"They're my nephews, Wil."

"Would you just allow me to thank you?"

"Pleasure, Wil. Now go away and let me sleep."

It was the following morning before Rowland finally emerged. He was still stiff and tender, and he was ravenous. Kate and the boys had not yet returned home—a precaution on the advice of her doctor who was concerned that, in her delicate condition, Kate would find the sight of the razed wing too distressing.

Lucy Bennett, however, was already back and determined to "muck in and help out". Rowland wasn't entirely certain what that entailed but it appeared to require an irritating level of positivity and good cheer.

Rowland was early to breakfast though he found his friends were already there, discussing the papers as they enjoyed eggs and bacon from the warming trays on the sideboard.

The Sydney newspapers as well as the local dailies reported the fire at one of the state's grandest estates in lurid detail. And the rescue of Ernest Sinclair was written up in mortifying and vaguely inaccurate hyperbole.

"Six-year-old Ernest Sinclair was snatched from the jaws of a certain and grisly death by his uncle, Rowland Sinclair of *Woodlands House*, Woollahra in Sydney, who, with no regard for his own safety, carried the boy through the flames and handed him to the waiting arms of his desperate mother, Mrs. Wilfred Sinclair, nee Baird, before collapsing from his injuries. Such acts of raw courage and self-sacrifice typify the bravery of the Sinclair family. Both Lt. Col. Wilfred Sinclair DSO and the late Lt. Aubrey Sinclair DSO were decorated during the Great War," Edna read aloud.

"*The Tribune*'s obviously employing novelists," Rowland muttered.

The Canberra Times carried a picture of Mrs. Kendall with Canon Hall, a list of the eminent persons, including the Prince of Wales, who had been guests at *Oaklea* in the past, as well as embellished prose on the laudable valour of Rowland Sinclair.

"This one here says you leapt off the roof with Ernest in your arms," Milton added, laughing. "Now would be a good time to stand for parliament, Rowly."

Rowland poured himself a cup of coffee from the silver service on the sideboard.

Edna sipped her tea. "Well I think it's quite lovely that the papers are saying nice things about Rowly for once."

"What do they say about Clyde?" Rowland asked, trying to evade further embarrassment by offering up his friend.

"Nothing at all," Milton said, flicking through his paper. "After all, he just saved the nanny and the younger son and did so in a manner that was somewhat conventional. You rescued the heir apparent by leaping off a burning building!"

Clyde smiled. "It all came out rather well then."

Milton sighed. "Perhaps the *Worker* will give Clyde a mention."

Arthur Sinclair cleared his throat, and walked into the dining room. "Well, well, if it isn't the man of the hour," he said, smiling broadly at Rowland.

"Good morning, Arthur," Rowland responded curtly, still irritated with his cousin.

"I must say, Rowland, you and Mr. Watson Jones are champions—good men to have on hand. Why I expect the whole district is talking about the other night's heroics."

He filled his plate from the selection of dishes on the sideboard. "Hopefully it will go some way towards showing the police the kind of decent and upstanding man with whom they are dealing." He winked at Rowland. "If I have my way, old boy, they'll stop making scurrilous allegations and pin a medal on your chest!"

"I don't suppose you've seen Wil this morning?" Rowland asked, hoping to change the subject. He assumed Arthur was trying to smooth over their previous disagreement, albeit rather clumsily.

"He left earlier to fetch Kate and the children. I believe Aunt Libby will return with them. Don't worry, old man, I've asked Mrs. Kendall to organise for the boys and their nanny to be housed somewhere in the main house or in one of the other wings."

"That's good of you," Rowland said.

"Of course, the garden party will have to be cancelled. Aunt Libby will be disappointed. You know how she looked forward to it, but under the circumstances."

"Garden party?" Edna asked.

"The annual *Oaklea* Boxing Day Garden Party in aid of the Red Cross, Miss Higgins," Arthur said proudly, though he'd never actually attended the event. "It's been a tradition here since poor Aubrey died."

The reference reminded Rowland. "What's become of Miss Walling's gardens? Did they survive the fire?"

"For the most part," Clyde replied. "Though by all accounts, we made a bit of a mess of the copper irrigation system. Still, those extra water lines and pumps she put in to establish the garden probably saved the house... not to mention you."

"Good morning!" Lucy Bennett walked in, stopping dead still when she saw Rowland. There was a collective slide of chairs as the gentlemen stood.

Arthur hastened to pull out a chair for Lucy. But she did not move, continuing to stare at Rowland. Finally she stammered. "It's… it's wonderful to see you out of bed, Ro… Mr. Sinclair."

"Thank you, Miss Bennett."

"What you did was just… simply… so…" She didn't finish, placing her hand over her mouth and turning away. "Excuse me," she choked before hurrying out.

At first nobody moved. Then Edna stood. "Should I go after her?" She asked more because the men seemed at such a loss than because she thought she could offer any comfort.

"I think not!" Arthur snapped. "You have caused that dear lady enough heartache!"

"For God's sake, Arthur!" Rowland said, exasperated.

Arthur pushed in his chair and stormed out of the room, presumably in pursuit of Lucy.

"What did he mean?" Edna asked, sincerely perplexed. "What on earth have I done to Lucy Bennett?"

Rowland returned to his breakfast. "Every family has at least one blasted fool. Arthur is ours."

16

A MOAN ON MANNERS

Shortcomings of Australian Life

By MACGRUMPUS

... Without grace and in the disagreeable manner that comes natural to me, I should like to write about the shortcomings of the Australian people. Having been a pernickety old man ever since I was about 14 years of age, I am extremely well qualified to tell Australians what bad manners they have... The worst manners in the world are in England; the second-worst in Australia... But England's bad manners arise from an offensive sense of superiority over lesser crawling things and a social system that makes most individuals snub those below them and fawn to those above. Australian bad manners come from sheer uncouthness. The poor brutes know no better...

Good Hearts; Crude Behaviour.

Australians are nice, solid chaps, with good hearts and all that sort of thing, but they are crude. To begin with they do not know how to behave; the Englishman does even if he doesn't; the Frenchman improvises brilliantly. Having mastered the elementary rules of good conduct, namely that you walk on the side of the lady nearest the traffic (even if her deaf ear is on that side) and that you "dip yer lid to a sheila" if you know her and give her a glad eye if you don't, the young Australian man goes no further with lessons in etiquette until the day before he wants to get married. Then he writes to a newspaper asking at what stage of the proceedings the bridegroom kisses the bridesmaids and whether you serve the nuts and raisins before the best man makes his speech. The young Australian girl takes no lessons in etiquette at all; she imitates a film star. Poor benighted beggars that we are, most of us grow up without knowing what to do when we are introduced, when to sit down or stand up, how to behave with aplomb when we have spilt coffee on a dress, how and when to apologise, whether to tuck the serviette under the chin or into the top of the pants, the correct position for the little finger in relation to a tea cup, or whether one should or should not show one's operation scars to a guest...

The West Australian, 1938

Rowland fished a deformed and charred lead soldier out of the ashes. Its comrades-in-arms had melted and fused in the inferno.

"I wonder what started the fire?" Clyde toed the blackened remains.

"Nanny de Waring thinks it might have been the vaporiser," Edna said, picking through the rubble. "Ewan had a cold you see, so she'd been burning it in the sunroom. She can't remember if she turned it off correctly before they all went to bed. Poor girl was beside herself."

"She told you all that?"

Edna nodded. "I found her here, yesterday, crying. She was afraid to go in and face Wilfred."

"Good Lord, why?" Rowland asked.

"She was certain he'd have her charged or sacked or both, for setting fire to *Oaklea*."

Rowland slipped the charred soldier into his pocket. "Did you tell her—"

"I'm afraid nothing I said seemed to give her any comfort at all," Edna admitted. "Fortunately, those lovely gardeners passed by."

"How exactly did the gardeners help?" Clyde was curious.

"Mr. Templeton said he'd heard of vaporisers malfunctioning before and they all agreed. Mr. Bates told a funny story about a burning circus tent. They were really very kind." Edna turned to Rowland concerned. "Wilfred wouldn't sack Miss de Waring, would he?"

Rowland smiled. "No, I don't think so." Wilfred was gruff, but he was a fair employer.

"Mr. Sinclair!" Wilfred's illustrious garden designer waved as she approached.

"Good morning, Miss Walling."

"*Good* morning? Well you are an intrepid optimist! How splendid to see you up and about, Mr. Sinclair." The garden designer shook his hand warmly. "The chaps and I were here helping to divert the irrigation pipes when the bay collapsed. Still don't know how you managed to come out of it so well."

"Thank you, Miss Walling... I say, did the fire ruin much of the new garden?"

"A lot of the groundcovers were trampled with so many people running about in the dark, but the structures have pretty well survived. Of course, we'll have to relay the irrigation system, but she should be coming up roses, not to mention hellebores, hydrangeas and alyssum, in no time!"

"Good show," Rowland said, laughing.

Jack Templeton came up behind them with a wheelbarrow. "How is Master Ernest, Mr. Sinclair?" he asked.

"I'm told he's well, Mr. Templeton," Rowland replied.

"Well, you tell him Jacko and Vic said hello."

"You could probably do that yourself, Mr. Templeton," Edna said, pointing to the dust cloud where the long oak-lined drive joined the main road. "I think that's them now."

Two Rolls Royces returned the absent Sinclairs to *Oaklea*, driving around to the front of the house from where the damage was not so evident.

Arthur Sinclair and Lucy Bennett stood ready to welcome them. Eager to avoid any unnecessary scenes, Rowland hung back, listening idly as Edna discussed plaster casting techniques with Walling and her crew.

Ernest jumped out of the car and tore around to see what had happened to his old bedroom. Rowland went after him, and found the boy standing at the edge of the destruction. Ernest kicked at the ash, wide-eyed. "Look at that! It's gone!"

"It is," Rowland agreed.

Silently Ernest reached up to take his uncle's hand and they stood there for a while.

"Rowly!"

Rowland turned to his brother's summons. Wilfred and Kate, it seemed, had also walked around to view the burned wing. They were talking to Rowland's friends near the half-constructed stone and timber arbour. Kate had Clyde's large calloused hand in both of hers as she spoke to him. His neck and ears were flushed pink and he shook his head as he attempted to deny any great part in the rescue of her children.

Rowland grinned. In his discomfort, Clyde had reverted to calling Kate "Ma'am" as if she were Queen Mary.

"You were all simply wonderful," Kate said, including Edna and Milton in her gratitude. "It terrifies me to imagine what might have happened if you hadn't been here." She glanced at Ewan who was in his father's arms. "This will be a very special Christmas, and if your families could possibly be persuaded to spare you, I hope you'll stay and share it with us at *Oaklea*."

Ernest ran to his mother, and she turned to notice Rowland.

"Hello Kate. How are you?"

Kate Sinclair gazed at her brother-in-law. Her eyes shone with barely contained tears. "Oh Rowly," she said. "I'm so sorry." She began to weep in earnest then.

Rowland looked to Wilfred in alarm.

Wilfred cleared his throat. "Katie, my dear, perhaps—"

Kate embraced Rowland. She composed herself a little. "We're deeply, deeply grateful, Rowly. I'm so very sorry for how cross and utterly unreasonable I've been with you. It was unfair. And I want to say that you and all your interesting friends will always be welcome in our home."

Rowland smiled faintly, quite sure Wilfred thought his wife was perhaps taking gratitude a step too far.

"If you hadn't rescued Ernest I'm not sure I could have..." Kate disintegrated completely into tears again.

Wilfred handed Ewan to Clyde while he took his young wife's hand. "Come on, Katie," he said gently. "The boys are both safe. You're overwrought and in need of a rest. Perhaps we'd better have a cup of tea before you donate *Oaklea* to the Communist Party."

Milton chuckled. Rowland might have too, if he hadn't been afraid of upsetting Kate further.

Edna started to walk towards the main house, calling back to Ernest, "Ernie, shall we go on ahead and tell Mrs. Kendall that we will need cake?"

Kate and Wilfred followed, each holding one of Ewan's hands as he toddled between them.

Milton clapped Rowland on the shoulder and whispered, "Oh! Too convincing—dangerously dear—In woman's eye the unanswerable tear!"

"Bit early for Byron isn't it, Milt?"

"And yet that's the second time this morning a woman's burst into tears at the sight of you," the poet said, slinging his arm companionably about Rowland's shoulders. "This new hero status of yours could prove to be awkwardly moist."

Much of that day passed quite peaceably, all things considered. Everybody stepped carefully and quietly about Kate, whom the past days' events had left quite fragile. Even Elisabeth Sinclair seemed to be particularly kind.

Arthur Sinclair decided to take another look at *Emoh Ruo* with a view to moving into the neighbouring homestead in the new year. Lucy Bennett offered to drive him out in her Riley, and so, for much of the afternoon, neither reproach nor tension disturbed the civility of *Oaklea*.

The telephone at *Oaklea* rang so often with well-wishers and acquaintances who had read of the fire that a maid was stationed permanently beside it to act as a secretary of sorts, offering assurances that the Sinclairs were all well though they were not at home to calls.

It was not until that evening that the problems arose, or they became aware of them at least.

They first noticed that Arthur and Lucy had not returned when Mrs. Kendall enquired about numbers for dinner.

"They might have stepped out for a meal," Milton suggested. "The Royal seems to have become quite fashionable. From what I understand, every man and his sister is dining there these days."

Wilfred glanced at his wife. "Arthur and Lucy seem to have become rather close."

"Oh… oh how lovely." Kate seemed uncertain. She asked Mrs. Kendall to set extra places in case they returned.

It was after dinner when Wilfred decided that it would be a good idea to look for them. Not wanting to alarm his wife, he took his brother aside.

"I'm sure it's unnecessary, Rowly, but would you drive out to *Emoh Ruo* to make sure Miss Bennett hasn't driven her car into a ditch or some such thing."

"Yes, of course. I'll take Milt and Clyde with me—Clyde's a good hand with motors and Milt can always push."

The yellow Mercedes arrived at *Emoh Ruo* just a minute before the two police cars. The house was dark. On the verandah, Arthur held a hurricane lamp and Lucy Bennett was smoking frenetically.

Rowland ran up the front steps. "Arthur? What's wrong?"

Arthur was pale, shaken. He pointed into the house.

Rowland took the hurricane lamp and walked inside. Though not on the same scale of grandeur as *Oaklea*, *Emoh Ruo* was a substantial homestead. The rooms were large and well appointed. Most of the furniture was covered with dust sheets. It was in the hallway that Rowland noticed the smell. He heard the police cars pull up as he stepped into the drawing room.

"Rowly, what the—Holy Mother of God!" Clyde stopped beside him. A body lay crumpled on the floor by the hearth, its head haloed by a pool of blood. The dead man's eyes were swollen shut, in a face that was cut and bruised. The stench was overpowering.

Milton's entry into the drawing room was marked with cursing. "Is he—?"

"I'd say so."

"Do you know who he is, Rowly?"

"Hayden. Charlie Hayden. He worked for my late father."

The informant's fists were balled and clenched, a strap looped loosely around his right hand.

"What is that?" Clyde bent over for a closer look.

"His belt," Rowland said quietly.

"Bloody oath!" Milton yanked Rowland back as Detective Angel entered the room with his weapon drawn.

"Stand clear!" he shouted checking behind the doors.

Gilbey and two fresh-faced constables followed him in. They all stared mutely at the body of the informant.

"Would you gentlemen step outside with the constables," Gilbey instructed. "Detective Angel and I will be with you in a moment."

The uniformed policemen escorted them out. Arthur Sinclair was seated on the steps with Lucy Bennett. She was crying, and he looked decidedly unwell.

"What happened?" Rowland asked his cousin.

Arthur swallowed. "I don't know. Lucy and I came in to see… and we found him." He wiped his mouth with a handkerchief. "I telephoned the police."

"From here?"

"Wil had the telephone reconnected before he offered me the house."

"Mr. Sinclair," Angel strode out of the entrance.

Both Sinclairs turned.

"Rowland Sinclair," Angel qualified. "Might we have a word?" He motioned back into the house.

"We'll be right here, Rowly," Milton said as Rowland followed the detective in. "Just call."

Angel led him to the billiard room. A single kerosene lamp now illuminated the chamber and cast strange elongated shadows onto the wall. "Do you have anything you wish to tell us, Mr. Sinclair?"

"About what?"

Gilbey sighed. "Do you know anything about this particularly unsavoury matter, sir?"

"No."

"Can you tell us when you last saw Mr. Hayden?"

"The day before yesterday. He turned up just as I was landing my biplane in the next paddock."

"What did he want, Mr. Sinclair?"

"I don't know... I told him to get off the property."

"And did he do so quietly?"

"Eventually."

"I see. Was any other person present who could corroborate your version of events?"

"Mr. Watson Jones, and my nephew Ernest."

Angel made a few notes.

"Can you tell us where you were yesterday, Mr. Sinclair?"

"I was in my bedroom asleep."

"That seems to be your standard alibi, Mr. Sinclair, as unreliable as it has already been proved."

Rowland did not respond.

"And where was your brother, Mr. Wilfred Sinclair, yesterday?"

"Wil? Why do you want to know where he was?"

"Just answer the question, sir."

"I don't know. As I said, I was asleep. Nevertheless, detective, I'm sure there are any number of people who could verify my brother's whereabouts."

Rowland did not miss the glance that Gilbey and Angel exchanged. It, more than anything, made him uneasy.

The detectives sent them back to *Oaklea* then, with a police car escort.

Clyde drove Lucy's Riley as both she and Arthur were too upset to take the wheel.

They returned to find that Kate and Elisabeth Sinclair had retired. Wilfred and Edna had been passing time listening to a broadcast of the Sane Democracy League, which had so amused Edna that she was laughing out loud when they came into the drawing room.

Rowland waited as Arthur explained the grim discovery at *Emoh Ruo*. Lucy Bennett had composed herself somewhat and sat beside Arthur offering details now and then.

Wilfred listened calmly. "You've had a very upsetting evening, Lucy. I can't tell you how sorry I am. Perhaps you should go up to bed. I'll have Mrs. Kendall bring you up some brandy and milk."

Lucy nodded tearfully. "You know me, Wilfred, always happy to muck in. If there's anything I can do…"

"There'll be plenty of time for that tomorrow," Wilfred replied firmly. "The police will most likely wish to speak to you again. It's probably best if you get a good night's rest."

For some reason, Wilfred did not try to similarly dismiss Edna. Perhaps he realised she would not so easily be sent away.

Once Lucy had gone, Wilfred questioned his brother. Rowland told him what he had been asked and what he had answered. Again, Wilfred listened, saying little.

"What's your assessment, Arthur?" he asked in the end.

Arthur pursed his lips. "It doesn't look good, Wilfred. They already assume Rowland had something to do with Uncle Henry's death. He was just a boy then, but now…"

"Wait a minute," Milton said, flaring. "He didn't kill anybody, then or now."

"I only meant that any chance the police would let sleeping dogs lie with respect to Uncle Henry has probably been blown by this latest murder," Arthur replied.

Wilfred tapped the arm of his chair as he thought. He glanced at his pocket watch. "There are some people I need to get out of bed," he said. He pointed sternly at his brother. "You, Rowland, are not to speak to the police again without a barrister present, do you understand? Now get some sleep, and I'll handle this."

17

HE BUYS HIS PRESENTS

—————◀▶—————

The Great Xmas Problem Solved
A MAN'S WAY
(By O. T. H.)

I AM one of the Christmas shoppers that the shops do not like. I do my Christmas shopping late to avoid the rush of those who do it early because they think they'll avoid the rush of those who do it late.

But, then, of course, I have a little idiosyncrasy that counterbalances that. I write down suggestions on the backs of envelopes, so that I can buy everything without a hitch. I put alongside the entries where I am going to buy them, and the prices I am going to pay. And then I lose the envelopes, and my Christmas shopping's done.

Today, though, I remembered that I had borrowed a handkerchief from a girl, and that at the time I had decided to give her a really good one back for Christmas. I went into a shop and said I wanted some handkerchiefs. They referred me to the next counter. I explained there that I wanted some good handkerchiefs. And that, of course, meant that I had to go to another counter.

THIS "KERCHIEF PROBLEM"

"I want to see some handkerchiefs, not too dear," I said, and was directed back to the first counter for not-too-dear sorts. They showed me some for 5/11 a dozen (marked down from 6/6), but I said that I wanted some a little better. They showed some more—25/11 a dozen. The girl said that any friend of mine—implying of course, that I was a Fine Old

English Gentleman who would have nothing shoddy—would appreciate those.

I worked it out quickly. That was 6/ for three. "No," I said. "They are a little too coarse." So they brought out some Irish linen handkerchiefs with white lace round the edges. "35/," the girl said. This was getting terrible. "Too gaudy," I said, hoping that they would have nothing plainer at a higher price. But they had. I said I would let the girl come in and choose her own.

So I created a new record. I am the only man in South Australia who has not bought a handkerchief to give someone this Christmas.

The News, 24 December 1931

Rowland had been staring at nothing in particular—more thinking out of the window rather than looking—when he caught sight of two figures in the moonlight. He could discern the red glow of a cigarette as the men strolled together in the muted luminosity and dense shadow of the summer night. He knew the figures, their shapes, their gaits. Wilfred, and Harry Simpson. It did not surprise him that they were talking in the garden—Harry would not set foot into the house. The original edict that the blue-eyed Wiradjuri boy never come to the "big house" had been Henry Sinclair's—perhaps a minor concession to the feelings of his wife. Of course, *Oaklea* under Wilfred would have welcomed Harry, but the stockman still refused.

There was a tap on the door of the bedroom. Rowland turned. His nephew seemed to be making a habit of going visiting in his pyjamas. "Come in, Ernie," he said quietly.

But it was Edna Higgins who slipped in, shutting the door quickly behind her. She was not Ernest, but she wore her pyjamas nevertheless. Actually, Rowland noted—by the monogram on the pocket and the fact that the sleeves had been rolled several times— they were his pyjamas.

He smiled. Convinced that male attire was more comfortable to work and sleep in, Edna had been blatantly helping herself to the clothing of the men she lived with since she'd moved into *Woodlands*. Milton complained bitterly that it took three washes to get her perfume out of his shirts.

"Ed... couldn't you sleep?"

"No," she said, standing at the window beside him. "Who's that?"

"Wil and Harry."

"What are they talking about, do you think?"

"Fish probably. Or perhaps Harry's telling Wil about one of his accident-prone hounds."

Edna laughed softly. She turned her back on the window and looked up at him. "Rowly, I'm really scared."

"Scared?" he asked, puzzled.

"Wilfred is too, I can tell. Whatever their reasons, the police want to say you killed your father. Maybe Mr. Hayden as well."

"They'll come to their senses, Ed."

"But what if they don't? What if they decide to arrest you? Remember what happened to Allie Dawe in London? If you hadn't helped her, she might have hanged."

"Ed, you're getting ahead—"

"I'm not. Rowly, please, I just want you to fight for yourself the way you did for Allie."

For a while he said nothing. Then, "This is not something I can talk about."

She ignored that, kicking off her slippers and settling herself cross-legged on his bed. Reaching out, she grabbed his hand and pulled him down beside her.

"Rowly," she said, taking both his hands now and locking her eyes on his, distracting his resolve with her closeness. "Did Wilfred kill your father?"

He wavered. "No... God, I don't know... Ed, can't you leave me—?"

"Rowly, please, I need to understand, that's all. Can't you just trust me?"

"I do trust you."

"Then tell me exactly what happened the day your father died. There may be something. Please."

Rowland rubbed his face. Finally he nodded, but he was at a loss as to where to start. It all seemed so complicated.

"What precisely happened when you returned home from school, Rowly?" Edna prompted.

"Wil had stepped out to meet someone. He was involved in politics even then..." Rowland's brow furrowed as he remembered the details. "Must've been someone of whom Father didn't approve or Wil would have brought him to the house." He laughed. "Perhaps Wil was a Communist back then."

Edna waited for him to continue, refusing to let him jest the subject away.

"My father called me into his study. I knew what I was in for. He shouted the bible at me for a while, then Hayden came in."

"And did Mr. Hayden say anything to you?"

"No. That wasn't how it worked." Rowland lay back on the bed, staring at the ceiling as he spoke. "I'd remove my shirt, Hayden would wrap the buckled end of that flaming surcingle once around his hand." Edna could sense the tension in Rowland's body, as if he were there again, waiting to be brutalised on his Father's command. "I would brace myself against the chair, Father would read from the Book of Psalms and Hayden would begin. It was the way it always was."

Edna desperately wanted to leave him alone, to let him forget. She steeled herself to continue. "But this time Wilfred intervened?"

Rowland nodded. "Yes, eventually. He must have returned."

"Do you remember what happened?"

"It's rather confused, to be honest. Wil punched Hayden. There was a lot of shouting… I don't know, Ed. I was barely conscious."

"Oh, Rowly." Edna's voice was hoarse. She traced her hand over his shoulders. They were broad now, and strong, but they wouldn't have been then. It hurt her heart to think of them bearing so much.

Rowland drew her close, touched by her tears, the way she wrapped her arms around him as though she were trying to protect him in retrospect. He kissed her cheek, his lips lingering just inches from hers. For a moment he forgot about everything else.

"No!" she said, pulling away and wiping her face angrily. "You're not to stop! Tell me what you remember next."

"Ed…"

"Please, Rowly."

He exhaled. "There was a doctor, Mrs. Kendall…" He glanced at the chaise by the window. "Wil sat right there, drinking whisky and smoking. I could barely look at him."

"Why?"

"I was ashamed, I suppose."

"Why would you be ashamed?" Edna asked gently.

"They'd completely broken me that night, Ed. My brother was a war hero… it was not something I wanted him to see."

"You were fifteen!"

"I'm sure Wil didn't think any less of me, Ed. I just felt less."

"What about your mother, Rowly? She speaks so lovingly of your father. Didn't she—?"

"My mother seems to have re-imagined life with my father, Ed. Back then she was terrified of him. She'd lock herself in her room whenever Father… is there any point to going over all this?"

"If you weren't here, in this room, when your father was shot, where were you, Rowly?"

"I was walking out."

"Walking out of where?"

"The house, everything. I wasn't thinking sensibly. I was scared and angry…"

"You were running away?"

"Not running… I could barely walk. I heard the gunshot when I was at the back door."

"What did you do, Rowly?"

"I went back into the house."

"To the study?"

"Yes."

"And?"

"My father was dead."

"Did you see anything else?"

Rowland said nothing.

"Who are you protecting?" Edna demanded, reading into his silence. "Wilfred…" she said accusingly. "You saw Wilfred, didn't you? With your father's body!"

He flinched. "Ed…"

"Did he tell you what he was doing there?"

"We've never talked about it."

"What? Never?" Edna stared at him, flabbergasted. "Not once?"

Rowland shrugged. "It's not a particularly pleasant subject."

"For pity's sake!" Edna was cross now. "Well then, what did you do?"

"I returned to my room. Wil came up later to inform me Father had passed."

"And nothing else?"

"He said he was sorry."

"Of course he was sorry," Edna said, determined to make Rowland see sense. "He'd just shot your father!"

"I don't know that. But honestly, Ed, I don't care."

"But the police believe you were responsible," she said, clenching her fists.

Rowland sat up. He tried to make her understand. "I was a boy, Ed. Wil was not. Wil has a wife and young family, and I do not."

"You have us!"

"You know that's not the same thing." He smiled. "Perhaps if you were to marry me…"

"How can you make jokes?" Edna's tears were hot and frustrated now. "You're an idiot, Rowly!"

He didn't take his eyes off her. Even crying and angry she was beautiful. If she'd said yes, he might well have sold his soul. "You're overreacting, sweetheart. If there's anyone who can sort this nonsense, it's Wil."

"And if he can't?"

"If he can't, I'm not going to offer up my brother to save myself."

"It's not fair, Rowly."

Rowland took the sculptress's hands. They were small in his, but her grip was strong. "You're underestimating Wilfred Sinclair."

"I hope so. God, I hope so."

Edna wiped her eyes with her sleeve. Rowland handed her a handkerchief. She stared at it blankly for a while, and then she laughed through her tears. "Oh, Rowly. You carry a monogrammed handkerchief in your pyjamas… how would you possibly cope in prison?"

"I don't expect I'll encounter quite so many weeping women there," he said as she giggled helplessly now.

He smiled, enjoying the respite. They talked for a while then about nothing in particular… Lucy and Arthur, the Sane Democracy

League, Edna Walling, Senator Charles Hardy and his many sisters. Aware that Lucy Bennett slept in the guestroom just across the hall, they whispered, and when Edna laughed, she buried her face in Rowland's shoulder to muffle the sound.

He might well have declared himself then, if his own future had not been so uncertain.

"I should go back to my room before we both fall asleep," Edna said climbing out of his bed.

"I say, Ed, did Clyde and Milt—" Rowland began drowsily, fighting the impulse to pull her back into his arms.

"They're worried about you, Rowly."

"Did they ask you to talk to me?"

"Yes." She rolled her eyes. "Milt told me to seduce the truth out of you if I had to."

Rowland groaned. "I wish I'd known. I wouldn't have been so blasted forthcoming."

The partners of Kent, Beswick and Associates were at *Oaklea* before breakfast. The police arrived soon after.

As the matter was no longer merely a thirteen-year-old murder, Gilbey and Angel were accompanied by a third detective, an investigative specialist, despatched from Sydney's Criminal Investigation Bureau.

"Colin! What are you doing here?" Rowland said as Detective Delaney presented himself.

"The commissioner sent me down to keep an eye on things," he said quietly as he shook Rowland's hand. "Gilbey and Angel are still calling the shots." He glanced over his shoulder to see that his colleagues were beginning the process of questioning the staff once again. "You're in trouble, Rowly."

"I gathered."

Delaney walked towards the stairs motioning for Rowland to follow. "Let them assume you're showing me where you were on the night of your father's death," he instructed under his breath.

Gilbey glanced up as they climbed the stairs, but returned to the dining room where Angel was already interviewing Lucy Bennett.

"Hell, Rowly," Delaney said when he was sure they were alone. "This is one unbelievable bloody mess."

"You're talking about Hayden?"

"That bastard *and* your father." Delaney glanced at his watch and got straight to the point. "Listen mate, I've read Hayden's statement. By themselves, there's not enough to arrest you for either murder. But together, it's a different matter. There are only two people who would want to kill both Henry Sinclair and Charles Hayden. And only one who has the reputation you do." Delaney shook his head. "Your brother has influential friends, but Eric Campbell and the New Guard are not without connections and, to top it all off, you've been making a habit of harassing and embarrassing members of parliament about what's happening in Germany, where it is rumoured you killed a man!"

Rowland grimaced. "I can see your point."

Delaney just looked at him.

"I didn't kill anybody, Colin."

"I wouldn't be here if I thought you had."

"So what now?"

Delaney sighed. "I'll do what I can. You say nothing. There'd be nobody in prison if criminals weren't stupid enough to confess."

"I haven't anything to confess, Col."

"A few of the boys know how to help you find something, Rowly."

"Splendid."

Wilfred stormed into the drawing room and picked up Ernest who was sobbing inconsolably. "What the devil have you done to my son?"

"Ernest has been assisting us with our enquiries, Mr. Sinclair." Detective Angel smiled at the child. "Thank you, Ernest. You've been a good and very helpful boy."

Ernest hid his face in his father's shoulder.

"What did you say to him?" Rowland demanded, entering the room to stand with Wilfred.

"It's not so much what we said to him, but what he told us, Mr. Sinclair." Angel read from his notebook. "Your nephew claims that two days ago he saw Rowland Sinclair strike the deceased, Charles Hayden, and threaten to kill him."

For several moments Rowland's young nephew wept into an otherwise stunned silence.

Maurice Kent, KC, of Kent, Beswick and Associates, spoke first. "Preposterous! You don't propose to use the allegation of an imaginative six-year-old to—"

"Are you saying the boy is lying, Mr. Kent?"

"He isn't," Rowland said. "He isn't lying." He reached over Wilfred's shoulder to tousle his nephew's hair. "It's all right, Ernie. That's exactly what happened."

Wilfred stared at his brother in dismay.

Delaney cursed under his breath.

Gilbey spoke to Wilfred. "Perhaps you'd like to take the boy out before we arrest your brother, sir?"

Rowland placed his hand on Wilfred's shoulder. "Go," he said quietly.

Gilbey triumphantly tapped a cigarette from his case and lit it, while he waited for Ernest to leave with his father. He was not the only one waiting. Clyde and Milton exploded.

"Are you out of your tiny mind?" Milton demanded of Gilbey.

"You can't arrest him for an outburst made in the heat of the moment," Clyde said with a warning glance at the poet.

"We're not arresting Mr. Sinclair for what he said, gentlemen; we're arresting him for the murders of Henry Sinclair and Charles Hayden," Gilbey replied coldly while Angel dealt with Rowland.

Edna appealed to Delaney. "Do something."

"There isn't anything I can do, Miss Higgins, even if it were appropriate. We'll have to take Mr. Sinclair back to Sydney."

"I'm going with you," Milton said defiantly. "We're not leaving Rowly alone with you jokers."

Delaney looked at Milton strangely. "I'm afraid you will not be able to accompany Mr. Sinclair unless, Mr. Isaacs, I had cause to arrest you, too."

Delaney's words needed only a breath to sink in. Milton took a generous swing at the detective making contact with Colin Delaney's jaw.

Delaney reacted quickly, seizing and pinning Milton in a movement that seemed far too easy. By the time Wilfred returned to the drawing room, both his brother and Milton Isaacs had been handcuffed.

18

WHEN BEING PHOTOGRAPHED

———— ◆ ————

Some people photograph well, but others do not look their best in a photograph. Probably one reason for an unsatisfactory portrait is that the sitter is too self-conscious. Another common fault is that the wrong kind of clothes are worn. To be a success, a photograph should be as natural as possible. Therefore, choose a natural pose and avoid an expression that is not familiar to you.

The Western Mail, 1932

"What the hell do you think you're doing?" Rowland whispered angrily as he and Milton were escorted out of the house to the waiting police cars, amidst a melee of argument and protest.

"I'm watching your back, Rowly... as much as possible anyway," Milton replied.

"What?"

Milton spoke quickly while the detectives were dealing with Wilfred and the Sinclair lawyers, not to mention Clyde, Edna and Arthur Sinclair all of whom were protesting the arrests in no uncertain terms. "Colin will ensure we're processed together. You haven't been to prison before, Rowly. I'm not letting you go alone."

"So, you hit Colin to get yourself arrested?"

"Believe me, I would much rather have hit that fool Gilbey, but he might not drop the charges against me when they finally realise you're completely innocent."

Rowland swore. "Whose idiotic idea was this?"

"Look, mate, I know the Sinclairs have all sorts of toffee-nosed, powerful friends, but inside Long Bay Prison my unsavoury connections are precisely what you'll need."

"Milt, you can't—"

One of the constables shoved Rowland away from the poet. "Enough chatter, Sinclair!"

With his hands cuffed behind his back, Rowland overbalanced. Another constable dragged him up while the first restrained Milton. Harry Simpson broke away from the watching workers.

"Hey!" he bellowed.

"I'm all right," Rowland said quickly, alarmed that Simpson, too, might want to join him in prison. "I tripped, that's all."

The scuffle may have ended then and there if Lenin hadn't rushed forth to protect his master.

Gilbey and Angel turned as the greyhound bounded towards their prisoners. Angel drew his weapon.

Edna screamed.

"For God's sake, he's harmless," Rowland shouted, trying to get to his dog. "Len, it's all right, mate. Lay down!"

Lenin continued to bark and snarl.

"Call off your mongrel or I'll shoot him, Sinclair."

"Lenin!" Edna grabbed the dog's collar. "Don't you dare shoot him," she said, furiously fronting the detective. "Don't you dare!"

Angel lowered his gun.

Elisabeth Sinclair walked out of the entrance doors. "Aubrey?" she said, confused when she saw her son in the grip of two constables. Her face drained of colour as she sighted the gun.

"Put that away you blasted fool!" Delaney barked at Angel.

Slowly, Angel returned his weapon to its holster.

"Aubrey?" Elisabeth said again. "Where are you going? What are the police doing here?"

Wilfred tried to calm his mother, but she would not be calmed. "Wilfred, you tell your brother to come in right now! Your father would never have allowed the police to come to the house." Then she caught sight of Harry Simpson. She stepped back in horror, trembling as jumbled memories surged. "What is that... that boy doing here, Wilfred? Your father wouldn't have allowed this."

Wilfred put his arm around their mother and turned her firmly back towards the door. He walked with her into the house.

Simpson grabbed Rowland's shoulder. "I'm sorry, Gagamin. We'll fix this."

"Harry," Rowland whispered urgently. "Make sure Wil doesn't do anything daft."

Angel grabbed Rowland before Harry Simpson could respond, and shoved him into the back of a waiting police car. Milton was pushed in beside him.

"I understand that you are upset, Miss Higgins, as are we all." Wilfred Sinclair did not look up as he waited for his call to Sir Adrian Knox to be connected. "But I really don't have the time to talk to you right now. Perhaps Kate might—"

"Mr. Sinclair, you are going to be able to sort this out, aren't you?" Edna said walking into the study regardless.

Wilfred put his hand over the receiver and barked at the sculptress. "Miss Higgins, I am endeavouring to keep my brother from the noose. I do not have time or patience for your histrionics."

Edna paled.

"Now, I would thank you to leave me to get on with it!" Wilfred returned to his telephone call and turned away from Edna. "Adrian. Wilfred Sinclair. How are you, old man?"

The sculptress left him alone, numbed by the implication of his words. She stopped in the hallway outside the study door and settled herself to wait.

She would let Wilfred Sinclair call his friends to Rowland's aid first, but she would talk to him.

The grandfather clock in the hall ticked away each moment that Edna waited, locked out of whatever it was Wilfred was doing. She felt sick. It was not until Wilfred had mentioned it that she'd contemplated the possibility that Rowland could hang over this.

Clyde was preparing the Federal for a trip to Sydney. They would leave Rowland's Mercedes at *Oaklea* and drive back in the old truck so that it could be returned to Milton's cousin. Edna watched the clock. An hour had passed since Wilfred had asked her to leave his office.

Arthur Sinclair walked down the hallway towards the study. "Miss Higgins, what in heaven's name are you doing here?"

"I'm waiting to speak to Mr. Sinclair."

"Wilfred's very busy. Perhaps I can take in a message for you?"

Edna took a step back. "I'd rather speak to him directly."

"Miss Higgins, do you really think it's good form to impose on the family right now?"

"I beg your pardon?"

"The legal and social ramifications of this scandal are significant for the Sinclairs, for us. I understand that you have been supported by my cousin for some time now, and it's natural that you are concerned about your own interests, but I really think—"

Edna glared at him. "I will speak to Rowland's brother," she said coldly.

Arthur fished inside his breast pocket. He pulled out a chequebook. "If it's money you're after—"

"Mr. Sinclair, I don't want your money," Edna said, her voice shaking with fury and horror.

The door to the study opened and suddenly Wilfred Sinclair was standing there. His eyes fell first on the chequebook before he looked from Arthur to Edna. "Miss Higgins, you're still here."

"I must speak to you, Mr. Sinclair. Alone."

Arthur frowned. "In the circumstances Miss Higgins, your demands are quite inappropriate."

Clyde cleared his throat as he walked down the hallway towards them. "The truck's ready, Ed. I'm just going upstairs to fetch our luggage."

"You're leaving?" Arthur said, clearly not grieved by the thought. "That's probably best. This is, after all, really none of your affair."

"You know, Mr. Sinclair," Clyde said, fronting Arthur angrily. "Rowly would have decked you for the way you just spoke to Miss Higgins. In his absence, I just might do that myself."

"The influence of you and your fellow ruffians on my poor cousin is clear, Mr. Watson Jones!" Arthur bit back.

Edna grabbed Clyde's arm before he could react.

Wilfred watched them thoughtfully. "Perhaps you'd best come in, Miss Higgins," he said.

"Wilfred—" Arthur began to protest.

Wilfred put up his hand for silence. "I won't be long, Arthur," he said stepping aside for Edna to pass and closing the door behind her.

He offered the sculptress a seat and took his place on the opposite side of his expansive desk. "What can I do for you, Miss Higgins?"

Edna gathered herself. She would not allow herself to be afraid of Wilfred, but what she had to say was difficult... not least because she knew that Rowland loved his brother.

"Mr. Sinclair, sir, I want you to give me your word that Rowland will not be convicted."

Wilfred sighed. "I will do my best, Miss Higgins."

"Not your best, Mr. Sinclair, your word."

"I am not God, Miss Higgins."

Edna bit her lip, steadying herself. "After everything Rowly went through at the hands of your father, how can you allow him to take the blame for you, Mr. Sinclair?"

"I beg your pardon!"

"I understand why you killed your father, Mr. Sinclair—you shot him to save Rowly—which is why I can't understand why you'd let him go to gaol now!"

Wilfred stared at her. "I'm not sure what insane theories you—"

"They've arrested Rowly, Mr. Sinclair!"

"I'm aware of that, Miss Higgins."

"But he's innocent. You know that, too! And he won't defend himself properly because he won't say anything that might incriminate you!"

"Me?"

"Rowly saw you with your father's body. He knows."

Wilfred's voice was icy. "Exactly what does he know, Miss Higgins?"

"That you... you killed your father," Edna said, unsure now whether she was doing the right thing. She'd always known Wilfred Sinclair was ruthless. Was she just making things worse for Rowland? She stood.

Wilfred wasn't looking at her. "Rowly, you bloody fool!" he muttered.

Edna backed towards the door.

"For pity's sake, Miss Higgins, sit down! I'm not going to hurt you!" Wilfred glanced up at the sculptress. On another day he might have been amused by how frightened she looked. "I thank you for bringing this to me. I can assure you that I will handle it."

"You'll tell the police it was you?"

"No." Wilfred stood. "If you'll forgive me, Miss Higgins, I must say goodbye to Kate and the boys before I, too, set off for Sydney."

By the time Rowland and Milton were delivered to Central Police Station, the Sinclair family's solicitors in Sydney were briefed and waiting for the arrival of their client. So too were the newspaper journalists and a jostling bevy of photographers.

"Head down, Rowly!" Milton warned, lunging in front of his friend.

The first flash exploded. Delaney closed in to obstruct the photographers as the prisoners were bustled inside the station.

They were taken to be processed, divested of all personal effects other than their clothes. The young constable raised a brow when Rowland handed over his watch. Still, he was not unduly impressed. Many of the more successful criminals had flash timepieces. Rumour had it that Tilly Devine's wristwatch was encrusted with rubies. More intriguing was the leather bound artist's sketchbook. The policeman flicked through its pages, telling himself that there might be a weapon concealed between the leaves. He checked page after page of intimate sketches, women in various stages of undress, studies that brought the blood to his cheeks. From Milton, he took a small volume of verse and a pocketknife.

The constable then took them into a grimy cell, where the wall had been clearly marked with heights. It was against this wall that a humourless police photographer took their mugshots. Milton complained bitterly that any image in right profile made his nose look large and demanded that a second shot be taken from the left.

From there they were taken to a second cell, empty but for a couple of battered bentwood chairs. The photographer returned.

"Where do you want us?" Milton asked when no instructions seemed forthcoming.

"Wherever you want for this snap," the young policeman replied.

"Really?" Rowland surveyed the cell sceptically.

"We want to photograph you natural-like."

"These are somewhat unnatural circumstances," Rowland replied.

"You'll get used to them. You can pose together if you want."

"Come on, Rowly," Milton urged placing one foot on the seat of the chair and adjusting his cravat. "It'll be a nice keepsake... like a postcard from Medlow Bath."

And so the photograph was taken: Milton with his arms and one leg in the air as he declared, "Well, they are gone, and here I must remain, this lime-tree bower my prison!" beside a clearly bemused Rowland, who smiled for the camera before he murmured, "Coleridge."

"Would you send us a couple of copies, my good man?" Milton asked as the photographer finished.

"I'm not supposed to," the constable said, quietly. He shook his head as he looked Milton up and down. "You do realise you've been arrested, don't you, sir?"

"I suppose that explains the cell," Milton replied, grinning broadly. "Go on... no one will know, and Mr. Sinclair, here, will make it worth your while, won't you, Rowly?"

Rowland laughed and groaned at the same time. Still it was somewhat comforting to have Milton treat being arrested like a holiday at the beach. "Yes, I'd be more than happy to compensate you for a memento of this special and memorable occasion," he said.

The police photographer grinned. "Tell ya what. If you get off I'll send you a couple of prints."

They thanked him as they were escorted out for finger printing.

Once fully processed, they were taken down to the cells to await further interrogation. The detectives were, it seemed, all busy dealing with the legal and administrative aftermath generated by the arrest of a man of Rowland Sinclair's background. There were enquiries and protestations by politicians, clergy and other men of standing, as well as missives of congratulations from those who considered Rowland Sinclair a menace. The young man's lawyers were laying siege to the legal system of the land in order to have him released. It was not surprising then that the detectives who brought this inundation of paperwork and scrutiny upon the Metropolitan Police were being asked for explanations of one sort or another.

19

HOSPITAL ESCAPEE

Arrested by City Police

Nellie Cameron, who escaped from the Newcastle Hospital some weeks ago in sensational circumstances, was recaptured by the consorting squad in Palmer Street last night.

The woman had been admitted to bail pending the hearing of her appeal against a sentence of a month's imprisonment for stealing. The appeal was dismissed, but Cameron in the meantime had disappeared. Some time later it was learned that she was an inmate in Newcastle Hospital, and that two men, one of whom was believed to be Frank Green, who has an unenviable police record, had been visiting her. Green had previously given an undertaking to leave the State. The Newcastle police intended to arrest the woman when she was discharged from hospital, but the night before she was to have been apprehended she left her bed during the visiting hours, and disappeared…

For some weeks the police have been searching for the woman in the belief that Green, with whom she associated, would be found with her. Last night Detective Browne, who was with other members of the consorting squad, noticed the woman in Palmer Street. He leaped from the police car and pursued her. Cameron ran to the door of a house nearby, but before she could open the door the policeman overtook and arrested her. The house to which she had run was searched, and a man was noticed climbing over the rear fence. It is believed that the man was Frank Green.

Cameron was taken to the Central Police Station, and this morning will be sent to Long Bay Penitentiary to undergo her sentence.

The Sydney Morning Herald, 1933

The holding cells at the Central Police Station were narrow and windowless. A cot hung against one wall, the ticking mattress stained with mould and God knows what else. Rowland and Milton were shoved into separate cells.

Rowland paced, more because he didn't want to touch the mattress than because he felt a particular need for physical movement. He reached for his handkerchief to wipe the finger print ink from his hands and he thought of Edna.

"Hey," the man in the cell opposite rose from his cot, a cigarette stuck to his lower lip. "Haven't seen you about. What are they trying to do you fer?"

Rowland hesitated. His fellow inmate looked distinctly unsavoury: a small, weasel-faced man whose pinched features were marked by violence, scarred by blades and malice. Still, it seemed rude not to respond.

"I've been arrested for murder."

The prisoner cocked his head like a dog. "You speak like a proper gentleman, friend." He smiled, a sly smile that did nothing to soften his face. "Green, Frank Green. I'd shake your hand if I could reach."

"How do you do, Mr. Green? Rowland Sinclair."

Green's eyes narrowed. "Who did you say you were?"

"Sinclair, Rowland Sinclair."

"You have some fancy joint in Woollahra?"

Rowland was startled. How did Green know where he lived?

"Well, who would have thought?" Green said, pressing his face against the bars of his own cell to get a closer look at Rowland. "I thought she'd made yer up!" He exploded into a rage of profanity and threats. "I'm gonna kill yer, Sinclair!"

Rowland stepped back, affronted though not unduly alarmed. Frank Green was not a particularly big chap and he was, in any case, confined to a separate cell. He did wonder, however, what he had done to offend the man.

A couple of other prisoners called out and demanded Green pipe down, further enraging him to a point of incoherent, frothing fury.

Only the arrival of Detective Colin Delaney did anything to curb the outpouring of frustrated vitriol. Delaney banged on the bars of Green's cell with a truncheon and instructed him, in terms that were neither polite nor ambiguous, to be quiet.

He had the lock-up sergeant let him into Rowland's cell. "You want to watch him, Rowly," Delaney warned under his breath.

"Who the hell is he?"

"Green... the Little Gunman."

"The Little Gunman? Who calls him that?"

"Himself mostly. He's a killer, Rowly, a murdering thug. What have you done to offend him?"

"No idea. I've never seen him before."

"Well, stay out of his way. You have enough problems."

"Tremendous. What now?"

"Tomorrow is Christmas Eve, you realise."

"Yes." Though, to be honest, it had not been at the forefront of his thoughts.

"It means we're not likely to get you into a committal hearing for a couple of days. They want to transfer you and Mr. Isaacs to Long Bay with the other remand prisoners until then."

"Christmas at Long Bay. Capital!"

"There is significant pressure to deny you bail altogether, which might mean you'll be in Long Bay until trial."

"What?"

"Your lawyers are trying to make sure it won't come to that. Look, Rowly, C.I.B. has also received information, from an anonymous source, that we should, in fact, be looking at your brother for this."

Rowland stiffened. Then he cursed.

"Steady on, Rowly," Delaney said. "Gilbey and Angel have no interest in anybody but you, for the moment. I just wanted you to know that the enemies aren't all yours."

"Colin, Wil has a wife who's expecting and a young family. I want him kept out of this."

"Don't worry about it, Rowly," Delaney said, thoughtfully. "It'd be a brave detective who'd accuse Wilfred Sinclair on the basis of an anonymous note."

"What exactly did the note say?"

"Something along the lines that Wilfred had persuaded your father to make him his sole heir, and having done that, he killed Henry Sinclair."

"That's preposterous. For one thing, I was not, and have never been, disinherited."

"Which is why we've not pursued that line of enquiry. I presume the note came from some disgruntled business associate of your brother's."

"I'm sure Wil has plenty of them."

"I've made sure the boys all know who you are," Delaney said, tapping a cigarette out of his case.

"Why?"

"Just so none of them takes you out back to reason with you."

"I see. What about Milt?"

"Mr. Isaacs has been a guest of this establishment before. He knows how things work." Delaney lit his cigarette. "If you need me, tell them that you want to confess, but only to Detective Delaney. They'll call me in quick smart."

"Thank you again, Colin." Rowland offered Delaney his hand.

The detective frowned. "You don't shake hands with a policeman in full view of other prisoners, Rowly—they'll assume you're a top off—you'll get yourself killed."

"Oh." Rowland dropped his hand. "Right."

"Now, I'll have a quiet word to the boys out at Long Bay. Make sure they keep you away from Green." He reached into his pocket and extracted Rowland's notebook. "Take this… it's corrupting the desk sergeant."

The Federal truck limped into the *Woodlands* drive. The journey had been slow and arduous and it was only Clyde's talent with motors, and routine tappet adjustments, that had ensured it did not stall entirely. They had spent many hours en route beside the road with Clyde bent under the bonnet.

Edna climbed out, travel-worn and stiff. Clyde lifted Lenin gingerly to the ground lest the hound jar his wound by jumping. He cursed both the Federal and Milton's cousin. The sojourn from Yass had taken them nearly a full day. They had slept in the truck somewhere near Moss Vale and stop-started all the way back to Woollahra.

Edna looked uneasily at the looming grandeur of *Woodlands House*. They had decorated for Christmas before they'd set out for *Oaklea*, hanging the jacarandas with dozens of whimsical terracotta angels and bronze-cast stars, but new wreaths and swags had been added in the time they'd been away. Edna bit her lower lip. It seemed strange arriving here with Rowland and Milton in gaol. "Oh Clyde, what are we going to tell Mary Brown?"

"I don't know," Clyde said grimly, grabbing their bags. "Maybe we should just say Rowly's still at *Oaklea*, that he'll be back soon. That way she won't hurt us."

Edna smiled. Clyde was only half-joking. Mary Brown was formidable and still treated Rowland's houseguests as if they were stray alley cats he'd brought home.

"Clyde," Edna began hesitantly. "Should we tell Detective Delaney about Wilfred?"

Clyde took a breath. "Rowly would never forgive us, Ed. I'll risk that if it's the only thing that will save him, but…" He closed his eyes wearily. "Come on, let's get washed up. Even Long Bay has standards."

It was only after Mary Brown opened the door and admitted them that they realised they would not be the only guests at *Woodlands House*.

"Edna, Mr. Watson Jones," Kate said, stepping out into the vestibule. "We had expected you to arrive before us, though we've been here scarcely an hour ourselves."

"Mrs. Sinclair." Clyde put down the suitcases and removed his hat.

"I wouldn't hear of Wil being away at Christmas," Kate explained before they could ask. "Not after the fire… and since he had to be here to help poor Rowly, we decided that we should all have Christmas in Sydney this year."

"Of course." Edna tried to muster enthusiasm. "What a lovely idea. Where is Mr. Sinclair?"

"He's already gone to the… to Rowly," she replied unable to bring herself to name the prison. "Arthur's stepped out too."

"Oh, well perhaps we should—"

"You must be tired," Kate said, observing the dishevelled state of them. "Why don't you two go and wash up while I have Mary organise some tea and refreshments?" She smiled nervously. "Wil is looking after Rowly. If I know my husband, he'll have Rowly released today."

A little reluctantly, Clyde and Edna agreed, washing and changing quickly.

Tea was served in the conservatory.

"Mary won't let us use the drawing room, for some reason," Kate whispered in explanation.

Edna smiled, despite herself. "Rowly uses the drawing room as a studio, Kate. It's probably a bit untidy."

"Goodness! We must go in and have a look!" Lucy Bennett declared as she came into the conservatory. She took a seat at the table, set out with tea and cakes on an Irish linen tablecloth. "Why hello again, Miss Higgins, Mr. Watson Jones. Do please sit down."

Edna glanced anxiously at Clyde, who responded by pulling out her chair.

"Shall I pour?" Lucy asked with the pot already in hand.

"Where are Ernest and Ewan?" Edna asked uncomfortably. "And Mrs. Sinclair?"

"Elisabeth is a bit tired after the trip. She's resting," Kate replied. "And Nanny de Waring took the boys to the beach—there's a puppet show. It hasn't been much of a Christmas for the poor little darlings."

Lucy handed Kate a cup of tea. "Well, we'll all muck in and make up for that now!" She looked around her. "I'm sure with a spot of extra work we could make this place festive. And next year, you can come to Arthur and me for Christmas—oh bother!" She clapped her hand over her mouth. "I s'pose the cat's out of the bag now," she said, giggling as she looked at Clyde and Edna. "It's not been announced of course."

"You and Mr. Sinclair are engaged?" Edna asked, trying to follow.

Lucy glanced at Kate and nodded emphatically. "We're extremely happy."

Edna and Clyde offered their somewhat bewildered congratulations.

"Arthur hasn't yet spoken to Colonel Bennett," Kate cautioned, awkwardly.

"I'm certain Pater will give us his blessing. And then," she took Kate's hands and squeaked, "we'll both be Mrs. Sinclairs."

Colour warmed Kate's cheeks. "Yes, that will be lovely."

"But you mustn't say a word to Rowland. Not a word—not now," Lucy continued, turning back to Clyde and Edna. "It would be cruel, another blow. We'll just wait to see how it all works out."

Edna's brow rose. "I'm sure Rowly will be delighted for you and his cousin, Miss Bennett, but, of course, we'll let you and Mr. Sinclair give Rowly the happy news yourselves."

They continued then to take tea in thoroughly civil but uncomfortable circumstances. Lucy talked of parties and the wording of engagement notices and made only occasional reference to Rowland and Milton being "away".

As soon as it was politely manageable, Clyde and Edna excused themselves, leaving Kate and Lucy to plan an autumn wedding at St Martins in Darling Point.

The altercation between prisoners Frank Green and Rowland Sinclair occurred as the lorry load of remand prisoners arrived at the Long Bay Penitentiary. Green was clearly surprised that his posh opponent knew how to fight.

Green was a ferocious street fighter; Sinclair a trained pugilist, but the spectacle was short-lived, interrupted by another prisoner who tried to soothe the Little Gunman with poetry and, of course, the guards, who eventually descended to teach both men a lesson.

In this, Green fared much worse than Rowland who had only taken a couple of blows of correction before another, more senior guard, intervened.

"That's Rowland Sinclair, you bloody fools!"

The punishment stopped there, for Rowland at least.

Of course, the inequity incensed Green who spat and raged about the injustice of the system, and accused Rowland of being a "grass and a top off".

Rowland and Milton were taken to the cell they were apparently to share in one of the double-storey wings, and locked in. Whether the particular confinement was some form of punishment for the fracas or merely to keep them out of Green's reach was hard to tell. The cell was noticeably larger, cleaner and less dank than the holding cell at Central. Long Bay was, after all, less than twenty years old—a modern penitentiary—which had at least started out with a reformist agenda. Once the guards left, Rowland told Milton of Frank Green's earlier threats.

The poet was less perplexed by Green's enmity. "He knew where you lived and said he thought *she* made you up? Flaming Nellie Cameron!"

"What has Nellie Cameron got to do with this?" The notorious young prostitute had visited *Woodlands* earlier that year with Phil the Jew, a gangster who for some reason believed and insisted that Rowland Sinclair was his friend. The Jew had presented the "services" of lovely Nellie to Rowland as a gift of sorts. She had not been unenthusiastic, but Rowland had declined, in a manner that was characteristically polite. He'd had her taken back to Darlinghurst in a chauffeur-driven Rolls Royce.

"Nellie is Frank Green's lover, Rowly... when he's not in prison, anyway. She's obviously embellished her encounter with you somewhat, and now he wants to kill you for it."

"What on earth does Green think I've done to her?"

"She's on the game, Rowly. I would say it's fairly obvious what he thinks you did."

"But she's—"

"Clearly the Little Gunman believes she entertained you for free, which is a different thing. Or perhaps she told him she had too good a time."

Rowland sighed. Still, he was reasonably confident he could handle Green if he was called on to do so.

"It's not in *here* you have to worry about Frank," Milton warned. "As you said, he knows where you live."

"Why's he here? Do you know?"

"Murder this time—shot a man in cold blood. Over Nellie, I'm told. You need to watch your back."

Rowland's smile was wry. "I'm in here for murder, too."

"Yes, but he actually did it."

Rowland looked at Milton uneasily. "If I had shot my father, would that have made me as reprehensible as Green?"

"Are you asking about you, or Wilfred?"

Rowland groaned, and rubbed his face.

"Look, Rowly," Milton said, moving to lean back on the wall beside his friend. "I get it. He's your brother. But has it ever occurred to you that he may have had reasons, other than protecting you, to kill your father?"

"Father and Wil were always at odds over business," Rowland replied. "Wil wanted to expand and modernise in a way Father considered reckless. But that argument started before the war. Why would he suddenly be driven to murder over it?"

"Your brother has a reputation for ruthlessness, Rowly. He didn't show that bastard Hayden any mercy."

Rowland's eyes darkened. "He didn't deserve any. Hayden made it sound like he was just some downtrodden pawn. That's not how

I remember it. He beat me senseless on a regular basis for five years. And then he'd brag to the other men, tell them how the boss' boy would beg." Rowland laughed bitterly. "That was before I realised begging just made it worse."

Milton shook his head in disbelief. "I always thought you had it so good, that you'd been dealt all the good cards."

Rowland shrugged. "Swings and roundabouts, Milt."

"I gotta hand it to you, Rowly," he said. "By anyone's standards your father was a bastard, treats you worse than a dog and then he gets gunned down in the next room, and you just straighten your tie and carry on. Maybe that's why your lot find it so easy to oppress the proletariat—you don't flinch."

"I don't know about that," Rowland said ruefully. "I was a bit of a firebrand for a long time, quite unreasonable to be honest."

Milton laughed. "What—because you wouldn't assume your place in the Graziers' Association, join the Country Party and marry an appropriate debutante?"

Rowland's eyes became distant as he thought back. "I was really angry when Wil shipped me to England. Not with him, just angry. I did my level best to get expelled again. It must have cost Wil a small fortune to ensure they kept me on. I joined the boxing club when I got to Oxford. I was getting into so many fights anyway, I thought I may as well."

"Yeah, but that sorted you out."

"Boxing taught me to control my temper a bit, I suppose, but I don't think I stopped being angry until I started painting. Even so, I haven't exactly been a bastion of respectability since."

"No… there is that, at least."

20

ON THE SCENT

(By L.W. LOWER)

The N.S.W. Police Association wants different uniforms of lighter material, open at the neck, with a collar and tie. They also want black buttons and badges. They'll be wanting feathers next. I would most certainly refuse to be arrested by a constable in a bow tie. And the possibility of being bailed up by a constable with a water-pistol full of eau de Cologne is not so remote as it seems.

"What do you mean by beaning that poor old gentleman with a bottle! You ought to be ashamed of yourself. I've a good mind to slap your face, you cad!"

"Oh, constable! How could you use such language to an old Goulburnian!"

"Were you at Goulburn? What year?"

"Last year. I matriculated in 1936, and have just completed a refresher course in the gaol bakery at Long Bay."

"Hmmm. Have you no respect for the old gaol tie?"

"I'm sorry, constable."

"Well, I don't want to get my new uniform creased, so I'll let you off this time. Don't do it again. Is my tie on straight?"

"I think it needs adjusting, just slightly. Allow me."

"Thank you. Now you go and apologise to the old gentleman. He seems to be conscious now."

There's no doubt about it. Clothes do make a difference.

The Daily News, 1939

W ork assignments in the penitentiary bakery were much sought after and usually reserved for those who co-operated particularly with the police. It was here that Rowland Sinclair and Elias Isaacs, who was otherwise known as "Milton", were sent. True to his word, Colin Delaney was doing what he could. Of course, they were not, at this stage, permitted to touch the bread and were put to work unloading sacks of flour and scrubbing bench tops.

"If Mary Brown could see you now," Milton grinned. It was obvious that Rowland had not even considered mopping a floor before. Indeed, he might never have actually witnessed the act. Such things were done invisibly in suburbs like Woollahra.

"Squeeze the mop out a bit first, otherwise you're just going to make mud, mate."

The baker's oven at Long Bay turned out enough loaves to feed the entire prison population on a normal day. This day, being Christmas Eve, it was twice as busy, due to the fact there would be no baking on Christmas Day itself. The comforting aroma of freshly baked bread would have been tempting to any man, but the bakery was manned by criminals. Guards watched to ensure the bakery workers did not help themselves to extra rations. Even so, the occasional inmate would return to his cell plumper for the secretion of buns smuggled out in his clothing to stock the prison's thriving black market.

Rowland observed, intrigued as always by the stories etched on the faces around him in hard lines and worn shadows, eyes wide and uneasy or squinted with rat-cunning. He could already identify the first-time offenders, and even distinguish between those who were simply making their prison debut, and those who'd actually offended for the first time. Almost unconsciously he reached for the notebook hidden inside his shirt.

"Oi! What are you doing?" A guard approached. Rowland pulled his hand away, wordlessly berating his own recklessness. Whilst

Delaney had arranged for him to have the notebook back he had been warned to let no one, guard or inmate, see it, lest his drawings incite some kind of riot in the community of men.

"What in the name of God are you doing, Sinclair?" the guard demanded. "You're supposed to mop the floor not create a bloody swamp!"

"Fair go!" Milton protested. "That mop is faulty."

"Shut your trap, Isaacs, or I'll shut it for you! Sinclair, you can come with me. Isaacs, you clean up whatever the hell he thought he was doing here."

Relieved that his notebook had not been discovered, Rowland allowed the guard to escort him out of the bakery. Who knew that surrounded by murderers and thieves, incompetent mopping would be such a cause for concern?

The guard handcuffed Rowland before taking him up to the entrance block. "Relax, Sinclair," he said, grinning. "We're not gonna hang you just yet. You have visitors."

Rowland was taken to a secure room into which his brother and his lawyers had been previously directed.

"Hello Wil," he said as he waited for the cuffs to be removed.

The guard left to take up his position outside the door. Wilfred shook Rowland's hand, noting the new bruise left on his brother's jaw. "You look like hell, Rowly."

Rowland glanced down at his prison uniform. "It is a smidgeon casual. Still, I could get used to not wearing a tie."

"Don't." Wilfred replied, unamused. "We'll have you out of here soon enough." He pointed at the bruise. "Are you all right?"

"Yes, I'm well."

Wilfred introduced the four gentlemen from Kent, Beswick's Sydney office.

"My colleagues and I are going to step out for a few minutes, Mr. Sinclair," Matthew Beswick announced, once the handshaking had been seen to. "I believe your brother would like a private word."

"Just tap on the door when you're ready for us," he said to Wilfred as they left to join the guard in a vigil outside the room.

Wilfred waited until Rowland was seated. "Rowly, your Miss Higgins came to see me."

"How is she?" Rowland asked, smiling at the thought of her.

"Impertinent," Wilfred replied, "but in this instance I am rather glad of her tendency to speak out of turn. She informs me that you believe I killed our father."

Rowland closed his eyes. He should have known Edna would take matters into her own hands. "She won't go to the authorities, Wil."

Wilfred rolled his eyes, exasperated. "Of course she will. Your band of hopeless, unemployed Communist malingerers will do whatever it takes to save you, we both know that. That long-haired layabout got himself arrested just so he could accompany you here!"

"Look Wil, I'll—"

"Rowly, I didn't shoot Father."

"What?"

"I didn't kill him. And it's only knowing that you believed I did that has made me realise that *you* didn't."

"You thought *I* killed Father?"

Wilfred sighed. "When I heard the gunshot, I went immediately to the study and found Father. I looked up and saw you in the doorway. You didn't say anything, you just backed away. I thought you'd finally had enough and…"

Rowland dropped his face into his hands and groaned. "My God, Wil, all these years, I thought you'd killed him. You said you were sorry."

"I thought I'd driven you to it."

"You? Why?"

Wilfred hesitated. He lit a cigarette. "Do you remember when I collected you from the siding that day? You asked me to help you. To intercede with Father on your behalf."

"Did I? I don't remember."

"I do. I was busy… that fellow Menzies was calling in to… Well, it doesn't matter now." Wilfred drew on his cigarette. "You asked me for help and I told you it was time you grew up and started accepting the consequences of your actions."

Rowland wasn't quite sure what to say. He vaguely remembered panicking as they neared *Oaklea*. He may have asked his brother for help.

"Rowly, I didn't know it had got that bad. I thought Father would probably give you a clip around the ear but I had no idea that he'd have you flogged like that—" Wilfred stubbed the cigarette out in an ashtray. "I knew I'd let you down. I thought I'd forced you to kill Father out of desperation and I've always wondered whether that's why we've never seemed able to get along."

Rowland dragged his hands through his hair, trying to absorb how enormously wrong they'd got it. "Wil, until a minute ago, I thought you'd killed Father to protect me. I was nothing but grateful." He smiled. "We don't always get along because you can be a pompous, insufferable git!"

Wilfred glared at him. "For pity's sake, Rowly, why did you think I shipped you to England before the funeral meats were cold, if it wasn't—"

"I expected you were sending me away because you didn't trust me not to say anything about your killing Father. I was a trifle put out about that, to be honest."

"Thirteen years and you've never said anything!"

"Neither have you. I assumed we had an understanding."

Wilfred cursed. "How are we going to explain this to Kent, Beswick without sounding like complete bloody fools?"

If the gentlemen of Kent, Beswick and Associates thought any less of their clients, they were polite enough not to mention it. In fact they responded with such comforting mumblings as "perfectly understandable" and "a difficult time after all". For the first time since Henry Sinclair died, his sons gave complete accounts of what they'd seen and done that evening up until they'd discovered his body.

Matthew Beswick, KC, stroked his beard thoughtfully. "We may need to consider, gentlemen, who else had cause to murder Henry Sinclair."

His associates murmured in agreement.

"You see, as elucidating as these revelations have been, they do nothing to mitigate your motives or opportunity to commit the murder. Nor do they provide you with any sort of alibi. Our best course of action may be to present the court with an alternative theory of the crime."

Rowland's brow rose. "Are you suggesting that we run our own investigation?"

"Now that neither of you gentlemen need fear incriminating the other, that may indeed be advisable."

Wilfred nodded curtly. "We shall look into it, Mr. Beswick, as soon as we get Rowly out of this godforsaken place."

Clearly frustrated, Wilfred gave Rowland the news that Delaney had heralded.

"I'm afraid that even with Sir Adrian's help, we are not going to be able to get you before a bail hearing any earlier than Boxing Day, Rowly."

"Don't worry about it, Wil," Rowland replied, grimacing nevertheless. "Aside from the uniform, it's not unlike boarding school."

Wilfred and the learned gentlemen of Kent, Beswick prepared to leave.

Rowland shook his brother's hand. "Merry Christmas, Wil. Give my love to Kate and the boys."

"Merry Christmas, Rowly. Keep your head down."

The guard had only just placed Rowland in handcuffs once again when another came in to say, somewhat irritably, that he had another visitor. "Someone's looking out for you, Sinclair. Your sister and her husband are here."

"My sister?"

Edna and Clyde were escorted in. The sculptress embraced Rowland and exclaimed, in an inflection that sounded uncannily like Kate's, that Mummy was very worried about him.

Rowland started to laugh.

Edna hugged him again and pretended to sob into his shoulder. "How can you be so terribly callous, Rowly?" she lamented. "Stop laughing!" she added quietly. "They only let family visit."

Rowland sobered, trying to look appropriately contrite until the guard, satisfied that Edna was in fact the prisoner's sister, closed the door.

Then Clyde grasped Rowland's hand warmly. He took in the prison uniform. "Never thought I'd see this day, Rowly. How are you? How's Milt?"

"He's well. Claims to be composing the *Ballad of Reading Gaol*." Rowland told them of his conversation with Wilfred—the revelations of omission.

Clyde laughed. Edna was cross.

"You spent thirteen years covering up for one another because you were too polite to talk about it!" she said hotly.

Rowland shifted uncomfortably. Put that way it was a little embarrassing. He looked sheepishly at the sculptress. "If it wasn't for my impertinent sister we'd probably still be doing so."

"Impertinent? Did Wilfred call me impertinent?" she demanded. "Well that's not polite at all!"

"So what now, Rowly?" Clyde asked, grinning. He was happy for his friend. While Rowland believed Wilfred was guilty, his hands were tied somewhat for fear of implicating his brother. Now they could do something.

"We'll have a look into who else might have killed my father and Hayden. I'm sure they both had any number of enemies."

"How long do you think they'll keep you here?"

"Not long. I'll be bailed on Boxing Day, I hope. Colin will drop the charges against Milt and we'll be home."

"Will you be all right, Rowly?" Edna touched the bruise on his cheek, frowning. Milton knew how to move in the most brutal places, but, despite everything Rowland had been through, there was something naive about him.

Rowland grabbed her hand from his face and kissed it. "Don't be silly. If anyone comes near me, Milt recites poetry at them. I'm probably the safest man in here!"

"And what is this, Sinclair?" Too short to be accepted into the police force, Guard Sergeant Withers had been at Long Bay since the penitentiary opened. He had seen all kinds of men come through its gates, some plagued by bad luck, others bad character. He was as yet

SULARI GENTILL

unsure into which category Rowland Sinclair fell. Withers held the notebook up under Rowland's nose.

Rowland hesitated. The guards had searched him after Clyde and Edna left, in case his sister had passed him some sort of contraband. In the process they'd discovered his notebook. Apparently, only long-term inmates were permitted to have writing materials. Of course, he couldn't admit that Delaney had given the notebook back to him, nor that he'd smuggled it into Long Bay. "It's just a sketchbook, Mr. Withers. My sister thought it might help me pass the time."

"Did she indeed?" Withers flipped through the pages. Rowland's sketches were both detailed and accurate enough to make the drawings of Edna recognisable to anyone who'd met her. Withers had met her. Rowland Sinclair's beautiful sister had caught the attention of all the guards.

The guard sergeant looked at Rowland contemptuously. "What kind of man looks at, let alone draws, his sister like this? Are you a pervert, Sinclair?"

Rowland cursed silently. There wasn't a lot he could say really. It did seem an odd way to draw one's sister.

"I'm onto you, Sinclair. You're not the first bloke to try and sneak his tart in here on some trumped up yarn."

Rowland bristled. "You may want to be careful, Mr. Withers."

The sergeant pushed his truncheon up under Rowland's chin. "I'm sorely tempted to close the door and teach you something about the rules right now."

Rowland looked down to meet the guard's eye. His right brow arched scornfully.

Withers swung and caught him in the ribs. The blow would not ordinarily have felled Rowland, but for its landing on the incompletely healed injuries he'd sustained in the fire. He crumpled, gasping. The guard seemed alarmed by the effects of what he'd thought a tap, and perhaps it was that which stayed his hand.

"You'd better hope you make bail, Sinclair!" Withers snarled. He lowered the truncheon and instructed two junior guards to return Rowland to his cell. The notebook he kept.

21

CHRISTMAS CLEANING

Most housewives like to have a special time of house cleaning and renovating prior to the Christmas season, and it gives one a feeling of quiet contentment to know that walls, if they have not been washed, have, at any rate been well brushed, cupboards have been done out and bait laid for destructive moths and silver fish, pictures have been polished, and fresh curtains adorn gleaming windows.

After your actual cleaning has been attended to, the paint or varnish pot is the next item to claim attention.

The Charleville Times, 1932

"Rowly! Bloody hell—what did those bastards do to you?" Milton was lying on the lower bunk when Rowland was pushed back into the cell. He got up to make way for his friend and helped him onto the cot.

Rowland lifted his prison tunic, gingerly testing the large area of bruising on his ribs. Milton winced. Rowland's torso was a startling canvas of black and blue. "Do you need a doctor, mate?"

Rowland straightened. "No."

Milton paced furiously. "They've no right—just because you can't mop."

Rowland smiled. "It wasn't that, Milt. The bruising is from the fire. Withers just reminded me it was there, that's all." He told

Milton what he'd been doing for the past couple of hours. His conversations with Wilfred, Clyde and Edna, and then Withers.

After Milton finished laughing, they talked of what they'd do next.

"We're going to have to find out who really shot your old man, Rowly."

"We?"

"You're not objective about this, Rowly. You've already proved that. Clyde and Ed and I will need to get involved this time."

"As opposed to every other time?" Rowland asked.

Milton ignored him. "We need to get back to *Oaklea* when we get out."

"*Oaklea*? Why?"

"It's the scene of the crime, old boy. It's where we have to start."

"The crime happened thirteen years ago. What evidence there was would be long gone by now."

"Even so. We need to figure out who exactly was there that night. Now that you're no longer worried about dropping Wilfred in it, you might be able to remember something useful."

"I don't know, Milt…"

"This meeting of Wilfred's, for example. Who was it with?"

"I believe Wil said his name was Menzies."

"Well, perhaps this bloke Menzies was involved."

"He didn't set foot on the property as far as I know," Rowland said, shaking his head.

"But perhaps the meeting was purposely engineered to get Wilfred off the property while your father was murdered."

Rowland frowned as he considered the idea. "But Wil was back at the house by the time Father was shot."

"You returned unexpectedly from school, remember? You should still have been away at Kings. The killer wouldn't have known that your father would be dealing with you that evening. Perhaps he was just waiting until he could get Henry Sinclair alone." Milton leaned back against the cold cement wall. "What about the servants?"

"What about them?"

"Perhaps one of them saw or heard something. Like you and Wilfred, they may have had reasons for not coming forward."

Rowland lay back, allowing Milton to carry on. A devotee of mystery novels, the poet's theories began to take on Christiesque twists, involving disguises, conspiracies and elaborate plots. Rowland was only half-listening, still getting used to the idea that Wilfred had not killed their father; that his brother had sent him away to protect him, rather than because he didn't trust him. For so many years, he had been shaped by the gratitude and the hurt that had come out of that night. He wondered what would have been different had he known. Perhaps nothing.

At six o'clock they were taken out of their cells and marched to another block for the evening meal. Amongst the prisoners Milton came into his own, diffusing any hostility and steering Rowland away from those who might have taken issue with him for one reason or another. Green glowered at them from the other side of the dining hall but he did not approach.

Rowland allowed the poet to recite the verse of Wilde, Keats, and Coleridge as his own. They were, after all, in a prison—stealing poetry was probably not an offence worth pointing out in the circumstances.

The diminutive guard sergeant oversaw the dining hall hawkishly. Rowland wondered if he'd ever see his notebook again. In its absence he tried to commit the features and manner of the men around him to memory.

After dinner the inmates were returned to their cells. The remand prisoners were escorted to the showers and given five minutes and a cake of soap. Rowland found the communal facilities less than dignified, but at least they weren't being fumigated again. By eight o'clock they were locked down for the night.

Despite the hour, both Rowland and Milton were grateful to find their rudimentary beds. Guards patrolled the corridors, conducting bed checks and moving on.

When Guard Sergeant Withers, flanked by two other guards, stopped outside his cell, Rowland assumed he was about to receive the promised lesson in rules. He sat up in the lower cot.

Withers unlocked the cell and strode in. Rowland stood slowly. Milton jumped down from the upper bunk. The two guards stationed themselves at the cell door so that any clear view of what was occurring inside the cell was obscured.

Rowland waited.

Withers reached inside his jacket and extracted the artist's notebook. "I've been looking through your book, Sinclair."

"I see," Rowland said eyeing the holstered truncheon warily.

"You draw bloody well, Sinclair... them pictures of your sister aside." He opened the notebook to a portrait of Detective Angel that Rowland had scribbled from memory. "I applied to join the police with Angel. Course he's a bit taller than me. Recognised him straight off. It's a damn good likeness."

Rowland said nothing, unsure where the conversation was headed.

"You know, Sinclair, it's Christmas Eve."

"Yes. Merry Christmas, Mr. Withers."

"It should be, Sinclair. I'm married to a fine woman. Saintly, she is. Though it's been a difficult year. Her folks have been ill and a guard don't bring home much, but she's never complained."

"It sounds like you're a lucky man," Rowland said awkwardly.

Withers lowered his voice, and stepping closer, spoke in confidence. "I'd put away a bit to buy her something nice for

Christmas. A surprise… a clock for the mantel. Mrs. Withers takes great pride in her mantel. But I had a bit of bad luck, you see, on the horses. A sure thing that had second thoughts."

Rowland's brow rose. Was the guard about to ask him for money? Was this some clumsy attempt at extortion? Briefly he met Milton's eye. The poet seemed equally at a loss.

"I feel real bad 'bout it—Christmas Eve and me with nothing for my beloved Patricia. But then I saw this book of yours and I thought to myself that Mrs. Withers would like nothing more than to have a real portrait for the mantel—like you see in posh houses. It'd make a fine Christmas gift."

The guard smiled, clearly pleased with his ingenuity.

"You'd like me to draw a portrait for you?" Rowland asked tentatively.

"Not for me, for Mrs. Withers."

"Of?"

"Of me, of course." The guard became vaguely defensive. "Mrs. Withers still finds me quite fetching… says I'm more handsome now than I were when we was courting. Saintly she is." He signalled one of his men who brought in a cardboard box. "We rustled up some blotting paper and a few pencils."

Rowland glanced at Milton. "I see."

"Will you do it, Sinclair?"

"Yes, I suppose I could… but I'll need decent light."

Withers nodded at the guard who remained outside the cell, and within minutes the lights were turned on. The prisoners whose cells were on the same circuit stirred and protested. The guard threatened them into silence.

"Right," Rowland said, pulling a roll of thick paper and a couple of pencils from the box. "We'd best get started."

The guard sergeant took up a position by the cell door, posing with his chin high and his hands on his hips—a man of authority, a gatekeeper of consequence.

After some discussion, and in the absence of an easel, Milton and the guard inside the cell stretched the paper out and held it against the cement wall. It was an awkward way to draw but with little other option Rowland made the best of it. He worked quickly, defining a loose composition before he began on the detail. In time he forgot the somewhat peculiar circumstances and became engrossed with the portrait. The haughty insecurity in Withers' demeanour intrigued him. Whenever the sergeant talked of his wife, his face became tender and he stood taller. It was that moment, that insight that Rowland endeavoured to capture.

Rubbing the back of his neck, Rowland looked again over his shoulder at his model, cross-hatching with the lead's point like he was making an etching.

For nearly two hours he worked, pausing only to allow the men serving as his easel to change position or stretch. Withers for his part barely moved, though Rowland invited him to relax once the structure of the portrait was complete. Aware that Rowland was not accustomed to working with an audience, Milton chatted, recited and even sang at one point, in an attempt to distract everybody else in the confined space.

Eventually Rowland stood back. "I'm afraid that's the best I can do without proper equipment."

So eager was Withers to see his portrait that he leapt from his pose by the door and jostled Rowland out of the way. He viewed the pencil sketch from various angles, touching his own face as he studied his features on the paper. "I think Mrs. Withers will be most satisfied, Sinclair."

"I hope so, Mr. Withers."

The guard sergeant handed him back his notebook. "I've already been offered a month's wages for that book, Sinclair. It's worth a fortune in here."

"I'm not trying to sell it, Mr. Withers."

"Well, considering how happy Mrs. Withers is going to be tomorrow, I'll try to make sure no one tries to kill you for it. Some of the blokes can get pretty desperate in here, and then there's the inmates."

Rowland laughed. There didn't seem to be any good purpose in protesting the difference between art and pornography just then. "Thank you."

"Just don't show anyone what's in it." Withers took the portrait in his hands, smiling warmly at his own image. "We'd better get on. Oh yes," he added as he stepped outside the cell. "Don't go to the dining hall tomorrow, stay in your cell."

"Why?" Rowland asked.

"Your brother's arranged for a special Christmas dinner to be brought in for you and Mr. Isaacs."

"Is that allowed?" Rowland asked, surprised. Long Bay was a prison after all.

Withers winked. "With any luck your sister will deliver it."

***

Edna and Clyde returned to *Woodlands* just as the furore erupted. They saw immediately as they entered that the doors to the drawing room had been thrown open. They could hear Arthur's voice, from within, speaking to Lucy Bennett and Kate Sinclair.

"I can only apologise, ladies. Rowland is clearly a very troubled young man. I only thank God that the children and Aunt Libby weren't with you."

Edna glanced warily at Clyde and stepped into the room Rowland had used as his studio. Lucy was in Arthur's arms, her face buried in his lapel as he tried to shield her from the horror.

Kate's face was flushed as she stared at the painting on the easel, clearly Edna, undeniably naked.

"Hello," Edna said. "What are you all doing in here?"

Kate's colour rose even higher as she looked at the sculptress. "Lucy thought… We were curious as to why Mary Brown did not want us to use this room. It was silly really…"

"Oh, I see," Edna said gravely, though her eyes gleamed merrily. "Mary doesn't really approve of the way Rowly paints."

"I would say the problem lies more with what he paints!" Arthur declared. "Good Lord!" He gaped at the portrait of Edna in the yellow leather armchair, her legs slung over one upholstered arm, almost beckoning, as she gazed brazenly from the canvas. "That's Uncle Henry's chair!"

Edna smiled mischievously. "It's most comfortable."

"Ed…" Clyde warned. The sculptress seemed unable to resist poking at ant nests.

"Please don't be concerned, Kate," Arthur declared valiantly. "I'll arrange for the paintings to be removed and the room returned to some sort of respectable order."

"You can't take Rowly's paintings!" Edna objected.

"You aren't in any position to issue directives in this house, Miss Higgins," Arthur replied coldly. "There are now ladies, not to mention children, staying at *Woodlands* during this festive season."

"Oh, Arthur, I don't know that we should—" Kate began.

"If the authorities see this they'll lock Rowland up without doubt!" Arthur said firmly. "We must save Cousin Rowland from himself."

"Where's Mr. Sinclair?" Edna directed the question at Kate. Arthur Sinclair needed taking down a peg or two. Wilfred knew

219

full well the way Rowland ran *Woodlands*, of what he painted. He didn't approve of it but other than the occasional rant, he did not interfere.

"In meetings with gentlemen from *Smith's Weekly*, *The Herald* and *The Times*," Kate replied. "Wil's determined to keep Rowly's arrest out of the papers for all our sakes."

Edna nodded. By gentlemen, she presumed Kate meant the proprietors and editors of the Sydney papers, most of whom moved or aspired to move in the same social and business circles as Wilfred Sinclair.

"I'll move Rowly's paintings," Clyde said suddenly. "He's particular about that sort of thing. I can make sure they're not damaged."

"You'll have to see to it tonight, Mr. Watson Jones—tomorrow's Christmas Day, for pity's sake! We'll want to put the tree in here!"

"As you wish, Mr. Sinclair," Clyde said tightly.

Kate was clearly distressed, whether by Rowland's paintings or the tension was hard to tell. "We could always use the ballroom for the tree... Perhaps we should wait for Wil?"

"Wilfred has more than enough to worry about with getting Rowland out of prison," Lucy said, leaving Arthur's side to take Kate's hand. "It's up to us to make sure everything's perfect when he gets back. If Rowland were here, I'm sure he would insist we put the tree in this room!"

And so it was decreed.

Mary Brown and the staff worked late into the night to ensure that Christmas at *Woodlands* was all that it should be. It had been many years since there had been children in the house at this time. The mansion was filled with the sweet aromas of baking, the grand staircase festooned with holly and ribbons, and every surface polished.

Edna helped Clyde move Rowland's canvases and equipment up to his room. Whatever didn't fit was moved into the rooms she and Clyde occupied. They worked silently, declining to join the family for dinner so that they could clear the drawing room as Arthur demanded. Neither said so out loud, but both felt strangely uncomfortable in the house which had been their home for years. It was not Arthur's antagonism towards them, but the sense that Rowland was no longer the master of his own house.

22

SENT TO GAOL

———— ◆ ————

WOMAN BREAKS BOND. SWEARS IN COURT

SYDNEY, Tuesday

Kate Leigh, or Barry, was sentenced to two years' imprisonment today for having broken a bond to remain away from Sydney for five years.

When the woman was convicted on a charge of dishonesty in June, she was released on condition that she did not come within 200 miles of Sydney for five years. She stated that she proposed to live at Dubbo.

Sergeant Bowie informed His Honour that the woman had been seen in a motor car at Surry Hills.

Leigh told His Honour that she was ill, but admitted that she had not seen a doctor. She was led out of the court after the sentence had been passed, swearing loudly.

The Canberra Times, 1933

Christmas Day at Long Bay began with an ecumenical service in the prison chapel. Rowland studied the arched stained-glass windows and ornate woodwork, mildly surprised by the skill of the craftsmen. The chapel had been built by inmates during the War—perhaps there had been a significant number of criminal carpenters back then.

Milton stood beside him in the pew. The poet was technically Jewish, and more accurately, entirely godless, but he did enjoy a good hymn whatever the denomination. He sang with gusto and rather too much flair for a house of God, amending the lyrics now and then when his memory failed. During the sermon he strove to be attentive, but soon fell into a doze, shouting "Amen" whenever he was made to stir.

After the service, the inmates were marched around the courtyard for half an hour and returned to their cells.

The prison was busy that day with the coming and going of visitors. Mid morning, they were taken out again and assembled in a large hall for a concert organised by the Benevolent Society and performed by the inmates themselves. The residents of the Women's Reformatory were brought in to ensure all seats were taken.

Kate Leigh, Darlinghurst's sly grog queen, arrived in a broad-brimmed hat and silver fox fur, sitting in the front row like a dignitary rather than an inmate. Loud in style and voice, Leigh had amassed a considerable fortune supplying alcohol outside the restricted hours through sly grog shops all over the inner city.

As they waited for the performance to begin, she distributed gifts and cake to her numerous friends in the men's prison. The guards left her alone, though the inmates were otherwise strictly segregated.

The concert opened with the not quite dulcet tones of Tony "The Canary" Vanzella, who it seemed was serving time for fraud. He tearfully dedicated his first aria to "Janice", expressing the wistful hope that she had forgiven him, before launching into a rendition of *O Sole Mio* that, sadly, was recognisable only by the lyrics.

"The fraud was sayin' 'e could sing!" Kate Leigh boomed. "It's us 'e should be asking for forgiveness... Give 'im the 'ook!" She led her fellow prisoners in a chorus of jeering. The Canary sang on regardless, bravely belting out notes with discordant passion until his tribute to Janice was complete.

After the reception that Vanzella received, a number of acts withdrew. The remainder were subject to Leigh's brutal critique, every utterance of which was greeted with uproarious laughter and approbation.

As the stage was being prepared for a group act, she moved unfettered in the hall whilst officers with batons kept all the other convicts in line. In the row in which the remand prisoners were seated, Kate Leigh stopped to offer Yuletide succour to Frank Green, who was apparently an ally in her long-running public war against the gangster madam, Tilly Devine. The chair beside his was quickly vacated for her. It creaked and strained as she settled her considerable form upon it.

"There sat a jolly giant, glorious to see..." Milton whispered wickedly.

Rowland smiled. "I doubt Dickens had Kate Leigh in mind for the Spirit of Christmas Present," he said, as they watched.

Leigh and Green both leaned forward and craned their necks to look towards Rowland.

Milton sighed. "Looks like Frank's telling her that you stole his girl."

The sly grog queen heaved herself up, and after wrapping a hand-knitted scarf around Green's neck, pushed her way through the chairs to Rowland and Milton.

"As I live and breathe!" She looked the poet up and down. "I always knew you'd never 'mount to any good, Milton Isaacs. Your nan must be 'eartbroken! I must call on 'er and see if there's anything I can do."

Milton glowered at Leigh and she smiled triumphantly, exposing the generous gap between her yellowing front teeth.

She turned to Rowland, grinning coyly. "Well, well, I did always wonder what 'appened to the gents who fell into me vegetable patch. Destroyed me silverbeet, you did, and not a ha'penny in compensation."

Rowland nodded politely. "How do you do, Miss Leigh?" He and Wilfred had encountered Kate Leigh's ire earlier that year when they fell off the roof of her sly groggery whilst escaping an unrelated band of villains. He'd discovered then that she'd known his late Uncle Rowland.

She beckoned him closer. "Just a word of advice, for old Sinkers' sake. Men who mess with Nellie Cameron have a 'abit of dying 'fore their time." She inhaled and smacked her lips as she looked into his blue eyes. "You smell real sweet for a bloke in 'ere. I can see why Nellie strayed, aside from 'er being an alley cat of course." She cackled wickedly. "I could show you a Merry Christmas if you like."

Rowland's face was unreadable. Valiantly so. Kate Leigh had made a similar offer when last they'd met. He was no more inclined to accept.

Milton laughed. "He turned down Nellie Cameron. What makes you think he'd take on an ugly old crone like you?"

"For pity's sake, Milt—" Rowland began, disconcerted by his friend's lack of basic courtesy.

But Leigh did not pause, hissing like a bloated serpent. "He's locked up now, there ain't as much on offer 'ere," she said, her voice lowering dangerously.

"He wouldn't be that desperate on the gallows, Kate!" Milton snorted.

She lunged at him, slapping his face with an almighty blow before cuffing him around the ear. Guards hurtled down the row to prevent a riot as prisoners rose in both support and fear of Leigh.

Withers pulled Kate Leigh off, but it was Rowland and Milton he had taken from the hall. They might have objected but the concert was making them long for the relative silence of their cell.

Kate Leigh laughed, and curtseyed clumsily as they were led away. "Good on yer, Mr. Withers, sir." She winked slyly at him. "There's a token of my respect waiting for you at the desk."

"Yes well, thank you. Now move along."

"You gentlemen 'ave a lovely Christmas," the sly grog queen shouted after Rowland and Milton. "Don't you forget to thank the good Lord for Mr. Withers 'ere—a prince among guards—and when you get out, feel free to come see old Kate for a 'elping 'and and a bit o' Christian comfort!"

The Long Bay crowd laughed and cheered, calling "God bless yer, Kate" and "Merry Christmas, luv."

"Kate Leigh's well known for *assisting with enquiries*," Milton muttered as they were locked into the cell. "Clearly being a dobber has its advantages. You'd think she ran the place."

They did not, however, languish in the cell for long before Withers opened the door. "Isaacs, Sinclair, you've got visitors!" he said, grinning.

Rowland and Milton were handcuffed for transfer to the entrance block visitation room. "And take that flaming book with you," Withers warned. "The blokes in this place aren't always honest."

Edna and Clyde were waiting for them. The handcuffs were removed and they were left to visit, though Withers returned shortly thereafter to announce that the dinner which Wilfred arranged had arrived.

"You can eat here," he said. "Best not to torture the other blokes in the block—the Long Bay kitchen does its best but… anyway, this way, your sister can stay."

"Thank you, Mr. Withers," Rowland said, a little surprised. Withers was unexpectedly considerate for a gaoler.

"Mrs. Withers is as pleased as punch with her Christmas

present," the guard said quietly. "Said she was proud to have such a fine-looking gentleman on her mantle. Saintly she is!"

Into the windowless room was delivered a feast of cold turkey, ham, lobster and a dozen or so side dishes, as well as a pudding so soaked with brandy that it served as after-dinner drinks.

Considering that two of their party were presently incarcerated, they had a merry time indeed. It was in fact the first Christmas dinner they'd all shared together and, despite the fact that it was in Long Bay Prison, it was spent in good company.

"Wilfred said he'd visit this afternoon," Clyde said. They had seen Rowland's brother briefly that morning. "He's sorry he can't—"

"I didn't expect him to miss Christmas morning and sitting down with his family, just to keep me company," Rowland said. "I feel bad enough about you all having Christmas at Long Bay as it is. I expect my sister-in-law was disappointed you didn't stay as well."

Edna glanced at Clyde.

Rowland noticed. "What?"

"The atmosphere at *Woodlands* is a bit tense at the moment," Clyde said carefully.

"I beg your pardon?"

Clyde informed Rowland about the clearing of his studio.

"And Arthur decided this?"

"I believe he thought he was protecting the womenfolk and children from your paintings."

Rowland cursed. "Arthur can be a surprising prig."

"Black sheep are not what they used to be," Milton sighed.

"Who does he think he is?" Rowland shook his head. "And Wilfred allowed—"

"Wilfred wasn't there, Rowly. I don't suppose he would have stood for it. They bullied poor Kate into agreeing really. We didn't want to upset her by making a fuss."

"That was probably wise," Rowland replied, "and kind. I'll remind Arthur that *Woodlands* is my house when I get back. He can do whatever he wants at *Emoh Ruo*."

Edna sighed. "I suspect he and Lucy have decided that they prefer *Woodlands*—" She gasped, pressing her lips together as she realised her slip.

"Lucy?" Rowland asked.

Clyde looked at the ceiling. "Lucy wanted to tell you herself, so act surprised when she does. She and Arthur are engaged."

"Really? Good Lord!" He laughed. "I guess any Sinclair will do!"

Clyde folded his arms and rocked back in his chair. "Rowly, mate, I'd be careful of that Arthur if I were you."

"Arthur? What do you mean?"

"I suspect he wants to replace you in more than just Lucy Bennett's affections."

Rowland smiled. "I feel rather like he's taken a bullet for me, with respect to Lucy."

"Well don't be too grateful, mate. I don't trust him."

Early on Boxing Day, Rowland Sinclair and Milton Isaacs were collected from Long Bay Penitentiary in a chauffeur-driven Rolls Royce. Wilfred had arranged for fresh suits and a barber to be sent into the gaol, so that anyone watching from outside the gates may well have assumed the smartly dressed, clean-cut young men were solicitors.

The charges against Milton had been dropped. Rowland was committed to face trial in April, and bailed into his brother's recognisance. The court was closed to the public and not attended by the press, and consequently the committal of Rowland Sinclair for murder was not yet a full-blown scandal.

They followed Wilfred's green Continental to *Woodlands House*. Ernest Sinclair met the small convoy at the gate, waving his father through and running beside the second motor car all the way up the long drive. On Rowland's instruction, the chauffeur drove very slowly to ensure the boy could keep up.

When they got to the house, Ernest opened his uncle's door. "Hello, Uncle Rowly."

"Hello, Ernie." Rowland shook the boy's extended hand.

"You missed Christmas, Uncle Rowly."

"Yes, I'm terribly sorry. I was—"

Ernest beckoned him down before he could finish and whispered in his ear. "I'm not supposed to know that you were in prison, Uncle Rowly. I'm just a child, you know."

"I see."

By then the rest of the family had emerged in a rather civilised cacophony. Even Elisabeth Sinclair came out to greet her son, though it was the wrong one she welcomed home.

To Rowland, his mother seemed to have become smaller in the few days he'd been away, and more deeply confused. He sat with her in the sunroom for a while, reassuring her that the presence of the police at *Oaklea* had been a mistake. She'd clearly found the incident distressing. Clinging to Rowland, she whispered, "The gun... I saw the gun. I thought he was going to kill you."

"Detective Angel is rather too quick on the draw, Mother. But he had no intention of shooting me." He put his hand on hers and rubbed gently. "I'm perfectly fine, you mustn't be upset."

Elisabeth reached up to straighten Rowland's tie. "Your father would have been so dreadfully proud of you, Aubrey. I do wish he might have lived to see the man you've become." She brushed the hair out of his face. "If only you'd comb your hair properly. Wilfred's hair is never out of place."

Rowland smiled, comforted that his mother was well enough to scold him. "Wil doesn't have as much hair to worry about," he said loudly.

Wilfred cleared his throat and glared across at his brother. He did not take kindly to being reminded that his hair was thinning.

Luncheon was, if anything, more extravagant than that which they'd eaten the day before, and served with the formality that Wilfred preferred, but which was rare under Rowland's stewardship of *Woodlands*. Indeed, usually neither Rowland nor his houseguests were in residence during Christmas. Still, the staff coped admirably presenting a table and a service that was both excellent and smooth. Some grumbled about the extra work, others relished the opportunity to do things properly and all were in any case assuaged by the generous sums which had been included in their Christmas envelopes.

The family and their guests retired to the drawing room for coffee and Rowland entered his studio for the first time since it had been made fit for polite company. The only painting which remained was the portrait of his father. Rowland's easels and paintboxes were gone and the paint-splattered rugs had been removed. The furniture and drapes too had been changed. An exquisitely decorated Christmas tree stood in the large bay window in which he usually posed his models.

"What do you think, old boy?" Arthur asked, beaming. "I've organised the painters for the new year."

"Painters?" Rowland looked slowly about the room. "I always thought I was a painter."

"For the walls." Arthur pointed out a splatter of viridian and another of ochre. "Miss Brown did her best, but we couldn't remove much of the damage. Repainting's the only way. I've asked Lucy to pick out the colours. There's nothing like a woman's touch."

Wilfred handed Rowland a drink. "Settle down, Rowly," he said under his breath. "They meant well."

Rowland forced a smile.

Wilfred stepped through the French doors onto the verandah, beckoning his brother to follow. They stood looking out over the manicured lawns.

"I'm afraid you are going to have to return to *Oaklea* with us, immediately after the New Year—terms of your bail."

"We were prepared for that," Rowland said.

Wilfred scowled. "Prepared? We?"

"You heard what Beswick said—our best plan is to find out who did, in actual fact, kill Father."

"And you need a band of Communists to do that?"

"Yes, yes I do."

Wilfred sighed. "Arthur won't like it."

"Since when does Arthur's—"

"Keep your shirt on, Rowly. I was simply warning you, not telling you not to bring them. After all, my dear wife already issued them an open invitation." Wilfred lit a cigarette. "It's just that I believe Arthur and Mr. Watson Jones, not to mention Miss Higgins, have had a falling out."

"Over what?"

"To be truthful, I suspect Arthur was out of line."

"Well he'd better bloody well apologise—" Rowland began furiously.

"I've spoken to him, Rowly."

"I'll do more than speak to him!"

"Arthur means well." Wilfred attempted to soothe his brother. "It was getting mixed up with a woman not unlike Miss Higgins that led to his own ruin."

"Ruin? For God's sake…"

"In his own way, he's trying to save you from making the same mistakes he did." Wilfred removed his glasses and, clenching the cigarette in his teeth, polished the lenses with his handkerchief. "Arthur worked tirelessly with our solicitors to secure your bail, Rowly. He's never doubted your innocence. Even I can't say that."

Rowland groaned. "Very well, I won't deck him. Not today anyway."

"We do have to talk about Dangar Geddes."

"What about it?"

Wilfred's influence and the Sinclairs' substantial shareholding in Dangar Geddes and Company had seen Rowland appointed to its board. He was far from the most enthusiastic, let alone diligent, director, but they had not as yet asked him to leave.

"You can't remain on the board whilst on bail," Wilfred said. "You'll have to stand down, for the time being at least. I thought perhaps Arthur could assume your place."

Clyde's warning that Arthur intended to replace him passed fleetingly through Rowland's mind. Perhaps. But Arthur was welcome to the Dangar Geddes board meetings. "Capital idea."

23

HUGH D. McINTOSH

---◆---

Again Declared Bankrupt

A second sequestration order against the estate of Hugh
Donald McIntosh was made yesterday by the Judge in
Bankruptcy. The petitioners for sequestration were the
defendants in the libel action brought by the respondent
against *The Truth* and *Sportsman Ltd* a writ for costs (£700)
which McIntosh had been ordered to pay having been
returned unsatisfied.

The Sydney Morning Herald, 1932

Mr. and Mrs. Wilfred Sinclair opted to spend New Year's Eve
in, with a small party of close friends and family, including
Lucy Bennett, her parents and Arthur Sinclair. A gracious dinner
was planned, an intimate first celebration of the very recent
engagement of Lucy and Arthur. Of course, the guest list did present
some awkwardness for the usual residents of *Woodlands House*,
considering their last encounter with the good Colonel Bennett. It
was not surprising then, that an alternative invitation, extended to
Rowland and his friends by none other than Hugh D. McIntosh,
was greeted with general approbation and relief.

Rowland had met Hugh McIntosh only once before. Norman
Lindsay had introduced the gentleman as a "denizen of the sporting

world" and the conversation had been struck with a discussion of the pugilistic arts. McIntosh promoted professional fights at the Sydney Stadium, which, it seemed, he had built. The man was a brash, gregarious raconteur, but there'd been a child-like exuberance about him that Rowland had found engaging. McIntosh had been quite proud that the press had dubbed him "Huge Deal", which he claimed was a resounding endorsement of his entrepreneurial prowess and not a moniker from which he resiled. He was, however, happy for Rowland to call him Mac.

At present, after a recent bankruptcy, McIntosh was managing *Bon Accord*, a fashionable guest house in the Blue Mountains, beside which, he'd built a nine-hole golf course. It was at *Bon Accord* that McIntosh was throwing his New Year's Eve party followed by a day of golf for those who survived to play on.

"Golf?" Milton exclaimed. "We don't play."

"Rowly does," Clyde replied. "His chip shot ain't half bad."

"Really?" Edna was surprised. She'd never known Rowland to play.

"Shall we go?" Rowland asked. "I'm told Mac's parties are reminiscent of Jay Gatsby's shindigs."

"Of course, we're going!" Milton declared. "What about the conditions of your bail?"

"I have to reside with Wilfred and I can't leave New South Wales. Otherwise I'm essentially free."

"And Wilfred?"

"I'm sure he'll be delighted to have us out of *Woodlands* while the Bennetts are here."

And so it was decided.

Edna removed the scarf which had held her copper tresses vaguely in place for the trip up to Springwood. The summer evening had been so warm and clear that they had travelled the entire forty-five miles with the top of Wilfred's Rolls Royce Phantom II well and truly down. Now she and Milton fought over the rear vision mirror to re-groom what disruption the wind had inflicted upon their hair. Clyde had used enough Brylcreem to make that unnecessary, and Rowland did not even think to check his reflection.

The party at *Bon Accord* was a fancy dress affair with guests directed to come as pagan gods and goddesses. Though only Milton had been particularly keen, they had all managed to procure costumes.

Milton had come as Pan, the goat-legged Greek god of the woodlands. He'd managed somehow to secure a set of short horns to his forehead in a manner that looked more demonic than anything else, and wore a toga long enough to hide the fact that his legs were inconveniently human. *Costumes on George* had turned Clyde into a gladiator, as Mars the Roman god of war. Rowland had chosen a Norse deity, mainly because their costumes involved trousers. Consequently he was attired in the leather vest and horned helmet of a Viking, while he purported to be dark-haired Loki.

Edna, like Milton, had chosen to be Greek. She wore a sheer white gown which was draped over one shoulder. Her hair was woven with a wreath of laurel and she carried both a bow and a golden apple. Rowland wasn't sure whether she was meant to be Athena or Aphrodite, but he was in no doubt that she was a goddess.

The celebration had well begun by the time the borrowed Rolls Royce joined the scores of vehicles parked in the drive and adjoining road. The way to the grand ballroom of *Bon Accord* was lined with lanterns shaped like birds in flight and suspended from wires strung between the trees.

Rowland grabbed Edna's hand as she stumbled. "Be careful Ed—the path's quite uneven here. You may need to watch your step."

"Just look up there, Rowly," she said, her eyes bright, and fixed upon the glowing flock which seemed to hover over them. "It's so utterly enchanting... How can you tell me to watch my feet instead?"

He laughed and offered Edna his arm to secure her balance while she took in the decorations. They made way for an Egyptian pantheon, and a man painted blue in the style of some Asiatic deity.

When they finally reached the entrance to the ballroom, they were received just inside the door by a gentleman who managed to be dapper despite being dressed as Neptune, complete with silver trident.

"Rowly Sinclair!" boomed the god of the sea. "How are you, slugger?"

"Hello, Mac," Rowland replied, shaking Neptune's hand. He introduced Hugh McIntosh to his friends, drawing them close to do so, as the room rang with the sounds of revelry backed by a twenty-piece orchestra.

McIntosh summoned a waiter and distributed glasses of French champagne while demanding Rowland and his friends enjoy themselves. He directed them to the buffet where a feast was presented in oversized horns of plenty and attended by staff dressed in togas.

Leaving Clyde and Milton to partake of the supper, Rowland took Edna onto the dance floor, where they quick-stepped and jazz-waltzed with Celtic immortals and elephant-headed divinities.

The party built momentum, fuelled intermittently by the infusion of some new spectacle to spur the merriments. Dancing girls, magicians, flaming delicacies and showers of glittering confetti cast from the upper floors—the guests were kept breathless by the sheer extravagance and energy of the event.

McIntosh had summoned his guests from the heights of society, from the world of professional boxing, politics and the theatre. They all had stories to tell about the fortunes, the schemes and the generosity of their host—accounts of commercial daring and financial courage. Tales which, lubricated by the champagne provided by their subject, were invariably affectionate and acclamatory.

At the stroke of midnight, the band played *Auld Lang Syne* and in a flurry of handshaking and new year's greetings, Rowland found the sculptress in his arms.

"Happy 1934, Rowly," she said, kissing him with slightly intoxicated abandon, before she was danced away in the cheering crowd and he was left with the lingering scent of roses and the taste of her on his lips.

Midnight did not signal any abatement of the celebrations, though as the first hours of the year passed the dancing slowed and the conversations became more sedate.

Rowland had not seen the Honourable Hugh Lygon since his first years at Oxford, though he did vaguely remember recent mention that the Englishman was in Australia. He'd faced the young aristocrat in the boxing ring once—a surprisingly brutal encounter considering that his opponent had been in the peculiar habit of carrying a large teddy bear about. It had sat in Lygon's corner throughout the match, watching the violence with sad glass eyes. On this occasion, Lygon was accompanied instead by his father—the disgraced Earl of Beauchamp—who had fled Britain after being charged with homosexuality. For some reason that defied usual social segregations, Milton and the Earl were acquainted, and though Lygon had no recollection of Rowland, Earl Beauchamp recognised Milton immediately. He asked after the poet's grandmother with whom he apparently shared a love of embroidery and needlework.

It was from the midst of this unexpectedly mundane conversation that Hugh McIntosh pulled Rowland aside. "I wouldn't mind a word, Rowly."

"Yes, of course," Rowland said, allowing his host to guide him into a quieter part of the house.

McIntosh looked over his shoulder to check they were more or less alone. "Rowland," he began, "I like you. You've always struck me as a man of vision."

Rowland regarded him quizzically, wondering if McIntosh was just slightly intoxicated.

"A simply extraordinary opportunity has recently come my way and I would like to give *you* an opportunity to invest!"

"Me?"

"As I said, my boy, I like you, and this is my way of making amends, I suppose."

"Amends? For what?"

"For the amount your cousin lost on the Al Foreman bout."

"Arthur bet on a boxing match?" Rowland tried to follow.

"No, no, the bout didn't take place. Foreman pulled out. Arthur was one of the gentlemen who financed me to bring him out. What happened could not have been foreseen. It was disastrous for us all, but I've always felt bad."

"Well then, shouldn't you be offering this opportunity to Arthur?"

McIntosh stroked his meticulously trimmed moustache. "I'm afraid Arthur will not take my calls, Rowly. Your cousin is not a forgiving man and he blames me for the disappointing outcome of our enterprise."

"Just how much did Arthur lose?"

"Quite a significant sum. He was forced to sell his legal firm, I believe. As I said, I feel bad."

"So you want me to financially back another fight?" Rowland asked.

"No—fight promotions are old hat! I've another idea, and slugger, I think this might be the best idea I ever had! It's simply inspired!" He put his arm around Rowland's shoulders. "Have you noticed the Black and White Milk Bar in Martin Place?"

"The Milk Bar?"

"Always a line clamouring at its door. Rowly, I am going to open Black and White Milk Bars all over England! I've some excellent business and political connections there, and on the Continent. We'll make a fortune. There's money in milk, my friend!"

They talked for a while after that, McIntosh outlining his proposal, building an empire with words and belief. Rowland listened, amused, intrigued and not entirely pessimistic about the idea's potential.

"Look, Mac, how about I speak to my brother about this?"

"Your brother? Why? Excuse me if this is a vulgar question, Rowly, but don't you have your own fortune?"

"Yes, of course, but business is Wil's talent. I'm just a painter."

"Painter… nonsense, you're an artist! Why Norman Lindsay claims you as his protégé, and Norman does not do that lightly! I was a humble pie maker once, but I have made fortunes, for myself and many others. They love me in England! I was invited to the royal wedding, you know!"

McIntosh was persuasive, but Rowland was steadfast. "You don't really expect me to commit that amount of money tonight, do you, Mac? I'm not sure I've drunk enough champagne to make that kind of investment!"

"Perhaps not," McIntosh conceded, slapping Rowland on the back. "I suppose I should be glad that my new partner is not a fool."

"Partner?"

"It's inevitable, Rowly, inevitable. This is too good a deal to pass up!"

It was only Milton's determination to wear plus fours that ensured they emerged the next morning after ringing in 1934 in such grand style. The poet roused his companions, and was clearly disappointed that Rowland and Clyde intended to golf in ordinary suits. Rowland was adamant that he'd had enough of fancy dress and Clyde was less polite.

The golfing party was surprisingly large, a merry, good-natured gaggle of tired, not entirely sober partygoers with thankfully few serious golfers. Out of the elaborate costumes of the night before, many guests became recognisable—actors, politicians, and celebrities of one kind or another. They all broke into smaller groups to play the eighteen hole course made up by the combination of McIntosh's nine holes with that of the Springwood Country Club. Eager caddies, assured of generous gratuities, lined up to carry custom golf bags.

Rowland and his companions formed a foursome on their own, carried their own clubs and spent the day playing a less than orthodox game of golf. Edna cheated, blatantly kicking her ball into more playable positions. Milton changed the rules and Clyde dug more divots than he hit balls. The game, such as it was, was punctuated with laughter and the frank conversation of people completely at ease in each other's company.

At some point during the pleasant amble, Rowland told his friends about the previous evening's conversation with Hugh McIntosh, omitting Arthur Sinclair's financial difficulties which were, after all, Arthur's business alone.

Milton frowned. "It'll be a sad day indeed when bars serve milk! What is the man thinking? I'll wager those crones from the Temperance League are behind this!"

Clyde swiped at the poet with his golf club. "I dunno, Rowly, everybody needs milk. It might just work. The Sinclairs could become dairymen."

"I suppose so." Rowland had never really considered how milk was procured before. He took his putt. "I wouldn't mind painting Mac, you know. There's something about his eyes, a distinct glint of insanity."

"Sounds like the perfect choice of business partner," Milton observed.

It was mid-afternoon by the time they returned to the *Bon Accord* to thank their host and take their leave. McIntosh would not allow them to depart without gifts of champagne, chocolates and a biography of the erstwhile premier of New South Wales. It seemed that Premier Lang had commissioned McIntosh to write the volume and, unhappy with its scandalous contents, had refused to pay him… which of course recommended the book in itself. He inscribed a volume for each of them with the same theatrical flourish with which he appeared to do everything. In Rowland's he wrote "To a fellow fighter… Milk Bars!"

Rowland smiled. "I won't forget, Mac."

24

A DARK ROOM

---◆---

Making It Cheerful

It is often thought that it is necessary only to decorate a dark room in light colours to make it appear much lighter. This is not the case always, because colour values are usually distorted in a room where there is not sufficient light to bring out their qualities. White and cream, for example, sometimes appear grey near a ceiling. Light blues look cold, and pale greens can take on a dirty tinge. One of the best shades is yellow, the more golden in tone the better, while pink, if it has a certain amount of yellow in it, is also good.

Examiner, 1934

The Sinclairs and other residents of *Woodlands House* remained in Sydney for just another day. With the frivolities of the festive season behind them, there were matters of homicide to be resolved in order to clear Rowland's name. For that it seemed appropriate to return to the place where the murders had been committed.

For Rowland, it was almost a relief to be returning to *Oaklea*. The hierarchy there was established and unchallenged. The grand mansion was the ancestral home of the Sinclairs, but Wilfred was undeniably its current master.

At *Woodlands* it had always been less clear. Rowland's staff had never stopped deferring to Wilfred, and now Arthur Sinclair was adding a further complication to the lines of authority, and with it, a predictable tension.

As they left *Woodlands House*, Rowland gave his housekeeper explicit instructions that the painters, when they arrived, were not even to enter his drawing room.

"Tell them to paint the dining room if they must paint something."

"The colours Miss Bennett chose..." Mary Brown asked hesitantly.

Rowland grimaced as he recalled the swatches of lavender and pink that Lucy Bennett had selected. "God, no! Tell them to paint it red, or black. Yes, tell them to paint it black."

"Oh, you can't mean that, sir!"

"I do." Rowland was aware that he was being a little childish, but his cousin's presumption irritated him. As much as he was loathe to carry on like some lord of the manor, *Woodlands* was his house.

With the Mercedes still garaged in Yass, Rowland and his friends caught the train from Central Station. Lenin travelled with them in the private first class compartment. It was not exactly within the rules of carriage but Rowland had paid the greyhound's fare several times over in gratuities intended to induce temporary blindness.

They played cards as they planned what they would do next.

"We're going to have to really look into your old man, Rowly," Milton said as he shuffled. "Try and find out who else hated him."

"How could we possibly do that?" Edna asked, taking up the cards he'd dealt her.

"Journals, diaries, letters, that sort of thing," Milton replied, turning to Rowland. "Do you know where we'd—"

Rowland glanced at his cards. "The lawyers... Wilfred perhaps." He frowned. "I don't know that anybody has used Father's study since he died. There may be some papers in there."

"We'll have a gander," Milton decided. "What about this bloke your brother was meeting?"

"Menzies?" Rowland shrugged. "Wil might know what happened to him, though I'm not sure how Wil will feel about your conspiracy theory, Milt."

"I shall just have to dazzle him with my razor sharp logic," Milton replied unperturbed.

"There's also Hayden," Clyde reminded them. "The police obviously assume whoever killed Henry Sinclair killed Charlie Hayden too."

"The police assume it's Rowly," Edna corrected.

"Perhaps the two murders aren't connected," Rowland said, tapping the window absently. He showed his cards and took the hand.

"I don't know, Rowly, they were both at *Oaklea*. It seems too coincidental to be unrelated."

"I suppose, but there were some thirteen years between the killings."

"We need to ascertain who, other than Rowly and Wilfred, was connected to both men." Milton abandoned the card game.

"That's everybody who worked at *Oaklea*, I suppose," Edna mused.

"Hayden was my father's manager," Rowland offered. "There are probably a few people that dealt with both of them in relation to the property."

"That shearer your father sacked... for teaching you to shear," Clyde raised the man tentatively. "He'd hate them both. Do you know what happened to him, Rowly?"

Rowland said nothing for a while. "John Barrett's a good bloke, Clyde."

Milton stiffened. "We talked about this, Rowly," he warned. "We can't just look at the people you don't like."

Rowland sighed. "He works on Wainwright's, the neighbouring property. Has done since Father sacked him."

"You've spoken to him?"

"He called by the day of Father's funeral. I saw him speaking to Harry." Rowland's eyes darkened. "I expect he was just expressing condolences or something of the like."

"Harry never told you?"

"I left for England soon after the funeral and, to be honest, Milt, I haven't really thought about it since."

"And other than that, have you spoken to Barrett?" Milton persisted.

Rowland shook his head. "We've exchanged the usual pleasantries in passing but nothing more than that. We don't really move in the same circles."

Milton conceded. "Fair enough."

Edna leaned into Rowland. She could sense his unease. "We won't say anything about anyone to the police unless we are absolutely sure, Rowly."

Rowland's smile was fleeting and tense. "I know. I'm sorry." He loosened his tie. "I just detest the idea of suspecting everybody who was ever kind to me."

"Of course you do," Edna said gently. "That's why we're here."

They changed the subject then—for Rowland's sake—because they knew that there was a great deal he felt but did not say, and because some things were buried for good reason. The conversation turned instead to art and life and the less consequential.

Dr. Selwyn Higgins, Edna's beloved, decidedly eccentric father, had been in Turkey since October, and had sent them each a fez for Christmas. Milton was wearing his despite the protests of his companions.

"Selwyn has excellent taste," he said, admiring his reflection in the window.

"You look like a flaming organ-grinder's monkey," Clyde muttered. "Just remember to take it off before we get to Yass Junction! You can't expect us to be seen with you wearing that!"

Rowland laughed and nudged Clyde. "Perhaps you should wear yours next time you step out with Miss Martinelli."

Clyde groaned. "If I thought it would work, mate, if I thought it would work…" He sighed. "Rosie wants to meet my mother and she's decided I have to speak to her father before Easter."

"Oh, Clyde." Edna rubbed his shoulder sympathetically. "That soon?"

"Your mother could well scare her off," Milton suggested optimistically.

"I don't want to do that. Well, not entirely. Rosie is a great girl. I just don't want to get married, not yet." Clyde discarded his cards miserably. "Anyway, it's far more likely that she and my mother will join forces, and then I'm doomed."

Rowland winced. "I thought your mother was still hoping you'd join the church. Doesn't she owe a son to God?"

"My brother, Tom, is talking about the seminary," Clyde replied resentfully. Clyde's Catholicism was of the unobtrusive sort, more traditional than theological. But it seemed he'd come to rely on the expectation that he would eventually enter the priesthood as his protection against the expectation that he would marry.

Milton placed a comforting hand on Clyde's shoulder. "Chin up, mate. If we can save Rowly from the gallows, we should be able to save you too. You'll just have to wait your turn."

Clearing of the scorched site of the fire was already well underway. Wilfred had retained an architect and a builder, both briefed to restore *Oaklea* as soon as possible. Edna Walling and her crew had also returned and their work in the gardens was proceeding with a renewed vigour.

As Arthur Sinclair had now spoken with Colonel Bennett and obtained his blessing, Lucy remained in Sydney to celebrate the good news with her family. She did, however, promise Kate and her fiancé that she would visit *Oaklea* again as soon as she was able.

Detectives Gilbey and Angel called by the day the family arrived back, to check that Rowland was indeed complying with the condition of his bail which stipulated that he live with Wilfred Sinclair. Rowland's passport had been surrendered to the court, but it was understood that men of Wilfred Sinclair's means and influence could obtain whatever paperwork they needed, and afford to lose the financial surety put up for bail.

Kent, Beswick and Associates also called to discuss strategy and update their clients.

In a dramatic demonstration of confidence in his brother's innocence, Wilfred Sinclair offered a ten-thousand-guinea reward for anyone who provided the police with information leading to the apprehension and conviction of Henry Sinclair's murderer. The move had perplexed Rowland at first until Delaney telephoned to report that the Criminal Investigation Bureau was being inundated with calls, letters, telegrams and witnesses all claiming to know who killed Henry Sinclair.

"We had a bloke in here yesterday, dobbing in his mother for doing away with your old man," the friendly detective said, laughing. "Gilbey and Angel will be working around the clock for months to follow up this lot!"

Alice Kendall welcomed Rowland back with joy and tears and apology. He was forced to eat close upon an entire batch of her shortbread before she would believe that it was not anything she had said which led to his arrest.

"You know I didn't shoot Father, don't you, Mrs. Kendall?" he asked when he'd finally calmed her.

The old housekeeper clasped her hands to her heart. "It's so good to hear you say that," she gasped. "I always knew it in my soul, but sometimes I wondered." She broke down again. "He could be such a cruel man. I wish I could have done more for you…"

Rowland took her hand. "I know Mrs. Kendall—I knew then too."

"I wanted to say something, but if he'd sacked me you would have had no one at all. I couldn't bear the thought of leaving you with that man."

"I know," he said, rubbing her hand. "I'm glad you didn't give him an excuse to take you away too."

He waited until she'd blown her nose. "Do you remember anything at all about that night? Could anyone else have been in the house?"

"Oh Mr. Rowland," she said, dabbing her eyes with the edge of her apron, "you know the kitchen door is always left open. It was then too. We kept a bigger staff in those days… people always coming and going. And then there were the gentlemen who came to see Mr. Sinclair."

"Wil?"

"No, no… your father."

"Who?"

"The accountants, the solicitors…" The housekeeper's whole face furrowed as she tried to remember. "As for the rest, I'm sure I don't know."

Rowland asked one more thing. "The guns, Mrs. Kendall. They used to be kept in the cupboard next to your pantry. Do you know if they were all accounted for after he died?"

Mrs. Kendall smiled. "Your father was not as particular or careful as your brother about the guns. There were several missing the night he died. Mr. Sinclair was always taking them out for some reason or another, and then forgetting to put them back. The maids would regularly find loaded pistols about the place." She clicked her tongue disapprovingly. "It's only since he died that there's even been a lock on the cupboard."

"So anyone may have taken one?"

"Anyone who knew where they were kept, or I suppose anyone who found one Mr. Sinclair had left about."

"And the gun Miss Walling found in the dam—do you remember when you last saw it in the cupboard?"

"I'm so sorry... I'm so useless," the old woman fretted now. "Until Mr. Sinclair was shot, we didn't really pay any mind to what was or was not in the gun cupboard."

Rowland dusted the shortbread crumbs from his tie. "That's probably as it should be, Mrs. Kendall."

* * *

Edna joined Milton and Clyde at the Mercedes. Clyde was bent under the bonnet checking oil or some such thing. He and Milton were deep in conversation. Edna caught the end of it.

"Why else would he tell Rowly he was sorry?"

"Wilfred wasn't talking about shooting Henry Sinclair," Edna said. "You know that."

"We weren't talking about Wilfred," Clyde said. "We were talking about Harry Simpson."

"Harry?"

"He told Rowly he was sorry just before the police took us away," Milton said, frowning. "It got me thinking."

"That's ridiculous, why would Harry kill Henry Sinclair?"

"Maybe he wanted Wilfred in charge."

"Why?"

"Wilfred made Harry manager," Milton reminded her.

"Don't be idiotic, Milt. Harry doesn't care about that sort of thing," Edna replied, cross.

"It was thirteen years ago, Ed. Perhaps Harry was different back then," Clyde ventured, though clearly the idea did not sit well. He liked the stockman, but still. "You know when Rowly first told him that his father's gun had been found, Harry asked how, not where or when—*how*."

"And Harry was damned upset when Rowly was arrested," Milton added.

"Naturally." Edna stared hard at the two men before her, wondering just how obtuse they were. "You do realise that Harry's not just any stockman, don't you?"

Clyde shifted uncomfortably. "Rowly's never… and Harry hasn't either…"

"Of course, he didn't… they wouldn't. It's probably impolite." Edna sighed. "But look at the way they are with each other. How could they not be?"

"They grew up together, Ed."

"Rowly's mother nearly fainted when she saw Harry."

"He's Aboriginal, Ed. Just because Rowly takes a man as he finds him, doesn't mean his mother does."

Milton interrupted. "It doesn't matter whether Harry's an ordinary stockman or Rowly's… or not. In fact, if he isn't, it's probably more likely that he killed old Mr. Sinclair and Hayden."

"I can't believe you're suggesting this!" Edna said furiously.

"I'm not suggesting anything, Ed," the poet said firmly. "But we have to consider every possibility and Harry is definitely a possibility."

25

"DEAR OLD FRUIT"

MODERN MARRIAGE PROPOSAL

Mr. A.E. Bell, a London solicitor, in a paper on "Is the Law an Ass?" at the Law Society's conference at Eastbourne recently, declared that in these days marriage settlements were mere pamphlets.

"Betrothed beings nowadays," he said, "court by telephone and 'marriage settlement' each other by letter." He gave an example of a super up-to-date marriage contract which read:

"Dear Old Fruit,—Suppose we park ourselves at the altar together; you shall have the run of my rabbit warren and all its gadgets. You know that my jolly old life has had something done to it; I mean to say that when old daddy time throws a monkey wrench into my works some giddy insurance company will hand you a cool thousand and you can have my bank overdraft and everything what's over.

All the best."

The Advertiser, 1928

"Oh for the love of God!" Wilfred muttered.

"What's wrong?" Rowland asked, wondering what Edna Walling had done now. He had accompanied his brother out into the dam paddock to inspect her progress. The works were significant: an arboretum was being planted on the open ground which sloped gently towards what would be a grand cobble-edged pond. The dam, which had been drained a few weeks before, had been partially refilled with soil. A massive mound of clay, which had once lined the dam, was awaiting use in sealing the new pond. A dozen men toiled with wheelbarrows and shovels and the garden designer directed proceedings from the midst of it all. It was none of this, however, that had prompted Wilfred's outburst.

Instead, it was the fact that Edna Higgins was on her knees beside the mound, sculpting figures with the clay lining of *his* pond. Her arms were caked with clay to the elbow, as were her feet and shins. Her shoes had been discarded on the grass a short distance away.

Rowland stopped, entranced. Edna seemed, to him, to be drawing shapes out from the earth, conjuring form from the dirt. There was a glorious immersion about her focus that enchanted him. Like a child absorbed, she took complete, abandoned joy in what she was doing, forgetting any regard for clothes or propriety. To Rowland this was when she was at her most beautiful—the uninhibited, uncontainable sprite who'd enslaved him from the first.

He reached inside his jacket for his notebook, determined to capture the moment, to record what he'd need to paint the sculptress like this. He found a tree stump just a few yards away, against which he settled. Accustomed to being Rowland's model, Edna ignored him entirely, when she noticed him at all.

Wilfred stared incredulously as his brother began to draw the woman playing with mud in his paddock. He threw his arms in the air and walked away.

For a time nobody bothered either artist or sculptress, as work on the paddock continued.

It was Jack Templeton who first wheeled his barrow up to Edna.

"Miss Higgins," he said, tipping his broad-brimmed hat.

"Hello, Mr. Templeton," Edna replied, brushing the hair from her face and smearing it with red clay in the process.

"Can I ask what you're doing there, Miss Higgins?"

She smiled. Templeton stepped closer, drawn by her.

"I saw people in the clay," she said, running her hand over one of the smooth bodies now sculpted into the mound; rounded fluid figures that spoke of the earth in form and substance.

"But Miss Walling said we have to use this clay to line the pond." Templeton stared in awe at what Edna had created.

"I know."

"But, this—it'll all be destroyed."

"No, they'll always be there in the clay. I've set them free now."

Templeton's brow rose. "You'd be pulling my leg, Miss Higgins."

Edna laughed. "No, I'm not. Well, maybe a little. I only wanted to see what they looked like. They can go into the pond now."

"But they'll be wrecked. No one will ever see them." Templeton sounded genuinely distressed.

"I've seen them," Edna replied. "You've seen them, and I think Rowly may even have drawn them…"

Rowland stood. "I don't know Ed. I wasn't really trying to capture your mud people." He looked critically through his sketches. "I may have caught them in the background."

Templeton was clearly startled by the presence of Rowland whom he'd apparently not noticed till then. One didn't expect graziers to be lying about in paddocks. "Mr. Sinclair, sir, I didn't see you there…"

"Hello, Templeton. Did you enjoy a good Christmas?" Rowland closed his notebook, stepping over to inspect more closely what Edna had carved into the walls of the mound.

"I did. I haven't spent Christmas in Yass for some time."

"You're from around here?" Rowland asked.

"Born and bred, sir. I lived here as a boy. The place hasn't changed all that much."

Rowland laughed. "Don't let Wil hear you say that. He's convinced that Yass is a shining example of progress and development. In fact, I'm sure he believes this is the real national capital."

Templeton grinned. "There are a few more people in town, I suppose, but the Sinclairs are still in charge." He looked back at Edna's sculptures. "I don't feel right just shovelling this into the pond. It's smashing."

Edna rescued her shoes from the grass. That smile again and both men caught their breath. "Why, thank you, Mr. Templeton. But it's not going to last anyway. There are too many impurities in the clay to fire it, even if we could build a big enough pit. Don't feel bad."

Templeton removed his hat and wiped his forehead, bewildered. "But then why did you—?"

"I saw them there when I looked at the clay and I just couldn't help myself—I had to dig them out," Edna explained confusing Templeton further.

Rowland understood. Edna often saw shapes that others could not—hints of form imprisoned within a medium. It was in her nature to liberate them.

Templeton picked up his shovel. Then, placed it back in the wheelbarrow, shaking his head vehemently. "I can't do it," he said. "I'll have to talk to Miss Walling."

"Oh dear," Edna said as they watched him go. "I didn't mean to make things difficult."

A laugh. Loud, deep and familiar. Harry Simpson strode across the paddock towards them. He stopped with his arms folded across his broad chest, gazing at the rotund figures protruding from the mound of clay, and chuckled. "Wil said Miss Higgins was playing in the mud. I had to come have a look."

"I'm so glad you did, Mr. Simpson," Edna retorted brightly. "You can help Rowly and me shovel them into the pond."

"I beg your pardon?"

"Mr. Templeton feels bad breaking them up, and he shouldn't. The pond needs to be lined and this was just an experiment." She picked up a handful of the clay soil and showed the stockman its consistency. Harry Simpson nodded sagely as if he knew what she was talking about. "I really was just messing around. They won't last," she said earnestly.

Simpson looked at Rowland, who was removing his jacket, resigned to the task ahead. "She does this kind of thing all the time, Harry. I don't think there's a cake of soap at *Woodlands* that Ed hasn't whittled into some creature or other. Sculptors, you know." He rolled up his sleeves. "We'd best get on with it before Arthur discovers there are naked mud people in the paddock!"

It was late afternoon by the time they finished breaking up the sculpted mound and wheelbarrowing it into the pond. Indeed, the enterprise might have taken a good deal longer if Clyde and Milton had not come out to help.

Alarmed both by the destruction of the sculptures and the fact that Rowland was shovelling dirt in a three-piece suit, Templeton returned with Victor Bates, who seemed as aghast as his workmate.

Touched by their concern, Edna showed the gardeners Rowland's sketchbook, in an attempt to explain that what she'd been doing was equivalent to an artist's sketch—a whim or a notion rather than a fully conceived work.

The burly workmen took in the contents of the notebook. Bates' mouth fell open and Templeton turned a quite interesting shade of pink. Rowland smiled, very much doubting that his sketches were actually making the point Edna intended.

Once the clay had been moved, they left the garden designer and her men to put it to the use for which it had been collected, and called by Simpson's cottage to clean up a fraction before returning to the main house. The men were still in a reasonable state, but Edna looked rather like she should have been part of her own sculpture.

Harry Simpson handed the muddy sculptress a towel and a cake of Sunlight soap. "Now that's to wash with, *not* to carve," he warned, breaking into a grin.

"I see Rowly's been telling tales," Edna replied, enjoying the sound of Simpson's giggle. It was ridiculous on a man so large and strong and otherwise rugged. Uninhibited and contagious. She could not hear it without smiling.

While Edna was inside the cottage trying to make herself presentable, the men waited on the verandah.

Simpson settled himself in the old squatters' chair and regarded Rowland sternly. "Why don't you hurry up and marry that girl?" he asked.

Both Clyde and Milton pulled up, startled. It was not that they were unaware of Rowland's enduring torch for the sculptress, but that they had decided long ago it was a matter best left alone.

Rowland looked at Simpson and responded plainly, if a little reluctantly. "I'm afraid she wouldn't have me, Harry."

"Afraid? Have I taught you nothing Gagamin?"

"Nothing at all."

"Don't be smart, Rowly!" The stockman would not have it. "You're not a bad catch. Aside from your current legal difficulties. You should ask her. Take flowers—no, chocolates. Take chocolates! And get down on one knee. I'm pretty sure that's what Wil did."

Rowland laughed.

"I'm serious, Rowly," Simpson persisted. "What are you waiting for?"

"Ed's not…" Rowland struggled to explain.

Clyde maintained a sympathetic silence, but Milton decided to help. "Ed's a complicated girl, Harry," he said. "She's not the marrying kind."

"But if Rowly told her—"

"It wouldn't end well, believe you me! I've known her since we were knee-high." Milton sighed, beckoning Simpson to lean closer, as he lowered his voice. "Ed's mother was a Dickensian kind of mad. Raised Ed to never belong to a man."

"But surely she can see…"

Milton shrugged. "Perhaps we're all products of our parents regrets. Ed won't settle down, Harry. Over the years, all the blokes daft enough to propose simply disappeared."

"What happened to them?" Simpson asked sceptically.

"Don't know. Some of them were barely more than boys—poor souls. Just know we never saw them again."

Rowland smiled. "I'm sure she didn't devour them, Harry."

"I wouldn't count on that," Milton muttered.

In an attempt to deflect the discussion, Rowland told Simpson about his and Milton's stint at Long Bay, and his rather elucidating conversation with Wilfred.

Simpson cursed, standing up. "You didn't shoot him? It wasn't you?" he said, incredulous. "Bloody oath!"

"You thought it was me, too?" Rowland groaned.

"Why do you reckon I threw the gun into the dam?"

Milton glanced at Clyde.

"I didn't know that you had, Harry. What were you doing at the house?"

"Wil sent one of the Kendall boys to fetch me—I got there just as Wil's mate left."

"What mate?"

"Some chap he was meeting with."

"Menzies—he was at the house?"

"Don't know his name, Rowly. Wil didn't exactly introduce me." Simpson rubbed the stubble on his jaw. "Wil told me what had happened, well, what he thought had happened. He gave me the gun, a silver candlestick and some other odds and ends to make it look like a robbery, and told me to get rid of the lot."

"And you threw it into the dam?" Milton asked.

"Yes. That dam's never run dry so I thought it would be safe at the bottom of it." Simpson leaned on the verandah rail, his shoulder up against Rowland's. "I'm sorry, Gagamin. We should have known you'd never…"

"Don't be too sorry, Harry," Rowland said. "I thought about it, I just didn't get the chance."

Simpson sighed. "You might need a better defence than that, mate."

"When Rowly was arrested," Milton asked carefully. "You said you were sorry. Why?"

Simpson glanced at Rowland. "That wasn't anything to do with the arrest," he said. "I was sorry I'd upset Mrs. Sinclair, is all. I know she isn't well anymore."

Rowland stared out towards the homestead. "She's forgotten me completely, but you, she remembers, even after all these years."

"As I said, Rowly," Simpson replied quietly. "I'm sorry."

Rowland found his brother in the library. Wilfred studied him disapprovingly as he poured them both a drink. "You decided to assist Miss Higgins, then?" he said, nodding disdainfully at the smears of clay and dirt on his brother's suit. "I suppose Kate's pond has been replaced with some monstrosity made of mud and sticks."

Rowland grinned. "No, your clay has been safely returned to the ignominy of being pond lining."

Wilfred shook his head, exasperated.

"Wil... I was just talking to Harry about the night Father died."

Wilfred looked up sharply.

"The chap you were meeting that night... Menzies. You brought him back here?"

Wilfred nodded. "Yes, that turned out to be rather a mistake."

"He was a business associate then?"

Wilfred said nothing for a moment. He stood up and closed the library door. "Bob Menzies and I were, at the time, vying for the hand of the same young woman."

Rowland choked on his gin. "What! Really?"

"We had both been pursuing a Melbourne girl—Miss Pattie Leckie—with some vigour. For pity's sake Rowly, stop looking so stunned! Did you suppose I was in a monastery before I married Kate?"

"No, I just didn't expect... Sorry, go on."

"Miss Leckie had at that stage accepted neither of us."

Rowland tried to follow. "So why exactly were you meeting with your rival for the young lady's affections?"

"To decide the question of Miss Leckie."

"I beg your pardon?"

"We met to resolve the issue of Miss Leckie's hand. Obviously we couldn't both prevail."

"You're not serious," Rowland said unable to mask his astonishment.

Wilfred rolled his eyes. "It was 1920, Rowly. We'd moved past pistols at dawn."

"So I assume you resolved to stand aside."

"It became clear that Mr. Menzies was much more committed to the proposition than I. He was desperate for Miss Leckie to accept him."

"And you conceded—just like that?" Rowland pressed, finding it difficult to believe his brother had walked away so easily.

"It was more of a negotiation," Wilfred said carefully. "I had business priorities, and Menzies felt his only chance lay with me stepping aside gracefully."

"Why?"

"Well, aside from the obvious, Bob Menzies didn't serve." Wilfred's tone made his disapproval clear. "He assumed I'd use the D.S.O. to unfair advantage, had some notion that Miss Leckie would be won with war medals."

"And what did he offer you in this negotiation?"

Wilfred scowled. "Not a great deal, if truth be told. He begged. It was bloody awkward. Embarrassing for all concerned."

"I see." Rowland tried not to smile. "So why did you bring him here?"

"He was so flaming grateful he insisted on dropping me back. I felt obliged to invite him in for a drink. We came in through the conservatory." Wilfred frowned, sipping his whisky sullenly. "Mrs. Kendall called me aside. She was in rather a state. I told Menzies to make himself comfortable in the drawing room, and went to Father's study."

"Harry saw him leave much later," Rowland said, "after Father had been shot. He must have been in the drawing room for hours."

Wilfred shrugged. "I'm not sure why he stayed, Rowly. To be honest, I forgot about him entirely." He swirled the whisky in his glass. "When I came back down, he was still there. God knows what he heard, or what he was doing. I apologised, he said he understood, I poured him another drink and then we heard the gunshot."

"He was with you when Father was shot? My God, Wil, why didn't you tell the police?"

Wilfred frowned. "I left him in the drawing room whilst I went to the study. I saw you... thought it was you... I was worried that Bob might have seen you too. I just wanted to get him out of there."

"And he was happy to simply go?"

"Bob Menzies was a barrister, Rowly. He was leading an important constitutional case before the High Court—his first, I believe. He couldn't be associated with any sort of scandal, however peripherally."

"And you've never spoken about it?" Rowland asked, not entirely unaware of the irony of the question.

"I was a guest at his wedding later that year. By that time the official version was that Father had been killed during a robbery by a person or persons unknown. He expressed his condolences. I congratulated him on his marriage."

"We should speak to him, Wil. Perhaps he saw something. At the very least he could alibi you."

Wilfred grimaced. "Menzies is the current Deputy Premier of Victoria, Rowly. And I very much doubt he'll want to be associated with scandal now any more than he did then." He pressed his fingers together pensively. "In any case, it's you who's been charged."

"Thus far," Rowland countered. He told his brother of the anonymous informant who insisted that it was Wilfred Sinclair that the police should be charging. "The only reason the police are not taking it seriously is that I was clearly not disinherited."

"Clearly."

"But they may yet come back to the theory, Wil."

"Let's not get ahead of ourselves, Rowly." Wilfred Sinclair's eyes darkened. "Did Detective Delaney have any idea who this informant was?"

"No, he just assumed it was some disgruntled business associate of yours."

Wilfred sighed. "I'll telephone Bob Menzies. To be honest, I'm now rather curious as to what he was doing all evening."

Rowland stood to leave. "I'd better wash up." He stopped, somehow compelled to ask. "If you'd had a rival for Kate's hand, would you have—"

"Negotiated?" Wilfred looked hard at him over the top of his spectacles. The barest hint of a smile played about his lips. "No. For Katie, it was always pistols at dawn."

Rowland nodded. "That's what I thought."

"Rowly," Wilfred said as his brother reached for the door handle, "I've not mentioned Miss Leckie to Kate."

"I see."

"Be a good chap and keep this conversation strictly between you and me."

"Menzies can alibi you, Wil."

"We'll deal with that if it becomes necessary. Right now I want nothing else to upset my wife, so let this be on the square."

26

SYDNEY WOOL SALES

———◆———

Prices Again Firmer

SYDNEY, Tuesday

Prices showed a farther hardening tendency on yesterday's improved rates at the wool sale today. The market was very animated, competition being well distributed. The buying on German account was again a prominent feature.

Greasy merino fleece sold to 35d. for five bales from Rylstone, and five bales from Yass. The offerings totalled 11,482 bales, of which 11,386 were sold at auction, while an additional 1296 were disposed of privately.

The Canberra Times, 10 January 1934

Henry Sinclair's study had been unused since the night he died nearly fourteen years before. Wilfred had bypassed his father's throne room, for a study nearer the library and further from Henry's shadow. The oak-panelled chamber was dusted weekly, but otherwise it remained untouched. Until now, Rowland had not set foot in it since the shooting. He drew the drapes allowing in the soft light of a wet summer's day.

Standing before his father's desk again felt strange. The perspective was different—he was taller now. The wall behind the desk was bare. It had once held the portrait of Henry which currently hung in the drawing room at *Woodlands*.

Rowland exhaled slowly. He was tense, there was an odd metallic taste in his mouth. He was suddenly glad that Wilfred would not hear of Communists rifling through their father's papers, and had insisted that any search be conducted without them.

The study was spacious, incorporating its own library and a sitting area where Henry would occasionally entertain business associates, and which was large enough to allow his manager to swing a leather strap against his son. The walls were decorated with photographs of prize-winning rams and the bookshelves burdened with trophies and ribbons from the Royal Easter Show. An inscribed five iron, which had been presented to Henry Sinclair by the Royal Sydney Golf Club, was mounted on the far wall beside various other commemorations of the gentleman's civic philanthropy.

Rowland loosened his tie. He didn't like being here, even now with his father long dead. As much as he tried to forget it, to never think of it, this part of his memory was still too clear.

He composed himself and began to go through the desk, not entirely sure what he expected to find.

In the beginning he searched carefully, putting everything back as it had been. But then he found his father's bible in the second drawer and something snapped. Cursing Henry Sinclair, Rowland pulled the drawer out and upturned it unceremoniously on the desk. He rummaged through the contents, discarding documents and calling cards onto the floor. He upended the next drawer, and the next, until the desk was buried in papers, massive ledgers and old inkwells.

The diary was in the bottom drawer, leather bound, embossed with the Sinclair crest.

Rowland flicked through to the Monday his father had died. Several meetings were entered in Henry's florid hand, including a large block of time marked simply "Rowland".

He stared at the page, his chest tightening. His father had made an appointment for him. Knowing what he intended to do to his son, Henry Sinclair had scheduled enough time to do the job properly.

Rowland slammed the diary shut and flung it across the room. For several minutes he could do nothing but seethe and swear. He racked his brain for some forgotten recollection. Was there something from that evening he'd forgotten, some clue as to who else was in the house? Parts of that night seemed vivid whilst others were confused. He was no longer sure how accurate his memories were.

He moved to the door and, turning back, determined where exactly he'd seen his father's body, and in what position. The Axminster carpet had been removed so there was no longer any indication that a man had bled and died on that spot. Assuming Wilfred had not moved the body, it seemed to him that the murderer must have been quite close to the door to the adjoining hallway when he fired the fatal shot. Henry Sinclair had died in front of the desk not behind it. Did that mean he was stepping forward to greet his attacker?

Rowland retrieved the diary from the floor, and, taking a steadying breath, turned back to the relevant page. The entries made for earlier the day Henry died were recorded in more detail. Rowland's eye caught on a notation for midday. "Mullins. Execution."

The door squeaked open and Ernest Sinclair peered timidly in. He stared agog at the papers and books strewn about the study, the empty drawers stacked on the desk in a precarious tower.

"Hello Ernie—what are you doing here?"

"I heard thumping. I thought it was the ghost."

"The ghost?"

Ernest walked in, Lenin padding contentedly behind him. "Nobody's allowed in this room, Uncle Rowly," he said gravely. He beckoned Rowland down and whispered. "Someone died in here. It's haunted."

"Haunted? Who told you that, mate?"

"It is, Uncle Rowly. Sometimes you can hear someone crying in here."

Rowland hesitated, unsure what to say. "There's no such thing as ghosts, Ernie."

"Yes there is!" Ernest declared. "I've heard it." He took his uncle's hand. "I'm not scared, though."

"Does your father know about this ghost?"

"Daddy said I was never to go in here."

"Because of the ghost?"

"I suppose."

"Perhaps we should talk to him," Rowland said, deciding that it was really up to Wilfred how much he told his son. He reached up with his free hand and took the golf club from its mounting.

"He might be cross," Ernest warned. "Nobody's allowed in this room."

Maintenance work in the holding yards at Wainwright's came to a momentary stop when the yellow Mercedes pulled up. Three men alighted. Most of the workers recognised the giant indigenous man with blue eyes. The man who slipped out from behind the steering wheel was a stranger, but looked like he may easily have been one of Simpson's stockmen. It was the third man who caused them to stop and look again.

For his part, Milton Isaacs considered the green velvet jacket and striped waistcoat a smart and fetching ensemble given a rural flair by the red kerchief he wore in place of his usual cravat.

Simpson led them up the steps onto the loading-stage and into the shearing shed just as the rain began. Though neither as large nor as well-equipped as *Oaklea*, Wainwright's still boasted a substantial shed of some twelve stands. Of course, the shearing was done, and the shed was currently empty, but for a single man undertaking maintenance on the mechanised stands and holding pens.

John Barrett looked up as the men from *Oaklea* came into his shed. Harry Simpson nodded. "John. How would you be?"

Barrett shook his hand. "Fit as a Mallee bull, Harry. Heard you've had a bit of strife at *Oaklea*."

"Could say that." Simpson introduced Milton Isaacs and Clyde Watson Jones, explaining that they were Rowland's friends from the city.

Barrett glanced at Milton and nodded as if that explained a few things.

Then Simpson and Barrett talked about the weather for a while.

Clyde and Milton waited, allowing Simpson to lead them through whatever parochial protocol was necessary. Finally Simpson raised the matter for which they'd come. "You know Charlie Hayden's body was found at *Emoh Ruo*."

Barrett sighed. "I heard. Bad business, but can't say I'm mourning. Been expecting the police to come talk to me."

"Why?"

"'Cos I didn't like the bugger… after that day in the shed. Wasn't no secret."

"What exactly happened, Mr. Barrett?" Clyde ventured. "We've heard Hayden's side of it." Perhaps Barrett would not think to be defensive if they asked about Charles Hayden instead.

"What's it to you?" Barrett was suspicious nevertheless.

"The police are looking at Rowly for it," Clyde replied, carefully omitting the fact that Rowland had already been arrested and charged.

Barrett frowned. "I don't know if what I could tell you would help him." He leant back against the stall and, taking out a tin of tobacco and some papers, rolled a cigarette. "The boy was back on holidays from that posh school they sent him to. Half me men had enlisted and we were trying to get the clip in. Rowland seemed a bit lost, used to watch. He had nothing better to do, I suppose." Barrett shrugged. "He was a good lad, quiet. Didn't try to throw his weight around like some of the graziers' boys do. We'd stopped for smoko, and I thought I'd teach him to shear, just for a lark. The kid surprised me—he might have made a shearer. Hayden told us to get back to work, I told him to bugger off. We still had fifteen minutes. He strode back with Mr. Sinclair in tow. Bloody coward!"

Barrett cupped his hands, lit up and drew deeply. He coughed and picked a few moist strands of tobacco from his cigarette. "Old Mr. Sinclair sacked me right out. Got Hayden to flog the boy then and there so that none of the other blokes would ever think 'bout talking to the boss's son again... for his sake, if not theirs." He shook his head. "Poor bloody kid. That bastard made sure the boy was too bloomin' humiliated to ever show his face in the shed again. There were a few of us who talked about killing Hayden then."

"What about Mr. Sinclair?"

"He was a mean, black-hearted mongrel. But what can you do? He was the boy's father. If he hadn't died I reckon he might have killed the kid in the end."

"Look, John," Simpson said. "Rowly doesn't want the police to even talk to you if it isn't necessary."

"I appreciate that."

"But we still need to know everything you can remember."

Barrett looked at Simpson. "Yeah, I can see what you're saying." He drew again on his cigarette. "I was in Sydney at the wool sales with Mr. Wainwright when we heard about Mr. Sinclair. We came back straight away."

"Why?"

"Mr. Wainwright was a mate of Mr. Wilfred Sinclair's. Had no time for the old man—that's why he was willing to give me a job, I suppose—but he thought he should show his respects."

"What about Hayden?" Milton asked.

"If I'd wanted to kill Hayden I'd have done it fifteen years ago. I heard he was back… bragging that he was finally evening the score, being compensated for what Wilfred Sinclair did to him."

"Compensated? How?"

"Dunno. He was shouting rounds at the *Commercial*. Certainly wasn't skint."

"Do you have any idea as to who might have wanted to kill him, Mr. Barrett?" Clyde asked.

Barrett dropped the stub of his cigarette and crushed it under his heel. "Look, not many people liked Hayden. He was a downright bully, a coward, but he picked his targets. You worked for him until Wilfred Sinclair sacked him, Harry—did he give you any grief?"

"No," Simpson admitted. "He stayed out of my way. I had no idea of what the boss was using him to do."

Barrett nodded. "He didn't take on any bloke who could stand up to him." The shearer folded his arms. "I wish I could help you. I liked the kid… used to think he had it made… and then that day in the shed." Barrett cursed. "My old man used to clip me round the ear too, and I'd come out and kick the dog. But I never saw Rowland do anything like that."

"No," Simpson said. "Rowly likes dogs."

Barrett snorted, shoving Simpson good-naturedly.

They took their leave of John Barrett then and sprinted through the rain, back to the Mercedes. Clyde started the engine, noting with not a small measure of trepidation that the dirt road was quickly turning to mud in the deluge. He drove slowly because visibility was poor.

"So what do you think?" Milton asked from the back seat.

"Rowly's right, Barrett didn't shoot anybody," Clyde replied, craning his head out of the window to see more clearly.

"No, I know that. I meant what he said about Hayden having money."

"What do you mean?" Simpson asked.

"Well, when Hayden first emerged we thought it odd that he should appear just when the gun was found. I'm starting to suspect we were right. It's more than coincidence."

Clyde nodded. "You may have a point. Delaney's been telling us from the beginning that the police have an anonymous informant."

"So who's behind this?" Simpson looked back at Milton.

"Do you suppose it might be Campbell and his Boo Guard?" Milton posed.

"Maybe," Clyde kept his eyes glued to what little road he could see. "Campbell's a solicitor. He'd certainly know how to stir up this kind of trouble. He'd probably also know how to access the original records on Henry's murder."

Milton frowned. "But how would he even know to look?"

"It was widely reported in the newspapers when it happened, as a burglary-cum-murder of course," Simpson informed them. "Lot of features on Wil taking over the reins of the Sinclair empire."

"So perhaps we're talking about Wilfred's enemies, not Rowly's," Milton suggested.

"But they're pointing at Rowly for murder, not Wil."

"Did you blokes see anybody the night Lenin was shot?" Milton asked suddenly.

"No. Why?"

"Just think we let that go too easily. Someone might have been trying to shoot Rowly."

"Wil's convinced it was just some fool shooting rabbits." Simpson's misgivings were apparent in his voice.

"Watch it, Clyde!" Milton warned as the Mercedes slid sideways in the mud.

Clyde reacted quickly, using the steering to bring the car back to the road and under control. "I worked in a gang of shearers once," he muttered, clearly brooding over what Barrett had described. "They were tough blokes—pretty bloody hard to shock, I'd say. God, poor Rowly. How could you do that to your own boy?"

"When Aubrey died, I gather the boss thought the Good Lord took him as atonement," Simpson said.

"Atonement for what exactly?"

Simpson raised his thick dark brow. "Past indiscretions. Aubrey and I were about the same age." He frowned thoughtfully. "As boys, we were all wary of the boss's walking cane," he confessed. "But I think the bible reading business must've started after Aubrey died. Perhaps he was flogging himself as much as Rowly."

"I dunno, Harry. It sounds to me like Henry Sinclair was just a mean, sadistic mongrel—what the hell?"

The car jolted as it collected a rut in the road.

Clyde swore. The wheels began to spin. He stopped the Mercedes and put it into reverse, but the back wheels didn't have traction. It seemed they were bogged. He cursed again.

Simpson turned towards Milton. "Looks like you and I are pushing, mate."

"No point in this rain," Clyde said. "We're stuck. We'll just have to wait till the rain stops and then chock the ruts with something."

Wilfred was on the back verandah with one of his managers. They spoke loudly over the pounding of the rain upon the tin roof as they discussed wool prices which had apparently recovered to record levels. The *Oaklea* bales were already in Sydney, safely stored at the Goldsborough Mort Woolstore, ready for auction whenever Wilfred gave the word. Despite the extraordinary prices, Wilfred was holding back most of the *Oaklea* clip, convinced the market would climb even further.

Ernest left Rowland's side and stood by his father, listening intently with his hands clasped behind his back. Rowland had no doubt that his nephew already knew far more than he did about wool. There was a solemn perspicacity about Ernest that more than anything else identified him as Wilfred's son.

Rowland, on the other hand, had difficulty even feigning interest in the finer points of wool classing, let alone breeding programmes. Generally, he just signed whatever Wilfred put in front of him, repaying his brother's commitment to expanding the Sinclair fortune by not interfering. Every now and then, Wilfred felt the need to drag him to a meeting or have him appointed to some board or sub-committee, but they both knew their roles.

The conversation moved from the wool clip to the weather, which had turned rather dramatically. Fortunately, the last of the cereal harvest was in and so the deluges of the past day would cause the property very little trouble. In time the manager tipped his hat and wished them all a good night.

Wilfred ruffled his son's hair. "And what have you two been up to?"

Ernest clammed up, clasping his hands over his mouth.

Rowland smiled. Clearly the boy was not a poker player.

Wilfred glanced at the presentation club in Rowland's hand. His brow arched. "What do you want with that?" he asked.

"I'm going to work on my chip shot."

Wilfred started to say something and then elected to stop. "I take it you were in Father's study?" he said instead.

Rowland nodded. "Yes."

"Did you go in?" Wilfred asked his son.

"Only to tell Uncle Rowly that he wasn't allowed in there." Ernest glanced nervously at Rowland. "Uncle Rowly didn't make the mess—it was like that when he got there."

"Just as well," Wilfred said, allowing Ernest's clumsy attempt to cover up for his uncle to pass without comment. "Did you find anything?" he asked, turning to Rowland.

"Perhaps… but Ernie told me something much more interesting."

On cue, Ernest told his father about the ghost.

Wilfred listened grimly. "I expect we should have a chat, Ernie. You have a few things backwards, old chap."

"Oh." Ernest's face fell. "So there's no ghost?"

"I very much doubt it."

Rowland leaned against a verandah post, listening. He was more than a little intrigued as to how his brother would handle Ernest's guileless curiosity.

Wilfred invited his son to sit, and took the squatters' chair opposite. "Your grandfather Sinclair died in that room, Ernie."

"When?"

"A long time ago, son. Before you were born. We don't talk about it because it upsets your grandmother."

"Doesn't it upset you?"

"Of course, but I'm a man. So are you. It's important that we are considerate of the ladies."

"Would Grandma cry if we talked about it?"

"Possibly."

"She doesn't cry when we talk about Uncle Aubrey, and he died. She thinks he's Uncle Rowly."

Wilfred sighed. "Your uncles look very much alike so your grandmother gets mixed up sometimes."

"Why don't you tell her?"

"Tell her what?"

"Which one's which."

Rowland couldn't help but smile as Wilfred began to look somewhat flustered.

"It's more complicated than that, Ernie, you'll understand when you're older."

"Grandma's older, and she's all mixed up."

"Now you're being cheeky, young man," Wilfred said sternly.

"Mr. Sinclair, excuse me, sir." Jack Templeton interrupted them, appearing quite suddenly from the deluge. He removed his hat and wiped the water from his eyes with muddy hands. "Miss Walling sent me to tell you, sir, that the rain is causing problems. We're just going to dig a trench to divert the overflow and minimise the damage until this is over."

"Yes, very good, Templeton. Carry on."

Templeton twisted his hat, shifting uncomfortably. "I'm afraid Miss Walling is having a few difficulties with Mr. McNair. He seems quite agitated, sir."

"McNair? What the dickens is he bellyaching about now?"

"I'm afraid, sir, that we haven't been able to work that out."

Rowland laughed. McNair, Wilfred's permanent gardener, had a particular mumbling manner of speaking which seemed to render only the random profanity comprehensible. Wilfred was the only person who understood the man.

Wilfred stood. "I best go out with you. If you'll wait here, I'll fetch a raincoat."

"Can I come too, Mr. Templeton?" Ernest asked, once his father had stepped inside.

Templeton squatted to speak with the boy face to face. "No, you'd best stop here in the dry like a good boy." He ruffled Ernest's hair. "When the rain stops, Vic and I will hang a swing for you in that elm tree, if you like."

27

YASS RIVER RISING

———◆———

The Yass River was running high at 6 p.m. last night, but had not reached dangerous proportions. However, very heavy rain commenced to fall shortly after 8 o'clock, and it was feared that a sudden rise was imminent.

Campers on the river bank have all shifted to higher ground, and it is thought that sufficient warning has been given to enable stock and property to be safeguarded.

The Canberra Times, 8 January 1934

It was quite late in the day when Milton arrived back at *Oaklea*. He was dripping, muddy and his green velvet jacket had clearly seen better days.

"Oh, Mr. Isaacs! What in heaven's name are you doing out in this rain?" Mrs. Kendall exclaimed as she opened the door.

"I drew the short straw, I'm afraid."

"Milt!" Edna joined the housekeeper in the vestibule. "Where have you been?"

"We got bogged," Milton said, stopping on the verandah. He removed his sodden jacket, wringing the water from the sleeves and muttering. "Thought we'd wait for the rain to stop, but it doesn't seem inclined to break any time soon."

"For goodness' sake, Mr. Isaacs, come in before you catch your death," Mrs. Kendall ordered.

Milton paused to shake his head like a wet dog, before crossing the threshold. "Harry Simpson said I should tell Mr. Sinclair to send one of his Caterpillars for them."

"Caterpillar?" Edna asked.

"It's a tractor," Rowland said from the hallway. "Good Lord, how long have you been stuck?"

"We gave up on the rain letting up an hour ago and they sent me for help."

"I'll drive out and get them," Rowland said, grabbing his hat from the hallstand.

"I'm afraid we took your car, Rowly."

"Oh." The alarm was evident on Rowland's face. "We'd better organise that Caterpillar and some tow chains then."

The available Caterpillar was stored in the same shed on *Emoh Ruo* in which the *Rule Britannia* was housed. It was, as luck would have it, not far from where the yellow Mercedes had become hopelessly bogged.

Jack Templeton volunteered to undertake the rescue. Wilfred sent the gardener out to collect the tractor on horseback, to avoid bogging another car, dismissing out of hand any notion that Rowland accompany him.

"I'm sure Templeton can manage to pull that Fritz monstrosity out on his own," he muttered.

Reluctantly Rowland conceded, giving Templeton instructions on where and how to attach the tow chain.

"Don't you worry, Mr. Sinclair," Templeton said as he set off in the rain yet again. "I'll be real gentle with her."

Wilfred snorted. He'd never quite reconciled his brother's insistence on keeping the German automobile. "Just let the man do his job," he growled. "Templeton's a good hand. I'm thinking about keeping him on once Miss Walling has finished up."

"Won't she need him?"

"Apparently he and the other one—Bates—are just filling in for one of her usual contractors. They asked me if I'd consider giving them jobs as gardeners. I don't need two, but I'm inclined to take Templeton on."

"What about McNair?" Rowland asked. He imagined the taciturn gardener might have something to say on the subject.

Wilfred sighed. "I'll talk to him. He could doubtless use some more help about the place. These blasted gardens will take some upkeep and I'm afraid poor old McNair just wants to plant pumpkins."

Rowland was waiting in the garage when Clyde brought in the Mercedes. Edna had come out to keep him company while Milton was recovering with a generous balloon of Wilfred's finest brandy. Harry Simpson had, of course, been dropped off at his cottage and Templeton was returning the Caterpillar and picking up his horse.

Clyde chuckled as Rowland fussed over the mud-splattered automobile. "She's fine, Rowly, just a bit wet."

Rowland patted the grille. "She does seem to have survived the indignity of it all."

"Perhaps you could draw her a hot bath!" Edna suggested, rolling her eyes. "It might calm her nerves."

"I'm glad you came out to check on her, actually," Clyde said as Rowland stood, satisfied his beloved car was none the worse for the experience. "I wanted to talk to you."

"How did you fair with John Barrett?" Rowland asked.

Clyde recounted the conversation. "It got us thinking again that perhaps Charlie Hayden appearing out of the blue wasn't just an inconvenient coincidence."

"You believe someone paid him to come back?"

"It makes sense, Rowly. Harry and I went over it while we were waiting for help to arrive."

"Harry believes there's someone behind all this too?" Rowland asked.

Clyde nodded. "What's more, Rowly, we don't think you should dismiss the fact that someone shot at you. It may not have been an accident."

Rowland leaned back on the bonnet of his car, his arms folded, and laughed ruefully. "That. No, it wasn't an accident."

"You know who shot Lenin?" Edna asked, aghast.

"As Clyde said, they were shooting at me—got Len by mistake. At first I couldn't for the life of me understand why Wil was so adamant it was some near-sighted rabbit hunter. I worked it out eventually."

"Not Wil?" Edna stepped back, appalled.

"No, of course not. Wil wouldn't have missed, for one thing. It was Lucy Bennett."

"Lucy Bennett shot at you?"

"I'm fairly sure. The colonel probably gave her a pistol to fend off Communists. She has a car, she knew I'd be walking back and she was rather vexed with me."

"But why would Wilfred want to—"

"Lucy is his wife's dearest friend. I expect Kate appealed to Wil on Lucy's behalf."

"And Wilfred... both of you... are willing to let it go at that?" Clyde joined Edna in her horror.

Rowland replied calmly. "I wasn't exactly thrilled about it, but it appears shooting a dog is not actually a crime in New South Wales. I don't know that making a fuss would have achieved anything."

"She tried to kill you!" It was hard to tell if Edna was angrier with Lucy Bennett or Rowland.

He grimaced. "Perhaps Miss Bennett just wished to let me know she was displeased. She was rather distraught."

"Before or after she tried to shoot you?"

Rowland smiled apologetically. "I'm convinced she's not dangerous. I expect Miss Bennett gave herself rather more of a shock than she did me."

"So you said nothing?"

"All things considered, it seemed like letting it go was the decent thing to do. I only bring it up so you know it's got nothing to do with the murders."

Silence.

Then Clyde sighed heavily, and pointed sternly at Rowland. "You, mate," he said, glancing sideways at Edna, "would be well advised to stop associating with women who shoot at you. The next one might not miss!"

The unrelenting rain ensured they were more or less confined to barracks for the next few days. It might not have been such an issue if the mix of guests at *Oaklea* were not so volatile. Arthur Sinclair made it clear that he believed his cousin Rowland's friends had no business imposing on the family yet again. He was polite, but hostile nonetheless, expressing his antipathy within the bounds of civility.

Clyde ignored him, while Milton seemed to find it amusing. Only Edna, for whom he reserved his most obviously contemptuous barbs, faltered occasionally. Inevitably Rowland exploded.

He invited Arthur to step outside. The rain, of course, meant they only got as far as the verandah.

"You would do well to remember, Arthur, that you are as much a guest here as my friends!"

"You think so, do you, Cousin Rowland?" Arthur spat. "What the Sinclairs now have was built by my father as much as yours."

"Mr. Watson Jones, Mr. Isaacs and Miss Higgins are here on my invitation and Kate's. They are here to help me establish what happened the night Father was killed."

"Don't be bloody daft, Rowland! Anyone can see you're being offered up for the greater good. You're finally going to do your part for this family!"

"What?"

Arthur regarded him with a kind of derisive pity. "Wilfred has been speaking to doctors. I suspect he's going to keep you out of prison by having you committed."

"That's preposterous!"

Arthur's expression softened. He grabbed Rowland's elbow and lowered his voice. "Look, Rowly, listen to me. Believe it or not, I am your friend, your ally. Twenty years ago, I was you—headstrong, irresponsible and moving with a bad crowd. I wouldn't listen to anyone until it was too late."

Rowland pulled away.

"Sinclair men have a common failing. We want to control our sons and brothers. Your father tried to do so, my father tried to do so and Wilfred is no different. If you don't fall into line, believe me, Wilfred will do something drastic!"

"You're an idiot, Arthur, and you don't know Wil at all!"

Arthur's smile was smug. "Wilfred and I have been working closely for months, Rowland. He's come to confide in me, and I know how he feels about having to support his feckless wastrel of a brother and the Communist scum with whom he associates!"

"I'm not sure why you believe it's any of your business, but Wilfred does not support me."

"You'll find he does, and all your friends. As for Miss Higgins—"

Rowland stopped him. "Is there any particular reason you're trying to get me to beat the hell out of you, Arthur?" The question was not rhetorical. It seemed to Rowland that his cousin was intentionally trying to goad him.

"For pity's sake, man, I'm trying to help you. Hasn't it occurred to you that there's a reason Wil's keeping your gold-digging—"

Rowland grabbed Arthur, ready to make good his threat.

"Rowly!" Wilfred stepped out on to the verandah and regarded the confrontation incredulously. "What on earth is going on here? Every time I turn around you're trying to thump Arthur. You're a grown man, for God's sake!"

For a fleeting moment Rowland thought about hitting his cousin anyway, but, in the end, he released him.

Arthur straightened his tie.

"Well?" Wilfred demanded.

Arthur cleared his throat and smoothed down his lapel. He sniffed. "You know, Wilfred, I think it might be best if I go to Sydney for a few days. Lucy will be pleased, I'm sure, and I can continue to do what I can for Rowland's defence."

Rowland caught himself before he responded in a manner quite ungracious.

Wilfred nodded. "Perhaps that wouldn't be such a bad idea. I suspect we're all getting a little short-tempered in the circumstances."

"Well then, I best telephone Lucy—let her know I'm coming." He looked at Rowland and put his hand out. "I apologise if I offended you, old chap. I sometimes forget that you've grown up. Shall we say no hard feelings?"

Rowland stared at his cousin's hand, still fuming. Reluctantly, because there was no way he could refuse without seeming churlish, he accepted the handshake. Wordlessly, he met Arthur's eyes. In them, he could see no sign of retreat.

Arthur took the train back to Sydney that afternoon. Elisabeth Sinclair was clearly saddened to see him depart, though he did so with promises that his absence would not be long. She clung to Rowland as she waved away the Rolls Royce. "I was rather getting used to having all my boys home again," she said, dabbing her eyes with a lace-edged handkerchief. "You mustn't leave me again, Aubrey. They'll simply have to carry on this dreadful war without you."

"Fortunately, Mother, the war's over," Rowland said quietly.

"So soon?" Elisabeth Sinclair sighed. "Well, it's just as well. Perhaps Arthur will be home shortly then. He looked so handsome in his uniform."

Rowland frowned. Arthur, of course, had not been wearing a uniform of any sort. To date, it was only her youngest son that his mother saw differently, incorrectly. The development worried him.

While Wilfred accompanied his cousin to the station, Rowland and his friends sat in the drawing room, drinking tea and playing euchre with Kate, while Ernest tore about pretending to be a plane. The conversation was relaxed and inconsequential. Kate's condition, her refined disposition and her allegiance to Lucy Bennett made it difficult to discuss anything frankly in her presence.

Elisabeth Sinclair sat on the settee with a book in her lap. Rowland watched the way she clutched the volume when her eyes became vague and frightened. The book gave her something to hold onto, as she tried to remember where she was and what she was doing.

He left the card game and sat beside her. She took his hand and held it silently for a while. He let her be as he brooded over his exchange with Arthur. His cousin's conviction that Wilfred was supporting him was perplexing. Of course Wilfred had managed and expanded his brother's assets with the greater Sinclair fortune, but…

Elisabeth Sinclair squeezed his hand. "You mustn't make your father angry, darling. You must be as good as you can be."

Rowland turned to her, startled. His mother would say those precise words to him when he was a child. Before she forgot who he was.

He looked into her eyes, searching for some faint spark of recognition.

"Aubrey?" she said.

But he saw her hesitate. "No Mother, it's Rowland. I'm Rowland."

She gazed up into his face and laughed. "Don't be silly, Rowland died."

"No, he didn't. I'm Rowland."

"You're being cruel," she hissed, pulling away from him, her lips and hands trembling. "You're playing wicked tricks, Aubrey!"

"Mother, please."

Elisabeth grabbed his lapel, disintegrating, sobbing. "I know you're Aubrey! I know!"

Ernest stopped pretending he was an aeroplane and ran to his mother.

"Yes, of course," Rowland said as he tried desperately to soothe her. "I was being silly."

Clyde stood and took Ernest from Kate. "What say we play cricket on the verandah, mate?" he said quietly. "We'll let Milt bowl since he can't bat to save his life."

Kate smiled uneasily, gratefully, as they took her son away while Rowland tried in vain to calm his mother who was now both angry and distressed. She lashed out, suddenly unsure who he was altogether.

On the face of it, Rowland stayed composed. Edna grabbed Kate's hand. "Perhaps we should call for a doctor," she said.

"That's a good idea, Miss Higgins," Wilfred Sinclair stepped into the room, having just returned from the station. He stopped only a moment to assess the situation. "Katie, my dear, I think you'd best telephone Maguire—I believe he's not yet returned to Sydney." He spoke evenly, almost severely to Elisabeth. "Mother, perhaps it's time you had a rest."

Elisabeth turned to Wilfred in what looked like terror. "No, Aubrey needs me... we're reading!"

Rowland glanced at his brother. "Yes, we are. Why don't I read to you for a while, Mother?" Gently, he teased the book from her hands. She stopped fighting him and settled, confused and shaking, back into the settee. "Yes, yes... read to me, darling. Your father would read to me from the bible, you know. He was such a strong man, and so handsome."

Rowland read, his voice low and metered, betraying almost nothing of his own disappointment and sorrow. It seemed to comfort her.

By the time Maguire arrived, Elisabeth Sinclair had become almost listless. Rowland carried his mother to her room so that the surgeon could treat her in private. She released her grip on her *Aubrey* only as the Laudanum with which the surgeon treated her began to take effect.

Not entirely sure what to do next, Rowland joined the makeshift game of cricket on the verandah. Milton handed him the soft rubber ball with no mention of what had just happened. "You bowl, Rowly. We have a young Bradman on our hands."

And so they played a game designed to entertain Ernest while breaking no windows, but which also served to distract his uncle a little.

They stopped when Maguire walked out of the house with Wilfred. Rowland tossed the ball back to Milton and joined them.

Frederick Maguire shook his hand. "I'll leave your brother to relay the details, Rowland, but it would be best if you don't go in to see your mother right now. Your presence seems to cause her a great deal of conflict and distress. It may be that she's beginning to remember you as Rowland rather than Aubrey. But that, in itself, is, of course, associated with her still unresolved grief. Mrs. Sinclair is very fragile at present. In fact, I would suggest her condition is at the lowest ebb I've seen."

"Of course, I won't see her. Thank you."

Maguire took his leave, brusquely in his fashion, before opening a black umbrella to stride out to his awaiting motorcar.

Wilfred polished his glasses which had apparently fogged in the moisture. He regarded Rowland sombrely. "We'd best have a word, Rowly."

28

DUCHESS OF YORK'S COUSIN AS AUTHORESS

---◆---

Twelve-year-old Sarah Bowes-Lyon on 'THE ART OF HORSEMANSHIP'

(By *The Daily News*' WOMAN WRITER ABROAD)

AUSTRALIANS have a literary treat in store for in London a book has been published which is the essence of "joie de vivre." Miss Sarah Bowes-Lyon, aged 12 years, a second cousin of the Duchess of York, with her book entitled 'Horsemanship As It Is Today,' is likely to achieve world sales and eclipse even 'The Young Visitors' by Daisy Ashford...

The etiquette of hunting is expounded at length. "Always have a very good breakfast, as you will only have your sandwiches for lunch," writes Sarah. "For lunch, it is a good thing to have some ginger biscuits, etc., in as well as they do not crumble as much as sandwiches, and take a few bits of plain chocolate to eat for the hack home. You must always start early for the meet, so that you will not be late if you are delayed on the way. When you get there, go and find your pony, and don't forget your sandwich case! If your hostess asks you in, always go and have some coffee, it is rude not to. Always say 'Good Morning' to the Master, and then the Hunt Servants... Anyway, when you get home from hunting have a hot bath, go to bed, sleep tight, and may you dream of... fox-hunting!"

The Daily News, 3 January 1934

Wilfred led Rowland into his own study.

"Drink?"

"Anything but whisky."

Wilfred poured him a generous glass of sherry and kept the Scotch for himself.

"I'm sorry, Wil, that was my fault."

"Why?"

"I thought she remembered me for a moment. I pushed her. It was stupid, selfish…"

Wilfred sighed. "We'll talk about Mother directly, but that's not why I called you in here. I want you to tell me what exactly went on between you and Arthur."

"That's between Arthur and me, Wil."

Wilfred's eyes flashed. "Don't be difficult, Rowly. The two of you were shouting at each other on the verandah—I doubt it was particularly confidential. We haven't time for bloody airs and graces."

"I suspect he was just trying to provoke me, Wil."

"For pity's sake, you're not going to hurt my feelings!"

"Very well." Rowland was not in any mood to quarrel over Arthur. "Our dear cousin seems to have got the wrong end of several sticks." He recounted the conversation, trying to be as fair as animosity would allow.

Wilfred listened carefully without interrupting. When Rowland finished, he stood and retrieved several pages of documents from a cedar cabinet, and placed the sheaf before his brother.

"What is this?"

"Father's last will. He'd signed it the day he died."

Rowland remembered the entry in his father's diary: *Mullins— Execution.* So, Henry Sinclair had not been scheduling the summary murder of some business rival. Relieved, he read through the first interminable sentence with its multiple whereases, moreovers, and thenceforths. "What is it you wish me to see, Wil?"

"Turn to the next page, second paragraph."

Rowland read. He sat up, startled. "He disinherited me," he said, in stunned disbelief.

Wilfred came around the desk and took a chair next to Rowland's. "Father, as a matter of course, disinherited one or the other of us regularly. Poor Ray Mullins must have drafted and redrafted Father's will on a monthly basis. It just so happened that he died that night just after he'd cut you off. If you recall, later that evening, he was adamant he'd disinherit me."

"So this is what Arthur meant when he said you were *supporting* me and my friends."

"I am certainly *not* supporting your Communist hordes!" Wilfred took the document out of Rowland's hands. "Look, Rowly, if I'd had my way you would never have known about this. When Father died, I restructured all our assets into the family trust from which you receive your income. The accountants will talk you through all the mundane details anytime you want."

Rowland shook his head. "All this time I thought…" He stared at his brother. "All these years you've been demanding I throw my friends out of *Woodlands*. You could simply have…"

Wilfred's jaw tensed. "Father controlled us with pounds and shillings. You were too young to know, but it was how he kept Aubrey and me in line—who we saw, what we did, what we thought. I came back from the war only to have him order me about like some…" Wilfred sipped his Scotch. "Now, I sincerely hope that one day you will come to your senses about the way you live, but I am not your keeper, Rowly. I reserve the right to be outraged, appalled and utterly furious with you as the need arises but what you do with *Woodlands* is your affair and your affair alone."

Rowland said nothing, strangely shaken.

"You may also recall that you were the sole beneficiary of Uncle Rowland's personal estate, however dubiously it was derived," Wilfred continued, watching him closely. "And you didn't think twice about having it consolidated into the Sinclair Family Trust. Let me be clear, Rowly, I will not tolerate you feeling beholden to me in any way!"

Rowland's brow rose. "It might be too late for that."

"I do not wish to ever talk about this again, Rowly. As I said, I would have rather you never knew, but Arthur's bringing it up with you has raised an entirely different issue."

Rowland rubbed his face. "What issue?"

"Ray Mullins, as you know, passed away ten years ago. I was the only other person to know the contents of this will which has been kept here under lock and key. I didn't tell Arthur but he was here, under this roof, while we were both in England last year."

"So he's been digging through your files?" Rowland asked.

"More than that, Rowly," Wilfred said. "You mentioned that the police have an anonymous informant who insists you were disinherited?"

"Yes, that's what Delaney said. You suspect it's Arthur?"

Wilfred nodded. "I'm afraid so."

"But why would he—?"

Wilfred tapped the desk with his fingers distractedly. "Perhaps he is angrier than he reveals about his own circumstances, perhaps he wishes to punish us somehow or perhaps he genuinely believes I killed Father. It doesn't really matter."

"Wil," Rowland said, recalling what Hugh McIntosh had revealed. "Do you know that Arthur made some unfortunate investments last year?"

Wilfred's eyes narrowed. "No, I didn't. I may need to ask the accountants to check our books for irregularities. I'm afraid I might have been too trusting where Arthur was concerned. Clearly the man is a cowan."

"Exactly how much does the bastard know about our affairs?" Rowland asked.

"I don't know, Rowly."

Rowland told his brother about John Barrett's information. Wilfred's face became harder.

"Could Arthur have found out about Hayden?" Rowland asked. "Could he have tracked him down?"

"Quite possibly. Arthur's a solicitor, he'd most likely know how to find a man."

"How long have you suspected him, Wil?"

"Obviously not long enough. It was this business about you being disinherited. Only someone with intimate access to and knowledge of our records would know there was ever an issue."

"Does Arthur know you've—?"

"No, I'm reasonably confident he believes that I supported his going to Sydney to keep you from breaking his nose." Wilfred sighed. "My most pressing problem is how I'm going to tell Kate that Lucy will have to find herself yet another Sinclair."

Rowland grimaced. He didn't envy his brother that. "So what now, Wil?"

"I'll be in touch with the solicitors directly to inform them that our dear cousin Arthur is to have no further access or authority. And I'll telephone the Commissioner of Police to apprise him of the fact that his informant is none other than Arthur Sinclair who has a vested interest in the outcome of your case, though to be honest, I can't think what it is."

"Arthur doesn't want me convicted, Wil," Rowland replied as he

thought back to the confrontation with his cousin. "I'm certain it's *you* he wants held responsible." He thought of something then. "If you were convicted, then your inheritance of Father's estate would be reversed, correct?"

"Yes."

"And I was explicitly disinherited. To whom would the estate revert then?"

Wilfred stared at him for a moment. He swore. "Why the hell didn't I see it?"

"Steady on, I'm not sure I see it yet."

"The residual clause. In Father's will, if the gift fails, the estate reverts to his brothers, or, if they are deceased, their male progeny. It was a similar clause that saw our father inherit Arthur's father's estate."

"But Arthur was disinherited."

"By his father. It doesn't affect *our* father's will."

"And Arthur would know this?"

"He's a solicitor, Rowly. We can probably assume he's as underhanded, mean-spirited and amoral as the best of his profession!"

"Which means we have to be more concerned about proving your innocence than mine."

"Possibly not. The solicitors have already warned me that if you're convicted I could easily be prosecuted as an accessory after the fact."

"And would that preclude you from inheriting?"

Wilfred paused. "I don't know. I'll have to ask them." He sighed. "Now to the other matter at hand. Tell me what precipitated mother becoming so suddenly unwell."

Rowland frowned, confessing his reckless demands on his mother's memory. "I'm so sorry, Wil. For a moment I really thought she might remember me."

Wilfred removed his glasses and polished them vigorously as he studied his brother. "It probably wasn't you, Rowly. Mother is getting worse, more fragile and difficult to deal with. She's lashed out at the servants and even Kate on a couple of occasions now. I was consulting doctors about Mother, not you."

Rowland regarded his brother with both sympathy and horror. "God, Wil, you're not considering—?"

"A sanatorium? I don't know, Rowly. Perhaps engaging the services of a private nurse will suffice."

"What did the doctors say?"

"Nothing particularly useful." Wilfred regarded Rowland gravely. "Look, Rowly, the immediate issue is that your presence is upsetting Mother. Perhaps she is finally beginning to realise you're not Aubrey."

Rowland stared moodily at his drink.

Wilfred continued. "I thought it might be a good time for you to take a little sojourn."

Rowland looked up. "Where?"

"To Melbourne. Kew to be exact." Wilfred handed Rowland a sealed envelope. "A letter of introduction to The Honourable Robert Menzies, KC, with a reminder that he is unlikely to move into federal politics without my support."

"You want me to personally deliver a… threat?" Rowland asked. "Don't you think that's a trifle—"

"I want you to find out exactly what he was doing on the night of Father's death, in the time I left him unattended in the drawing room."

"Gilbey and Angel call in every second day, Wil. If they find I'm not here…"

"What if you take the plane? Could you fly there and back in twenty-four hours?"

"Yes, of course, if I could find a place to land *Doris*. I can't exactly park her in front of his house."

"Leave that to me."

Rowland opened the shed doors on *Emoh Ruo* half an hour after Gilbey and Angel left the property, having once again confirmed he had not fled. Clyde insisted on checking over the *Rule Britannia*, his caution justified by the discovery of an issue with the push rods.

"This might have brought down the aeroplane," Clyde grumbled as he attended to the problem which, fortunately, was relatively simple to remedy.

"We checked the push rods after I took her up last time," Rowland said, perplexed.

"Do you suppose someone's been tampering with the plane?" Clyde asked, wiping the grease off his hands.

Rowland shrugged. "It's more likely we missed something."

"Perhaps." Clyde's manner made it clear that he did not think it more likely at all.

Rowland climbed up onto the wing and pulled the extra cap and goggles from the cockpit. Though he had initially resisted involving his friend in the current escapade, Clyde had insisted. With Milton and Edna backing Clyde, Rowland had given in.

No one had come to see them off. Indeed, very few people knew they were going. Rowland had taken to his bed the day before, with what the helpful Maguire proclaimed was flu. Kate, in her delicate condition, was banned from that part of the house, as were the servants and the rest of the household. Rowland was purportedly being tended by a specialist nurse and Maguire himself. Edna and Milton, who might otherwise have been likely to risk contagion, were party to the ruse, and so did nothing to challenge or breach the quarantine.

When the detectives had arrived that morning, Rowland had spoken to them from his sick bed, coughing and spluttering in what was quite a reasonable impersonation of a man who was seriously unwell.

Clyde had left the house on the pretext of catching the train to Batlow via Cootamundra. Wilfred allowed him to take one of the farm vehicles. Rowland had been secreted on the payload.

And so to everyone whom the police might question, Rowland Sinclair lay ill in his bed while Clyde Watson Jones was visiting his mother.

They parked the Chevrolet Capital in the shed and taxied the *Rule Britannia* out into the paddock. The weather was fair, the sky clear and the winds ideal in both strength and direction. The Gipsy Moth took off into the nor'-easterly without incident and turned south for the hop to Melbourne with a refuelling stop at Wangaratta.

Finding *Eldonvale*, where Wilfred had arranged for them to land, was not difficult from the air. Both Rowland and Clyde had charted their route carefully, following the railway lines and then the Yarra River. The house was distinctive, boasting turrets and spires in the style of a European castle. A short runway had been cut into the natural bushland behind the tennis courts. *Rule Britannia* approached from the south, touching down surprisingly softly before slowing to a gentle stop.

"Hello, it's the cavalry," Clyde said as several riders on horseback charged towards them.

He and Rowland climbed out of the cockpit and dropped onto the tarred ground.

"Well, well, you must be young Rowly Sinclair!" A gentleman in hunting pinks slipped down from the lead horse to shake Rowland's hand. He spoke with a distinct highland brogue.

"Colonel Mouat?" Rowland regarded his brother's old friend and comrade curiously. Gregory Mouat had apparently been Wilfred's commanding officer during the War. He was a compact, affable sort of chap who grinned broadly at them both through a neatly trimmed salt and pepper beard. Rowland wasn't entirely sure how much Mouat knew about their current purpose.

"Colonel? Good heavens, laddie, nobody's called me that since the war!" He reached up and slapped Rowland heartily on the back. "I canna' know who you mean unless you call me Haggis!"

"I beg your pardon?"

"Haggis, all the lads call me Haggis." He laughed loudly to demonstrate his approval of the joke.

"Yes, of course… Haggis."

The other riders dismounted now, and Mouat introduced his wife, a tall blonde he called "Apples" for some reason he did not specify. Rowland elected to call her Mrs. Mouat.

"Wilf was at pains to point out that you'll be in a tearing hurry, so I have a car waiting. There's a driver too—if you want him—but I see you've brought your own," Mouat said, nodding at Clyde. The Mouats left their horses with the other riders and walked Rowland and Clyde past the tennis courts to a gleaming Cadillac parked in the drive.

"We had hoped to be slightly less conspicuous, sir," Clyde ventured hesitantly.

"My good man, you're going to Kew. Anything but the latest limousine will be highly conspicuous, I can tell you that!"

"We do wish we could stop to take a drink with you before you go," Mrs. Mouat apologised. "But if we don't get back into the chase, we'll never catch the hounds and the lads will get away."

"The lads?" Rowland couldn't help but ask. It seemed rather a friendly term by which to refer to foxes.

"Young Tom and Samuel," Mrs. Mouat said. "Our eldest is abroad, so it's just the bairns."

"You're hunting your sons?"

"Oh aye, Haggis, daft as he is, won't kill anything but Germans. But the hounds will follow the lads you see. You would'na know it wasn't a real hunt."

Mouat concurred with his wife. "Our Tom's become quite swift. Could run for Australia, that lad!"

Rowland glanced at Clyde who was clearly bemused. "We'd best not keep you, then. Thank you kindly for your help and your hospitality, Mrs. Mouat, Mr... Haggis."

"Not at all, laddie. Only too glad to do old Wilf a good turn." Mouat checked his watch. "I've made an appointment for you with Dag Menzies. He may be under the impression you're a delegate from the Graziers' Association—plenty of votes in that. I'll see that your bird's refuelled and ready to go, once we catch the lads."

29

The Presbyterian Church, Cotham Road, looked beautiful with its decorations of arum lilies and white roses, done by the ladies of the congregation in honour of the marriage of Miss Pattie Maie Leckie, oldest daughter of Mr. John W. Leckie (ex M.H.R. for Indi), "Indi," Manningtree Road, Hawthorn, to Mr. Robert Gordon Menzies, third son of Mr. James Menzies, M.L.A., which was celebrated on Monday evening, Sept. 27th, by the Rev J.H. Anderson.

The graceful bride, who was given away by her father, wore a beautiful gown of ivory satin, made with pannier draperies, held with clusters of exquisite handmade silver flowers, and a softly folded corsage with georgette sleeves. The bridesmaids were the Misses Coryn and Gwenyth Leckie, sisters of the bride, and Miss Ruth Gosman. The reception was held at the Grand Hotel, the guests being received by Mr. and Mrs. Leckie (stepmother of the bride).

Alexandra and Yea Standard, 22 October 1920

Not yet forty, the Deputy Premier of Victoria was still a young man but already he looked every inch a statesman. He moved and spoke with a careful gravity and received Rowland with the friendly formality of the political stage.

Clyde, as Rowland's driver, had remained with the car. They had decided on the journey from *Eldonvale* that Menzies may be more forthcoming to Rowland alone.

Rowland waited until they were in Menzies' study with the door closed before he informed the Deputy Premier that he had nothing to do with the Graziers' Association.

Menzies stood, alarmed.

Rowland handed him Wilfred's letter before Menzies called for help. He scanned it hastily and then sat down in the leather upholstered captain's chair behind his desk.

"Please, do sit down, Mr. Sinclair."

Rowland took the armchair facing the desk. The study was not much different in style from Wilfred's—conservative, ordered and quietly opulent.

"Your brother, with whom I have had a long-standing acquaintance, believes there is a matter with which I can help you. I'll do my best, of course, but I must tell you I don't often meet with clients personally at this stage of proceedings. It is more usual that a barrister is briefed by advising solicitors."

"It's not your professional assistance I require, Mr. Menzies."

"I see."

"I don't know if you recall, sir, but you visited my family property, *Oaklea*, in early 1920, to meet with my brother."

"To be precise, Mr. Sinclair, I stopped in for a quick drink after I'd met with your brother at his club in town."

"You remember it then?"

"I may." Menzies remained cautious.

"Wil tells me that he was forced to leave you alone in the drawing room whilst he dealt with an incident demanding his immediate attention."

Menzies' eyes glinted suspiciously from beneath dark, upswept brows. "Yes, yes. I believe he might have, but I wasn't alone."

"I beg your pardon, sir?"

"Wilfred was gone for quite a long time as I recall. Mrs. Sinclair, your charming mother, kept me company."

"My mother! She was in the drawing room?"

"She came down shortly after Wilfred left to attend whatever business called him away. I'm afraid Mrs. Sinclair was rather cross that Wilfred would have abandoned a guest in her house and insisted on keeping me company."

"You were with my mother all that time?" Rowland asked, surprised. "Wil said he was gone for hours."

"Perhaps two," Menzies agreed. "Mrs. Sinclair was fortunately a gracious and vibrant conversationalist. At her insistence, we shared a bottle of your father's finest cognac and talked about your late brother."

"Aubrey?"

Menzies sighed. "It seems your brother and I were the same age. Your dear mother did not want him to go to war. Like my own mother, she felt her elder son was sacrifice enough."

"Both my brothers served," Rowland said. "Aubrey died in France."

"My brothers served also. Fortunately they both came back. My mother was successful in keeping me out of service, a fact which my political enemies have always been eager to exploit, but it seems your father insisted that Aubrey do his duty."

Rowland frowned. He remembered only that his brothers had all enlisted. He had not thought about whether they wanted to go— he'd always assumed they did. "I see. But Wil didn't see Mother there with you when he—"

"I'm afraid she became distressed… the talk of Aubrey, I suppose. She excused herself shortly before your brother returned. I was about to leave when Wilfred appeared and offered me another drink."

"And then you heard the gunshot which killed my father." A cold realisation spread from the pit of Rowland's stomach.

"At the time I was aware only that it was a gunshot," Menzies said, his posture defensive. "For all I knew it might have been one of the workmen shooting at a fox."

"That would be unusual *inside* the house, don't you think?"

"I suppose, in hindsight. Wilfred left for a couple of minutes and then returned to suggest it might be politic to leave before I became unwittingly embroiled in an unsavoury affair that might be used, by my legal adversaries of the time, to discredit me."

"I don't suppose you recall seeing anyone else in the house while you were there, sir?"

"The housekeeper when we first came in, but otherwise no."

Rowland bit his lip uneasily.

"I understand," Menzies said hesitantly into the silence, "that your father was murdered by an intruder that evening."

"Yes, sir. I'm afraid the culprit was never found."

"My sympathies, Mr. Sinclair, and to your good mother. May I ask, sir, why you are looking into this tragic matter now?"

"The gun used to kill my father has only recently been found and retrieved," Rowland replied. "We hoped it might lead to some resolution." He stood. "Thank you, Mr. Menzies. I do appreciate your time."

Menzies walked Rowland to the door. It was as they shook hands in the vestibule that Mrs. Menzies came out in search of her husband. Bob Menzies introduced Rowland to his wife.

"Rowland is Wilfred Sinclair's younger brother, Pattie."

"Of course. I'd have recognised those glorious blue Sinclair eyes anywhere," Pattie Menzies said, smiling. "How is Wilfred?"

"He's well, Mrs. Menzies. About to become a father again."

Pattie Menzies laughed. "It's hard to imagine Wilfred as a father. He was such a rogue!"

Rowland's brow rose. Rogue was not a word he would ever have associated with Wilfred.

"Now my dear," Menzies said sternly, "we mustn't slander the man to his own brother."

With not a little curiosity, Rowland regarded the woman Wilfred had once sought to marry. She stood by Menzies with a kind of complementary confidence he'd never seen in shy Kate Sinclair. His sister-in-law had always seemed uncertain of her place.

Pattie asked after Kate, whom, it seemed, she looked forward to meeting when "Bob made the move to Canberra." The Deputy Premier's wife was a perfect hostess, warm and charming with not a word or gesture out of place. The ideal partner for a man in pursuit of power.

And yet Wilfred had fallen in love with a slip of a girl. Rowland was glad. He was very fond of Kate and always charmed by how unreservedly beguiled Wilfred was with his young wife.

After a courteous sufficiency of pleasantries had been exchanged, Rowland took his leave of Mr. and Mrs. Menzies and returned to the Cadillac which awaited him in the drive.

"Well?" Clyde asked once the Menzies' house was well behind them.

Rowland stared silently at the road ahead.

"Did you discover anything?" Clyde persisted.

Rowland groaned. "Yes."

"Brilliant!"

"Actually no. It isn't."

Clyde glanced at his friend. Rowland looked wretched. "Rowly, are you all right, mate?"

Rowland dropped his head back against the seat. He rubbed his face and spoke candidly, trusting Clyde to guard his confidence. "I think my mother might have shot him, Clyde."

"What? Why?"

Rowland recounted his conversation with Robert Menzies.

"But your mother, Rowly." Clyde pulled the car over to the side of the road and switched off the engine. "Why would she want to kill your father? It doesn't make sense."

Rowland closed his eyes. "She was terrified of him, Clyde."

"Did he—?"

"I'm not sure. I didn't ever see him raise a hand against her, but I was at school during the term."

"And when he'd lay into you... or get Hayden to?"

"She'd lock herself in her room. The next morning we'd both pretend it hadn't happened." Rowland spoke quietly. He felt strangely ashamed. "Mother didn't have a lot to do with me after Aubrey died anyway. Not until I returned from England, when she decided I *was* Aubrey."

"Well if she was so scared of your father, and so indifferent to what was happening to you, why would she suddenly find the courage to brandish a gun and shoot the bastard?"

"Maybe she wasn't as indifferent as she seemed," Rowland said wistfully. "Or perhaps she blamed my father for insisting Aubrey enlist." He smiled sadly. "Most likely it was the bottle of cognac she shared with Menzies. The thing is, Clyde, it makes more sense than anything else."

"But what about Hayden?" Clyde said. "You don't believe your mother made her way to *Emoh Ruo* and beat him to death, do you?"

"Well no. That would be utterly absurd. Someone else killed Hayden."

Clyde watched Rowland carefully. "Do you know who?"

"No but..." He bit his lip anxiously. "We should get back. I need to talk to Wil."

Clyde started the car. If what Rowland suspected proved correct, it was the worst possible news for many reasons. Aside from the tragedy of it, Rowland's best chance of clearing his own name was to find and expose the actual killer. But he was unlikely to offer his mother to the detectives, as an alternative. "Don't worry, mate," Clyde said, glancing sideways at Rowland. "We'll think of something."

By the time they returned to *Eldonvale*, the Mouats had managed to hunt down their sons.

"This has to be the oddest bloody thing I've seen your lot get up to," Clyde whispered as Mouat recounted the number of fences they'd needed to jump to be there at the "kill".

Rowland smiled. "It's the same as a drag hunt in principle, I guess. It's the fact that they don't want to actually kill things that's unusual."

True to his word, Mouat had refuelled the *Rule Britannia*. Given the earlier trouble with the push rods, Clyde and Rowland ran a particularly careful check on the workings of the Gipsy Moth. Finding nothing untoward, they prepared to leave.

Mrs. Mouat presented them with a large basket containing sandwiches, an apple pie, a flask of tea, a white linen tablecloth, napery and two silver candlesticks. Rowland thanked her though he was unsure why and where she thought he and Clyde would stop for so elegant a picnic. He helped himself to a corned beef sandwich before he climbed into the cockpit and left the remainder of the basket to his passenger.

The day was still relatively clear though wispy cloud was accumulating to the north. Rowland switched on the fuel and waited while Clyde swung the propeller until the engine kicked over, removed the chocks and climbed into the passenger seat. The Mouats stood by the runway to wave them off.

By the time they took off from Wangaratta, after refuelling, the weather had come in. The valiant Gipsy Moth fought strong headwinds all the way back to Yass. Rowland had never before flown in such difficult conditions. The ply and canvas body of the *Rule Britannia* creaked and strained against the battering squalls. They did not make good time at all and it was nearly completely dark by the time they reached the Yass shire.

Rowland cursed, trying to keep calm. He did not see how he could land at *Oaklea* in the dark, but they were very low on fuel now, and diverting was not an option. The weather was only making the situation more grim.

It was then he saw the lights—two rows distinctly visible through the rain, marking a runway of sorts. He throttled back the engine and began his descent. They landed hard, bouncing as Rowland struggled to keep the wheels even and the nose up. The *Rule Britannia* slipped and fishtailed dangerously. Someone pressed a car horn. And then, finally, she stopped.

Rowland took his hand off the joystick, gasping, relieved. He turned to check that his passenger was all right. Clyde looked shaken and wet but otherwise he seemed intact.

"Rowly!" Harry Simpson ran up to the plane.

Rowland climbed out, dragging off his cap and goggles. "Harry! What are you doing here?"

"When the weather turned, Wil thought you might need some help," Simpson shouted over the engines of the dozen vehicles—an assortment of trucks and even Wilfred's Rolls Royce Continental— which idled in the paddock with their headlamps on. "We rounded up all the motors on the property and a few hurricane lamps and hoped you'd land before too long."

"We may have to fire up the Caterpillar to get everyone out," Rowland said as he and Clyde trudged through the mud after Simpson.

Simpson opened the door of one of the trucks and indicated they should get in. "That's not the worst of our problems, Rowly. Delaney rang. Some bastard tipped off the police that you'd breached your bail conditions. Gilbey and Angel are on their way to *Oaklea*—they may be there already. We've got to get you back."

Rowland swore. A breach would see him returned to Long Bay until trial. "Who tipped off the police?" he asked as Simpson put the truck into gear.

"Anonymous apparently."

The police cars were already parked in the drive when they reached *Oaklea*. Simpson took the farm truck to the back of the house.

"We'll just say I was out inspecting sheep with you," Rowland said to Simpson.

"Rowly, nobody inspects sheep in the rain."

"They won't know that. We've been inspecting sheep all day and got caught in the rain."

"What exactly were you inspecting them for?" Simpson asked, shaking his head.

"I don't know, condition, colour, the length of their skirts… make something up."

"I can't go in," Simpson said, stopping. "Tell them where to find me and I'll tell them about sheep."

Rowland didn't argue.

"Oh Rowly, thank goodness you're here." Edna ran out of the door to intercept them. "You can't come in. The police are here."

"I know."

"Wilfred and Dr. Maguire have already told them you're in your room dangerously ill—they're arguing on the staircase right now—you can't just walk in from outside."

"Is there any way of getting to your room without using the main staircase?" Clyde asked.

Rowland sighed. "Not through the house. I'll have to climb up through the window."

"Are you mad? It's on the second storey!"

"I had that room when I was a boy." Rowland smiled. "Believe me, I've climbed in and out that way often." He loosened his tie. "I'll need a couple of minutes."

Edna nodded. "I'll see if I can help Wilfred and Dr. Maguire convince them you're contagious." She turned to Clyde and Simpson. "Can you gentlemen please see that he doesn't break his neck?"

Rowland was already on his way to the window. He assessed the task. The tree and the drainpipe he'd always used as a boy were still there, the lattice looked distinctly more rickety than he remembered but he presumed the wisteria vine had strengthened to compensate. He was lucky, he supposed, that Edna Walling had not decided to remove it.

He handed his jacket to Clyde, rolled up his sleeves and began. The apricot tree helped him scale the ground floor quite easily. The next storey was more difficult. The drainpipe was wet, as was the vine. Still, somehow, he made it to the ledge of his window. He'd disabled the latch himself when he was twelve and to his relief it had not been repaired. Even so, opening the window was tricky as it required him to take all his weight with one arm whilst he pushed the window up. The trellis cracked beneath his right foot and, for a moment, he slipped. Clyde swore. Rowland scrambled, regaining his footing on the wisteria and dragging himself up through the open window. He was reminded that he had grown a fair bit since he'd last tried this.

He could hear Wil and Maguire arguing with the detectives in the hallway. Rowland ripped off his clothes and bundled them into the cupboard, before throwing on his robe. He opened the door to the room and stepped out. "What is going on out here? How's a man to get any sleep?" he demanded.

The four men quarrelling in the hallway fell silent and stared at him.

"Mr. Sinclair, how are you feeling?" Maguire asked eventually.

"Bloody awful," Rowland replied, coughing violently.

"He's wet!" Gilbey said suspiciously. "He's soaking wet."

"That, you fool, would be the fever," Maguire said curtly. "Come on, Mr. Sinclair, we'd best get you back to bed before you have a complete relapse." He turned to Gilbey and Angel. "If you're satisfied, gentlemen, Mr. Sinclair is a very unwell man and should not be on his feet!" He ushered Rowland back into the bedroom and slammed the door.

30

GOOD MANNERS AT HOME

———◆———

Practical jokes are rarely indulged in by persons of nice perceptions, and teasing passes the bounds of good taste when it ceases to be a matter of pure fun from all sides. Inquisitiveness is always bad form. "Whom is your letter from?" "What makes your eyes so red?" are interferences with one's rightful privacy. A closed door should be respected and give assurance of seclusion.

Camperdown Chronicle, 1933

Rowland inspected his jaw in the shaving mirror before finally rinsing his razor in the porcelain basin of his washstand. He glanced out of the window and saw that the police cars were no longer parked in the drive. Towelling off his face he selected a tie, relieved he no longer had to feign being mortally ill. He tied the Windsor knot with expert and practised speed and grabbed a clean jacket from the wardrobe.

Ernest was outside his door when he opened it to go down. "Uncle Rowly, you're back!"

"I was never away, just a mite unwell."

"Yes, you were away!" Ernest accused. "You weren't here!"

Rowland knelt to look his nephew in the face. "You're right, Ernie, but that was a secret. How did you know I wasn't here?"

"I came to see you, and I waited and waited and waited… and then I let myself into your room."

"Did you indeed?" Wilfred said reprovingly, as he entered the hallway.

Ernest stepped back and bit his lip.

"Ernie, what have I told you about respecting people's privacy?" Wilfred said, folding his arms as he looked down at his son. "You were told to stay out of your uncle's room!"

Ernest's lower lip wobbled under his father's censorious gaze. "I wanted to give him the picture."

"What picture?"

"I made Uncle Rowly a picture of Lenin and me to help him feel better, but he wasn't there!"

"I'm sorry I wasn't there, mate," Rowland said, still kneeling. "I had an errand to run."

"When you were sick?"

"I felt a bit better so I ducked out. Ernie, did you tell anyone I wasn't here?"

"I told Mr. Isaacs. He said that sometimes you like to sleep under the bed, but that he was sure you were there and would I like to play cricket."

"I see. Did you tell anyone else?"

"Only Aunt Lucy."

At this, the Sinclair brothers exchanged a glance.

"She telephoned and I spoke to her while Mrs. Kendall fetched Mummy. Aunt Lucy asked about you, Uncle Rowly, and where you were and I told her you weren't under the bed because I went back and checked." Ernest looked very much like he was about to cry now.

Rowland smiled. "I don't sleep under the bed, Ernie. I don't know where Mr. Isaacs gets such preposterous ideas. Perhaps we should go have words with him for pulling your leg so abominably!"

Ernest nodded.

"I think that first you and I need to have a word about obedience and discretion, Ernest," Wilfred said taking his son by the shoulders and turning him firmly in the opposite direction. "You go to your room and wait for me. I'll be there directly."

Rowland stood as they watched Ernest dawdle away, his shoulders slumped and his head hung as if he were walking to the gallows.

Rowland looked at his brother uneasily. "Wil, he didn't mean—"

"If you'd really been sick, Rowly, he might have endangered himself by going into your room when he'd been told not to."

"But Wil, you're not planning to—"

"Rowly," Wilfred interrupted, sighing. "I have never had cause, and hope never to have cause, to discipline my sons with anything more severe than a cross talking-to. Ernie has a flair for the dramatic and he's worked out that you're a soft touch." He shook his head. "I shudder to think what lawless brats you'll raise one day!"

⸻

Nobody commented on Rowland's sudden and almost miraculous recovery. Even Kate let it pass without comment. She possibly realised that there was more to it, but Kate had always trusted that her husband would tell her what she needed to know about his machinations, and the rest was best left alone.

Wilfred came down with Ernest a few minutes later. The boy held his father's hand as he apologised to Rowland. "I'm sorry I invaded your piracy, Uncle Rowly."

Rowland smiled. "Privacy, Ernie. I haven't plundered the coastline in a while."

Ernest nodded solemnly. "I'll never come in without knocking again."

"Without knocking and being invited in," Wilfred corrected, in case Ernest was creating a loophole for himself.

Rowland winked at his nephew. "That's good of you, old chap."

Ernest handed him a sheet of paper. It was the picture for which he had risked disobeying his father. Rowland smiled as he studied the drawing. Ernest had never drawn for him before, preferring to watch as Rowland sketched. The picture was full of whimsy and vibrance—naive attention to some detail, and the complete disregard of others. Lenin had been faithfully represented with only one ear, and numerous scars, though it seemed he was the size of a pony.

"Do you like it, Uncle Rowly?"

"Very much."

"Will you put it on your wall?"

"I will indeed. I'll hang it proudly alongside the Picasso."

"What's a Car So?"

"Picasso. He's a very famous artist who's devoted his life to trying to draw like this."

"Do you think I could be a famous artist too, Uncle Rowly?"

Wilfred cleared his throat, clearly alarmed by the thought. "I believe that's Mrs. Kendall calling you for bed, son. You'd best run along now."

Ernest beckoned Rowland down and whispered in his ear. "I'm glad you're not really going to die, Uncle Rowly."

Rowland met the child's wide eyes, startled. Ernest had obviously taken his uncle's supposed illness more seriously than they'd anticipated. "I'm sorry I worried you, mate."

"That's all right, Uncle Rowly." Ernest regarded Rowland gravely. "You shouldn't go out in the rain though. You'll catch death."

"I'm afraid I forgot how impressionable Ernie is," Wilfred said as the boy trotted off. "He's become very fond of you, Rowly, and his imagination is, well, six years old. I'm afraid he was convinced you'd contracted some fatal disease."

"To be fair, we did go to some lengths to create that impression," Rowland reminded him.

"Yes, I suppose we did." He removed his spectacles and extracted a handkerchief with which to polish them. "So, did you manage to speak to Bob Menzies?"

Rowland nodded.

"And?"

"We should talk."

Wilfred frowned. "Come into the library where we won't be disturbed."

In the privacy of the library, Rowland told his brother in some detail of his conversation with Robert Menzies. Wilfred swore, obviously drawing the same conclusion that Rowland had.

"Did Father insist that Aubrey enlist?" Rowland asked.

"Yes, but he also insisted I enlist. That was Father. He never spoke without insisting or demanding. Aubrey would have joined anyway. We all thought it would be over by Christmas. He never thought he'd die."

"But—"

"Mother was always particularly protective of Aubrey, and he was only nineteen when we went." Wilfred was lost in his own thoughts for a moment. "I didn't even think to wonder where she was that night."

"Wil, did Father… did he ever strike Mother?" Rowland struggled with the question because he dreaded the answer.

Wilfred's eyes darkened and he spoke candidly. "Yes. They used to quarrel, mostly about Harry. He'd take a belt to her… until Aubrey and I were old enough to intervene."

"Did no one else try to do anything?"

"Uncle Rowland did. He tried to reason with Father on several occasions, but it isn't the kind of thing people talk about."

Rowland clenched his fists, frustrated. "I can't remember."

"You were younger then than Ernie is now, Rowly. Harry's mother passed away around that time, and after that Mother and Father didn't quarrel so much." He sighed. "When we went to war, we really thought it would be all right—for Mother and you. Father had been content to disinherit us now and then for years. We didn't think he'd… I can't tell you how sorry, I am."

"What could you have done, Wil?" Rowland replied bitterly. "Short of shooting him before you left." He stared absently into the distance. "Do you suppose he'd started to… to batter her again?"

"Perhaps she was simply in terror that he would," Wilfred said gently, "or perhaps she was trying to protect you in her way."

Rowland swallowed. "Do you think she remembers, Wil? Do you think she's starting to remember?"

Wilfred rubbed his temple wearily. "I'm not certain. How could we ever be certain of what's going on in Mother's mind? The nurse informed me this morning that some of the Laudanum Maguire prescribed is missing."

"Laudanum? Who would—"

"I can't imagine any of the servants would steal Laudanum. The nurse fears it was Mother herself."

"I don't understand…"

"Maguire suspects Mother may be more depressed than we know. If she's remembering… realising… We're just keeping a very close eye on her."

Rowland stared at his brother. "My God, what are we going to do, Wil?"

"If this gets worse we may be forced to consider a sanatorium. I wouldn't make that decision without you, Rowly, but you should be prepared for the fact that we may have no other option."

Rowland groaned. "What about the police? We can't…"

"I'm not sure. I'll speak to our solicitors. Let's not panic just yet."

Wilfred lit a cigarette and for a moment there was silence as he fortified himself with the first draw. "Perhaps we should concentrate on who killed Charlie Hayden," he suggested. "It was, after all, on the strength of Hayden's murder that they arrested you." Wilfred sat back, tapping the arm of his chair absently, thoughtfully. "What do you remember from the scene?"

Rowland thought back. "Hayden had a belt in his hand," he said.

"A belt?"

Rowland nodded. "Like he was preparing to flog someone again."

"At *Emoh Ruo*? You don't think he'd taken a child to—"

"What child? I'm sure I wasn't the only kid he took a belt to over the years but he's not been back to the Yass district since you suggested he leave. Even if he came across a worker's son and decided to give him a hiding for some reason or another, what the hell would they be doing in *Emoh Ruo*?"

Wilfred sighed. "Was there anything else unusual or worthy of note?"

Rowland paused. "Oh, Arthur. He was there, with Lucy."

"Of course. Arthur found the body."

"So he says."

"You're suggesting Arthur may have killed Hayden?"

"Let's face facts, Wil—he's deceived us from the beginning. Plotted against you while living in your house."

"But murder? What possible reason could he have to murder Hayden?"

"If he did find Hayden and bring him to Yass, perhaps Hayden was trying to blackmail him. Perhaps they fell out, or Hayden attacked him first—"

"Arthur's a solicitor, for pity's sake—Hayden was beaten to death."

"Granted," Rowland conceded, "it's not a particularly lawyerly way of despatching someone, but from what I saw, it looked like Hayden had fallen and hit his head on the hearth. Someone was angry enough to hit him a few times but they may not have intended to kill him entirely."

"But Miss Bennett was with him, Rowly."

"Miss Bennett questioned your six-year-old son about my whereabouts and reported my absence to Arthur. I don't think there's any question where her allegiances lie."

"She telephoned to speak to Kate. It wasn't a conspiracy. She may have mentioned what Ernest told her to Arthur, but I doubt the poor girl has any idea what he's up to."

Rowland said nothing.

"She's Kate's dearest friend," Wilfred added.

"And she's marrying the man who wants to have you incarcerated and assume ownership of *Oaklea*. For heaven's sake, she's already started redecorating *Woodlands*!"

Wilfred pressed his fingers together pensively. "I do hope you're wrong on that count, Rowly. Kate's making arrangements to go to Sydney to help Lucy plan this blasted wedding."

"Perhaps we should put our cards on the table, Wil."

"Confront Arthur? What would that possibly achieve?"

Rowland wasn't sure. "Lucy Bennett should know the kind of man she's marrying."

"It's very gallant of you to be concerned about Miss Bennett," Wilfred observed.

"What can I say? I'm protective of the women who try to shoot me."

Wilfred sighed, abandoning the charade that some incompetent rabbit hunter had shot at his brother. He took another cigarette from the mahogany box on the table and stubbed out the remains of the first. "Perhaps it would be useful to acquaint Arthur with what it means to go to war against the Sinclairs."

"Arthur is a Sinclair, Wil," Rowland reminded him.

"Not once I'm finished."

31

WRONGED GIRLS

There is also to be considered the fiction of the law which does not allow a girl to sue for seduction. She can only do so through her father or guardian. And to maintain an action it must be shown that the relationship of master and servant exists. Technically the action is by the father for the loss of his daughter's services. But if those services cannot be proved the action fails.

The Mercury, 3 March 1934

Rowland checked over his biplane, making sure she had been returned to the shed in good order. The *Rule Britannia* was a little muddy but otherwise none the worse for landing in the storm.

"We may have to give her a spit shine," Clyde declared, inspecting the fuselage, "but considering how we landed, she's not too bad."

Milton jumped down from the Caterpillar parked on the other side of the shed. It too was caked in fresh red mud, having been called on to pull out a number of the vehicles that had been stranded after forming the makeshift airstrip.

Edna wandered out of the shed, thoroughly bored with the talk of engines and machines. She could see the *Emoh Ruo* homestead further up the hill. Rowland joined her.

"Shall we walk up?" he asked, glancing dubiously at the sky. It had stopped raining but the clouds had not yet parted.

"I'm sure we'll be all right," Edna said. She called out for Clyde and Milton to hurry.

They had decided to take another look at the place where Charlie Hayden had been killed in the hope that some new clue would present itself.

It was not so much that Rowland was convinced that his cousin had killed Hayden but his mind was open to the possibility.

He unlocked the front door and held it open for Edna to enter.

"Whose furniture is this?" Edna asked, peering under the dust cloths.

"I presume the previous owners'. They sold the place lock, stock and barrel to Wil."

"Everything?" Edna asked.

"I believe Jefferies hanged himself. After that, his wife just wanted to leave. There was a colossal amount of debt."

"Oh. How terribly sad. They lost everything."

Rowland nodded. "Pretty close to."

They followed Clyde and Milton into the room where Hayden had been found. The body had been removed, of course, but otherwise the room was undisturbed. They inspected it in the light of day: the blood was still visible, dried brown on the hearth and the rug adjacent.

In these surrounds, an image of Hayden's body was easily conjured. Rowland described what he could remember for Edna.

"Look how far into the room he was standing," Edna mused. "If someone had come in suddenly, surely he would have turned and walked towards the door."

Milton agreed. "He was meeting with someone. But why here? How did he get in?"

"Perhaps whoever he was meeting possessed a key or knew where a spare was hidden," Edna suggested.

Clyde stepped out the distance between the door and the hearth. "What do you think, Rowly? Arthur seemed pretty shaken when we got here. Perhaps it wasn't just because he found the body."

Rowland frowned. "It would be easier to believe if Arthur didn't have Lucy Bennett with him. Surely if you were going to kill someone, you wouldn't take a witness."

"Unless he didn't plan to kill Hayden. Perhaps something happened that made Arthur panic and hit him?"

"Maybe he was trying to prevent Hayden revealing their association to Lucy?" Edna suggested. "He does seem genuinely keen on her."

"The belt," Milton said. "That's why the police thought immediately it was you."

Clyde looked Rowland up and down. "He'd be a bloody idiot to try to take a belt to Rowly now," he said.

"Yes," Milton continued. "But maybe someone wanted to point the police in Rowly's direction. Surely it wouldn't be difficult to remove a dead man's belt and place it in his hand."

Rowland shook his head. "He had it wrapped around his hand in exactly the same way—"

"Arthur was there when Hayden told his story," Clyde reminded him. "He knew exactly what the mongrel did and how he did it."

Rowland considered the poet's theory. "It's possible, but I genuinely can't see Lucy going along with it. She's much more likely to have screamed the place down."

Milton shrugged. "Perhaps she didn't see him do it. She might have been waiting dutifully in the car. Did you ask her what she saw?"

"No. She hasn't really spoken more than a few words to me since I refused to marry her."

"Well, we may have to talk to her," Milton said firmly.

"Wilfred's arranged for Arthur and his fiancée to come to luncheon at *Oaklea* tomorrow," Rowland replied. "Though it might be a little tricky separating them."

Edna laughed. "Nonsense. You Sinclairs clear the room of women whenever you're afraid you may swear!" She winked at Rowland. "You announce that you wish to speak *frankly*, and everyone will gasp and agree that it's better if Lucy visits with Kate for a while. We'll speak to her then."

Rowland wished he could accuse the sculptress of exaggerating, but, to be honest, it was as good a plan as any.

There was a garden party at *Oaklea* that afternoon, hosted by Mr. and Mrs. Wilfred Sinclair to thank all those who had helped extinguish the fire. Two marquees had been erected on the lawns. A ten-piece band used the verandah as a makeshift stage overlooking a portable parquetry dance floor, specially laid for the event. White-clothed tables bore a feast of prettily iced cakes, finger sandwiches and cold meats on tiered silver platters as workers and townspeople in their Sunday best arrived to receive the gratitude of the Sinclairs.

Kate stood by her husband's side, shaking hands and welcoming guests. In the shadow of Wilfred's powerful and protective presence, she seemed small despite the fullness of her belly.

Rowland smiled as he watched Wilfred whisper in Kate's ear, gently moving her hair out of the way. The gesture was perfectly proper, but intimate and tender nevertheless. Kate blushed, and Wilfred carried on with the business of shaking hands.

Deciding that they should not cause any more disruption at *Oaklea* than absolutely necessary, Edna had bullied Milton into one of Rowland's suits for the occasion. Initially the poet resisted the "three-piece uniform of the Capitalist establishment" but eventually he conceded, making the best of it by adopting what he considered a complementary persona. He proved quite a popular figure, reciting poetry with the refined lilt of someone who regularly moved in the same circles as Wilfred Sinclair.

"Do you recognise the bloke Milt's talking to?" Clyde asked, handing Rowland a drink.

"I believe that's Dave Jessop."

"He's one of the blokes that tried to tar and feather Milt a couple of years ago, isn't he?"

Rowland sipped his drink. "I'd say at least half the chaps here were among the mob that tried to tar and feather Milt."

"And yet, not one of them seems to recognise him."

"Small mercies."

Wilfred stood on the elevated deck of the gazebo to deliver a few words of thanks. With Ernest holding tightly to his hand, he spoke of his gratitude to all those who had risked their lives to save *Oaklea*, his sons and their nanny. His words were greeted with enthusiastic applause and echoed with shouts of "hear, hear" and calls for cheers.

That formality completed, the band struck up again and the festivities resumed. This was not the usual crowd who graced Sinclair functions but a more eclectic gathering of farm workers, fire fighters and neighbours. The guests seemed, to Rowland, a touch inhibited, perhaps intimidated.

He offered Edna his hand. "Shall we begin the dancing?" he said, glancing at the empty dance floor.

She curtsied. "I'd be delighted, Mr. Sinclair."

The sculptress slipped easily into his arms, as she always had, and they christened the new dance floor with a quickstep.

Soon other couples joined them and the gathering seemed to relax. Rowland managed to keep Edna to himself for three brackets, but inevitably some young man worked up the courage to cut in.

The party had been in swing for some hours when Rowland ducked into the house to check on his mother. Elisabeth Sinclair watched the celebrations from her window comfortably settled on a chaise with a cup of tea. Wilfred had arranged for a nurse to be her companion at all times now.

Rowland stopped with his mother for a while, pointing out people with whom she might be acquainted in the crowd. He neither looked for nor made any attempt to remind her who he really was, unwilling to risk another breakdown.

"We hosted some very grand parties when your father was alive, before the war. I had a blue gown I'd wear for balls. It was considered very daring in its day…"

Rowland listened, wondering how his refined, gracious mother could have been driven to murder, and how they were going to protect her without ending up in prison themselves.

It was Elisabeth Sinclair who eventually urged him, or rather Aubrey, to return to the party, suggesting that he might meet a suitable young lady. He laughed, refilling her teacup and kissing her cheek before he left.

Rowland headed back outside through the kitchen so he could reassure Lenin, who had been confined there for the party, that he had not been forgotten. When he heard the scrabbling, he opened the door quickly, concerned the hound was helping himself to some painstakingly prepared culinary delicacy.

"Mr. Sinclair!" Nanny de Waring sprang back from Jack Templeton, fumbling frantically with the pearl buttons of her blouse.

Rowland turned away while she made herself decent. She apologised hysterically. Rowland did so out of courtesy.

"Charlotte… Miss de Waring is not to blame, Mr. Sinclair, sir," Templeton said gallantly. "It was me. I—"

"If you were forcing yourself upon Miss de Waring, Templeton, then you and I would have a problem. Otherwise, it's not really my concern."

"Oh, Mr. Sinclair," the young nanny sobbed, smoothing her hair back into place. "If you can only forgive me… it won't happen again."

Rowland smiled. "I'm neither your father nor your priest, Miss de Waring."

"This is my day off," she offered in mitigation. "There was no one in the kitchen and—"

"Not quite no one," Rowland said, bending to rub Lenin behind the ear. The hound opened one eye and grunted. "But Len doesn't seem particularly scandalised. You could probably buy his silence with bacon."

"We got carried away, Mr. Sinclair," Templeton explained. "We didn't mean to—"

"This is a rather risky spot to get carried away, Mr. Templeton, don't you think? I'm sure there are more private, not to mention appropriate, locations on *Oaklea* for… courting," Rowland grimaced, wondering when he'd become so stuffy. Courting! For pity's sake!

Perhaps Templeton sensed Rowland Sinclair was having trouble being in any way critical. "Do you have any recommendations, sir?" he asked rather impudently. Charlotte de Waring blushed but she didn't protest.

Despite a vague notion that he *should* be offended, or at least disapproving, Rowland laughed. "There's a folly on *Emoh Ruo* near the creek, looks like a Delphic temple. Some mad notion of the previous owners'. It's a bit overgrown now. I don't think anyone's been there in years."

"You won't be requiring it yourself?" Templeton asked, his eyes twinkling, in what Wilfred would have considered an unacceptable show of familiarity.

"No, I'm afraid not," Rowland replied.

Rowland returned to the garden party which, by then, was winding down.

"Where have you been, Rowly?" Edna asked. She was flushed with the consequential exertion of repeated invitations to dance.

Rowland told her quietly of the tryst upon which he'd stumbled. Edna giggled. "Good Lord, they're lucky it was you and not Wil."

Rowland nodded. Wilfred might well have objected, and quite strenuously, to his children's nanny entertaining the gardener in such a manner.

"The irresistibly handsome, mysterious gardener," Edna said dreamily. "It's all rather like Lawrence's *Lady Chatterley's Lover*."

Rowland's eyes sharpened. "Templeton? You think he's han— mysterious?"

Edna smiled wickedly. "Well, he's not nearly so mysterious as you, darling, but yes, I can see why he'd intrigue Nanny de Waring."

32

SUCCESS TO HITLER

Rev. W.E. Hurst's Wish

"We wish, with our whole hearts, that Herr Hitler will be successful in the tremendous and revolutionary experiment which he is undertaking at the present time, and that he will succeed in bringing the world a little nearer to what our Lord intended it to be, a society of friends."

These remarks were made by the Rev. W.E. Hurst, President of the Queensland branch of the Australian League of Nations Union, at a reception given by the branch to the commander, Captain Baron Harsdorf von Enderndorf, and officers of the Karlsruhe, at Mt. Coot-tha on Saturday morning.

The Rev. Mr. Hurst said he had been very much impressed with the remarks of Commander von Enderndorf and First Officer Schiller in regard to Herr Hitler in an interview appearing in the Press. The members of the branch greatly sympathised with Germany in the terrible and unjust conditions which had been imposed on her, and they wished Herr Hitler success in the task before him.

BROKEN PROMISES

There were a large number of persons in this country who felt that Germany had been treated very unfairly and unjustly by the world generally. Other nations gave a pledge that they would disarm to the extent they had forced Germany to do, and they had not done so. The present unrest in Europe, he believed, was mainly due to those broken promises. It had been said that all the trouble of the world today could be traced to the war. He refused to believe that; it was not right to impute war guilt to any one nation when there were others in it.

Courier Mail, 16 January 1934

Rowland woke early. He'd slept fitfully. The last weeks since his father's gun had been found seemed to have halted the normal course of his life. He was frustrated, angry that his father had risen from the grave to cause more pain and misery.

What Rowland had seen in Germany still haunted him; the brutality of the Nazi regime, the administrative ruthlessness of it. Before the question of Henry Sinclair's death had been resurrected, he had been trying his level best to get someone to listen. Not successfully of course. His concerns had been dismissed and belittled, at best he'd elicited a plea of powerlessness, but at least he'd been doing something.

Rowland showered and dressed, quickly. He and Wilfred would meet with their cousin and Lucy Bennett today. He wondered if Arthur had realised that his true intentions had been discovered. Perhaps not. Wilfred had been playing their cards close.

It seemed no one had yet come down to breakfast, and so, rather than eat alone, Rowland grabbed the newspaper from the sideboard and stepped out onto the verandah. The marquees had been taken down and all the lawns returned to their pristine manicured custom. From this part of the verandah the fire damage, and consequent reconstruction work, was not visible. In the distance, Rowland could see Edna Walling, pacing out distances while she made notes. Opening the paper he wondered what the garden designer thought of all the drama at *Oaklea*. Was she concerned that her clients could be murderers, or was that not as important as the harmony of the landscape she was creating?

"Good morning," Milton joined him. "What are you doing out here?" he asked, dropping his elbows on to the rail beside Rowland's.

"Just wondering when this will all be over," Rowland murmured. "April's a long time away, Milt. You and Clyde and Ed can't just put your own lives on hold for that long."

"We can put our lives on hold long enough to see you cleared, mate."

Rowland handed him the paper pointing out an article on the upcoming celebrations of the Nazis' first year in power in Germany, and another on the love of the German people for their führer, which wished the German Chancellor every success. "With an indictment for murder over my head, I'll have no hope of persuading anyone Hitler's is a despicable regime."

"You'll be acquitted, Rowly."

"But it will always be there." He cursed. "Nobody seemed keen to listen to me, anyway," he admitted. "Not with so many eminent, upstanding citizens extolling the virtues of Hitler's Germany."

For a while, Milton studied him silently. "Do you remember Egon Kisch?" he asked finally.

"Of course." Kisch had been one of the men who had given them refuge in Germany when they were wanted by the Brownshirts.

"Egon's fled Germany. He's trying to spread the word about the reality under the Nazis."

"It's a shame we can't get him to come to Sydney."

Milton looked intently at him. "It has been suggested."

"Really? By whom?"

Milton hesitated again. "The Australian chapter of the World Movement Against War and Fascism. They were established by Comintern—the Communist International."

Rowland was not surprised by his friend's reluctance. Milton was a Communist, fervent and committed, but, despite a certain sympathy, Rowland Sinclair was not. Neither attempted to change the other. And whilst Milton had lived in his house, enjoyed his hospitality and borrowed his clothes for years, he had never once asked Rowland for money towards his cause.

But this was different. It was Rowland who asked. "What exactly are they proposing, Milt?"

"The movement wants to bring Egon out for some events at the end of the year to coincide with the centenary of Melbourne and the royal tour—they just need to fund it."

"Are you a member of this movement?"

"Yes."

"Will they let me join without being a Communist?"

"Fellow travellers are always welcome," Milton replied. "Particularly those with your resources. But are you sure you want to—"

"Egon might be able to convince people of what European Fascism really means," Rowland said, remembering how the journalist had persuaded his comrades to risk everything to help them. "Nothing that I'm doing is working. It's worth a try."

"Wilfred won't like this."

"Doubtless. But I think it's a better investment than milk bars."

Milton pressed his shoulder. "I'll let them know."

———————

Arthur Sinclair and Lucy Bennett arrived in her powder blue Riley. Rowland's friends retired discreetly to the conservatory with Ewan, who was in disgrace, having chewed his brother's toy plane into a woody pulp. Elisabeth Sinclair and her nurse, a sensible quiet woman who was both firm and unobtrusive with her charge, sat in the sunshine embroidering.

Kate waited with her husband and brother-in-law to receive the newly engaged couple in the drawing room.

If Arthur knew that his cousins had discovered his manoeuvres he gave no indication of it, greeting them all with enthusiasm and jocularity.

Kate greeted her old friend warmly.

"Oh Kate, you're simply enormous!" Lucy effused. "What do you think? Heir, mare or spare? They say you can tell because girls steal beauty from their mothers." She laughed.

"Must be a boy then," Wilfred said curtly.

Kate blushed deeply. "I might just speak to Mrs. Kendall about luncheon," she said. "If you'll all excuse me for just a moment."

Rowland smiled. Any oblique compliment from Wilfred seemed invariably to compel his sister-in-law to leave the room. It had always been thus. Rowland imagined it had made courting her very awkward... and yet Wilfred had managed it.

"I'll come too," Lucy called after Kate. "It'll give us a chance to talk about the wedding while you gentlemen deal with business," she said, smiling at her fiancé.

"I'm afraid there's been a terrible cock-up with the painters at *Woodlands*, Rowland old boy," Arthur said after Lucy had left. "Lucy and I called in there yesterday and I'll be blowed if some fool hasn't painted the dining room black! Black! It looks positively ghoulish! Some blasted tradesman trying to ensure he gets paid twice for the same job, I expect. But don't you worry, Lucy and I will sort it when we get back. She's quite the little homemaker!"

"Stay the hell out of my house," Rowland said coldly.

"I beg your pardon?"

"We have become aware," Wilfred said calmly, "that you, Arthur, have been acting as some kind of informant to the police."

"I see." It seemed Arthur was not going to bother to deny it. He showed no sign of remorse or embarrassment. "Well how long did you expect to get away with murder, Wilfred?"

"Neither Rowly nor I had anything to do with our father's death," Wilfred replied, "so I hope you've not promised Miss Bennett the Sinclair estate in return for her hand."

"You deny it? Hardly a surprise." Arthur rolled his eyes.

"You've lived under Wilfred's roof, eaten with his family, taken his charity," Rowland snarled. "And the whole time you were—"

Arthur snapped. "Charity? A good part of this estate should always have been mine. Your conniving dictator of a father stole my inheritance!"

"And so now you're seeking justice for *him*," Rowland came back furiously. "And to do that you paid that vermin Charlie Hayden to come back to Yass."

"If the police had been doing their job, if Wilfred hadn't run him out of town, they would have taken his statement years ago."

"I believe we've been fair to you, Arthur," Wilfred said. "I settled your debts, gave you a new start… a house."

"Yes. Under obligation to the largesse of the great Wilfred Sinclair for what should rightfully have been mine in the first place!" Arthur hissed. "I found Charlie Hayden's name in the ledgers. It was the fact that you'd sacked a long-serving employee so summarily the day after Uncle Henry was murdered that made me wonder."

"But it went rather wrong, didn't it, Arthur?" Rowland said stepping towards his cousin. "Hayden tried to blackmail you, or pull out. He forced you to kill him."

"Me?" Arthur poked Rowland in the chest. "How dare you try to pin your crimes on me!"

"He was found at *Emoh Ruo* where you were about to set up house. You found his body."

"May I remind you that Miss Bennett was with me the entire time."

"She looked terribly distressed—was that because she'd just witnessed you kill a man?"

"Don't be bloody daft. The body was cold by the time we found it. I can't say I blame you for killing Hayden, all things considered, but don't think for one second that I'll take the blame. You and Wilfred have it all worked out, don't you? He kills Uncle Henry, secures the entire estate for himself, and then keeps you and your useless unemployed set in return for your silence!"

"Look, you idiot, Wil was with someone when Father was shot. He has an alibi!" Rowland blurted.

For the first time, Arthur looked startled. "What alibi? Who?"

Wilfred placed a hand on his brother's shoulder. "Perhaps, Arthur, it would be best if you left. Lucy, of course, is welcome to stay." His eyes flashed fury though his voice was steady. "You will find all the lines of credit I arranged for you have been revoked. You are not welcome here, or at *Woodlands*. Do not expect any further consideration from the Sinclairs."

"I am a Sinclair, you bloody fool!"

"We'll see."

At that point Kate and Lucy returned.

"Wil?" Kate stepped back, subconsciously repelled by the hostility in the room.

"Arthur is leaving, my dear."

"But why?" Lucy demanded. "What's happened?"

"Because he's a duplicitous...scoundrel," Rowland replied, controlling his language with some effort.

"You're just jealous!" Lucy said, moving to Arthur's side and entwining her arm in his.

Rowland laughed. He didn't mean to, but that particular accusation was more ridiculous than all the others which had been levelled at him of late.

Lucy erupted. "You, Rowland Sinclair, are an amoral, spoiled, cruel child. You are not half the man your cousin is!"

"Oh Lucy!" Kate said shocked.

"I regret to inform you, Miss Bennett," Wilfred said gravely, "that your fiancé has been conspiring against us all the time he has been a guest in my house. He has violated our trust and any sense of honour."

"Because he wants to get back what's rightfully his?" Lucy demanded. "Because he wants to see justice done after all these years?"

Silence, both stunned and appalled. None of them had really thought Lucy Bennett knew what Arthur had been up to. That she was complicit was something for which they were completely unprepared.

Kate gasped. It was more a cry. Wilfred moved immediately to help her into a chair.

"Lucy, you can't mean that," she pleaded.

"I believe Arthur!" Lucy replied, unmoved by her friend's distress. "I saw what Rowland did to that poor man we found at *Emoh Ruo* and I only thank God that I didn't accept him. I should have listened to Pater from the beginning."

"For pity's sake, Miss Bennett, you're the one that tried to shoot me!" Rowland said, exasperated.

Lucy inhaled. Her horror and fury was tinged with panic. "Arthur darling, I should like to leave now," she said.

Wilfred took Kate up to bed and stayed with her, explaining, and comforting his wife who was deeply hurt and unnerved by the betrayal of both Arthur Sinclair and Lucy Bennett.

Rowland told his friends about the exchange. "Did you manage to speak to Lucy?" he asked.

Edna moaned. "She wouldn't stop talking, but only about weddings and china patterns. Even Kate couldn't get a word in."

"It doesn't matter. Miss Bennett has made it clear that she's going to stand with Arthur on this."

"Why's he doing this, Rowly?" Edna asked. "You're his family."

"I don't know, years of feeling cheated, I guess. And he seems to genuinely believe Wilfred killed Father... or at least he did when the shouting started. He knows Wil has an alibi now."

"What do you think, Rowly?" Clyde asked. "Could Arthur have killed Hayden?"

Rowland grimaced. "He makes a valid point—the body was cold when he found it. Hayden was probably killed the previous day or early that morning. He could have done it then, I suppose, but why would he then go back to the scene, with Lucy no less?"

"Perhaps he left something incriminating at *Emoh Ruo* and went back to retrieve it."

"He could have done that on his own—without Lucy. Arthur paid Hayden to return, but I don't think he killed him."

"So we're back to no idea!" Clyde said, groaning.

Wilfred came into the conservatory. He seemed weary.

"How's Kate?" Rowland asked, pulling his brother aside.

"I might telephone her doctor. This kind of stress is not good for her with the baby due in less than a month."

"Is there anything we can do, Mr. Sinclair?" Edna asked. "Anything at all?"

"Thank you, Miss Higgins." He glanced at Ewan who was sitting in Clyde's lap chewing on a wooden block. "Perhaps if you take the boys up to visit with her, it might be a welcome distraction."

"Of course." Edna took Ewan from Clyde. "Where's Ernie?"

33

VERSES FROM BAIRNS

BOBBY'S SWING

Bobby King he had a swing
In an apple tree
All day long you heard this song,
"Will someone please swing me?"

When mother said, "Time for bed"
Bobby used to cling,
Hands tight, with all his might
To his treasured swing.

But at last, all warnings past
Father had his way.
And Bobby King he lost that swing
Through failing to obey.

Cairns Post, 1932

"Ernie's in the garden with the nanny. They said something about a swing," Milton said, standing. "You take Ewan up, Ed, I'll go find him."

"I'll give you a hand," Clyde said. "The swing is in the elm tree, if I recall."

Rowland poured his brother a drink.

"Maurice Kent is of the firm opinion that Mother would be declared unfit to stand trial even if the Crown elected to prosecute," he said quietly, accepting the glass of whisky. "On the whole, he doesn't believe they'd have enough evidence. In fact their case against *you* is, at best, extremely flimsy and would be completely unsustainable if it wasn't for the Hayden murder."

"So what are they saying?"

"If we could show that you couldn't have killed Hayden, then the indictment for Father's murder would more than likely also go away."

"But I could have killed him, Wil. I wasn't under lock and key that day after the fire, and while it's unlikely that I slipped out without anyone noticing, it's not impossible."

"Which leaves us with finding the real murderer. You accused Arthur…"

"Yes, I did suspect it might have been him at one point, but I doubt it now. To be honest, I doubt he could have beaten Hayden to death."

"What, physically?"

"That too, but I doubt he was angry enough. I saw the body. Hayden had been battered—it wasn't just one punch. It must have been someone with a serious grudge… like me, I suppose."

"Very well," Wilfred decided. "We'll look into who had reason to hate Hayden… other than you and me."

Milton returned while they were discussing how to proceed. "Clyde's still looking," he said, "but there's no sign of them. Miss Walling and her crew don't seem to have seen them either. Miss de Waring wouldn't have taken Ernie on a picnic somewhere, would she?"

Wilfred sighed. "I wouldn't have thought she'd do so without notifying us, but I'm afraid she's the silliest young woman we've ever had look after the boys." He stood, pacing irritably. "If I hadn't served with her father…"

"I'll go out and search with you," Rowland volunteered. "They couldn't be too far. Is Lenin with them?"

"Yes, I believe so."

"That's how we'll locate them then." Rowland grabbed his hat.

They headed into the garden shouting for Lenin rather than Ernest or Nanny de Waring, in the hope that the dog's single ear might prove more keen by virtue of the fact that it was attached to a greyhound. It took only a few shouts to elicit a responding bark.

Relieved, Rowland followed the sound to the fence near the front of the property. Lenin barked madly as he approached.

"Settle down, old boy." Rowland untied his dog from the fencepost. "What the dickens are you doing out here? And where are Ernie and Miss de Waring?"

He called for Ernest a couple of times, succeeding only in startling a flock of cockatoos from the gums along the fence-line.

Lenin panted, squirming excitedly and jumping up upon his master. "Come on, we'd best get back," Rowland said, worried now. What would the boy and his nanny have been doing so close to the road?

He sprinted back to the house.

"You found Lenin," Milton said as Rowland and the greyhound reached the house garden. "Where's—"

"I don't know," Rowland replied, catching his breath. "Someone had tied Len to the house yard fence. There's no sign of either Ernie or Miss de Waring."

"Bloody hell!"

"Look, could you check again with the gardener?" Rowland said grimly. "Someone must have seen them."

Rowland found his brother in his study. "Wil, we have a problem." He told Wilfred of their failure to find either Ernest or the nanny.

Wilfred paled but he wasted no time. He phoned Harry Simpson and the other managers immediately, directing that every man on *Oaklea* down tools and join the search. And then he telephoned the police.

"She's probably taken him on some ramble and got lost," Wilfred said gruffly. "Let's not worry Kate. We'll probably find them within the hour."

Rowland said nothing. He hoped his brother was right. *Oaklea* was vast—how far could a six-year-old and his nanny possibly have walked by themselves?

"Perhaps one of them has been hurt... a snake..." Wilfred stopped. "Dear God."

Rowland pressed his brother's shoulder. "Come on, Wil, we'll join the search."

Outside Harry Simpson was already organising teams to scour the property in every direction. Rowland spotted Jack Templeton—he looked white and shaken.

"She wouldn't have gone far, Mr. Sinclair," he said. "Mrs. Sinclair had given her the afternoon off. We were going to the flicks in Yass just as soon as I got through with planting the elm trees."

"When did you last see her, Templeton?"

"This morning. She was speaking to Mr. Sinclair."

"Wil?"

"No, the other one."

Rowland thanked him, already striding back to Wilfred who was standing over maps, barking orders and directing men.

He told his brother what he'd ascertained from Templeton. "Where did Arthur and Lucy go from here, Wil?"

"I don't know," Wilfred said angrily. "Sydney I presume, though they may have stopped in Yass for lunch." He started towards the house, motioning for his brother to follow. "Rowly would you telephone the police again—see if they can find them." He paused as they stepped through the front door, removing his glasses and pinching the bridge of his nose. "I'm going up to advise Kate," he said slowly. "All these people here... she'll sense something." He faltered. "Would you mind asking Miss Higgins to stay with Kate?"

Rowland nodded, unnerved by his brother's fear. He had never seen Wilfred afraid.

Once he'd spoken to the police, Rowland ran upstairs to find Edna. She was waiting outside Kate's bedroom with Ewan, while Wilfred broke the news to his wife. Edna threw herself into Rowland's arms. Ewan protested as he was squashed between them.

"Sorry mate," Rowland said, taking his godson from the sculptress. He put one arm around Edna and told her more completely what was happening.

She looked up at him in horror. "Oh, Rowly, how could this happen?"

"I don't know, Ed. *Oaklea's* an extensive property and there are still a few uncleared patches and gullies. I wandered off when I was younger than Ernie. I'm told it took nearly six hours to find me."

"But Miss de Waring is with him."

"I hope she is. Perhaps he wandered off and she's looking for him." Rowland watched vaguely as Ewan played with his tiepin. "They can't have just vanished."

Edna glanced at the closed door behind which Wilfred was telling his wife that their eldest son was missing. "Poor Kate. She's already so upset about Lucy." The sculptress wiped her eyes and kissed Ewan's chubby hand. "We'll have to look after your mummy, won't we darling?"

"Thank you, Ed. You're a brick."

"Rowly, why don't you take *Doris* up over *Oaklea*? You might see something from the air."

"That's a capital idea, Ed," he said. "Ernie can't see a plane without waving like a lunatic." Grateful to have something he could do, he smiled and kissed the sculptress on the forehead.

Wilfred cleared his throat as he stepped out of the bedroom. He looked haggard, desperate.

Edna took Ewan from Rowland. She paused at the door, placing her hand gently on Wilfred's arm. He seemed startled. "I'll stay with Kate, Mr. Sinclair."

"Yes, thank you, Miss Higgins. The doctor will be here shortly."

Rowland told Wilfred of Edna's suggestion as they descended the stairs.

Wilfred checked his pocket watch. "We have a couple of hours before sunset. I'll go up with you. I can look while you fly the plane."

Rowland didn't argue, concluding that Wilfred needed to do something practical as much as he did.

Outside, Rowland looked for Clyde but it seemed he'd departed with a hastily recruited search party led by Harry Simpson. He spotted Jack Templeton who had just returned from an unsuccessful search with Bob Bowman's group and beckoned him over.

"Look, Templeton, Wil and I are going to take the plane up, see if we can spot them. Would you give me a hand, pull away the chocks, that sort of thing?"

"Of course, Mr. Sinclair. Anything to help. I can't believe they've just vanished." The young gardener choked on his words. He looked wretched.

"Thank you, Jack," Rowland said. "We'll find them, we'll find them both."

Rowland parked the Mercedes outside the shed and opened the doors. Wilfred and Templeton followed him in. He climbed onto the wing, rummaging in the cockpit for the second cap and goggles. "There's a pair of binoculars in the car. It might be a good idea to take them," he said, reaching into the passenger compartment.

"Hey, we still need to get the plane out," he called as he heard the doors swing shut, darkening the shed's interior.

"Rowly." Wilfred's voice.

Rowland turned. It took a few seconds for his eyes to adjust to the diminished light inside the now closed shed.

"Don't move, Rowland. Not an inch."

Templeton's voice...but different—angry, confident. The gardener had one hand on the back of Wilfred's collar, the other held the revolver he pressed against Wilfred's skull.

"What the hell—?"

"Come down from there, slowly now, 'cos believe me I'd be quite happy to shoot your bastard of a brother."

"Come on, Jack, steady..." Rowland did as the gardener asked, his mind working frantically to understand what was going on.

Templeton motioned him over to the Caterpillar. "You'll find a rope on the seat. Give it to Mr. Sinclair here."

Again Rowland had no other choice but to do as he was told.

Templeton pushed Wilfred forward. "Now tie Rowland to that post over there. Either one of you tries anything and I'll shoot you both, I swear."

"What do you want, Templeton?" Wilfred asked as he bound Rowland to the post. He tied the knots securely, but carefully ensured there was just a little give in the bonds.

Templeton waited till he finished, and then with the gun trained on Wilfred, he stepped behind the post to test the knots. He noticed the slight slackness. The gardener didn't hesitate, stepping back suddenly and shooting Rowland in the upper arm. The bullet chipped the post after tearing through Rowland's flesh.

Both Sinclairs swore, Rowland in pain and Wilfred in horror. Instinctively Rowland struggled against the rope. His arm was on fire but he could still move his hand. Desperately he tried to loosen the bonds while the chance existed. It did not exist for long enough.

"Let's try again, Mr. Sinclair. If you don't tie him up properly this time I'll be forced to immobilise him by other means." Templeton pointed the revolver at Rowland's head.

Having evidence that Templeton would carry out his threat, Wilfred tightened the bonds. Rowland cursed as his arm was pulled back. "I'm sorry, Rowly," Wilfred said quietly. Then to Templeton, "He's bleeding, he needs a doctor."

"No, he doesn't," Jack Templeton said firmly. "Now you."

"I can't tie myself up, you idiot," Wilfred said, taking out his handkerchief and clamping it against the bloody wound on Rowland's arm. Removing his own tie, Wilfred used it to bind the handkerchief in place.

Templeton moved towards the Caterpillar. "Before you decide to be heroic, Mr. Sinclair, you may wish to remember that your brother cannot run or duck and I'm a pretty good shot." He kicked out a bag stashed behind the tractor and without taking his eyes from Wilfred or his gun from Rowland, extracted a pair of handcuffs. "Turn around, Mr. Sinclair, and put your hands behind your back."

Wilfred didn't move.

"I could just shoot out your kneecaps," Templeton said, aiming the gun accordingly.

"Wil," Rowland said. "Do what he wants."

Slowly, Wilfred turned and placed his hands behind him.

Templeton pressed the muzzle of the gun on Wilfred's neck and secured the handcuffs. With both Sinclairs now restrained, he seemed to relax slightly. He shoved Wilfred back against the post to which Rowland was tied and forced him onto his knees.

"What do you want, Templeton?" Rowland asked this time. The initial shock of pain was settling and he was focussing again.

"You don't remember me at all do you, Rowland?" Templeton stepped up to him.

"Should I?"

"I used to live here, was born here, in fact. We even played together once or twice before your father forbade it."

Rowland said nothing.

"Of course, why would you remember me? I was one of the workers' kids. Not good enough for you uppity Sinclairs to remember or even think about!"

Rowland stared at him, trying to force some sort of recognition... and then it came. More a guess than a realisation. "You're one of Charlie Hayden's boys!"

34

AID FOR ORPHANAGES

The man who called himself Jack Templeton smiled. "Yes. Charlie was my dear old dad."

Rowland winced. "I didn't kill your father."

"I know, I finished the bastard myself."

Both Rowland and Wilfred stared at him. Templeton seemed to relish their bewilderment, their attention.

"I'd just tracked Charlie to Queensland, drinking himself to death in Toowoomba," he said, "when suddenly, he takes off! The old soaks who drank with him reckoned he'd come into some money." Templeton sneered. "I wasn't going to let the old mongrel get away from me, so I followed. Could have knocked me dead when I realised he'd come back to Yass. And then, I heard Miss Walling was looking for some men to help with Lord Wilfred's fancy gardens."

"He recognised you?" Rowland asked, remembering that Hayden had waited on the verandah for Kate with a full view of the gardens in which Edna Walling and her men were working.

"Oh yes. Wanted me to help him extort a little something extra from you Sinclairs. When I refused, the drunken fool thought he might be able to persuade me with a thrashing. But I'm not a boy anymore."

"If you know we had nothing to do with your father's death, what the hell are you doing?" Wilfred demanded. "My God man, I don't have time for this—I have to find my son!"

"My issue, Mr. Sinclair, is with you—what you did."

"What I… because I sacked your father?"

"You did more than sack him, Mr. Sinclair, you destroyed him, you exiled him, and in the process you destroyed his family, my family." Templeton pushed the revolver muzzle up under Wilfred's chin. "My old man wasn't such a bad bloke until your bloody father instructed him to flog Rowland here. Then dad decided that if it was good enough for the Sinclairs, his own boys could probably benefit from having the living dickens belted out of them. But you never thought about that, did you?"

"How the devil was he supposed to know?" Rowland said in his brother's defence. "He didn't even know about what was happening to me."

"Yes, but once he found out, he sorted it, didn't he? Whichever one of you killed old Henry, life got much better for you after that, didn't it, Rowland? But it got a helluva lot worse for us! We lost everything!"

"What did you expect me to do?" Wilfred said, meeting Templeton's eye. "There are still scars on Rowly's back from what your father did that night. Did you really expect me to keep him on?"

"No, I would have thanked you if you'd shot him along with your own father. But you didn't, did you? You punished all of us. We were destitute. My mother took her own life. My brother and I went to an orphanage. We didn't think life could get any worse, but it did. It did. And neither of you ever even wondered what had happened to Charlie Hayden's lads."

Rowland tried to reason with him. "Look, Templeton, we didn't know. Perhaps we should have thought about you but it was a helluva time and we were doing the best we could…"

"It was me who sacked your father," Wilfred said. "That was all me. It was nothing to do with Rowly, or my son."

Templeton laughed. "What my father did was nothing to do with me either, but I paid for it."

"For God's sake, Templeton, he's a little boy!" Rowland pleaded.

"You don't deserve to be a father, Sinclair!" Templeton spat at Wilfred. "In the end you're the same man your father was. How many times have you belted that poor kid?"

Wilfred pulled back, stunned by the thought.

"Jack," Rowland said, seeing hope in the accusation—Templeton was ironically trying to protect Ernest on some level. "Wil's never laid a hand on the boys… not to hurt them."

"How would you know?" Templeton retorted. "He claims not to have known what was happening to you. Maybe you're as oblivious as he was."

"What do you want, Templeton?" Wilfred asked. His voice was strained, unsteady. "If it's money, I'll give you whatever you want—name your price, just, for God's sake, give me back my son."

"Can't do that. I'm not stupid, Mr. Sinclair. I know this isn't going to end well for me. Afraid it's not going to end well for you either." He poked Wilfred with the barrel of the revolver. "I was just going to stick around and enjoy watching you grieve, like I grieved for my mother. Don't even know where they buried her. A pauper's grave somewhere I expect—a stark contrast to the marble monument you erected for your father. I thought it would be fitting to watch you with no grave to mourn. But somehow, I don't think taking your son will be enough. I'll have to shoot you."

"What have you done with Ernest?" Rowland demanded as he watched his brother turn grey with grief and terror. "I know you haven't hurt him, Jack. You liked him, he liked you!" Rowland was speaking as much to Wilfred as their captor.

"I did like him, but you're wrong."

Rowland struggled against the urgency of his own anguish, stemming it with denial and a desperation to save his brother.

Jack Templeton took aim at the back of Wilfred's head.

Wilfred barely moved, defeated by the loss of his son.

Rowland shouted, straining against the rope, ignoring the physical pain as he threatened and begged. "Stop, Jack, please! I can fly you out of here. Kate—Mrs. Sinclair's about to have a baby... for pity's sake, man!"

Templeton turned on him. "Shut up!" he screamed. "Shut the hell up. I can't think!"

"I can fly you to Queensland. You'll have such a head start they'll never find you! Just stop."

Templeton aimed at Wilfred again, but he hesitated. "What about your arm?" he said.

SULARI GENTILL

"I'm all right," Rowland replied, seeing Templeton's resolve weaken. "I can fly."

Templeton took a knife from his belt and cut the ropes binding Rowland. "Get the plane ready. Try anything and I'll kill your brother."

Pushing the Gipsy Moth out of the shed by himself proved to be a challenge. Rowland didn't think he was badly wounded, but moving his arm was painful. He'd hoped that, out of frustration or impatience, Templeton might be tempted to help, to let down his guard and point the gun away from Wilfred. Instead the gardener secured Wilfred to the post while Rowland used the Caterpillar to pull the plane out.

Eventually the *Rule Britannia* was ready and waiting on the flat of the paddock outside, but still in view of the shed. Rowland climbed up onto the fuselage to switch on the fuel lines. Templeton backed out of the shed and clambered into the second cockpit, the revolver now aimed directly at Rowland.

"What are you doing?" he demanded as Rowland moved to jump off.

"I have to swing the propeller to start the engine or we are not going anywhere."

"Remember that I've got the gun. Try anything and I'll get out of the plane and shoot your brother."

"Yes, you've made that perfectly clear."

From his elevated position on the fuselage, Rowland had caught sight of the convoy in the distance. He dropped onto the ground before Templeton saw it too. Out of the corner of his eye, he could see Wilfred struggling against the ropes. Determined to keep Templeton in the biplane, he spun the propeller.

Now Jack Templeton saw the vehicles hurtling down the farm lane to *Emoh Ruo*. "Get in!" he shouted. "Get in and fly this bloody contraption!"

Rowland declined in terms that were profane and certain. He ducked, ready for the shot this time. A second shot splintered the propeller blade. He moved under the fuselage.

The motorcars reached the gate. Templeton launched himself out of the cockpit and ran for the shed. Rowland went after him, charging him to the ground just short of the doors. They grappled for the gun. Rowland slammed Templeton's hand to the ground as the gardener pulled the trigger.

Rowland wasn't sure where that bullet went, nor the next. Pinning Templeton, he forced open the gardener's hand and disarmed him. And then he punched him, repeatedly.

It was Clyde who pulled Rowland off.

"What have you done with him, you bastard?" Rowland was desperate. "What the hell have you done with Ernie?"

Templeton shook his head. Rowland lunged for him again.

Milton helped Clyde hold Rowland back this time, and it took the both of them. Detective Gilbey arrested Jack Templeton. Delaney uncuffed Wilfred, but held him back, in an effort to ensure that he, too, did not attack the prisoner.

"Rowly, you're bleeding," Clyde said, noticing the wound.

Rowland staggered, a little light-headed now. Milton steadied him.

"How did you—" Rowland began.

"We found Miss de Waring… the nanny," Delaney replied.

"Thank God," Wilfred said quietly. "She and Ernest are unhurt?"

Delaney flinched. "Ernest wasn't with her, Mr. Sinclair. We located Miss de Waring at the railway station waiting for Mr. Templeton. She said he was coming out to meet her as soon as he'd taken Ernest back to the house. They were planning to elope."

Nobody spoke as Wilfred Sinclair approached Templeton; nobody tried to stop him. "I understand, Templeton. I understand my part in all this. I swear I will do what I can for you, but for the love of God, man, tell me where my son is."

Rowland watched Templeton's face. First surprise and then the return of suspicion. His eyes hardened. "Drag the dams," he said.

35

CHILDBIRTH AT HOME

———◆———

Possible Hospital Danger
OPINION OF DOCTOR

Is Dr. H.G. Dain (chairman of the British Medical Association Committee on the National Maternity Service Scheme) right in stating that women are safer in childbirth at their own homes than they are in maternity hospitals? Dr. Dain declares that the danger from puerperal fever is great in hospitals, and that freedom from it in the home outweighs other disadvantages.

The News, 1930

Silently, Maguire stitched and dressed the lesion in Rowland's arm. Having passed cleanly through the flesh, the bullet, at least, had done no lasting damage. The rest of it was the worst kind of mess.

Wilfred sat behind the desk staring at a glass of whisky and smoking. Periodically he retrieved the watch from his pocket and checked the time, monitoring the hours since he'd last seen his son. Maguire finished with Rowland, and, pausing only to press Wilfred's shoulder, left them alone.

"He was lying, Wil, I know he was lying." Rowland said vehemently, pulling his blood-stained shirt back on. He slung the tie angrily around his neck.

"Then where is Ernie?" Wilfred's voice was brittle, ravaged with the enormity of his tragedy. "Every skerrick of the property's been systematically searched, every building, every shed, every flaming hollow log…"

"What about Bates? He and Templeton were friends. Perhaps—"

"The police have questioned him. Bates didn't know Templeton before they were both hired here. He doesn't know anything."

Rowland closed his eyes. This was unbearable. "There must be places we've not yet looked."

"There are," Wilfred replied. "The dams."

"Wil, no." Rowland turned away. He could not bring himself to think of his nephew as gone. It was incomprehensible. "Templeton liked him. He wouldn't have hurt him."

"You say that because that's what you want to believe!" Wilfred lashed out. "You and your set see only what you wish to see—good when it suits you, evil when it doesn't. Why the hell didn't you tell me Templeton was having an affair with Ernest's nanny?"

Rowland faltered. He was flogging himself for that already. "It didn't seem to be any of our business…"

"None of our business!" Wilfred stood and came after his brother. "Since when is the immoral conduct of the woman I have entrusted with the care of my children not my business, Rowly?" He exploded, grabbing Rowland by the collar. "If I'd known… but no—you decide that it's perfectly acceptable for my staff to engage in the kind of debauchery to which you and your Communist ne'er-do-wells devote your miserable lives!"

"Wil, I'm sorry—"

"You're always sorry. It's never your fault." Wilfred seized Rowland's arms, shaking him. "Bloody hell, Rowly! That bastard's murdered my son and all you can offer is that he liked him!"

Rowland felt each of his brother's words more keenly than any blow. He knew that Wilfred was near crazed with grief, but that did little to shield him.

"I don't know that I can forgive you for this, Rowly." Wilfred couldn't stop. "If you'd said something we would have at least been wary—"

"I don't know that I'll ever forgive myself, Wil. I'm sorry. I know that's worth nothing now. Oh God, if I could change it…"

Wilfred stopped, aware suddenly that his hand was wet. He looked down at his grip on Rowland's arm. The stitches had broken, the wound had reopened. Blood now seeped anew through the gauze and fabric and Wilfred's fingers. He stepped back, jarred, recognising the damage in Rowland's eyes and, even in the blackness of his own sorrow, regretting that he'd inflicted it.

"God, Rowly," Wilfred's voice broke now. "I don't know how I'm going to tell Kate."

<hr>

In time the Sinclair brothers emerged from Wilfred's study together. They didn't speak. What resemblance they bore to each other was accentuated by a wretched grief, and yet they were both contained, rigid with the grim need to carry on. The sleeve of Rowland's jacket was torn, but the blood stains were less visible on the dark wool fabric and his tie was straight. Maguire had repaired the stitches on his arm without once asking how they'd come to be disturbed. Wilfred started up the stairs to speak with his wife.

Rowland wandered into the drawing room, unsure what to do. He extracted his notebook more out of habit than any idea of sketching. Folded in its pages, he found the drawing that Ernest had presented to him so solemnly.

It was some while later that his friends found him there, staring at the picture, unable to move away from it. Edna simply curled up on the couch beside him. Absently he put his arm around her.

"How's Kate?" he asked.

"She was holding up… terrified but… Wilfred's with her now… She refuses to believe the worst."

Rowland blanched. Unsure whether he could say anything without swearing, he said nothing.

Edna rested her head on his shoulder. "We're so sorry, Rowly." Her tears were hot and wet as they soaked through his shirt. He held onto her. It was easier to comfort Edna.

Clyde and Milton sat opposite. Milton broke. "I'm sorry we pulled you off the scheming bastard, Rowly. We should have let you beat the useless life out of him. We should have helped!"

"Milt…" Clyde cautioned, unsure that Rowland was ready to discuss the man who killed his nephew.

But the poet saw the guilt in Rowland's anguish. "He fooled us all, Rowly. He seemed like a good bloke. God, the mongrel even joined the search, knowing…"

Rowland looked sharply at the poet. "That's right… Templeton joined the search from the very beginning…" he said slowly. Wilfred's words came back. Every part of the property has been systematically searched. "What part of Oaklea did Templeton search?" Rowland asked, straightening. "Did he go anywhere in particular?"

Milton glanced at Clyde. "Not Oaklea. Templeton headed out with one of the first groups to Emoh Ruo."

"Dammit!" Rowland closed the notebook. "Dammit! How could I…?" He stood. "I'm a flaming idiot!"

"Rowly, what is it?" Edna asked.

"I think I know where he took Ernie." Rowland cursed, furious that he had not seen it before. "Of course, Ernie wouldn't be found if Templeton made sure he was the one that searched there, if he reported back that there was nothing there..."

Clyde stood. "What do you—it doesn't matter. I'll get Wilfred."

"No!" Rowland grabbed his arm. "Wil's barely hanging on. If I'm wrong..."

"Let's go," Edna said, standing. "It's dark."

For the second time that day the yellow Mercedes pulled up outside the shed at *Emoh Ruo*. They took torches for they would go on foot from there.

Setting out across the paddock they headed towards the creek in search of the folly which Rowland had recommended to the young lovers in *Oaklea*'s kitchen. It was not difficult to find once you knew it was there. A crumbling concrete structure built to resemble a classical temple, it was a folly in more senses than one. Erected before the war when Jefferies had been fascinated with ancient architecture, it became a symbol of the whimsical self-indulgent expenditure that saw him lose everything in the end.

The dark outline of the faux relic became visible as they reached the top of the gully in which it was hidden.

Rowland broke into a run. "Ernie! Ernest! Can you hear me?"

There was no response.

Almost completely hidden among a thicket of willows, the building was much larger than it had seemed at first—cement columns on a parapet and large stone blocks arranged to look like ruins.

"Rowly—over here." Clyde shone the beam of his torch on a new padlock which secured a wooden door to the only walled part of the folly. The blackberry which had started to engulf the building was disturbed here, recently removed.

Rowland banged on the door and called Ernest's name again. Still no reply. "We'll force the door," he said.

"You've just been stitched back together," Milton reminded him. "Clyde and I will do it."

The padlock may have been new, but the latch itself was old and rusted. It gave way almost immediately and the door moved in. Then came the blast, a boom that seemed to shake the walls of the folly. Clyde and Milton recoiled, dropping to the ground, and Rowland turned to shield Edna. But the explosion seemed contained, confined within the building. Nobody came out.

Rowland moved first. "Ernie!"

Milton grabbed him before he reached the door. "Rowly—stop! You don't know what else he's rigged up in there."

"Ernie could be hurt…"

"Just be careful, Rowly. Go slowly."

Rowland nodded. "You chaps and Ed stand back." Gently, very gradually, he pushed open the door. Plaster showered down from the ceiling. Clyde handed him a torch.

Rowland played the beam of light around what was a windowless cabin. A shotgun lay smoking on the floor, the gardener's twine which had been used to rig it, a tangled mess. The bullets had hit the wall above the door—perhaps the Enfield had jerked up when it discharged.

They all stepped in now, adding their torches to the search to find Ernest motionless on what seemed to be a sheepskin in the far corner.

Rowland reached him first and bent to lift the boy into his arms, terrified that his body would be cold and rigid.

"He's breathing," he said, leaning back against the wall, suddenly weak. But his grip on Ernest was sure.

"Oh Ernie…" Edna stroked the boy's head. "Why won't he wake up? Oh God, was he hurt when the gun went off?"

Milton swung his torch back to the shotgun and the place where the bullets had impacted. The damage seemed fairly contained to the door's side of the room. "Can you find an injury? Is he bleeding?"

Edna checked the child quickly. "No."

Clyde retrieved an enamelled tin cup from the floor and sniffed it. "Templeton must have given him something."

"Probably Laudanum," Rowland said, remembering his mother's missing medication. Perhaps Templeton had asked Nanny de Waring to procure it for him somehow.

Milton removed his jacket and placed it over Ernest as he lay in Rowland's arms. Though the boy's eyes remained closed, he murmured and sighed.

"Come on, mate," Rowland said as he carried his nephew out. "There are some people at *Oaklea* who desperately need to see you."

———   ———

Clyde raced the Mercedes back to *Oaklea*, blasting the horn with Milton singing the Internationale in full voice out of the window so that by the time they pulled into the driveway, half the household had emerged to investigate the commotion.

Rowland handed Ernest to his father.

There was a moment when Wilfred simply stared at his brother and the band of grinning Communists who had ensconced themselves in his home.

"Templeton must have given him a sedative of some sort, Mr. Sinclair," Edna said, beaming, unable to contain her joy, "but he's already starting to stir."

"How—" Wilfred began.

"We'll explain later," Rowland said. "Take him to Kate."

———   ———

The kitchen at *Oaklea* had rarely been so festive. Rowland and his friends had felt the need to celebrate Ernest's return, but aware that *Oaklea* was not theirs they had abandoned the more formal parts of the house for Mrs. Kendall's kitchen. There they celebrated with the servants of the grand house, toasting young Ernest and drinking heartily to his health. Milton brought down the gramophone and Wilfred's record collection, and they danced to Crosby, Armstrong and Duke Ellington. In time, the party spilled out onto the back lawn, and Edna Walling and her workers and even Harry Simpson joined the impromptu celebrations. Alice Kendall opened her pantry, feeding all comers.

It was past midnight when Wilfred came down to find his brother. He watched quietly for a while as Rowland danced with Edna, and Milton led yet another toast to Ernest Aubrey Baird Sinclair who, he announced, would one day be Prime Minister of the Workers' Republic of Australia.

Rowland was a little merry when Wilfred approached them on the verandah which had become a dance floor. "Good Lord, Wil!" he said, catching Edna around the waist as she came out of a twirl. "You're the last person I'd expect to cut in!"

"I think it's you Mr. Sinclair wants, Rowly," Edna said, laughing.

Rowland's brow rose. "You can't dance with me, Wil... I'm a man."

Wilfred rolled his eyes, but he smiled, clapping his brother on the shoulder. "I do beg your pardon, Miss Higgins, but I would like to speak to Rowly while he's just vaguely sober."

Milton overheard from the tabletop from which he had been making toasts and raised his glass yet again, declaring defiantly, "Fill all the glasses there for why, should every creature drink but I, why, Man of Morals, tell me why?"

"Cowley," Rowland responded.

"Of course, you may speak with Rowly, Mr. Sinclair," Edna said, removing Rowland's hand from her waist. "I hope we haven't disturbed you and Mrs. Sinclair. We are all just so happy that Ernest is home and safe."

Wilfred nodded. "It's not at all inappropriate, Miss Higgins. If Mr. Isaacs has not already ransacked my cellar, please let him know that he's very welcome to do so."

Wilfred beckoned his brother to follow, pausing only to ask Mrs. Kendall to bring a pot of coffee to his study as soon as possible.

It was in the hallway that Rowland first heard the screams. Wilfred only just grabbed him before he ran upstairs.

"Wil, that's Kate!" he said. Clearly, she was being attacked.

"I know, Rowly," Wilfred said calmly. "The baby's coming. It is a couple of weeks early but, with all that's happened..."

Another blood-curdling scream.

"For God's sake, Wil, that can't be right," Rowland said, glancing up to the staircase. "We can't just allow..."

"Her doctor and the midwives are with her, Rowly, don't worry—it's all well in hand."

Rowland blanched as Kate screamed again. "What the hell are they doing to her?"

"I'm afraid this part of the business can be rather grim," Wilfred said. "Let me assure you, Rowly, this is one occasion on which you cannot charge in to save the day."

Rowland clenched his hands in his hair, horrified. "God Wil, how do you stand it?"

Wilfred sighed. "Usually, I drink. But right now I need you to sober up a little."

He took Rowland into his study and, when the pot of coffee arrived, poured him a cup. "How's your arm?" he asked.

"It stopped hurting a couple of drinks ago," Rowland replied, hoping the coffee wasn't going to reverse that particular effect. He told his brother where they had found Ernest and why he had thought to look there. Rowland braced himself for Wilfred's fury, but he was honest about his part in it. "I'm sorry, Wil. I told Templeton about the folly to give him and Miss de Waring somewhere private to... meet."

Wilfred blinked. "Look, Rowly," he said finally. "I'm not thrilled that you felt the need to assist in the corruption of a young woman, but perhaps if Templeton hadn't known about the folly, Ernie would, in fact, have ended up in the dam." He closed his eyes. The thought was still too recently real. "I intend to say this again when you are not compromised by drink, but thank you. If Ernie had woken before you got there, he may have tried the door himself. Thank you for not despairing, as I had."

Rowland flinched as another agonised scream penetrated the door of Wilfred's study. It was by far, more sobering than the coffee. "How long does—?"

"Hard to say, but each of the boys took several hours."

"Good Lord... I think I might need another drink."

"Not yet. There are some people we need to talk to."

"Now? Who?"

"Arthur and Lucy are waiting for us in the drawing room."

36

ANOTHER PRINCE IN THE BRITISH ROYAL FAMILY

It is an interesting piece of news, especially to women. The arrival of a baby in any home—or should it be a private hospital?—is an item of conversation among the women in the neighbourhood. They must see the infant. Of course, it is cute—all babies are cute—and so, like its mother or father, even though it might not resemble either parent. This interest in other people's children is a feminine characteristic. Father celebrates the arrival of a baby in a different way. He invites his friends to the bar counter for a drink, the ceremony being known as wetting the baby's head. It is worthy of note that this enthusiasm on the part of father cools off as later children come to share his pay roll and add to his anxieties.

The News, 1935

Elisabeth Sinclair had been entertaining her nephew and his fiancée while they waited. Lucy looked distressed and quite frightened by the sounds of childbirth which intermittently reached the drawing room. It was an awkward time to visit.

"Should I look in on Kate?" Elisabeth asked as she stood to leave. The nurse, now her shadow, stood also.

"No." Wilfred was firm. "The doctor has it all in hand. You should try to get some sleep, Mother."

"I'm not sure I will be able to, with the noise." She reached up and stroked Rowland's cheek warmly. "I remember when you were born," she said. "Wilfred burst in with a stick because he thought I was being murdered in my bed. How it made me laugh. He was always so protective."

She said goodnight and left them to it.

"I expect she was talking about Aubrey's birth," Rowland murmured. He had not heard the story before.

"No, it was yours," Wilfred said, frowning. "It was Aubrey who charged in with the stick though, not me."

Arthur Sinclair began. "Look, Wilfred, can I start by saying how distressed Lucy and I genuinely were when the police told us about Ernest being missing. We came straight back to see if we could help. Whatever's gone on between us, we were—are—very fond of the little dickens!"

"The police questioned us like common criminals," Lucy said tearfully. "I can't believe you thought for a moment that we would be involved in a kidnapping like that. I'm Ewan's godmother!"

"Templeton indicated he'd seen you talking to the nanny. At the time we had no idea of his involvement," Wilfred said brusquely.

"She congratulated us on our engagement," Lucy said. "Said she was getting married too, and introduced us to Mr. Templeton. It was rather unusual to have servants be so familiar."

"You spoke to Templeton?"

"He gave me an envelope," Arthur replied. "Said it was something he found that belonged to me. I put it in my pocket for later. I assumed I'd dropped something in the garden."

"What was it?" Rowland asked.

Arthur hesitated. "To be honest, I only thought to look in it when we heard that Templeton was involved in Ernest's disappearance. It was the last payment I'd made to Hayden. I gave it to him the morning after the fire."

"I see," Wilfred said coldly. "You are aware, I hope, that Hayden was Jack Templeton's father, and that Templeton killed him that day."

"Yes," Arthur replied.

"Perhaps you're also aware that your duplicity, your headlong pursuit of what you consider your birthright may have ended in a tragedy much greater than the death of my father."

Arthur glanced at Lucy. He took her hand. "A couple of days after I went back to Sydney, I received a message from a barrister I briefed occasionally when I was in practice in Melbourne. I had other things on my mind, so I didn't think to return the call until Lucy and I had come back to Yass, and were waiting for news of Ernest. I telephoned him from the Royal. I believe you gentlemen both know him... Dag—that is, Robert—Menzies."

"Yes," Wilfred's eyes narrowed shrewdly. "I am acquainted with the man."

"He told me he'd recently had a visit from my cousin."

Both Rowland and Wilfred stiffened, aware that this breach of bail could see Rowland sent back to Long Bay until trial.

"Bob told me what you'd discussed," Arthur continued. "Whatever you may think of me now, Wilfred, let me say that I acted on a conviction that you'd killed Uncle Henry."

"I see. And what Menzies told you has led you to doubt that conviction?" Wilfred posed impassively.

"He was with you when the gun was fired. I don't know how I could not doubt it. He also told me about his conversation with Aunt Libby that evening."

"Did he? And what do you plan to do with this information?"

Arthur Sinclair paused. "I intend to withdraw any allegations I've made against you and Rowland, both formally and informally. Now that Templeton has confessed to murdering his father, the case against Rowland will fall apart anyway. There is nothing to be gained for anyone by pursuing this matter any further and I believe we shall all have to be happy with calling Uncle Henry's murder an unsolvable mystery."

"What do you want in return, Arthur?" Wilfred asked bluntly.

"I presume there's too much water under the bridge for us ever to be friends again?"

"You presume correctly."

"Then let us settle this like gentlemen at least. I'm getting married. I would like to be able to afford to do so."

Wilfred glared at his cousin. "Very well," he said in the end. "We have property in Northern Queensland. Its value is equivalent to what you might have hoped to receive from your father's estate had he not disinherited you. I'll sign it over to you on the condition that you and Lucy go and never darken my doorstep again."

"Haven't you had enough of exiling people, Wilfred?"

"The offer is fair, Arthur. My son may have died as a result of the events you put into train."

"Those events were put into train long before I came upon the scene. What if we refuse?"

"Then you will get nothing."

"I know things, Wilfred."

"Indeed. May I remind you, Arthur, that your beloved fiancée tried to shoot my brother in a fit of pique and passion? You may recall I took her gun from her that night? Do not test me. I am being more than fair."

Rowland watched the exchange uneasily. Wilfred was almost emotionless as he negotiated with Arthur Sinclair. There was a ruthlessness about him, but it was tempered. The offer was fair. Arthur vacillated. Lucy cried. She appealed to Rowland, first apologising for shooting at him, then accusing him of jealousy, of exacting revenge by banishing them to the wilds of Queensland. Wilfred would not be moved.

In the end, Arthur accepted. The deal was struck and Wilfred escorted his cousin and Lucy Bennett to the door.

He returned to the drawing room to find Rowland waiting. Both men winced as Kate screamed again. Wilfred glanced anxiously behind him and left the door open. "I thought you might have gone back to your party," he said, clearly distracted.

Rowland shook his head. "We should talk about Mother, Wil."

"What about Mother?"

"I think she should come and reside with me at *Woodlands*."

"Absolutely not!"

Rowland took a deep breath. He had fully expected his brother to resist, he was prepared to make his case. "Wil, it's safer for everybody if Mother comes with me."

"Safer? Good Lord, Rowly, Mother isn't a danger to anyone."

"Let's make sure. You have two little boys and soon there'll be a new baby. Mother has always made Kate nervous. Now that we know, let's just be sure."

"You're not suggesting Mother would hurt Kate? That's—"

"No, of course not. I just mean that the anxiety can't be good for either of them. Besides, I think Kate's entitled to be mistress of her own house. That'll always be difficult with Mother playing empress dowager here."

Wilfred sat down opposite his brother. "Rowly, *Woodlands* is not an appropriate residence for a lady—"

Rowland smiled. "It'll be fine, Wil. I'll make sure she's gone to bed before we do anything particularly debauched."

"This is not a joke, Rowly!"

"Look, Wil, let's just try it for a while. She can always come back if it doesn't work out."

Kate screamed again. Rowland could see the perspiration beading on Wilfred's brow. This evening was his best chance of changing his brother's mind. "I'll have the south wing made ready for her and the nurses. She'll have her own part of the house—privacy if she wants it. The people who live with me may be Communists but they are adults. They understand about Mother, and I don't keep any weapons in the house."

Wilfred reared. "Mother is not some crazed gun-wielding lunatic!"

"I'm not saying that, Wil. But we don't know what caused her to shoot Father. We can't ask her, we can't be sure what exactly happened. So let's be careful. You've got to allow me to do my bit."

Wilfred wavered.

"You can't possibly think that I'd neglect or be unkind to our mother?" Rowland pressed.

"No. No, I don't think that."

"Then, let's try it. It's got to be preferable to a sanatorium."

A particularly long and agonised cry. Wilfred stood, pacing now. "Perhaps having Mother with you will help you settle down... grow up a little, finally take responsibility," he said gruffly.

Rowland shrugged. He didn't want to trick Wilfred into relenting. "I'll still be me, Wil. But Mother can call me Aubrey or whatever else she wishes. I believe coming back to Sydney might do her good. She can lunch at the Queens' Club, have a day at the races, visit the beach at Thirroul. I think being occupied might suit her."

"I don't think you realise how difficult Mother can be, Rowly."

"All the more reason she should come with me, I think. If it doesn't work, Wil, we'll figure something else out, but we should try."

Wilfred groaned. "I can't believe I'm agreeing to this. Perhaps I'm the one who should be committed!"

———————

Rowland watched amused as Edna held his new nephew. She and Kate sat in one of the newly installed garden seats. The sculptress's face was set determinedly as she cradled the child stiffly in her arms. Milton nudged Rowland, grinning. They both knew Edna was afraid of babies. She was fine with children, though she tended to treat them like cats—plying them with milk when in doubt—but babies terrified her.

On that score Rowland could sympathise. Newborns were odd, fragile creatures—quite slippery if you weren't careful. Fortunately nobody expected men to hold babies, so he had been spared the awkwardness of it all.

Gilbert Ambrose Baird Sinclair had come into the world in the early hours of the morning after his brother had been feared dead. And so he arrived at a time when grief and joy had already visited his parents in close succession.

Wilfred Sinclair was as besotted with young Gilbert as he was with each of his sons. The child's head had been wetted with champagne and the silver spoon placed firmly in his mouth. In the wake of recent events, Wilfred had retained two new nannies, both middle-aged, hefty, severe-faced women who would be unlikely to elope with gardeners. They rarely allowed the children out of their sights, hovering, ready to pounce on any would-be abductor. Milton swore they were carrying pistols in their garters.

Gilbert was ten days old now.

Clyde closed and secured the bonnet of the Mercedes, satisfied that everything was in order for the journey to *Woodlands House*. He and Milton were taking the motorcar while Edna flew back with Rowland in the *Rule Britannia*. Wilfred insisted upon escorting Elisabeth Sinclair to Sydney himself a week hence, giving his brother time to prepare for her arrival. For her part, Elisabeth seemed quite pleased to be moving back to Woollahra with Aubrey.

Wilfred came out with Ernest and Ewan in tow. He and the boys would take Rowland and Edna to *Emoh Ruo* once Milton and Clyde were on their way. They all waited patiently as twenty-month-old Ewan navigated the steps, refusing any sort of assistance.

Then Wilfred shook hands with the Communists. He had always been polite, but there was, on this occasion, a restrained and cautious warmth to his farewell. Even so, he was unlikely to ever entirely approve of Rowland's left-wing friends.

Being a practical rather than effusive man, not given to expansive expressions of gratitude, he had instead commissioned Clyde Watson Jones to produce a series of paintings depicting the gardens Edna Walling had created at *Oaklea*. Wilfred wanted a detailed record of the grounds as they matured, and of course, his brother refused to paint trees. Edna too, had been commissioned to create a bronze sculpture for the pond with the stipulation that nakedness be avoided at all costs. For Milton, there was little Wilfred could do as the poet seemed to do so little, but Wilfred Sinclair was a man with a long memory and his debts were always settled in the end.

"Righto, Rowly," Milton called as he opened the driver's side door. "We'll leave you and Ed to Heaven's ebon vault, studded with stars unutterably bright, through which the moon's unclouded grandeur rolls!"

"You and Shelley can rest assured we'll be back in Sydney well before nightfall," Rowland said, laughing.

The poet waved and Clyde pressed the horn as they set off.

Young Ernest chased the Mercedes down the drive and the nannies chased him.

THE CLARK ART EXHIBITION

NOTES ON THE ARTISTS

The following are additional notes on the artists represented at the exhibition of pictures in the possession of Mr. E.M. Clarke, now being exhibited in Hobart:

WILLIAM BECKWITH McINNES
William B. McInnes was born at Malvern in 1889. He began his art studies at the early age of 14 at the Melbourne Gallery, where he worked first under Fred McCubbin, and afterwards under Bernard Hall. In 1912 he went to Europe and stayed for two years during which time he devoted himself almost entirely to landscape. This was new ground for young McInnes as hitherto he had been trained chiefly as a portrait painter. McInnes has a fine sense of colour and a keen eye for the essential in a landscape, and is extraordinarily dexterous in his handling. McInnes has had the distinction of winning the Archibald Prize for three consecutive years. He has had many commissions as a portrait painter and has painted several notable "group" pictures.

The Mercury, 1926

Rowland poured drinks from the pitcher of chilled punch that Mary Brown had left on the sideboard. He and his friends had spent a good part of the day painting the black walls of the dining room, using white pigment to inscribe dense, detailed figures and patterns. Milton had contributed borrowed verse along the line where the wall joined the skirting boards and cornices. The result was dramatic, somewhat Beardsleyesque, and quite breathtaking.

The exercise had been a whim, begun in jest, but had quickly consumed them all. The residents of *Woodlands House* had never before applied their art together, blending their styles and ideas into a single, quite extraordinary piece upon the four walls of the room.

While they'd worked, they had discussed the issue of Rosalina Martinelli and her determination to marry Clyde with what they all considered an unseemly haste. Strategies were postulated, debated and eventually dismissed for one reason or another. Keeping Rowland out of gaol, it seemed, was less problematic than keeping Clyde out of wedlock.

Eventually they withdrew to Rowland's studio with their drinks. Rowland's paintings had been returned to the walls and it once again looked familiar, if somewhat tidier than usual.

Mary Brown brought in a platter of sandwiches and cakes since the dining room could not be used for eating. She communicated her disapproval of the unusual redecoration through a series of world-weary sighs.

Rowland grinned. His housekeeper's disapprobation felt comfortingly normal after the past weeks.

Despite Wilfred's misgivings about the manner in which his brother ran *Woodlands*, Rowland had directed that they should carry on as usual. He was certain that his mother, when she arrived, would simply get used to them, ignoring anything that did not match the world in her mind. She appeared not to notice, after all, that everybody else called him Rowland in her determination that he was Aubrey. It was only when the fantasy was directly challenged by him that she seemed to break down.

His friends were unperturbed about the impending addition to the household. Indeed Milton declared openly that his grandmother was madder than Rowland's mother any day. "It's not just pistols you have to keep from my granny, mate," he confided. "We've been hiding the knives for years. Upper class lunacy has nothing on the proletariat variety!"

"What's that?" Edna asked as Clyde lugged in a large flat box which had just been delivered to the door. The sculptress wore overalls, and a shirt belonging to one or another of the gentlemen she lived with. Her hair was pulled back under a scarf and yet the only indication that she'd been painting was the faint smear of white on cheek. Rowland's unprotected suit was, on the other hand, completely splattered. Lenin too, had, in solidarity with his master, collected several drips of white paint on his brindle coat.

"This," Milton said, gleefully cutting open the box, "is the portrait that Rowly and I had done at Central Police Station."

"You don't sit for portraits in a prison!"

Milton made space and sat the large framed photograph on the mantel, stepping back to admire it.

"You can't put that up here!" Clyde exclaimed.

"Why not? It's an excellent photograph," Milton said. "Captures a certain camaraderie, a joie de vivre in the face of injustice!"

"There's a height scale on the wall... it's a police mugshot!"

"I like it," Rowland said, tilting his head to consider the image. "It's a very fitting memento."

"Wilfred won't like it."

"Wil never looks too closely at what's on my walls. I think it frightens him."

Edna sat cross-legged on the armchair with a sandwich. Henry Sinclair's portrait stared thunderously down from the wall. Now that she knew, she could make out William McInnes' signature. "Rowly, do you keep that painting because it's a McInnes?" she asked. Rowland was a portrait painter after all. The quality of McInnes' work might well have overridden the subject of it.

Rowland glanced up from his notebook. He had been sketching the sculptress, but that was not unusual. "In a manner of speaking." He closed the notebook and stood to examine the oil painting. "I was about twelve when my father sat for McInnes. He came to the house. When Father wasn't actually sitting, I'd watch McInnes work. It was my first experience of portraiture."

"So that's why you hang it here?"

Rowland smiled. "It's also my first foray into painting."

"You painted this?" Edna asked surprised. Aside from the fact that the portrait was not the work of a child, Rowland's style was different.

"Of course not." He beckoned her over. Standing her before him, he put his hands on her shoulders to direct her gaze. "Do you see anything odd about that painting? A mistake perhaps?"

They all stared at the portrait. Clyde picked it first. "There's a highlight on his earlobe that doesn't belong," he said, pointing out the dot of titanium white paint. "It doesn't really fit with the direction of the light."

"After that day in the woolshed when Father sacked John Barrett and… well you know the story."

"Yes," Edna said leaning back against him.

"I was forbidden to set foot outside the house. McInnes called me into the room he was using, to show me the finished painting before anyone else. He felt sorry for me, I suppose." Rowland frowned slightly. "Then he left the room for some reason I can't recall."

"And you painted that highlight to flaw the portrait?" Edna asked tentatively.

"Actually I painted pearl earrings and a tiara on his head."

They turned to gape at him. Milton laughed first. "Bloody oath, Rowly, you had a death wish, but I'm so proud of you!"

"What happened?" Edna said fearfully. She did not want to hear again that Rowland had been barbarically punished.

"McInnes painted over it. My father never saw what I'd done," Rowland replied. "But he left that point of white so I'd always know there were earrings and a tiara under there. Sometimes that helped."

Edna looked back at the painting, seeing it differently suddenly. It was more Rowland than his father now. A symbol of a boy's defiance, a precursor to the man he'd become. She smiled, delighted. "Does Wilfred know?"

"No. Wil believes I hang the painting here to taunt my father's image with naked women in his favourite armchair."

"Will you ever tell him the truth?"

"Good Lord, no!"

"But with everything that's happened..."

"With everything that's happened," Rowland said, laughing, "I'm rather looking forward to going back to not talking about things again."

Epilogue

Jack Templeton revealed the whereabouts of Ernest Sinclair within twelve hours of his arrest. He had, as Rowland suspected, always liked the boy and intended him no direct harm. Of course, Ernest had, by that time, already been rescued by his uncle and a band of Communists.

Templeton was duly charged with the murder of his father, Charles Hayden, and the kidnapping of Ernest Sinclair. On the charge of murder, the defence argued successfully for mitigation, and he was convicted of the lesser charge of manslaughter as well as that of kidnapping. The charges against Rowland Sinclair were dropped.

Elisabeth Sinclair sent out beautifully illuminated cards announcing her return to Sydney. Three nurses moved with her and worked tirelessly in shifts to ensure she had around-the-clock care. While she was never again the toast of Sydney society, Elisabeth settled well at Woodlands enjoying the idiosyncrasies of her son's social connections. She established a particular rapport with Milton Isaacs, whom she believed to be related somehow to Sir Isaac Isaacs, the then governor-general. For his part, Milton did nothing to disillusion her.

Once established, the grounds and parklands developed by Edna Walling at *Oaklea* became a showpiece of garden design. The rose beds that Wilfred Sinclair had planted for his new bride remained, an eccentricity of box-edged formality in the rambling country estate.

———————◆———————

The picture Ernest Sinclair drew for his uncle was duly framed and hung beside the Picasso at *Woodlands House*. It remained the pride of Rowland's collection.

———————◆———————

The Sane Democracy League continued to pursue Rowland Sinclair in an attempt to recruit him, his fortune and his connections to their cause. Rowland continued to resist. On occasion, however, Milton Isaacs would attend one of their debates or information sessions for his own amusement.

———————◆———————

Colonel Eric Campbell unsuccessfully contested the 1935 State Election in the seat of Lane Cove for the Centre Party. The party failed to win a single seat.

———————◆———————

After a plebiscite in August 1934, the dual role of Chancellor and Leader of Germany was confirmed upon Adolf Hitler, with an overwhelming majority. Hitler formally became the dictator of Germany.

———————◆———————

Rowland Sinclair joined the Movement Against War and Fascism as a fellow traveller, quietly putting his resources behind bringing Egon Kisch to Australia for the Anti-War Congress of 1934.

With his brother's blessing, Rowland Sinclair invested in Hugh D. McIntosh's milk bar venture which, initially at least, made the fortunes McIntosh predicted.

The Hon. Robert Gordon Menzies, KC, made the move to federal politics, successfully contesting the seat of Kooyong in September 1934. By October he'd been appointed the Minister for Industry and Attorney-General in the Lyons government. As Attorney-General he played a significant part in the attempt to deny entry to Egon Kisch—the Communist journalist in exile from Germany—who arrived on Australian shores in November of that year. In that respect he and Rowland Sinclair found themselves opposed.

In the absence of any reliable evidence, Henry Sinclair's murder remained unsolved, and amongst his sons, unmentioned.

Acknowledgements

For six books now, Rowland Sinclair has been my constant companion. But we have not been unchaperoned. I'd like to acknowledge here those real people whose company along the way has been entirely proper and deeply valued, and whose contributions to this work, and the sanity of its writer, must not go unmentioned.

My husband Michael, collaborator, counsel and enabler, against whom so many ideas have been bounced that he's beginning to dent.

My Dad, who read this manuscript whilst undergoing chemotherapy, who allows nothing to shake his belief in my work, and who never misses an opportunity to pass on my books (as several nurses and the odd doctor will attest).

My sister, Devini, who is my role model for sibling loyalty and support.

My sons, Edmund and Atticus, just because they're awesome.

Leith and Jason Henry, who have always had my back, who are involved in my books as friends, as readers and as inspiration.

Sarah Kynaston and Lesley Bocquet with whom I've discussed the unfolding plot of A Murder Unmentioned over numerous cups of coffee, and for whom, I have therefore spoiled this book. Sorry. Cheryl Bousfield, whose enthusiasm for my books has been a constant from the very first.

Scorners of the ground, David Tennant, Steve Eather and Kristen Alexander, who made sure Rowland's Gipsy Moth did not crash—unless it was supposed to. Fellow traveller, Nigel E. S. Irvine, who directed me to the appropriate gaol. Malcolm Stradwick who allowed me to give him the third degree when necessary.

My extraordinary friends in the writing community, who have made me welcome among them. The solitary nature of writing is countered by the wonderful solidarity of writers. I remain buoyed by your compassion, your generosity and your idealism.

Deonie Fiford, my editor. This would be so much more terrifying a venture without the confidence instilled by the knowledge that Deonie won't let me slip. My cover designer, Sofya Karmazina, who has given all the Rowland Sinclair books a 'face' upon which the world can look. Desanka Vukelich, who proofreads my manuscripts into something worthy of print.

All those readers, reviewers and bloggers who have allowed me the privilege of their attention, and who have given Rowland Sinclair an existence that is independent of me. You are truly appreciated.

The people of Batlow and its surrounds, many of whom have lent their names to this novel. There is nothing as fortifying as hometown support.

The Greens, Ali, John, Jenny and Marty, and the talented team at Pantera Press. You have given me a writer's life, and for the rest of that life, I will be grateful.

If you liked *A Murder Unmentioned* then look out for
the next book in the Rowland Sinclair Series

Give the Devil His Due

When Rowland Sinclair is invited to take his yellow Mercedes onto
the Maroubra Speedway, popularly known as the Killer Track, he
agrees without caution or reserve.

But then people start to die…

The body of a journalist covering the race is found in a House of
Horrors, an English blueblood with Blackshirt affiliations is killed
on the race track… and it seems that someone has Rowland in their
sights.

A strange young reporter preoccupied with black magic, a
mysterious vagabond, an up-and-coming actor by the name of
Flynn, and ruthless bookmakers all add mayhem to the mix.

With danger presenting at every turn, and the brakes long since
disengaged, Rowland Sinclair hurtles towards disaster with an artist,
a poet and brazen sculptress along for the ride.

Please Enjoy this Excerpt from

Give the Devil His Due

1

DASHED TO DEATH

———————➤◆◄———————

MAROUBRA SPEEDWAY SENSATION

SYDNEY, Monday

The Maroubra speedway has claimed another victim. R. G. (Phil) Garlick, well-known racing driver, dashed over the embankment, crashed into an electric light standard and was then hurled 20 feet to his death during the final of the All Powers Handicap on Saturday night.

Garlick was trying to pass Hope Bartlett and was travelling at 93 miles an hour when the car swerved and left the track. He was dead when help arrived.

The dreadful fatality is the sole topic among motorists today. There is a difference of opinion as to the safety of the track, but the view is held that it is necessary to make some alterations in order to obviate the likelihood of any further accidents of a similar nature.

The Richmond River Express and
Casino Kyogle Advertiser, 1927

Rowland Sinclair's dealings with the press were rarely so civil. To date, his appearances in the pages of Sydney's newspapers had been, at best, reluctant, and more frequently, the subject of legal proceedings for libel. On this occasion, however, Rowland's conversation with Crispin White of *Smith's Weekly* began most cordially.

The reporter was, in fact, the fourth whom Rowland had received that day. Heavily built, White's broad, lax countenance belied the wily acuity of his manner. A newshound who resembled a somewhat over-fed lap dog, but a newshound nonetheless.

Crispin White had written about the wealthy young artist before. He'd covered the various skirmishes and scandals in which the gentleman had become embroiled over the preceding years. More recently he'd reported on Rowland Sinclair's arrest for murder, though the charges had been dropped and the story conveniently buried on page twelve when the family's solicitors had contacted his editor. White might have been bitter if he were not so intrigued by the polite, unassuming man who seemed to somehow wield the might of the establishment without abiding by any of its rules.

Woodlands House, where White was calling on Sinclair, had once been among the premier homes of Sydney's better suburbs, a sandstone declaration of tradition, privilege and stately decorum. These days, however, the Woollahra mansion and its acreage were rumoured to be teeming with naked women and Communists. Regrettably, White had not been able to verify that personally, having been met at the gatehouse by a servant and escorted directly to the converted stables where his subject was waiting.

Though he could not attest to the state of the main house, the reporter had noted the nude sculptures that challenged decency throughout the grounds—urns with breasts, naked nymphs and lovers entwined in the fountain. All very fine indeed, and exquisitely improper.

White's pencil scratched quickly to capture an impression of Sinclair himself. Tall, athletic build, clean cut—good jawline despite the determination of the upper classes to breed out chins—dark hair, and blue eyes... startlingly, intensely blue. They would print a photograph with the article of course, but the writer's words would be the only thing to convey colour. Sinclair wore a dark grey three-piece suit, expensively tailored. There was a conspicuous smear of yellow paint on the sleeve, and several on the waistcoat.

Rowland offered Crispin White his hand. "Rowland Sinclair, Mr. White. How d'you do?"

If White's hand had not been in Rowland's grip, he would have duly recorded that Sinclair's handshake was both firm and single handed. His inflection was certainly refined but not excessively so, and his smile, slightly bashful.

"I am sorry to receive you out here," Rowland apologised. "It must seem a little irregular, but I thought you might like to see the old girl." He stood back to allow White to behold the gleaming yellow 1927 Mercedes S-Class.

The reporter walked around the vehicle, making the admiring noises that were clearly expected. In a few weeks, Rowland Sinclair would take his prized automobile out on the notorious Maroubra Speedway—for a charity race in aid of the Red Cross. Plainly, Sinclair believed the motorcar deserved equal billing in any media profile.

"German engineering." There was a slight reproach in White's voice, an unspecified criticism.

Those blue eyes regarded him sharply. "Yes," Rowland said. "The Germans make excellent automobiles."

"It's never bothered you then…?" White asked, identifying an angle and pursuing it now. "I believe you lost a brother in the Great War didn't you, Mr. Sinclair?"

"Aubrey, from what I remember, was not shot by a Mercedes, Mr. White."

"But how would he feel about his brother driving a German motorcar, Mr. Sinclair?"

Rowland sighed. "I think you'll find the war is over."

"I understand you were in Germany last year," White continued. "Is that when you acquired your vehicle?"

"No. I won her in a card game when I was at Oxford."

White's face lifted. This was good. "You don't say! So you're not averse to a game of chance, Mr. Sinclair?"

"I don't know that poker is a game of chance. Not if it's played well."

"But you don't object to a wager?"

Rowland paused and studied the reporter. He laughed suddenly, shaking his head. "Just what are you trying to get me to say, Mr. White?"

The reporter's smile was sly. "Something wicked would do very nicely, Mr. Sinclair."

"Why?"

"Every contest needs a villain to stir emotion and get the public involved—someone to boo and hiss. It's all part of the show."

"And you've decided the villain ought to be me?"

"Well, you are driving the German car."

Rowland couldn't quite tell whether Crispin White was in earnest.

White grinned. "Just pulling yer leg, sir, but you understand your car may upset the odd digger. I'm not prejudiced myself, but some folks don't see it that way."

"Quite." Rowland leaned back against the mudguard of his car, his arms folded as he tried to discern just how badly this interview was going.

White tapped the lead of his pencil against the notebook. "So, tell me Mr. Sinclair, how did you get involved in this charity race caper?"

"My mother," he replied, thankful the reporter was moving on. "She's a patron of the Red Cross."

White made a note. "Can't fault a man who loves his mother," he said with a breathy note of disappointment.

"Mr. White, if it is necessary to portray me as some kind of melodrama villain, I'm sure you'll need to look no further than the archives of your paper." Rowland couldn't help but be slightly amused by the reporter's approach.

"Are you asking me to leave, Mr. Sinclair?"

"Not at all. We could continue to stand here while you ask ridiculous questions, or you could join me at the house for a liquid refreshment."

White's large head bounced from side to side as he considered the proposition. "A drink you say? Inside the house?"

Rowland smiled. He could see that White had not yet given up on uncovering a scandal. One had to admire the man's commitment. "If you'd care to follow me, Mr. White?"

White did indeed care to do so, and they walked amiably to the conservatory via the meandering wisteria walk. "Good Lord, they're women!" the reporter murmured, reaching out to touch the cast posts that supported the arched iron trellis upon which the wisteria was trained. He pulled his hand back hastily when it came too close to the small pert breasts of one elongated figure.

"You can touch it," Rowland said, entertained by White's reaction. "Miss Higgins' work is designed to be handled." He ran his fingers over the curve of a sculpted hip in demonstration. "She likes to try out ideas here before she finalises a commission. You'll find a walkway strikingly similar to this one, though somewhat bigger, at the Botanical Gardens in Adelaide."

"Miss Higgins resides here, then?" White asked, puffing to keep pace with Rowland's long stride. Of course, he knew full well that Edna Higgins was a member of the hedonistic artistic set who had taken up residence at *Woodlands House* where they lived at

Sinclair's expense. Some said she was his mistress, an opportunistic Communist siren with her eyes not only on Rowland Sinclair's fortune, but his political soul.

Rowland's response was brief and affirmative, his tone warned against any attempt to pursue the enquiry.

He offered White one of the wicker armchairs that furnished the conservatory through which they entered the house. The early evening was decidedly crisp but the room caught the fading light. Sunset bathed the parquetry floor in a warm glow, and patterned it with a lace of shadows thrown by fretwork brackets.

"I'm famished," Rowland said, pulling on the servants' bell. "Are you hungry, Mr. White?"

"Oh... I... Yes, I am actually," White said, surprised by the invitation. Sinclair seemed an exceedingly unaffected sort of chap, but perhaps he was trying to sway the coverage in his favour. Well, he'd find that Crispin White was not going to lose his objectivity so easily.

Rowland's summons was answered by a strong, straight woman, well into middle age, whom he called Mary. She addressed him as Master Rowly, as if he were a child, and when he told her that Mr. White would be joining him for dinner, she responded with a sigh.

"Since it's just the two of us, we might eat in here, Mary."

The housekeeper shook her head firmly. "Mr. Watson Jones telephoned to say he and Miss Higgins will be back for dinner after all, Master Rowly."

"Oh." Rowland glanced at White. He hadn't intended to give the press quite so much access to his personal life, but it was probably too late now to withdraw the invitation. "I guess we'll have to use the dining room then."

"I'm not sure when exactly they intend to come in, sir."

"I daresay they'll be back directly." Rowland responded to the unspoken complaint in Mary Brown's voice. The housekeeper believed tardiness to be a symptom of ill-breeding. "Mr. White and I might have a drink while we wait."

All this White dutifully recorded in his notebook.

A large misshapen greyhound padded into the conservatory, pausing to nuzzle Rowland's hand before turning to investigate his guest.

"Lenin's harmless," Rowland said when White pulled back.

"I've heard Lenin called many things but never harmless," White muttered as the bony one-eared dog tried to climb into his lap.

"Len, lay down," Rowland commanded, handing the reporter a glass of sherry.

The hound obeyed, settling at Rowland's feet with a distinct air of indignation.

"So, tell me, Mr. Sinclair,"—White was all business again—"have you raced before?"

"No," Rowland admitted. "But this is a charity invitational. I'm hoping at least a few of the other drivers will be equally inept."

"Well-heeled men with supercharged cars and no sense. A certain recipe for disaster, wouldn't you say?"

"It's for a jolly good cause, Mr. White."

"I don't suppose you're bothered by rumours that the Maroubra Speedway is cursed?"

"Cursed?" Rowland laughed. "My good man, you can't be serious?"

"Seven men have lost their lives on the circuit—it's been called the killer track."

"Rowly, where are you?" A woman's voice. White sat up. This was more like it.

Rowland stood and called into the vestibule adjoining the main hallway. "In here, Ed."

Despite rumours that the women at *Woodlands House* were customarily naked, the young lady who walked in was attired—a plain green frock, not drab yet certainly not the latest style. But she could well have worn a sack… indeed, the simplicity of her dress only served to accentuate the fact that she was beautiful—unusually, unforgettably so. There was a complete lack of self-consciousness in the way she moved: a natural informal grace. She'd already removed her hat, shaking out tresses of burnished copper as she greeted Sinclair with casual warmth.

White swallowed, hastily closing his notebook as he stood. Rowland introduced him to Miss Edna Higgins and Mr. Clyde Watson Jones.

It was only at that point that White even noticed Watson Jones—solid, sturdy with a face that wore the years plainly and the calloused hands of a worker. "Sorry we're so late, Rowly." Clyde helped himself to sherry. "Ed came across some bloke trying to drown a sack of kittens and their mother in the harbour. She insisted I rescue them… wanted me to thump the bloke too—"

"Oh do stop complaining, Clyde. You didn't even get wet!" Edna said, perching on the arm of Rowland's chair.

"Where are they?" Rowland asked. "These felines that Clyde liberated."

Edna directed her smile at Rowland. "Out in the tack room," she said. The old tack shed near the stables had served as Edna's studio for some years now. "Clyde thought we should give you a chance to tell Mary before we brought them into the kitchen. She's still cross about Lenin."

Rowland blanched. His housekeeper did not approve of his tendency to give refuge to what she called "ill-bred strays".

The Red Flag, sung stridently, boomed down the hallway.

"Good! Milt's back," Rowland said. "I'm ravenous."

The revolutionary anthem grew louder and a second voice became discernible, female, thin and tentative with the words. Milton Isaacs walked in laughing with an elderly woman on his arm. He was not a subtle presence, with dark hair that fell long to his purple velvet lapel, under which sat a carefully knotted gold cravat. His companion was elegantly dressed in a tweed skirt suit, her soft white hair coiffed neatly beneath a brown felt hat.

The seated gentleman stood. "Mother," Rowland said, alarmed. He did not want White's profile on him to invade his mother's privacy.

"Aubrey, my darling, I've had the most thrilling afternoon with your Mr. Isaacs." Elisabeth Sinclair resided in her own wing of *Woodlands House*, with her own staff, including three private nurses. She had for some time been suffering from a malady of mind that often left her confused and distressed. Elisabeth had forgotten a great deal, including the existence of her youngest son, insisting instead that Rowland was his late brother, Aubrey. Some days were worse than others. Today, however, she seemed well. Her cheeks were infused with rosy colour and she beamed like an excited girl. "We've been to a splendid show at the Domain!"

"It wasn't really a show, Mrs. Sinclair—" Milton began.

"May I introduce Mr. Crispin White from *Smith's Weekly*." Rowland interrupted before Milton could reveal that he'd taken Elisabeth Sinclair to a Communist Party rally. "Mr. White will be our guest for dinner."

Milton frowned as he regarded the reporter. "Crispin?"

"Elias Isaacs... I didn't know... Hello," White pulled at the already loosened knot in his tie.

Rowland's brow rose. It appeared the reporter was well enough acquainted with Milton to know his real name. The reunion did not appear to be a fond one, but neither seemed about to elaborate.

"Will you be joining us tonight, Mother?" he asked.

"I believe I shall decline, darling. I've had such an exciting afternoon with Mr. Isaacs, I think I might need a quiet night. I'll leave you young people to it. You'll all forgive me my old age, I hope?"

"Of course," Rowland said, relieved.

"I have drunken deep of joy, and I will taste no other wine tonight," Milton proclaimed, turning his back on White to escort the old lady from the conservatory.

"Shelley," Rowland said quietly. Milton's reputation as a poet was built principally on a talent for quoting the works of the romantic bards and a practice of not actually attributing the words. He didn't seem to feel obliged to write anything himself. Rowland smiled as he heard his mother object, "I don't think a small glass of cognac before bed will do me any harm, Mr. Isaacs."

Edna glanced at Rowland. The tension between Milton and White had been unmistakable. She shrugged slightly, clearly unaware of its cause and taking White's arm, she allowed their guest to escort her to dinner.

The reporter paused as they entered the dining room, gazing at the high walls around him with undisguised awe. Stylised figures and intricate patterns were defined with white paint on a background of black—naked women, mythical beasts, peacocks given movement in the candlelight. Every square inch of the walls was rendered in this way. It was ethereally beautiful and startling.

"Is this…? Did you paint—?"

"It was a collaboration," Rowland said, pulling out a chair for Edna. "An experiment of sorts."

"I feel a little like I've stepped through the looking glass." White sat down, glancing over his shoulder. "I must say it's the first time I'll have dinner with the devil."

Edna laughed. "Oh I'm sure that's not true, Mr. White!" She patted his arm reassuringly. "You're a newspaperman after all. And that's not the devil, you know. It's a faun. Rowly was having a phase with mythology."

"I trust you're not planning to report that Rowland Sinclair has a painting of the devil in his dining room, Mr. White," Clyde said, clearly disturbed by the possibility.

"Yes, if Clyde's mother reads that in *Smith's Weekly* she'll drag him home by the ear!" Milton rejoined them. There was a note of wariness, a warning in the jest.

Clyde didn't bother to deny it. His mother would do that if she thought his soul was at risk... or if she knew he wasn't attending mass regularly. He leaned over to Rowland while White was distracted by Edna's explanation of the wall's design, or perhaps just by Edna herself.

"You invited a newspaper reporter to dinner?" he whispered accusingly.

"I didn't expect that any of you would be home," Rowland replied.

Milton threw an arm around Rowland's shoulder. "You're not ashamed of us are you, old chap?"

Rowland smiled. "I take it you and White are acquainted."

"A long time ago, Rowly."

"He knew you as Elias."

"And I knew him as Crispin Weissen. Perhaps he's reformed."

Sign up to The Crime & Mystery Club's newsletter and get the ebook of *Give the Devil His Due* for FREE.

bit.ly/GivetheDevil

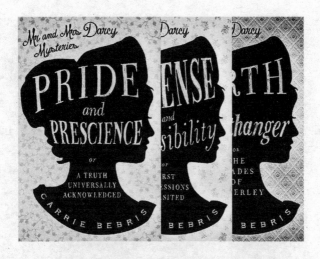

If you enjoyed this Rowland Sinclair mystery, you may
enjoy Carrie Bebris' Mr and Mrs Darcy Mystery Series!

In the best Austen tradition with Regency backdrops,
moody country houses, and delightful characterization –
plus an added twist of murder and mayhem...

Pride & Prescience
Suspense and Sensibility
North by Northanger

Sulari Gentill is the author of the award-winning and best-selling Rowland Sinclair Mysteries, the Greek mythology adventure series The Hero Trilogy, and winner of the Best Crime award at the 2018 Ned Kelly Awards, Crossing the Lines.

She set out to study astrophysics, graduated in law, and then abandoned her legal career to write books instead of contracts. Born in Sri Lanka, Sulari learned to speak English in Zambia, grew up in Brisbane and now lives in the foothills of the Snowy Mountains of NSW where, with her historian husband, she grows French black truffles, cares for a variety of animals and raises two wild colonial boys. Sulari also paints, but only well enough to know she should write, preferably in her pyjamas.